SHADOW TICKET

ALSO BY THOMAS PYNCHON

V.

The Crying of Lot 49

Gravity's Rainbow

Slow Learner

Vineland

Mason & Dixon

Against the Day

Inherent Vice

Bleeding Edge

SHADOW TICKET

Thomas Pynchon

JONATHAN CAPE
LONDON

1 3 5 7 9 10 8 6 4 2

Jonathan Cape, an imprint of Vintage, is part of
the Penguin Random House group of companies

Vintage, Penguin Random House UK,
One Embassy Gardens, 8 Viaduct Gardens, London SW11 7BW

penguin.co.uk/vintage
global.penguinrandomhouse.com

First published in Great Britain by Jonathan Cape in 2025
First published in the United States of America by Penguin Press in 2025

Copyright © Thomas Pynchon 2025

The moral right of the author has been asserted

Designed by Amanda Dewey

Penguin Random House values and supports copyright. Copyright fuels creativity, encourages diverse voices, promotes freedom of expression and supports a vibrant culture. Thank you for purchasing an authorised edition of this book and for respecting intellectual property laws by not reproducing, scanning or distributing any part of it by any means without permission. You are supporting authors and enabling Penguin Random House to continue to publish books for everyone. No part of this book may be used or reproduced in any manner for the purpose of training artificial intelligence technologies or systems. In accordance with Article 4(3) of the DSM Directive 2019/790, Penguin Random House expressly reserves this work from the text and data mining exception.

Printed and bound in Great Britain by Clays Ltd, Elcograf S.p.A.

The authorised representative in the EEA is Penguin Random House Ireland,
Morrison Chambers, 32 Nassau Street, Dublin D02 YH68

A CIP catalogue record for this book is available from the British Library

HB ISBN 9781787336339
TPB ISBN 9781787336346

Penguin Random House is committed to a sustainable future
for our business, our readers and our planet. This book is
made from Forest Stewardship Council® certified paper.

"Supernatural, perhaps. Baloney . . . perhaps not."

—BELA LUGOSI,
in *The Black Cat* (1934)

SHADOW TICKET

1

When trouble comes to town, it usually takes the North Shore Line. What with tough times down the Lake in Chicago, changes in the wind, Prohibition repeal just around the corner, Big Al in the federal pokey in Atlanta, Outfit affairs grown jumpy and unpredictable, anybody needing an excuse to get out of town in a hurry comes breezing up here to Milwaukee, where it seldom gets more serious than somebody stole somebody's fish.

Hicks McTaggart has been ankling around the Third Ward all day keeping an eye on a couple of tourists in Borsalinos and black camel hair overcoats up from the home office at 22nd and Wabash down the Lake, the Chicago Outfit handling whatever needs to be taken care of in Milwaukee since Vito Guardalabene cashed in his chips ten years ago, though Vito's successor Pete Guardalabene is still considered head man in the Ward, gets his picture in the social pages smiling at weddings and so forth.

Loitering in the alleyway in back of Pasquale's Bella Palermo, Hicks can hear sounds of noodle-flexing sociability, smell spaghetti sauce and garlic frying and sfinciuni bagherese baking over an olive-branch fire, and it's making him hungry, though this close to payday his lunch menu is a thermos of coffee and a buttermilk cruller stashed in a pocket someplace.

The explosion when it comes seems to be from somewhere across the river and nearer the Lake. Forks and glassware pause between tabletop and mouth, as if everybody's observing a moment of stillness, and nobody seems surprised.

It's still the topic of conversation a little later when everybody comes piling out into the street.

"Come up lookin for a little peace and quiet, next thing you know . . ."

"Startin to sound like Chicago around here."

Everybody is looking at everybody else like they're all in on something. Beyond familiarity or indifference, some deep mischief is at work.

Over the next few hours till the happiness twins are back on the train again, Hicks gets to hear a number of different stories, related to gangland matrimonials or hooch heists everybody's heard about before, not much of it helpful, even at the combination drug and hardware store plus lunch counter known as Oriental Drugs, heart and soul of the East Side and Hicks's usual source of reliable lowdown in Milwaukee, and sometimes lunch when it isn't too close to payday, which sends him instead over to Otto's Oasis, a speak disguised as a neighborhood Imbisswagen, with a refreshments list ranging from hours-old bathtub product to blockade-run imports of the real McCoy, where by dumb luck he happens to arrive next to the kitchen door just at the exact moment Otto's wife Hildegard is bringing a platterful of free lunch items out to the bar area, so while others are making grabs at Hildegard, Hicks, still brooding about the Sicilian food back at Pasquale's, manages to divert enough eats his way to see him through a couple more hours at least.

LATER BACK AT the Unamalgamated Ops detective agency, Hicks finds his boss, Boynt Crosstown, waiting on the doorsill, shoes beating a nervous eight to the bar.

"Flash bulletin," grabbing Hicks and pretending to pull him by the necktie through the length of the shop and into his office, "just a minute's all I ask."

Hicks trying to stay professional, "Don't suppose you happened to hear anything back around lunchtime . . ."

"Pineapples come and pineapples go, never mind that Santa Flavia Chamber of Commerce meeting, write me a memo, small change anymore, got us a ticket just in and it's a lulu, I'm telling you this is the one'll put us all swimming in the gravy . . ." and so forth.

"Wish you wouldn't come to work when you're like this, Boynt."

"Sure, sure, well, this isn't just daydreaming through the Depression for a change, I guarantee you there's money in this, big money, I've *seen* it!"

With Boynt this usually turns out to be an illegible IOU written in pencil on a wet bar napkin. Hicks tries to keep the doubts out of his face.

"This time it's the goods, right there on the table, and green? Wisconsin before they started logging it off should only've been this green."

"Too bad about my mattress, already over legal capacity, corners of bills hanging out, sure you understand—"

"You always worked too cheap," Boynt headwagging, "even before the Crash you were dime-a-dance." Reaching for a switch on his intercom, "Thessalie, would you mind fetching us in that file?"

"Whole different tax bracket up there in Shorewood, you people, ain't it." Boynt has come in for a major share of the class needling around here, which goes on at industrial sewing-machine tempo and pretty much nonstop, ever since a page from his confidential file mysteriously folded itself one day into a paper airplane and went sailing into the room where the mimeograph machine is, and before you could blink, copies found their way to everybody in the office, announcing Boynt's yearly income at a bit north of ten grand, plus profit sharing in a number of side ventures we may someday hear the end of but not anytime soon.

Thessalie Wayward comes breezing in with a file folder of some size, which Boynt opens dramatically. Hicks spots a familiar tabloid clipping.

"What's this, ol' Bruno back in the picture once more?" referring to local multimillionaire Bruno Airmont, known throughout the dairy industry as the Al Capone of Cheese in Exile since one middle of the night not that many years ago having packed a trunk full of banknotes and skipped, "Supposed to be taking it easy in a hammock," Hicks pretends to recall, "some remote tropical island nobody's sure which, drinkin Singapore Slings out of a fire hose. What's up, retirement's making him a li'l restless?"

"Actually this one's more about his daughter Daphne, with whom, if I'm not too misinformed, you have some history."

"Long time ago," reaching smokes out of his shirt pocket, latching one onto his lip, lighting up. "What's she up to now?"

"Seems your old romance has just run off with a clarinet player in a swing band."

"Keepin busy. Last I saw, she was supposed to be engaged to some North Shore loophound."

"Just off the phone in fact with that happy fiancé himself, G. Rodney Flaunch of the Glencoe Flaunches, acting as spokesman for an assortment of interested parties who've just hired us, and let me point out, for this crowd the fee scale doesn't seem like much of an object."

"And the job would be . . ."

"To locate Miss Airmont wherever she's off to, smooth-talk her out of her involvement with this clarinet player, bring her back. Simple pickup and delivery."

"Lot of fun for somebody, too bad that matrimonials, as you'll recall, were never my line—"

Back when he was getting into the business, one of the first things Hicks noticed was how many pre-divorcées just in Milwaukee and Waukesha counties alone seemed disposed to linger over forbidden liquids, going into all the intimate details as if mistaking him for a lawyer that doesn't charge much, with muscle thrown in for free, leading to romantic outcomes easy to imagine, except for the ones Hicks never saw coming, after enough of which he found himself more than ready to hand matrimonials off to energetic junior hires like Zbig Dubinsky, who regards the invention of the trouser-front zipper as a major advance in civilization and can put up with any long sad story that promises the least possibility of domestic cinder disposal.

Ignoring which as usual, Boynt continues.

"Except for your personal connection with the lady, of course—excuse me, what's this expression on your face?"

"This? Close attention, I think."

"No, if it's anything it's 'poor old Boynt,' and insincere at that. Who are you to act so virtuous? You're the one with the glamorous, some might even say lurid, past here."

"Making me even less qualified—"

Sudden commotion in the outer office now, as in through the door without an appointment comes running Skeet Wheeler, a flyweight juvenile in a porkpie hat, with Thessalie close behind attempting grabs which Skeet doesn't seem all that eager to avoid.

"Hicksie! Ya gotta do somethin! You heard it, right?"

"Sure, everybody in town must've heard it, but what was it?" Anybody has the straight dope it'll be Skeet.

"Stuffy Keegan's hooch wagon—somebody rolled a bomb, blew it all to hell."

"Language," Boynt murmurs.

"Stuffy's all right?"

"Nobody's sayin nothin, the hush is on. If he hasn't skipped town, if he's still alive, he ain't advertising."

Hicks has known, at least kept a mental file on, Stuffy Keegan since his early career as a petty offender and eventually MPD snitch who can be bought for a song, which is seldom "Puttin' on the Ritz." By the standards of these times and this neck of the woods, Stuffy's rap sheet, while technically criminal, is nothing special except for the number of paranoid lapses of judgment including the one that landed him here to begin with. Out on some otherwise routine run, possibly owing to lack of sleep, he began to observe in the rearview mirror growing numbers of law enforcement which, even if that's what it really was, might not really've been planning to pull Stuffy over, or even notice him at all, but by the time he got to Waukesha it was too much for his nerves, so he found a telephone and called the police and asked them to just please come and get it over with.

"It was highway coppers, I tell ya, a whole armored division, lights 'n' sirens 'n'—"

"Sure, Mr. Keegan, we understand, now don't worry, we'll take steps."

Convinced there was something screwy about his rearview mirror, every time he looked into which now he had started seeing something he didn't want to see, Stuffy traded in the rig he was driving for a REO Speed Wagon with a normal rearview mirror, soon familiar among the tattered convoys out in the wind between here, Detroit, and Toledo carrying a load typically of pint bottles, whose rectangular cross-section allowed more to fit into the limited cargo space, bought for $2 in Canada, sold on this side for $7 to retailers who then diluted the contents two, sometimes three to one. Return trips from Toledo often brought a wagonload of Lake Erie perch under ice, to be listed on local fish-joint menus as "Lake Michigan perch," the real critter having in recent years been pretty much fished out.

"That rig," Skeet looking forlorn, "got him out of so many bad situations . . . Called it his li'l tramp freighter of the streets and in the end a blown-up wreck with zero resale value."

"Getting sentimental, kid, better watch 'at, once."

Boynt meanwhile, having run his usual unsociable O-O of Skeet, "Recall there's a Depression on, we can only afford so much pro bono work anymore, there was a memo, I handed you it myself." Taking the runaway cheez heiress file, tapping Hicks gently on the head with it, handing it over and stepping back into his office. "Soon as you've had a look through this, Hicks, let me know what you think." Doesn't quite slam the door, but there is some emphasis to the way it shuts.

"Was that steam comin out his ears? Did I barge in on somethin again?"

"Nothin that can't wait. New watch, I see."

"Hamilton, glows in the dark too."

"Pretty classy there, Skeet."

"Can't help it, she just thinks I'm cute. Her way of showing it."

"Uh-huh." As likely lifted off somebody staggering out of a speak, but with Skeet you never know, so Hicks only makes with the avuncular beaming. Skeet is one of the modern young breed of dip, no longer interested in the pocket watches of the old and inattentive, finding more challenge in lifting a watch right off of a wrist in broad daylight, where any trick buckle or extra keeper can slow you down by some fatal splinter of a second.

Skeet lights up a cigar stub that never seems to change length much, the very blackest of Italo fumigators, dense as a rock, goes out if you don't keep puffing on it so after a while you let it go out, but keep it in your kisser anyway.

"OK, how do we approach this?" coming out of somewhere with a snub nose service .32, and pretending to check to see if it's loaded.

"Gosh sakes, Skeet."

"Kids' Special."

"You've been firing this thing much?"

"Only out at the dump so far. But keep your shirt on, one of these days you'll be readin all about it on the front page of the *Journal*."

Hicks used to talk like this back in high school. For a minute and a half he's taking a bounce back in time, and looking at himself as a kid.

"OK, OK now, Skeet, now about this bomb, what'd be your guess?"

"There was some talk of a Third Ward type of person."

"Uh-uh." Out with the cautionary finger. "Still want to be a detective when you grow up, first thing to learn is keep an open mind. Maybe for the MPD and them, bomb always equals Italian no matter what, but in real life there's bomb rollers in all parts of town, even among the German and Polish races. Now what about money, social life, how much does Stuffy owe and who to and is he carryin on with some big shot's sweetie."

"Love life among the grown-ups, better ask a newsie, you really want to know. Those guys are the ones that get around."

Though Skeet doesn't read the papers much, he manages to follow gang wars like some kids follow pennant races, carrying in his wallet a photo of Al Capone, clipped from the *Journal*, across which Skeet, or somebody, has inscribed, "To my old goombah Skeet, who taught me everything I know, regards and tanti auguri, always, Al."

Mostly his news of current events comes from keeping an ear aimed at the radio and staying in everyday touch with the kid underworld—drifters, truants, and guttersnipes, newsboys at every corner and streetcar stop—who in turn have antennas of their own out. "It's like Mussolini," Skeet explains, "the little ones report to bigger kids, who report to me, then I report to you, then on up the pyramid."

"And . . . the Mussolini here again being who, Pete Guardalabene?"

"You know better. Pete is no more'n mid-level, same for Joe Vallone—both bein run like everybody else in this burg by remote control from Chicago."

Hicks and Skeet go back a couple years, to one of those spells of bank robberies and pineapple detonations that now and then would sweep through town, leaving civilian nervous wreckage in its wake. Hicks had put his nose into a recently stuck up bank on Wisconsin Avenue on behalf of a client whose bank account had just disappeared, either in the robbery or into some soon to be ex-spousal pocketbook.

Before he can find somebody to talk to there's a sudden loud bang and people are running in all directions, screaming "They're here again" and "Run for your life" and so forth. Hicks moves into a corner of the floor plan not likely to be run around in much and waits. No Sicilians waving sawed-offs, no smell of burned powder, no fire brigades or bloody casualties in the picture. Check and double check . . . he waits. Soon from behind an artificial palm tree emerges a small though energetic urchin with a pocketful of rubber balloons and a supply of pins. As Hicks watches, he stealthily blows up a balloon, ties the neck off, scans around for likely targets, notices Hicks has been watching him.

"Uh-oh."

"Things in this town not jittery enough for you?"

"Don't turn me in, mister, I'm only a kid."

"Sure you are, you're kiddin me right now, go on, get outa here."

"You just saved me," adds the kid, "from industrial school, Green Bay, maybe worse."

"You still here? Go on, vamoose."

"You may not pay everything you owe, but some of us do."

Since then Skeet has just kept showing up out of the city mobility, quiet, unannounced, slowly to be revealed as a would-be apprentice with all the desire, maybe even some of the chops already, but still no idea what could be waiting just over the next doorsill, who thinks he wants, heaven help him, to be a detective someday. Not, he's quick to point out, a common field op like Hicks, "More of a class act, like Sherlock Holmes and them."

"There you go."

"If it's not professional," Skeet figures now, "this truck bomb, it must be amateur?"

"Amateur, frankly," Hicks shrugging, "ain't nearly as much fun, short money, doubtful tomato quality, too much work, too little of a return—"

"Yeah, but aside from that . . ."

"You always need to go for the big time, kid, every time—ya listenin to me? Glamour! high rolling, high explosives, high danger level—"

"You're some hell of a guide through the minefields of youth, Hicksie."

Far as he knows, Skeet was one of those Christmas babies left in a straw box for the MPD to find. There were a number of these cop shelters all over Milwaukee where a beat-pounder could step in out of the cold weather for a minute or two—any longer than that, you were apt to be jolted awake by some phone dispatcher whose idea of fun is sneaking upside your head in the middle of the night and banging on a gong. The little shacks had hay all over the floor to keep those flat feet warm and door-kicking-ready, reminding people so much of the manger in Bethlehem that when the Depression struck in earnest it became a practice at Christmas for desperate parents to leave babies not only at church doorsteps but also in these MPD straw boxes, with hay all piled around. A Christmas crèche with beat coppers standing in for the animals.

Skeet came to learn about outdoor city light and how much and how little to expect from it in the way of comfort—plate glass window reflections, penumbras of lampposts at the ends of trolley lines to the edges of suburbs still officially to be named—haunting given stretches of sidewalk just as the shops close down and the girls come out dazy and chattering, cigarette smoke and perfume in the slowly more intensifying light of the evening street, immersed too deep in lives that Skeet could never quite see any plausible way to step into . . . A Milwaukee bildungsroman, as they call it locally.

Skeet was to bounce his way through a string of his mother's domestic arrangements, motherly enough instincts but little to no judgment in the matter of boyfriend material, with unintended consequences few of which worked out well, though there were exceptions.

"What's that smell? Like rubber burning? What's the oven doing on 375 degrees?"

"I noticed you weren't hooking into the pocket so good, Knuckles—"

"Tell me it ain't so."

"Wanted to get it really clean for you," Skeet kept trying to explain, as Knuckles yanked open the oven door, revealing through the billows of smoke a reeking and out-of-round ex–bowling ball. "Oh—no, what'd I do?"

Which is where a normal Milwaukeean would've brought out some pocket revolver and settled things on the spot, confident that no local jury would call it anything but justifiable homicide. Instead Knuckles thought he saw an educational opening.

"First thing anybody learns in this town is never put a bowling ball in any oven over a hundred degrees, what kind of upbringing you been getting anyways?" Jerking his head dramatically at the now unrollable Mineralite blob. "That used to be a custom ball, cost me 20 smackers, kid, that's half of what's left of your childhood settin pins, nickel a game and be thankful this ain't Cleveland, you'd only get 4¢."

So began Skeet's pinsetting career, which would before long come to be described all over town as "illustrious." A tough monkey with a number of speeds to his gearbox, Skeet quickly learned his way around a bowling environment unforgiving as any on the planet. Meantime, Knuckles having bid farewell, presently a new gent appeared who turned out to be not so parentally inclined. The blissful pair moved up to Shorewood leaving Skeet on his own, and good riddance.

As word spread, Skeet found himself in demand for all-night private sessions, trusted by bowling alley owners to keep order and lock up and even to acquire his own small crew of assistants. The tips kept rolling in, literally, the practice being to stuff dollar bills into the thumb and finger holes and roll the ball back gently, even respectfully, to the pinboy. After a while Skeet began betting on kegler outcomes here and out of town and before long this had grown to a sizable sum which Skeet had the good sense to keep out of the stock market and inside a safe-deposit box at Northern Trust.

JUST AS HICKS is rolling a form into the Underwood, Boynt bounces back in to cast a disappointed eye.

"Starting a ticket, I knew it."

"Pay dirt here," nonchalantly, "Wait and see."

"Uh, huh." Boynt is wearing his You Poor Fish look, which he thinks is motivational, but isn't. "You know what happens around here any time our productivity curve even thinks about headin down Illinois way, back office just sends in more of their time-motion snoopers. That what you want? Bifocal lenses everyplace you turn?"

"Relax, Boynt, I'll keep this all off the swindle sheets . . ."

"Hicks, I'm a hard case, pity doesn't come to me easily, but this is pitiful. These clients of yours—living at the edge of desperation, yet always managing to find you, and you know why that is, of course you do, don't you, Hicks?"

"Prohibition?" Just a guess. Boynt blames everything on Prohibition.

"Because you're a sap! A Board of Idiots approved and certified sap!—have I mentioned that before, I forget."

"You mean in so many words?"

"Taken in by every two-bit crybaby comes pissing and moaning in under the door, no intention of ever paying on time, if at all, 'course not, why should anybody worry about overdue notices when they're only coming from a sap?"

"Does this mean there goes my year-end bonus again?"

"Oh, and by the way, this truck bomb, before you type up your ticket? oddly enough I'm just off the phone with Badger All-Risk Fiduciary Life as well as the local Teutonia Society, and guess what, each of them just hired us to look into that very same incident, each thinking the other did it, and how's that for peculiar, huh?"

"See, Boss? What'd I tell you?"

"When was that, I may not've been listening." Boynt heads for his desk drawer, where if this was Chicago you would expect to find a pint of Old Log Cabin but here in Milwaukee it's more likely to be Korbel brandy, a bottle of which Boynt now hauls out, looks at thoughtfully a while . . . "Nah, too early yet," and stashes back in the drawer.

2

The crime scene, turns out, is in District 2, down the south side. You can still smell it. In the middle of a big scorch mark sits what's left of Stuffy's Speed Wagon, blackened fragments scattered across the pavement, dozens of detectives walking around aimless yet thoughtful, including a few from the bomb squad. "Hicks, don't tell me you too? Criminy, they're all comin outa th' millwork for this one."

"Me and who else?"

"Federal kiddies that nobody's ever heard of."

"Not the prohis."

"They look more like bootleggers, except the suits are cheaper."

Skeet, tagging along, spots a ball bearing among the wreckage, slides it into his pocket.

"What do you want that for, could be evidence."

"Steelies. These can bring up to a dime apiece. Chicago Latin kids, they'll pay top dollar for anything. Why, you thought it was something sentimental?"

Back at the district station house, another of these eccentric midwestern cop outposts running to turrets, steeples, several colors of stone and brick ranging from cream to dark crimson, upstairs in the captain's office, passing around a bottle of Mistletoe gin.

"IMOPIO job, no question." Rhymes with Pinocchio.

"Howzat?"

"Infernal Machine Of Presumed Italian Origin."

"Somebody got the radio on? Is that accordion music, why, it, it sounds almost like 'Way Marie' . . ."

"Well? It's what they do, ain't it. Remember these are the people who invented the meatball, the bocce ball—rolling objects, it comes naturally to them."

"There's the problem," a bomb squad old-timer nods, "mode of delivery. Typical Italo whizbang tends to be absentee, time-delayed, slow-dripping acid, two-dollar Ingersoll slow-dripping acid, wired into the ignition, but seldom if ever rolled down the street by hand like it's Bensinger's Recreation out here or somethin, which any li'l pebble can throw your shot off, ain't it, not the usual leaf-and-a-half special, capeesh, wanna roll it under a truck, has to be some local genius who can read this pavement like a golf green."

"Or else precision-engineered, custom-built, self-correcting, maybe a li'l gyroscope inside."

"You got it. Which is why this caper's got German storm kiddies written all over it."

"Or how about, somebody's going to some trouble to make it *look* Italian."

"Uh-oh, who let the deep thinker in?"

Talk unavoidably spiraling back through time to 1917 and the bomb that went off at Central Station, downtown.

"A wop football in the station house, for Chrissakes. Safest place in Milwaukee you'da thought—nothing could touch us. Headquarters, throne of God, no bomb would dare to go off."

"Just after roll call, I'm heading out to the street—suddenly all hell. Go running back in, no lights, everybody screaming and yelling . . . it's really bad, blood, smoke . . . Worst thing was, we did it to ourselves, it wasn't even meant for us, civilians find it planted next to some little church in the Third Ward, some strictly inter-Italian beef, bring it downtown, instead of 'Get it the hell outa here!' the desk sergeant thinks some detectives might like to have a look, so it ends up in the assembly room, and . . ."

"Second thoughts about staying on the job after that, you can bet. Pull the hook early, get into a safer line of work."

"But that's the thing, ain't it. Nobody knew what safe meant anymore." Hicks must've had a funny look on his face.

"Sure, Hicks, your Uncle Lefty must've told you the story a couple hundred times before, maybe to you it's just cops, but there are things we can't ever share with any civilian, whatever we hear downtown, whatever we don't hear, it's all a closed circle. We're MPD. Ever since that fateful night it's always the force are gonna have first call, before all others, forever. Does that include God? Maybe. Arguments on both sides."

"Just about to ask," Hicks politely.

ALONG WITH HIS soda-jerk career and a sideline in medicinal alcohol, Hoagie Hivnak runs unclassified ads you won't always find in the *Journal*. Hicks, making his way past a couple of prohis collecting their weekly payoff, what appear to be large cartons full of ice-cream cones, gets to the Ideal Pharmacy in the lull between lunchtime and school letting out, and in the bright downstairs, the pleasantly chemical drugstore odor, multicolored syrup bottles, chrome fountain hardware vanishing down the counter into mirrored distance, finding Hoagie alone behind an empty counter trying not to drift into dreamland.

Grown older through Prohibition, Hoagie has still somehow not lost the adenoidal brashness of the prewar teenage soda jerk he started off as.

"Thirty years ago this was no place for kids, the words 'soda fountain' would send mothers all over town into fits, worse than 'opium den.'" Leapers and sleigh riders one end of the counter to the other lingering all day over house formulas with cocaine as the main ingredient, once a common sight in Milwaukee till the spoilsports at the Food and Drug brought the hammer down, like a preview of Prohibition, "and now it's all this wholesome family trade. Talk about depression."

Hicks slides onto a stool and pretends to look over the menu on the wall.

"How about a banana split, everything except the pineapple, which I'm suddenly allergic to after that one the other day."

The veteran seltzer jockey comes alert, and they commence their familiar novelty foxtrot, a bar and a half into which Hicks manages to find a $2 bill and, trying not to think of what it might've bought him, like lunch for a week, watches it vanish before Hoagie even touches it. Magic. "Still want the sundae, that's another two bits."

"Maybe just pull me a phosphate, now I'm suddenly on a budget."

"Good call 'cause there's nothin much to tell, heard it when it went off but down here couldn't even say what direction. You know the usual racial categories as well as me, but in this case that truck wasn't hit with no goombah grenade. Maybe you want to look closer to your own all-American type of neighborhood."

"Howzat?"

"Spend your whole day around ice cream, you can begin to grow philosophical. You figure a state with two million dairy cows, a certain percent of that milk will be going into ice cream, nickel a cone, been that way forever. But it turns out there's milk and then there's milk. The kind you drink from a bottle is more expensive than the kind they use to make butter and cheese and ice cream out of. A two-price system is what they call it. Now we got syndicates of Bolshevik farmers looking to make it all one price, meaning the cost per scoop of ice cream goes up 70, 80 percent, next thing we're looking at a dime cone, the banana split you thought you wanted goes up to 30, 40, 50 cents, no end in sight. Who's got money like that to spend?"

"Sounds serious, Hoagie."

"It's civil war."

"Over ice-cream cones?"

"Could be the one spark that sets it all off. Won't take much. Milk is the universal American drink, ain't it, bigger than beer, even in Milwaukee. Don't believe me, talk to your pals up on Yankee Hill. Track down Bruno Airmont wherever he's got to."

Bruno. "Seriously?"

"Why do you think he skipped when he did? Maybe he heard somethin rollin down the tracks we can't yet. You're the private investigator, laughing boy. Go investigate."

3

After drifting around the Near North Side, putting his head in Smoky Gooden's policy joint, passing some genial semiprofessional chitchat with elements of the MPD Morals Squad on their way in and out, listening in on a Bronzeville establishment or two, the Flame, the Polka Dot, the Moonglow, Hicks rolls into Arleen's Orchid Lounge a little before midnight. As jake with the world as it ever gets, extra pack of Spuds in his pocket, truck just in from Canada, rain whispering on the sheet metal out back, and April Randazzo about to begin a set, sporting an indigo number from some rag joint in Chicago that isn't Goldblatt's. Doesn't look bad on her.

Over the last year or so Hicks and April have become a recognized couple on assorted dance floors around Milwaukee and further down the Lake. Sometimes a camera girl will tiptoe up and snap them together dancing, and when the prints come back he's amazed at how often the shot has caught April not quite smiling, that'd be too much to ask, but at least visibly relaxed, as if thinking the hard part of her day is over, one of those good-as-sincere surrenders to the swing 'n' sway, the night out, the time she's having so far.

They met at the Aragon Ballroom in Chicago, near the el, half a clam to get in, cork, felt, and spring-cushioned floor, palm trees, archways, tile, the Spanish palace courtyard treatment, secret tunnel to nearby Capone hangout The Green Mill, only white people allowed in.

First thing Hicks runs into is a floor patrolman in a tuxedo who's just been prying apart a couple he thinks have been dancing "too close," the male half of which has promptly disappeared, leaving a presentable young woman who turns out to be April. "All's I'm saying," gripping her sleeveless arm in a less than hospitable way, it seems to Hicks, "is you and your boyfriend wherever he's got to might find it more comfortable at the Arcadia, Dreamland, the Savoy. Places like that don't mind Lindy-hopping or the more experimental types of jazz band, but we have this sort of house policy, you see . . ."

"Problem here?" Hicks's hands, ordinarily sedate, beginning to tighten into fists.

"Thanks, but I wasn't looking for police activities tonight," April in a whisper over her shoulder, "if that's OK?"

"See what I can do. First of all, pal, you can leave go of the lady, and get back to your junior prom out there."

"Excuse me—"

"You're excused."

Apparently having taken a good look at Hicks for the first time, the floor man nods and withdraws.

"Well," remarks April.

"Yeah. Care to cut a rug?"

"Not here. Somehow this joint has lost its charm."

They end up eventually at a black-and-tan ballroom somewhat south of here where the music is closer to jazz and the dancing experimental as anything in town.

The band at some point decide it'll be fun to play in 5/4. "Hey, it's the Half and Half. You know it?" April turns out to be the first he's met who ever heard of the step, let alone actually dances it, which according to Mr. and Mrs. Vernon Castle calls for a 1-2-3, 1-2 beat. The rest of the floor is suddenly unoccupied. Hicks and April remain, looking at each other, not for the first time but seems like it.

"Come on," giving her a spin and there they are alone in a follow spot, April content to be led for a change, though she can count 1-2-3, 1-2 as well as this customer here who's started putting in all these dips and hesitations, no doubt to keep her awake. Well. A break at least from the cement mixers she usually finds herself out tripping with.

At the end of the number there's even a little applause. April smiles back and nods. "For years that was my dream—to be one of those girls in a nightclub scene, all dolled up, out on a date, across a table from some dreamboat, just a little out of focus, having the best time in the world."

"Me, a dreamboat, really?"

"Or to put it another way . . ."

However, a few more dances and drinks on into the evening—

"Oh my! Is that for me?"

"Thought you'd never notice."

A pause, which he has the sense to wait through. "Maybe it's the time of night a girl needs something to hold on to."

"Go ahead, it won't mind."

"Oh, of course that'd be only one extra problem for you, I guess, easy in and out, get it over with quick as possible . . ."

"Who said easy?"

"Could've fooled me."

"Anybody around here likely to get fooled, Toots, it'd be me."

Pretending to recoil in sympathy, "Ooh! Poo-uh, lay-umb! Can I help?"

"You mean, by somehow not playing me for a sap? You'd really do that for me?"

"No. Not even if I knew you better."

"Let's hope that don't happen."

Yeah, let's hope.

She is squinting at him, suspicion all over that photogenic kisser. The full-scale Wabash Avenue once-over and then some. Has he ever been scrutinized quite this close before? Normally at about this point there begins to drift across the face of the broad in the scene a look of evasiveness Hicks has grown used to, followed by some form of "How cheapened has my life become that I have to put up with attention from palookas like this?" Except now, for once, it doesn't happen—moments tick by as it slowly dawns on him that here's a woman who's finding a way to withhold her annoyance with him so skillfully that it's invisible even to an old rejection whiz like himself. When did this happen last, a tomato he's hardly met going to so much trouble? Ever? He could be paying a professional actress union scale to perform this small act of mercy, and here's this April here giving it away for free. Not a thunderbolt, maybe, but at least a wave of gratitude slopping over him . . .

AS THEY GET to know each other better, Hicks discovers that though April is more streetwise than the crowd she usually runs with, careful with her money, not about to say no to a drink now and then, usually now, where her sentimental eye chart goes running off into a dangerous blur is in connection with married men. A gold-accented ring finger has the same effect on April as a jigging spoon on a Lake trout, especially when kept on while kidding around, good as a framed copy of a marriage license hanging up on a love-nest wall.

For a while Hicks tended to sympathize with the wandering husbands, although soon he found he was beginning to take it personally.

"Don't know. I see enough of it at work already, don't I. Crazy wives, jealous husbands, even when there's nothing going on, it's like they still want it to be."

"How about you?"

"Just happy to see you when I see you."

"Not sure how I feel about that."

"What, I'm not crazy enough? You want me creeping around outside your window in the middle of the night? Cross-eyes? Napoleon hat? Got one of those, I could wear it for you."

While not as common as a nose or needle habit, April's married-man fixation does bring along its own set of health risks. Wronged spouses within easy reach of firearms can no longer be ruled out of the national domestic melodrama, where the list of everyday household appliances now routinely includes hardware such as the Colt .32 used by the recently famous Mrs. Myrtle Bennett of Kansas City, who in the course of an otherwise friendly bridge game shot her husband dead for coming up two tricks short on a contract, delivering her into headlines nationwide.

"Everything," April has remarked wistfully to Hicks more than once, "right here for you, more romance than you'll find outside the movies, until I remember this one little item, this ringless finger here..."

"So... when we're kidding around, all that ooh, that aah, you mean that's just an act? Thought you were havin a good time there. My sweetie." Pulling out a hip flask from which he pours not hooch but some slow green liquid, rubs it between his hands, runs both hands through his hair as an intensely herbal aroma fills the room, begins to comb it into place...

"Putting some time in on your hair there, Sport."

"A shine you can see your face in. Lasts for days, glows in the dark."

"Show me," reaching for the light switch.

"Hmm... maybe not as shiny as that. But long as we're here..."

This is absolutely not the serious footloose-husband make-believe she's comfortable with, too breezy, Hicks being the last type of dating material she should be getting anywhere near, in fact, but she can't help herself. A big ape with a light touch. The light touch fools women into thinking he's sensitive, which he isn't.

"Nice thing with you," sez April, "is I never have to be nervous about my stockings. Any other night out all it takes is him thinking about it and zing! Runs, like that. Price of a steak, out the window. Dollar bills with these li'l... wings on them. But you, all those pile-driver activities you're so fond of and yet you never so much as put a wrinkle."

"Shouldn't tell me things like that, Cupcake, you know what happens. Now I'll just have to get impolite about it."

"Oh! You animal."

"She noticed," making a grab.

"Dammit now, Hicks, you ape."

"Hearing that one a lot this week."

"Oh, who'd that be?"

"Just one of those workday episodes, maybe somebody you know, maybe not."

"How likely am I to know anybody at, well, your level, I'm sure, and stop that—you hear me? you're making such a big assumption..."

"Me, I'm a perfect gentleman. You want to come on down off of there?"

"Oh, Hicks. If only you would just be married, to somebody, some nice girl, Lutheran, Catholic, don't matter, Polish, Irish, long as you do the deed in a real church . . . Even got the hoop right here for you, shoplifted straight from the top sparkler joint on Wabash, your exact finger size and all, just waiting . . . Only get married, one li'l 'I do,' and then I'd be more in love with you than you could ever dream."

Can't help narrowing his eyes a little. Is she serious? "Yeah but, but ain't there somethin . . . immoral about it, somehow? This wife I'd have to be running around on, this Polish trick, supposin I even fall in love with her or somethin, things like that happen, and what then?"

"Oh, but they all love their wives, it's part of the deal. Something I may need to talk about someday with somebody, though maybe not with you."

"So, these cute little hopefuls you keep sending around . . ."

"Sooner or later, one of them's gonna hit the spot, you know, you might as well get prepared for that, 'cause you can't hold out forever." With the big smudged eyes.

"Check. Some beauty parade. Last one you tried to fix me up with, that Euphorbia? I'm still shakin."

"Oh," a mischievous gleam, "keep telling you, she had a license for that."

"I can see what you're looking to promote me into, don't you know that's a private op's bread and butter, waiting all night across the street in the rain turning to snow for some window to light up and then go dark again. That's a holy sacrament I wouldn't wish on anybody, Toots."

After raiding the icebox, waiting for April to finish with the makeup and so forth, Hicks sits gazing at a calendar on April's kitchen wall advertising Mazda light bulbs, with one of those hyperilluminated Maxfield Parrish pictures of girls not what you'd call dressed for outdoor activities posing on rocks, in a steep and unforgiving landscape—cute, even innocent, but what are these two doing out here to begin with?

"And how's moy, ick-oo *pwoyvate dick*?" April has this habit of unexpectedly squeaking into a high-pitched flapper voice which men then have the choice of pretending is cute and going along with, or remembering they're out of smokes or parked illegally someplace blocks away from.

Always another big selling point about Hicks is how it's never worked on him, the baby-vamp vocalizing, the off-key attempts to rezone the boundaries of jailbait terrain. Just about every grown woman in Milwaukee has at least tried it on, a few drifting so far into it that you could argue they never came back out again.

"Only one thing, um, April, is, not tonight with this, OK . . ."

"No ick-oo dirl talk? Ooh! Hicksie-wicksie! What'oo poo-uh Apwiw do?"

"Well, let's see, you could do Louise Brooks, or Clara Bow—"

"They're from back before the talkies. Silent."

"*That's* the word I'm tryin to think of—"

"Now don't—"

"Don't what again?"

"You no-account, you lowlife— Aah!"

"I know you do. Me too. Any time you say—high noon in Schuster's window, shopping day of your choice." As close as Hicks gets to blurting thoughtless endearments. The preferred way to deal with this kind of thing is grab her and start dancing to music on the radio, though of course the room really isn't set up for dance numbers, you can't get carefree with the kicks and turns, you keep running into lamps, furniture, slippery little throw rugs. Some call it clutter, April calls it "the nesting instinct," something she must've read about in some dames' magazine. Within four bars they're sure to run afoul of an end table.

Just about then, on comes one of those motivational songs all over the airwaves lately about the joys of suburban married life. Hicks grabs yesterday's *Journal*, rolls it into a megaphone, and starts to croon along,

> When the shadows come driftin up the highway,
> another day, another dollar, I guess,
> Is when you'll find me headin back
> to that asphalt-shingle shack, and
> my little Missus, Middle-
> Clas-siness . . .
> forget that gum-snappin gal from the gashouse,

'n' keep your poutin pluto-cratic prin-cess,
Just gimme-that cute hootchy-koo,
I'm ree-ferring to, that's my—
Little Missus, Middle-
Clas-siness . . .

[bridge]

No more Saturday nights at the hush-hush,
No more soakin' my socks in the sink,
Now I'm all normalized, just like,
a mil-lion other guys, feelin so
satisfied, as we go slid-in'
o-ver-that brink, y'know,
It's on-ly a bungalow, in Wau-wato-sa . . .
                            But oh, so
co-zy when the sun's in the west . . .
Average mug, regular dame, oh did-I-for-get
to mention-her-name? Well, it's
My little Missus Middle-
Classiness, oh yes, she's—my
little Missus—

"You son of a bitch."

"Come on, it's only a song . . ."

"You're in trouble, Hicks."

"Long as it's with you, Angelface."

"You're in big trouble and you don't know it."

"Fine one to talk."

"Lounge lizards and wayward hubbies, Lunchmeat, forget all them, this time it's serious."

"To the great life lesson Money Talks," as Boynt has often lectured him, "is now added Lesson Two—Romantic Partners Stray. For reasons that continue to escape me you keep questioning both these principles, which happen to form the bedrock of our profession, choosing again and again not to cash in whenever a sure thing is handed to you on a plate, and continuing to believe against all evidence in true and faithful love, although to look at you nobody'd ever know it. Another romantic chump."

By the time Hicks understands he should've been paying closer attention to what's been going on, the moment has arrived when April is using the movies as an alibi for her whereabouts, a regression to high school Hicks would never have expected.

"*The Public Enemy*, again? It's three in the morning."

"They've started running it all night, round the clock, young American womanhood, you know, we can't get enough of *that Jimmy*, knocked all gaga in fact, plenty there to swoon over, case I haven't drooled enough about him to you already."

"Only part I remember's that grapefruit really . . . don't spoze you'd happen to have one around . . ."

EACH NIGHT IN HER GIG at Arleen's Orchid Lounge, whenever midnight happens to fall, April sings what's gotten to be her trademark ballad, backed by a minor-key semi-Cuban arrangement for accordion, saxes, banjo-uke, melancholically muted trumpet—

> Midnight in Milwaukee,
> Not exactly Paris,
> Not exactly swilling champagne, twirling yer
> cane, down the Champs-Élysées . . .
> Ev'ry hour's so blue now,
> How much, can it matter,
> Might as well be suds in a stein,
> Any time, night or day . . .

[bridge]

> Down along the Lake,
> nothing much awake,
> Till it almost seems . . .

[fill phrases from the band]

    Harp lights by the shore
    whisp'ring *je t'adore,*
    how could it be more
    than a doorway to dreams?
                    . . . even
    in Chicago,
    Any town but this one,
    Couldn't we be kids again,
    With our hearts in Par-ee?
                  So long to Mil-wau-
    -kee . . . Lonely
    night-times, adieu . . . hmmm
    Quite a dream, yes, you'd say,
    Enchantée, bonne soirée . . . oh get away
    from me, you—
               ol' mid-
    -night . . . in Milwaukee . . .

"Back when I didn't know any better, laying on the tremolo, thought it would get me noticed, what it did was drive 'em screaming from the room, till one day over the radio along comes Annette Hanshaw, and some curtain in my mind just suddenly goes up . . .

"Not another of these white thrushes who thinks she can sing—Annette thinks she *can't* sing, may not really know how she affects people. Made me rethink my whole approach. Got to see the insincerity in it. Anytime you think you hear the least little vibrato from me—"

"I should kick you," Hicks helpfully.

"Thanks, maybe lift an eyebrow anyway, that'd help."

Even visitors in from Illinois grasp right away how much respect April rates around Arleen's, enough to go easy with the yakking and tabletop sound effects and sometimes even look like they're listening. The band personnel changes night to night, refugees from rooftop and upper-story ballroom floors in the area, pit bands from vaudeville houses halfway through conversion to talkie palaces, sidemen from territory bands, rotating between here and Chicago, depending on the whims of bill collectors, ex- and current wives.

If you stay late enough, everybody shows up here. Musicians out on the variety circuits drop around after their paying gigs to sit in with the regulars. Bennie Moten personnel in matching three-piece suits and two-tone Oxfords, including the new piano player "Count" Basie, from whom you're apt to hear "Rumba Negro" more than once before dawn comes filtering up over the Lake. Jabbo Smith and Zilner Randolph going after high F's and G's not without some jugular risk, while in the back at any moment might be standing in wait some hopeful kid, his own instrument bouncing back highlights, his face still in shadows he's never felt at home in, as if, when the spot finds him at last, as he steps into the full light, he'll turn out to be somebody we already think we know . . .

"*Bel lavoro*, that load you threw us in the Lake." As out of a cloud of La Corona smoke now appears Lino "the Dump Truck" Trapanese, in a pearl-gray suit and custom homburg in pale maroon, beaming at Hicks like it's been years. Weekends Lino is most likely to be found up here in Bronzeville, putting up with remarks like "Took you for more of a 'Come Back to Sorrento' type of fella."

Hicks, long flagged among the police at all levels as Uncooperative, has enjoyed some attention from the other side of the law, tough parties like Lino here bending an eye kindly on Hicks's work life, maybe not down at it like the angels but at least sideways from time to time.

"Don't know if you can use this," Lino now behind the hand without the cigar and into Hicks's ear only, "even if you can't, it ain't me you heard it from—"

"D and D, Lino, that's me."

"*Um piccolo consiglio*. Yer Uncle Lefty? Funny stuff goin on," gazing intently, as if trying to send thought patterns through empty space.

After a while, "*Bene?*" inquires Hicks.

"Not for me to say."

"Thanks, Lino."

Since the early bad old days of street war, hand bombs and tommy-g fire syncopating the dark hours, Hicks has learned to look at these hot tips as letters of intent from Beyond, hasty, most often in rough draft, a sort of bargain-counter faith, which working ops down at his own level have been given in place of prayers unanswered. He decides to pay a family visit.

4

Next evening, halfway up the porch steps, here comes Uncle Lefty, fixing his nephew with a bright and wary look, as if beaming a professional high sign between criminals.

As Hicks learns from Aunt Peony presently in the kitchen, seems Lefty has been creeping in at late hours, imperfectly alibied by bowling-league politics, without the least detectable smell of beer, though with signs of intoxication all the same, an unforthcoming glitter, a reluctance to lower his voice or to back away, as if daring anybody in the house who might still be awake to ask him where he's been and what he's been up to. "And especially for you tonight, Hicks, he's doing the cooking."

"Here again," Uncle Lefty down at his end of the table well into third or fourth helpings, all but pitchforking around the sauerkraut, "is my Surprise Casserole you liked so much last time." Hicks can detect sport peppers, canned pineapple, almost-familiar pork parts marinated in Uncle Lefty's private cure, based on wildcat beer from a glazed-crock studio just across the Viaduct.

Seems like the chief topic of supper conversation is going to be Adolf Hitler, children present or not. This being Wisconsin, where you find more varieties of social thought than Heinz has pickles, over the years German American politics has only kept growing into a game more and more complicated, in some cases even deadly.

"Now," according to Uncle Lefty, "the MPD finds we gotta deal not only with the Reds, who've been troublesome forever, but also with the Hitler movement. Sometime soon they're headin for a showdown, more than just pushing and shoving like out in West Allis lately, but real blood on the streets of Milwaukee, let's hope not too much higher than trouser-cuff level, till one party prevails."

"'Prevails.' And you think the, um . . ." Hicks pulling his hair down briefly over one eye.

"Der Führer," gently, "is der future, Hicks. Just the other day the *Journal* calls him 'that intelligent young German Fascist.'"

"They called me Boy Inspiration of the Year once, look where it got me."

"You can't trust the newsreels, you only think you've seen him, the Jews who control the movie business only allow footage that will make him look crazy or comical, funny little guy, funny walk, funny mustache, German Charlie Chaplin, how serious could he be? But there also exist *other Hitler movies*, yes, some even filmed in color, home movies, a warmer, gayer Hitler, impulsive, unorthodox, says whatever comes into his head, what's wrong with that?"

"Jumpin up and down all nutty and screaming the minute anybody brings up the topic of Jews, sure, everybody's welcome to their own sense of humor. Swell casserole here, by the way."

"Had the recipe for years, from another beat cop I was walking partners with out in Sixth District. Sort of thing you get to talking about, walking a beat, especially if it's cold. Recipes. Kitchens of our youth. So forth."

"Very domestic," Aunt Peony poking at her food, "those straw boxes they fall asleep in, pictures on the walls, all done up, chintz curtains, the works." Since they got married, Peony's conversation has steadily been taking on an edge, her natural nerve coming out to shine, as if some maidenly spirit, searching and pious, has set out on a trip Peony has no plans herself to make, toward a destiny quietly lifted away from her when she wasn't looking . . .

"Around Baraboo, even the sweetest of girls, the most carefully brought up you can imagine, could still, one day, all at once, just . . . well, run away with the circus."

Her tactful way of mentioning her sister Grace, Hicks's mother. Peony and Grace grew up in the Driftless Area, a patch of Wisconsin never visited by glaciers, so that its terrain tends to be a little less flat and ground down than the rest of the state, free of the rubble, known as drift, that glaciers leave behind them.

Soon as they could figure how to bring their thumbs out of their mouths and into the wind, the girls fell into a practice of hitchhiking over to Baraboo every weekend, hanging around the circus people who wintered there, feeding the menagerie critters, hopelessly mooning after knife-throwers, acrobats, and mind readers, wondering just what was supposed to happen to them between now and whenever it got to a choice between run away some first of May with one of the shows or join the relentless spiral drain down to Milwaukee and find some city work, which is eventually what happened, and how Grace met Eddie McTaggart and Peony met Detlef Flaschner and got married, a double ceremony in fact, and not a day went by afterward that one or the other didn't wonder if she made the right call. This spell of matrimonial normality continued till Grace resumed an old Baraboo romance with an elephant trainer who learned his trade at the Carl Hagenbeck zoo in Hamburg from assorted stars of the profession, always talking about moving back to Europe, working the big circuses, hobnobbing with plutes and nobility, presented at court, someday owning and running his own herd. A dreamer though you'd never know it to look at him. "When other boys got sentimental they talked about all the children you were going to have, with Max it was more likely to be elephants."

Eddie, heartbroken, headed west, went silent, has kept that way since. Hicks was taken in by Aunt Peony and Uncle Lefty, or as far in as you can take somebody with one foot by then already out the door.

The logical field to get into after North Division High, it seemed to Hicks, was strikebreaking, being basically the same thing only better pay and always hiring. At the time in Wisconsin not a week went by there wasn't a strike at least being voted on someplace, plenty of opportunity to kick asses on behalf of management.

Before he knew it he'd picked up a certain notoriety as a corporate thug, fighting his way through one picket line after another so he could go on beating people up all shift long, a routine that may not've made much sense but was straightforward enough, asking nothing of Hicks but to be solid and in the way.

Any promise of industrial uncertainty inside half a tankful's driving radius and the call, almost telepathic, would go out and there'd be Hicks upside some piece of company fence out in outer Wisconsin someplace, into shoving matches all along the flare-lit fence lines, soon moving on to fists and saps.

It didn't get as political for Hicks as it did for some. "Bolshevik" was a popular insult being thrown around at strikes and marches, meaning people whose heads he was being paid to bust, but it took a while before he learned it was a Russian word and not Polish and he still isn't sure what it means.

Over that summer the papers were full of Sacco and Vanzetti, the usual bleeding hearts out in the street carrying signs and pissing and moaning ain't it awful. Houses in the Third Ward, enough so you noticed, draped in black. Somehow it must have all passed without much effect on Hicks that he can remember. He did notice nerves were on edge in the speaks, more nose-to-nose screaming and the sort of thing you expect on dim-lit patches of roadhouse parking lot later in the evenings. Mention was often made of the MPD station-house bomb of 1917 and its Italian origin.

Sometimes you're the Polack, sometimes you're the goon . . . find yourself tangling with boys you used to work alongside of, if you think that don't hurt . . . A lousy summer, on into and through the fall and if there ever had been any thrill factor for Hicks it was beginning to wear off. One night with the usual American Legion reinforcements away at some kind of annual raccoon feast, Hicks joins a disgruntled busload of colleagues headed into Sheboygan County. Running late to begin with, the bus gets pulled over by wheel coppers who take them for Communist agitators, delaying them further. By the time they reach the picket line, it's already dark, light snow on the ground picking up shadows easy to read as early bloodstains, and Hicks is in a doubtful mood. The management stooge in charge at the plant is having a nervous episode and taking it out on everybody.

"All right, listen up, some of you stay in the building, but most of you'll be outside the fence, the gates will be locked behind you. They'll be open again after you've done what you're being paid to do. Any problems?"

"The noises we keep hearing—is any of that guns?"

"Who would be that stupid?"

"Ain't stupid that worries us, Boss."

"Any of you ladies get too jittery, feel free to take cover, just keep in mind we'll consider that break time and dock you for it."

It was gunfire, all right. Coming from plant property. Five minutes out on the perimeter, the shrill glare of lights all up and down the fence suddenly goes dark. As if permission is being granted to do what comes next under cover of darkness.

"Get the feeling somebody's being set up here?"

One particular striker shorter than Hicks and wearing glasses, ordinarily the daily double of who not to go after, a wisenheimer with a mouth on him, somehow cannot be chased off or brought down. Hicks after a while is starting to take this personally. "Wait a minute, I know you. The famous Muscles McTaggart, ain't it. Why, you're nothin but a big creampuff, what happened to you? you were the certified wrath of God once, a part of history, what is it, your mother's been yellin at you? Kickin you with those combat boots," and so forth.

Hicks realizes later he really was angry enough to finish off the four-eyed troublemaker and just leave the body where it fell, another unfortunate casualty of failed labor relations. The pale blur of a face, eyes fixed on what would've been the upraised lead-filled beavertail sap, MPD issue though technically not legal . . . except that just for this moment Hicks seems to've somehow, strangely, misplaced it—nevertheless continuing to swing backhand and blind at where he last thought he saw the striker's head, only nothing connects, apparently because the sap Hicks thought he was holding isn't there anymore. Overswinging, he loses his balance, staggers, nearly falls . . . in the time it takes him to get normal again, somehow mysteriously something has changed.

The truculent little Bolshevik has been observing this with interest. "Go ahead," snickering, "take your time, I ain't afraida you."

"Not packing any heat there, I hope, li'l feller."

"If I was, you'd be dead already."

"My lucky day but maybe you can tell me— Hey, well where'd he go?"

"I would've flattened the little runt," Hicks is advised helpfully. "How can a man live with verbal abuse like that?"

IN FACT IT would take a couple of days for Hicks to understand that the strange feeling he couldn't get a handle on was relief at not having killed somebody, slow-arriving because it seemed too much to hope for, one of those opportunities for second thoughts that with luck sometimes can come along. It felt almost like flying. Like the kindliest judge out of the sappiest movie in history beaming over his eyeglasses, "Case dismissed."

Still leaving the mystery of where'd that beavertail get to, there one second and gone the next? Failing to fetch its target a blow that if it had connected would've killed him, Hicks had been that possessed by rage.

Presently he found himself falling into the strange habit of stepping between strikers and strikebreakers, if he was cranked up enough by then from the day's activities it didn't seem that much more dangerous, just an added direction to be jumped on from. Eventually the day arrived that when the call went out, Hicks found a way not to show up. Even when he could've used the money. Strangely, unexpectedly, out from under the obligation to go and bust heads, even if only for this one job.

Fellow tough guys are puzzled. "What a clambake you missed, dozens of casualties, nice payday too, peeled off of a flash roll the size of a spare tire, where were you?"

"BBH." Bowling Ball Hospital out on Highway 41, looking in on the progress of his prize Brunswick Mineralite ball, which is having weight distribution troubles, "Drilling, plugging, went on for hours, emergency call in fact, they had to send an ambulance." A converted Model T depot hack with little bowling-ball-sized gurneys and everybody in white coats.

DURING ONE JITTERY period visiting different local factories, for chances of steady security work, Hicks heard about U-Ops and decided to have a look. They didn't throw him out on his ear, a refreshing development, though there were a couple of trick questions.

"What'd be your idea of the next career step after industrial goon squad, Mr. McTaggart?"

Hicks gets nervous when anybody mentions next steps. Sooner or later the step turns out to be off the edge of some bluff and into the Lake. "I give up, tell me."

No reply, just a sweeping look around at the little office they were in.

Somehow next thing he knows Hicks is deep in a Sheepshead marathon, which goes on all weekend. Nobody's ever been promoted at U-Ops, let alone hired in the first place, without some proficiency at the game. The rules of Sheepshead, which not many outside Milwaukee find easy to follow, are somehow here inside the city limits inscribed into the local brain from birth. Not just playing for nickels, trick-taking and scoring points, Sheepshead engages with deeper matters of destiny, like having to figure out or blindly guess who among a number of players your partner is supposed to be, "As with life in general, always better to guess right, of course, though it's all those poor souls who never do that keep us private ops in business, ain't it."

Private eyes of the 1930s are emerging from an era of labor unrest and entering one of spousal infidelity, encouraged if not enabled by Prohibition, as Boynt, who blames Prohibition for everything, sliding into a bloviational W. C. Fields delivery, is quick to point out and happy to explain at further length.

"You wanna know why there's suddenly all these private coppers around, is it's Prohibition. Created so much disrespect for city police, state and federal law, that we now have this rush of customers more than ready to turn to private-sector stiffs like us before they'll trust the Milwaukee PD, despite which it's dumb, overfed coppers who are destined to inherit earthly power, you can bet the rent on that, the private eyes and postcollegiate dilettantes of today will be long scattered, lost, slid back down into the inventory of uncounted jobless—oh. Wait. Nothing personal, forgot your Uncle Lefty, with whom I share a melancholy piece of history, almost a stretch in jail," Boynt begins, and so on into another hooch-soaked evening, Boynt without even the common courtesy to stay at the office and break out his own, dragging Hicks instead from one nocturnal hush-hush to another, many of them unsuspected by Hicks till now.

"Yes, to look at it you'd think, easygoing, midwestern, nothin much going on, but step around the corner, try another angle, and it's a different story. What finds its way into which pockets, what and sometimes who gets deep-sixed in the Lake after midnight, what happens to Negroes down in the precinct houses. Hitler kiddies, Sicilian mob, secret hallways and exit tunnels, smoke too thick to see through, half a dozen different languages, any lowlife thinks they can turn a nickel always after you for somethin, there's your wholesome Cream City, kid, mental hygiene paradise but underneath running off of a heartbeat crazy as hell, that's if it had a heart which it don't . . .

"This isn't about bringing crooks to justice, did you think that's what we do? Not likely. We try any of that, licenses are sure to get pulled. What we do is, it's only investigation. It's like going to the movies. Sit quietly, eat popcorn, get educated. Solving murder mysteries, that's for cops. Lawyers, judges, those who want to see somebody do time or get hanged for whatever it is." In business since the days of the Haymarket bomb frame-up and the Rolling Mills Massacre, the Unamalgamated shop has always turned a brisk dollar from strong-arm jobs on behalf of management against labor, sometimes brutal and one-sided, sometimes fatal, no doubt, though why should offices back or front need to keep count, or even know that much?

"We're kind of a transition zone between working for the owners and saddling up to go steal a payroll from them. With the grand old days of union busting moved on west, now it's wandering spouses, beer-related intrigue, a little freelancing whenever the Outfit shows up needing some cheap labor, smaller-scale, what you could even call intimate sometimes, though potentially just as harmful to your health."

It also happened around this time that one day a paper match cover on the sidewalk fatefully caught Hicks's eye. "Learn Oriental Attitude and regain control of your life." Of course Hicks picked it up, filled it out, mailed it in, some address in Chicago, keenly curious till he saw what the complete twelve-week course was going to cost him.

There did turn out to be a lower-cost option, a 35¢ instruction manual in comic-book form full of speech balloons, which though translated from Japanese into English was still indecipherable to Hicks, who, strangely gripped nevertheless, read all the way through, several times.

"Just as well," Uncle Lefty helpfully, "when and if you finally go down there in person to get your diploma, maybe they hypnotize you into forgetting you ever took the course. There you are, all stuffed full of Oriental Attitude, and how will you ever know?"

"Thanks, Onk."

But something must have been filtering through anyway. Hicks was slowly becoming aware at this time of what you could call a change in outlook, finding himself mysteriously in and out of the Toy Building down on 2nd Street or Nan King, a new south side joint, places that specialized in chop suey and dancing, not his usual idea of a Saturday night, and on another unexpected weekend in Chicago actually required to mediate, without understanding a word of Chinese, between On Leongs and Hip Sings regarding their uneasy arrangements about who's supposed to get the opium trade and who the needle drugs such as cocaine, also receiving on top of a tidy fee from both parties a number of chain mail undershirts which turn out to be useful when wandering into moments of Chicago street recreation . . .

Maybe not as solid a voice as Dick Powell, not bad as a hoofer—yet as if in his sleep, he has somehow aged from a bright-eyed juvenile song-and-dance artist into a street-hardened, less often shaved and brilliantined specimen, one that the most level-headed of starlets these days might have trouble keeping still for even a couple bars of being crooned to by, Hicks finds himself ambling along the old worn pathways that lead into whatever the label "civilian" is currently being used for, a nationwide consensus including house chores on weekends, a dutiful ear to the radio, a disinclination to pick up any lengthier of a rap sheet than he's already got. Even all day on into overtime and half the night on his feet and in motion, Hicks has begun to feel a kind of spiritual heavysetness sneaking up on him. Sometimes he'll go a week without hearing a gunshot. Even desperate enough between shifts to go into the office and listen to police traffic on the Thrill Box. Who wouldn't start to get nostalgic for the high-adventure escapades of earlier Prohibition days?

After a while others begin to notice, especially those Hicks once would've had little problem doing damage to but now found himself thinking twice about even frowning at. For all he knows, Oriental Attitude might be saving their lives, not to mention redefining his own—who knows if even one more assault beef on his record could be the fatal one to tilt him into a completely different life story?

"You've somehow come to safety, Hicks," it seems to his aunt Peony, "safe in the featherbed of your destiny, not by refraining from violence but by embracing it, surviving it." With, however, that trademark Aunt Peony reckless glint.

"Nah. Don't feel like that at all. Whatever it means."

"Hicks, it's as plain as the nose on your face. If you'd only stop to think."

Stop doing what, was the problem, but she wouldn't get specific. It kept going back to the last strike he worked, and the four-eyed Bolshevik he meant to kill but didn't. He kept trying to find somebody to talk to about it, even Boynt, though the boss wasn't too sympathetic. "Look at your rap sheet. Never tried, never even booked, street legal forever including the streets of heaven, count your blessings, get over it."

"Maybe I killed somebody, Boynt, maybe more than once, and never knew it."

"You always know when you've done it. If you're not sure, assume you didn't. Guilt's all it is. Have you been to the company brain-croakers about this yet?"

"Back office says no dice, insurance only covers the one annual checkup, psycho ain't included."

"So . . . untreated guilt complex, mm-hmm. Some lucky voodoo artist out there's looking at hours of gainful employment. Save the bellyaching, Hicks, I've heard it all."

"And what would you do in my place?"

"Why not have a word with Thessalie. Even the back office listens to her."

Good idea. Thessalie happens to have worked as a stage mentalist, till talking pictures put the whammy on vaudeville, "And now I'm reduced to this. You think it isn't humiliating? All this carnal-relations stuff? Typing 'penis' every day? Not like I have a choice. A shot at anything, any toilet anywhere, any death trail from here on south of the border—say, wouldn't I jump at it. But you see what's happening to vaudeville, they're even tearing down the Majestic now, for Pete's sake, it's the double whammy, the talkies arrive exactly the same time as the Depression. Some coincidence, huh. Almost like somebody's trying to get rid of us old troupers."

Whenever it becomes necessary to trace the history of physical cash, it's Thessalie who's likely to get the midnight phone call . . . paid off on the Q.T. one job at a time in—what else?—overhandled currency, typically $2 bills loaded with enough resentment, remorse, lust, anxiety sometimes to send an unwary psychometrist swooning nearly to collapse.

"Strange thing," Uncle Lefty reluctantly admits, "but she seems to be the genuine goods." Though the MPD have never been that crazy about psychics, whom they like to blame for fondling evidence, smudging prints, compromising bloodstains, Thessalie has been enough help with a number of cases that she's widely sought-after now by city police here and down the Lake, whenever what they think they see with their own eyes isn't enough . . . nothing in writing of course.

5

Hicks and Thessalie meet one day at Velocity Lunch, a quiet joint with an upstairs you can loiter in and not be bothered, meet briefly for a hand-off, or for hours of matrimonial business, even to eat at. Lunch dramas passing like storm fronts, pies in glass cases slowly losing their a.m. allure, grill artists taking care of various counterside chores while whatever they're flipping is in midair rotating end over end. Fluorescent light through Today's Special, a vivid green salad centerpiece the size and shape of a human brain, molded in lime Jell-O, versions of which have actually been observed to glow. "We used to dim down the lights before bringing it in to the table, but eating it in the dark made too many people uncomfortable."

Thessalie is a nice enough trick if brainy and resourceful is your type. Although knowing what men are thinking about doesn't take supernatural powers, still it has often put a certain kibosh on her social life, which she doesn't mind complaining about. The mind-reader angle doesn't strike Hicks as much of a selling point either. So maybe he's a little nervous.

After a brief guess at Hicks's arm length, she sets her purse out of reach and switches on a smile. "Boynt mentioned you have something on your mind you want to talk about."

Him and his big mouth. "Thessalie, if you ain't just the spit of that Joan Blondell."

"Widely remarked on, and don't change the subject."

"Just that I wouldn't know how to—"

"It's OK, no taboos, you can ask me anything, long as it isn't state capitals."

"Well . . . say you're just about to . . . you know, give somebody the business, OK, only it doesn't happen, not because your aim is off, see, but because your weapon all of a sudden somehow isn't . . . uh . . ."

"Isn't there any more? Sure, happens a lot, an often heard excuse. 'It withdrew into its own space, it asported to safety.'"

"It, um . . . ?"

"Asported. When something disappears suddenly off to someplace else, in the business that's called an asport. Coming in at you the other way, appearing out of nowhere, that's an 'apport.' Happens in séances a lot, kind of side effect. Ass and app, as we say."

"This was outdoors, during a strike. Solid one minute, there in my hand, then . . ." Small shrug, palms up and empty, "I had a pretty good look around, figuring I dropped it someplace, but—"

"A firearm of some kind."

"A beavertail. Kind of a loaded sap."

"Been out socially with a number of them. How long ago's this been now?"

"Dunno, a while."

"And it's still on your mind."

"Thing is, is if I'd ever connected, I would've killed somebody."

"Someone who was trying to kill you?"

"Yes, maybe no . . ."

"Well, and this vanishing beavertail, did it ever come back?"

"A little later that night. Looked in my pocket and there it was again."

"Again? Or there all the time?"

"No, that's how I knew to look, was I could feel the extra weight, when it came back."

"Narrows it down to temporary amnesia, or ass and app. Less likely, maybe something out there didn't want you to commit the assault, some unnamed force. Grace of God, another technical term we use."

"Presbyterian, myself."

"Well, and the beavertail—how about the next time you had occasion to use it?"

"Never did. That was around the time I pretty much quit working strikes. Ended up hiring on at the U-Ops instead."

"Where now you get to pack a revolver instead of a sap. Nice career step."

"Sure, but I still have to sign for it, plus ammo." It took Hicks a while to get comfortable carrying heat. First time Boynt sent him off on a case, handing over a little S&W .32, "These li'l Smiths here, Federal B of I loves 'em. Better set aside some room in your pocket."

"Loose in my pocket? What if I have an accident?"

"Good to see you respect that—here, this is called the safety, OK?"

"Thanks, Boynt."

"Now," Thessalie continuing, "I can look this up, but since you've been with the U-Ops, how many rounds would you say you've fired, total?"

"Hmm, ten, twelve maybe, haven't been keeping count, who wants to know?"

"Hit anybody?"

"Hard to say." Explaining how he tries not to show up heavy but if he has to, never to aim that straight. Usually it's been at night, or during some fog, once or twice returning fire, but mostly just expending ammo into an unlighted distance. Maybe a couple of over-the-shoulder type blind shots while he was running the other way.

"And the sap, you still don't have it around by any chance."

"Long gone, sorry."

"Too bad. Sometimes it takes no more than lightly touching an object to read the traces of where it's been and who with and what they've been up to. We want to believe that objects are pure, innocent, when the truth is that they lie open to every vibration that comes their way, law-abiding, criminal, everything in between . . ."

"Wait, you're saying an object can have a living personality? Same as you and me?"

"Same as me, I hope not. Same as you, maybe *you* better hope not. But if a human soul can be defined as a structure of memories, if to 'read' an object is somehow to gain access to what it remembers, then how can we begrudge it a soul?"

"Lemme think about that." Soon as he figures out what it means, of course. "And this ass 'n' app, now, this instant skip, are these objects doing it all on their own? or is there somebody doing it to them?"

"Some apportists believe that it's all them—others think of themselves only as go-betweens, mediums, stooging for unseen forces."

"Like some special . . . gift, or . . ."

"Not the word that comes to mind, a gift is usually free, whatever this is has a price tag stuck onto it whose amount might surprise you. Speaking of which, including the professional discount, this'll be ten dollars U.S."

"What? Where am I supposed to find—"

"Try inside your hatband, toward the back, new bill, folded twice, you want the serial number?"

"Forgot that was there," trying to blink away some temporary brain fog, handing over the sawbuck. "That's amazing, Thessalie, could revolutionize the whole field of daylight robbery, how do you—wait, second thought, don't tell me."

"All right, but listen—whatever it was, apports or whatever, you were lucky once. Just don't count on luck every time. If you're going to be carrying a weapon, it'd also help to have some insurance."

"Like what?"

"Talk to Lew Basnight." Get him to teach you the Curly Bill Spin. Something every gunslinger should know."

"Somehow I took you for more of a nonviolent type."

"A couple of times it saved my life. Talk to Lew."

6

Approaching the critical hour when many a private op would prefer, after more than enough little homeopathic snorts of gunsmoke, to head indoors to a safe desk in some upstairs office, Lew Basnight on the other hand continues to think of office work as early retirement, and intends to die on the job, out in the field. "Is where they'll find me, weeks later, years, maybe never, someplace unknown, middle of chasin down one more no-hope lead everybody's long forgotten. Gumshoe's Grave. There's a tattoo parlor in Chicago up North Clark could do you somethin along those lines if you're interested."

Lew can usually be found decorating the mahogany at Otto's Oasis, the only place in town willing to assemble for him a Doc Holliday—Old Overholt, Doc's preferred brand, plus Nehi peach soda, in recognition of his native Georgia, plus maybe a half jigger of absinthe if available, to put an edge on it, over ice. In public a kindly old geezer but in fact an unreconstructed veteran of the Old West at its least merciful, another of those hard cases who didn't settle for law-abiding when it did, returning as the nights go deepening to memories of his outlaw youth.

"See, at the time you had a number of corrals in Tombstone, there was the Mighty Fantastic Corral, deluxe indoor stalls, gourmet nosebags, what they call 'oat cuisine,' and right around the corner in the same price range the Just as Stupendous Corral, but then if you didn't want to spend that much money, why there was always . . ."

Lew is happy to show Hicks the famous gunhand maneuver named after and taught to him in person by Curly Bill Brocius, one of the Clanton gang.

"Pretty straightforward, just pretend you're handing over your heater butt first, but remember to keep your finger in the trigger guard so when least expected you can spin the sucker around and shoot whoever's trying to take it away from you. There you go. Just like that. Keep practicin with different weapons till you can do it without thinking, which around Chicago is usually the case."

"Thought you'd be back in California by now, Lew."

There is rumored to be an ex–Mrs. Lew Basnight, living on the Near North Side, remarried back in early Prohibition to an Outfit subcontractor whom Lew still considers himself under obligation to protect her from. Given Lew's history of conflict resolution, this has her feeling like some kind of widow in waiting, and refusing to talk to or even have much at all to do with him. Lew understands this and doesn't understand exactly. But it could be what's keeping him back East.

"You think if I had a choice I'd stay here any longer than I have to?" Gazing out the window where some snow has begun to fall.

"This? only Lake effect, too early for anything more."

"Gets earlier every year. After you put some time in you'll start to notice. Normally with the corporate circuit ride they've got me doin, by the time this kinda stuff starts in I'm already on board the ol' Chief and rollin on into the sunset. Don't think I'm homsesick or nothin just because you find me now and then with my head down the Victrola horn listenin to Al Jolson sing 'Home in Pasadena.' Didn't even get out there till late in life, after years of dancin the Pinkertonian around what only a couple of old-timers were still callin the Wild West anymore. Hell, I'm ready to go back, the minute this damn blizzard lets up I'm on my way, train station's just down the street, pack a bag, get my hat steamed, step aboard, no effort at all, a man could do it in his sleep," which in fact sometimes Lew does, lucid dreaming that he's flown in from strange suburban distances, past radio antennas and skyscrapers, down the gloomy city canyons, skimming echo to echo, banking into the Dearborn station, flown invisible, ticketless, right onto the Santa Fe Chief. And away. Away, so easy . . .

"Thanks for showing me the move, Lew. Thessalie thinks it'll keep me safe like it does for her."

"That one? she'd've been fine without it, hell if it was her against Curly Bill, I wouldn't take the bet. Just don't oversell yourself on safety, kid. No damn such thing."

"Now you tell me."

"Just so long as you ain't another one of these metaphysical detectives, out looking for Revelation. Get to reading too much crime fiction in the magazines, start thinking it's all about who done it. What really happened. Hidden history. Oh, yeah. Seeing all the cards at the end of a hand. For some, that kinda thing gets religious mighty quick."

"I have enough to worry about with real life."

"Well good luck, sonny. Hate to tell you but the only time 'real' comes into it is when they're shooting at you. In practice, 'real' means dead—anything else, there's always room for some conversation."

7

The Hollywood talkie *Dracula* opened last year in Chicago on Valentine's Day, which happened to fall on a Saturday. April's idea of a romantic date.

"I was thinking more like a candlelight dinner at the Villa Venice," said Hicks. "You sure you want to go all the way into Chicago, considering what tends to happen there on Valentine's Day—"

"Ha! I knew it, superstitious is one thing, Lunchmeat, but that kind of talk is just howling at the moon."

"Come on, Cuban band, gondola ride out on the river, it's the classiest rendezvous between Chicago and Milwaukee."

"It's a ritzed-up speak with a two-dollar cover."

"Three on Saturday."

"Where would you find that kind of money?"

"Twenty-six game, lucky couple of rolls."

"Uh-huh, what was her name?"

"No, wait, I forgot, it was the dog races."

"I don't want your money, I want that silver screen as I share a romantic bucket of popcorn with the man who—or let me put it another way . . ." Suddenly looking nervous. Hicks had an idea why, though he wished he didn't.

"Hmm, well, OK, but this picture is supposed to be kind of terrifying, so promise if you get scared you'll come sit on my lap."

So they rode into Chicago, and were spared any Outfit-related violence, but what there was was Count Dracula, big as a movie screen, once or twice during whose activities it was Hicks who considered jumping into April's lap. By the time it was over she'd eaten six cubic feet of popcorn and was using his tie to wipe the butter off her fingers with.

"Romantic enough for you?"

"Just want to swoon," April confirms. "Mmm, that Bela Lugosi, some kinda Hungarian oomph there, all right."

"So Jimmy Cagney's about to have his heart broken."

"Hayseeds like you could learn something."

"Bite your neck? I can do that, c'mere."

"Hicks, you need more culture, a more Continental approach to life and love. At least find out what Bela's putting on his hair," and so forth.

William Powell, James Cagney, now this. Hicks figures he's in for weeks of sighing, movie magazines gathering in uneasy stacks, and whispers of "Oh, Bela!" in her sleep.

Soon she is sending away to Johnson Smith down in Racine for a set of Glow-in-the-Dark Vampire Choppers, 35¢ postpaid. They prove to be less of a hit in the bedroom than over at Uncle Lefty's, where no sooner does Hicks clip on the strangely radiant fangs than he's buried in a rush of juvenile hilarity . . .

Though Hicks had been still hoping for the Villa Venice, they didn't get much further that night than one of the no-name drink-and-dance joints out northwest, which was also where and how he finally got the official word about Don Peppino Infernacci, something Lino Trapanese has been hinting around about for the better part of a year now. The minute April heads for the ladies' toilet, Don Peppino's chief enforcer, Angie "Vumvum" Voltaggio, an infrequent shaver in a glossy suit known for a readiness to bring out his "ukulele" on any pretext and spray a pattern, here tonight hosting a small party of two dozen, blaming his loosened tongue on the Gaglioppo, blurts out what's news to nobody, that April Randazzo is in fact the promised bride of evil, known locally as Don Peppino—and not only publicly dizzy about but actually preparing at any moment to go running off with her abductor. No kindly mob elder, more like a shark, brute force, no apologies. Dangerous. And what kind of dimwit does Hicks have to be that he doesn't know that already?

Couple days later there's a follow-up visit from Don Peppino's boys. Being Wisconsin torpedoes, they go about their daily mischief with the innocent demeanor of farm kids just arrived in town, causing strangers they may have business with to confuse stolid with harmless, often with dismaying results.

"Yelling 'get lost' is often not the recommended course of action," as it says in the Gumshoe's Manual, so Hicks only raises his eyebrows in a friendly way.

". . . put the bump on you? Not us, not our specialty. We'd have to go find and hire somebody for that, could take weeks. And the paperwork, *lascia perdere*."

"This is just a friendly word to the wise."

"Or in your case, the otherwise."

"It's about your social life."

"A certain Bronzeville canary of your acquaintance."

"I think he gets it."

"On the other hand, yiz out shoppin for a wood kimono, maybe we could help."

"Pink would look cuter on him, ain't it."

Having run into this once or twice, Hicks is hep that they're trying to crank him up enough that he blows his top and goes after one of them, providing an excuse to bring out the hardware. Seeing he hasn't been getting enough exercise lately, this begins, actually, not to look like such a bad idea. Nunzi, perhaps the more reflective of the two, seems at last to pick this up and gives his partner Dominic's arm a warning tap.

"Maybe you're startin to miss the accident ward again, *minghiun*, 'cause right now you are *so close* . . ."

"Say, I can handle this big creampuff." Dominic goes rushing in at Hicks. It doesn't last long. Presently, Dominic is lying inert though breathing next to a beaverboard partition wall, which now has a dent from where he's just been slammed into it.

"Seemed in pretty good shape," Hicks pretending to flick blood from his sleeve, "you might want them to have a look at him down at County General, just to be sure."

"You mind signing this release form for Don Peppino, he likes to see some proof we didn't just go off someplace and roll a couple of frames."

IN HICKS'S EXPERIENCE, wide but not always educational, of a cross-section of womanhood in our time, most of them, he's noticed, haven't had much, if any, idea of how to fight. Not in the grimly verbal married way, but more like physically grabassing, throwing real punches and kicks. April has been a welcome exception, making Vumvum's news especially saddening because no such amorous round-and-round is likely to be in the cards anytime soon for her with Don Peppino, who's been known to take back-talk, even unwelcome gestures, very much amiss.

He'll carry her off down the MKR Corridor to Little Cosenza, some love *casinetto* down there stupendous in its level of tastelessness, into a horrible domesticity that Hicks gets nauseous even thinking he might begin to think about. Tongue-biting and gaze-lowering. Weekend after weekend, giant, labor-intensive social-hall lasagnas—Wisconsin lasagnas, with dead raccoon somewhere in the recipe, like the Delafield American Legion only more garlic and oregano possibly . . .

Happy Valentine's Day. Vumvum is eager to add details a few days later when he and Hicks run into each other at Fahrflung's Sporting Goods, down an alleyway from the interurban station at 6th and Michigan, Canoes, Tents, Camping Supplies, and in Vumvum's case today, Submachine Gun Accessories. Vumvum has just purchased a Cutts compensator or muzzle brake to keep his aim from drifting upward during lengthier bursts, "25 clams, but Don Peppino is off on one of his cost-cutting routines trying to save money on ammo. Thousand rounds a minute, nickel per round, it adds up, see."

"From the presence or absence of a Cutts compensator," as the Gumshoe's Manual points out, "the alert operative can often gain valuable insight into the character of a Thompson user, though here, time being understandably of the essence, speed is recommended."

Once a few years back in Waukesha County, Hicks, observing Vumvum chased by rival gang elements and headed his way like a runaway express train, stepped in pretending to be lost and looking for directions, allowing Vumvum to highball on into the custody of the sheriff's department and only a little less leisure-time whoopee in his life, instead of becoming the next notch on the butt of somebody's *lupara*. For which Vumvum if not eternally grateful found himself from then on strangely unhomicidal when in Hicks's company.

"He's a lord of the underworld," Hicks points out now, "you can't tell me she's with him of her own free will."

"I just did," Vumvum replies. "Could have somethin to do with Don Peppino's got the biggest *minghiuzza* in the criminal trades, major league fungo stick, always in use and not just for practice pop-ups neither, you capeesh?"

Taking a few seconds to light up, "Useful information, Vumvum, to be sure, why hasn't somebody mentioned this sooner?"

"Never know how dimensions that personal will go over with people. Reactions vary." A strange capacity for sentiment has somehow found its way into Vumvum's face, which Hicks up till now, being reluctant to look that close, has failed to notice. "*Goomara* mentality," angling his head before shaking it, "not for me to speculate. Been keeping a close eye but it don't look like she's tryin too hard to get away, even if Don Peppino deliberately lets her misbehave, so he can scold her for it later. Not that she ain't caught on to that, not much gets past her."

An uncomfortably throbbing patch of silence, which Hicks takes to be Vumvum's unwillingness to discuss how much April might be enjoying herself with the 'Ndrangheta heavyweight, who has considered often enough getting athletic with Hicks about it, though preferably not in person. "Vumvum, seriously, how worried should I be about Twinkletoes?"

"Well, dancing is vertical whoopee, Boss, everybody knows that."

"Education," smacking Vumvum amiably upside the head, "ain't it grand. Vumvum, now, total honesty, do I seem to you the violently jealous type?"

"Padrino, this far down the chain nobody gives *ungazz* about that emotional stuff."

8

Hicks gets a note from Skeet. "Come on down the Viaduct, somebody there you might want to talk to."

He finds Skeet and some fellow gang members waiting under the Holton Street Viaduct for the fog to lift, along with a few girls grown wary of the evening shift looking for some daylight trade. Streetcars go banging overhead. "C'mon." Skeet leads him into an abandoned lot surrounded by darkened walls, paint of old advertising weathered away, windows that could have anything just behind them. Or nothing for years. Civilians drift to and fro mostly idle, a few collecting lookout fees.

"Welcome to the clubhouse."

Cobwebs of purple light from radio tubes with imperfect vacuums inside. A dozen speakers going at once, cop traffic and shipping transmissions from out on the Lake, foreign voices from even further away crackling in and out. Pieces of electrical gear blinking and chirping at each other, like a lab in a movie belonging to a scientist not entirely in his right mind— Type 19 dual triodes from incompletely assembled Doerle Twinplex kits lying around everyplace, including where they're likely to be sat on. Radio equipment, some of it bright and new as if just boosted, "Top-notch and 1929-compliant," according to Skeet, "we steal only from the best." All clear as daylight to an eye electrically fly, leaving the rest of us to squint, frown, try to make some sense out of it while not looking too lost, for among this pack of juvenile offenders, street-corner musicians, and policy runners can also be found a number of "hams" or amateur radio operators, either licensed or hoping to be, including a couple of young ladies just graduated from Mary Texanna Loomis's Radio College in Washington, D.C., in touch with other enthusiasts around the world, via waves the average civilian still has little idea of, waves they have learned, sometimes at a certain cost, to ride and respect. They lurk at the fringes of frequency bands public and private, listen in on and try to decipher secret messages, sell some of what they learn, use some of it themselves for purposes of mischief, or, as the Hellraisers think of it, "practical joking."

Not surprisingly, interested parties can be found, usually after dark, prowling around in little panel trucks with rotating loop antennas on top trying to get a fix on sources of transmission, obsessed by what these kids might find out, who they might be talking to about it . . . bootleggers, lately more and more making use of encrypted radio traffic, being of particular federal concern.

Everybody is smoking Camels and Luckies, Dutch Masters and El Productos stolen off the Milwaukee Road freights that come rolling through town. The joint is wallpapered with publicity stills of Goldwyn Girls in their unmentionables, prominent among them the platinum trick or, as Skeet prefers, desperately adorable goddess Toby Wing. "This here is the all-time definition of cute with a capital Q!"

A back room with its own back room, "First workspace in my life that *has* a toilet," sez Skeet, "instead of is one. The mad scientist's lab I always dreamed about."

"Mad scientist like—angry? Or—" crossing his eyes and putting out his tongue at an angle.

"Both." Helpfully.

Around midday Hughes, one of the Negro policy runners, shows up, taking a breather before the next round of betting resumes, sporting a hand-me-down drape suit retailored at the waist and ankles from one of his father's. Accompanied by Bensonhurst, a small, shaggy mutt, mostly Norwich terrier, that Hughes was supposed to drown as a puppy but couldn't bring himself to. "White gentleman pays me four bits to do the job. Face to face, couldn't do it and Benny knew I couldn't, ain't that right, Benny, hay-ull no.

Thought about giving the money back, but we blew it all on Ken-L Ration instead."

A furious torrent of dots and dashes from a shortwave set back in a corner. "German naval code again," explains a kid named Drover in a set of earphones who's been monitoring, a very bright young science whiz who had to lie about his age to get into Shorewood High School and is currently sitting in on physics classes at Marquette, now and then getting in a round of speed chess with the professor, Árpád Élő, the top player in Milwaukee. "Family are happier when I'm out of the house, any trouble I'm headed for I ought to be able to avoid if I'm as bright as everybody keeps telling me, don't you think?"

"Uh-huh, what's with all these wires comin out of this ukulele here?"

"Listen." Eight quick bars of "On the Sunny Side of the Street" on amplified uke.

"It's coming over the radio, how's that work?"

"Kid out in Waukesha showed me, you take a record needle, wire it up to the speaker here, see? You want the real Tom Swift, it's this Lester kid, calls himself Red, playing hillbilly guitar up and down Bluemound Road for nickels and dimes, drive-ins, roadhouse parking lots, gets to where he needs to be heard over the traffic, so he figured this out."

"White kid named Red on Bluemound Road, check and triple check, pretty patriotic, ain't it."

"Also known as the Wizard of Waukesha. Me, I'm just another brass-pounder, but this kid's the goods, I tell ya."

"Hicksie, you got a minute?" It's Skeet, dragging over who, natch, but the till recently incommunicado Stuffy Keegan.

"Well, Stuffy. Sorry about the truck."

"Hope you ain't working for anybody that's looking for me."

"Couple of clients naturally curious about who did it and why, wondering who'll try to collect the insurance, nothin more personal than that."

"See, when it blew I was supposed to been in it. Last-minute yen for a Giant Bar, pulled over, just about to step in the candy store, feeling around for change, suddenly ka-blooey, all hell, whizzin around my ears, thought it was giant mosquitoes but it was pieces of my rig. Somehow I begin to get this feelin . . ."

"MPD say they're on the case, some think it's the Outfit, some say the Nazi Youth."

"Two different kinds of trouble, ain't it, one you end up dead, the other dead and in hell."

"Just in time, Stuffy," Drover back at the shortwave equipment. "Your sub just showed up again."

Stuffy finds another set of earphones and jacks in.

"His what?" sez Hicks.

"The U-13," Drover explains. "An unsurrendered Austro-Hungarian submarine. Supposed to be broken up by terms of the Versailles Treaty, but somehow they dodged it."

"Where are they?"

"Out in the Lake someplace. Closer to the other side where there's less ice."

"A submarine in Lake Michigan. Come on, kid."

"Hmm, traffic's light tonight, everybody must be down below at the bowling alley."

"The, um . . ."

"There's a big tournament on."

"Bowling alley on a submarine, Drover?"

"Sure, quite common in fact, you never heard of *20,000 Leagues Under the Sea*?"

Stuffy meantime has gone off into some trance of his own, as if monitoring the U-13 could be no more weird or peculiar than listening to a normal radio show over a Thrill Box of unconventional design.

"Each episode," Stuffy explains later, "the U-13 visits a different port of call. A different chore. Pickup and delivery, tobacco, dope, guns, hooch, live passengers with their papers not always in order who need to be here or there in a hurry and don't mind being stashed with the cargo."

"Anybody we might know, Stuffy?"

"Sure—and if I tell ya, you'll get all agitated, with your lousy cop reflexes, start calling names, mania this, phobia that, unnatural emotions, and givin me that look. Yeah, right there, that one."

"Your personal affair, Stuffy, man wants to be U-boat happy, what's it to me?"

"Yeah, well, they're picking me up tonight."

"This . . . U-boat . . ."

Drover looks back over his shoulder, catching Hicks's eye, points his thumb at one earphone, nods, goes back to monitoring traffic.

"Just came by to say so long. To people I can still trust."

"Where they takin you, Stuffy?" Hicks tries but it still comes out like you talk to crazy people.

"To where it's safe."

"Mind if me and Drover tag along?" sez Skeet.

EVENING ON THE LAKE, ice fishers either preparing to spend the night or heading back to shore, Stuffy indicates a shack in the distance, "That's the rendezvous point, but you guys ought to stay here. Far as the Lake's OK if you want, but any further forget it, they tell me no witnesses allowed."

Stuffy bids everyone a good night that sounds like a goodbye, trudges off alone in the direction of Grand Rapids, Michigan, crunching, squeaking over the ice into the darkness, as the coast of Wisconsin slips step by step away behind him . . .

They watch him till it's too dark.

"Looked like a fishing shack," sez Skeet.

"You think he's gone bughouse?"

"No more than he ever was."

"Maybe we better . . ."

They hurry out onto the ice. Nothing much to see when they finally reach the shack, which is strangely un-winterbeaten, some firewood stacked under a tarp, wheels, a towing hitch . . .

"Door's open," Skeet reports.

"Anybody home?" Hicks loud but friendly. Nothing inside. Ashes in a cold woodstove, scatter of cigarette butts on the floor, Stuffy nowhere in sight.

"Where'd he go, then?"

Picking up a penciled note, "If you're here and I'm not, means I'm on my way and time you were on yours. Head toward the city lights, brighter the better, keep going, try not to look back."

About halfway back to shore, "Uh-oh, what's this?"

Lights beneath the ice. In from the unscaled distance, dim halos each slowly sharpening, outlining a sleek black underwater shape, making a careful approach, brighter as they glide closer.

"Is it what I think it is?"

"All black, can't make out too much detail through the ice, but it has to be Stuffy's sub," Skeet less casual than normal.

"You've seen it before?"

"Fits the description according to Stuffy."

The jet-black apparition slows, slides underneath them and matches their course and speed. When they pause, it pauses. After a short while Drover notices one light in particular, blinking unevenly on and off. "Seems to be Morse code," Drover with a concentrated look. "Yeah, it sez, 'Now you're all up to speed, suckers. BCNU, Stuffy.'"

"He's on board that, whatever that is?"

"I didn't see nothin," sez Skeet. "You guys?"

AS DAYS PASS without further word, suspicions grow that Stuffy has been taken aboard the U-13 and into its history of pickups and deliveries, back to his old contraband-running ways, assigned a sleeping space, standing watches regularly . . .

"You know how crazy that sounds."

"What's the un-crazy story then?"

Shrug. "Maybe we just don't want to hear about it."

"We've all been looking at the same blotters, if he's silent key and it's a ghost we saw then there'd be a coroner's verdict someplace, likely Chicago, hit-and-run victim not used to big-city traffic, Milwaukee being notorious for its inattentive pedestrians, 'Jaywalkee,' as it's known to the wisemouths of the County of Cook . . ."

"Times Stuffy thought he wasn't here anymore—that they really did get him when they blew up the truck. Kept saying things like 'Maybe I'm a ghost now and I'm haunting you.'"

"Thanks, Skeet. If it's creepy stories tonight, I hope somebody remembered to bring the marshmallows."

9

Skeet shows up at the office next day with an out-of-town tomato who causes a certain commotion. Thessalie asks her where she buys her shoes. Zbig Dubinski has his hat off and his hair combed and has changed into his Lucky Necktie. Boynt has a grimly professional smile on. "It figures," he mutters. "Child enticement now."

"Beg your pardon," she points out, "I'm over eighteen even if I don't look it."

Boynt was talking about Skeet, but understands when to keep shtum.

Small hat at a provocative angle, blindingly platinum cocktail bob, belted city dress with sleeve dimensions seen typically only in movies dames go to. Calls herself Fancy Vivid. Apparently she and Stuffy met on one of his trips to Detroit, where she was working as a chorine in the house revue at the Club Palermo, a Hamtramck joint just off of what the papers liked to call the Joseph Campau midway of sin, with its own secret escape tunnel that let you out into some church basement blocks away. One of those recreational centers where you're apt to find Grosse Pointe aristocracy mixing with line workers between shifts from the Dodge Main plant, college kids from Ann Arbor, tourists from farther afield.

We're . . .
step-pin out-of-our step-ins, so long
silk, 'n' ray-yon, 'n'
lace— 'Cause

all-a-girl needs to look
hep in's, just
that smile she's got on, her, fa-a-a-ce!

So don't

bo-ther frisk-in-for weap-ons,
You won't even find lonja-ra-y-y . . .
Cause we're steppin' out of our
step-ins, and skip-
steppin the night a-way!

"Don't suppose you'd go for a friendly snort, Miss Vivid—"

"Oh call me Fancy. Actually not teetotal but after years, well, months, of pretending to sip champagne, I do seem to've picked up something of an honest-to-goodness *ginger ale habit* . . ."

"I'll have a look in the icebox," Zbig already on the way.

"Oh thanks so much, Vernor's if you've got any, Canadian style tends to be a little too much on the brut side for me. But what I really—"

"She's trying to find Stuffy Keegan," Skeet explains.

"There seems to be an uncommon amount of interest in the whereabouts of Mr. Keegan," sez Boynt. "I expect his likeness to appear at any moment on post office walls across the land."

"Don't know what I can afford to pay you. Skeet seemed to feel we could work the fee out somehow. This is where you people work? It looks like the ladies' lounge at Hudson's. The Budget Store, not the big one."

"Stuffy could be in on some federal beef," Hicks points out. "The B of I's been after him for a while, so if all you want to know is his whereabouts—"

"Besides what else?"

"If it's not a skip, if he didn't take something you want back."

She gazes at him steadily for a long time. April looks like this when she's getting ready to sing. "Something, yeah," Fancy Vivid in a whisper. "My heart."

Oh. "Not to get too personal, but . . . you and Stuffy . . . you're sayin this is the goods—"

"Sure," an eyebrow maneuver for and so what. "Can't always see the appeal there myself . . . He does have a mean streak, not with me so much but now and then there'll be some middle-of-the-night phone call, you know, some forlorn li'l face in a powder-room mirror, that kinda thing."

"You're sure this is Stuffy we're talking about."

"I know—two-bit con artist, thinks he's figured out an angle or two, never knows the going price on anything. Takes more trouble than it's worth over some li'l handful of change, which he never believes it'll work anyway, and when it does, it's like a miracle, the look on his face . . . so innocent. That's what gets me, you know, that innocence, and you'd have to be a colder customer than me not to just want to . . . oh . . ."

"Here, use this."

"You're sure? the day just started, some other Miss Waterworks might come along."

"It's OK, we have to keep a pocketful of spares, it all gets charged to overhead."

A silent beat and a half.

"He ever say anything to you about a submarine?" Hicks wonders about the same time Fancy asks, "He ever say anything to you about a submarine?"

"Kept wanting to know if I'd ever been on one, if I'd like to go for a ride on one. At first I thought it was some kind of sex talk."

"And . . ."

"Swore he wasn't making it up. Said it could be our cruise to salvation."

Later, looking through an unhelpful file, Hicks nods into a half-minute dream about Stuffy. They're in Chicago, or something calling itself that, up North Clark, across the suicides' bridge, deep in that part of the North Side known as The Shadows.

An intense black-and-white glare, a pattern of arc light through girderwork announcing that they are entering a region not for everyone. What seems to be the old county jailhouse over on Dearborn, haunted to saturation by the unquiet spirits of hanged men and women, white, Negro, and American Indian—Stuffy's been sleeping in the execution room, passing his daylight hours out on West Madison trying to blend in.

Unwelcome visitors, faces indistinct.

"Hicks, what's going on, hey?"

Hicks as surprised as anybody.

"For Chrissake they're gonna—"

"They took my heater, Stuffy, what'm I supposed to do?"

"Enough, enough. Say good night to your pal, unless you want in on this too."

"Stuffy, I'll see what I can do, I'll call the office—" But Stuffy's attention has moved elsewhere, as if he's caught a glimpse of the next world and can't look away.

A power failure, all the lights go out, all comfortable illusion of busy Loop activity fades to darkness, silence. How many more times is Hicks going to let somebody down like this, somebody who trusted him? He blinks awake.

Only a dream, he has to keep reminding himself all day till he's out of range of coffee urns and news of the day. Only a dream.

10

Next time Hicks is over to the Flaschners for what turns out to be another novelty casserole, he finds Uncle Lefty in a reminiscent yet strangely gemütlich state of mind.

". . . poised to *overthrow the U.S. government*? Itself? *Ja*? one word from the Kaiser, no questions asked—straight into action, half a million nationwide."

"Don't think I ever heard this one before."

"Oh *ja*, twenty years ago. Old news. History. Loyal German youth, waiting for the order to rise up. Woodrow Wilson, General Pershing? pushovers, kid, scared to death. Us, we kept the U.S. out of that War for three years."

"And now, you're telling me, there's 'ese old-time Kaiser Bill guerrilla units, which never . . . officially—"

Nod, finger to lips. "Some got demobilized, of course, older cadres, but . . . well, maybe not all." With his well-known mischievous smile that you wouldn't necessarily want to smile back at. "Come on out with me tonight and see. You're gatted up? That little snub-nose they let you carry?"

"And the reason you're asking . . . ?"

"Somebody may want to frisk you. Procedure, nothing personal."

Uncle Lefty has tactfully avoided mentioning that the streetcar route takes them across the Menomonee Valley via the Wells Street Viaduct, 90 feet up, iron, black, rickety in the wind, not for nervous passengers or even those with their wits about them who'd prefer to get across in one piece.

"Hope you're not too uncomfortable up here, Hicks?"

"Who, me? Nerves of steel."

"Not even half a mile. Over before you know it."

"That's what I'm worried about."

"Took your aunt Peony up here on our first date. Proposed to her in fact."

"She went for it?"

"Well, she said let's see when we get to the other end."

"Yeah? And . . ."

"Says she's still waiting."

"What's that mean?"

"Your guess is as good as mine."

Before Hicks knows it they're out in the far northwest somewhere, a bleak stretch not yet assigned a district number, an all-night beat out of a sergeant's most ill-tempered threat, out in onshore winds not expected to get much above freezing, straw boxes few and far between, apt around any corner to find yourself up the wrong end of a roscoe from somebody you knew in sixth grade.

"There, look," nodding out the window, "there it is, kid." Visible for miles across the bleak night prairie, the neon announcement NEW NUREMBERG LANES, not the traditional German typeface you see so much of around town but modern sans serif, straight from the soon to be new and improved Old Country, four or five different colors from deep violet to blood orange, bowling balls flickering left to right, pins scattering, reassembling, again and again, silently except for an electrical drone fading up slowly louder the closer to it you get.

The streetcar lets them off right in front. Inside it's expensively designed as a movie set. Shoe-check girls in matching outfits, working in pairs, one for the rubber-sole side, one for leather. A different pair of girls available for southpaws. A custom ball-laundering station. Lounge areas saturated in blue twilight, smelling like beer fumes, tobacco smoke, and hot griddle grease, a constant wood percussion from lanes near and far, echoes receding into the blur. All normal as club soda, yet somehow . . . *too normal*, yes something is making a chill creep across Hicks's scalp, the Sombrero of

Uneasiness, as it's known in the racket. Something here is off. A bowling alley is supposed to be an oasis of beer and sociability, busy with cheerful keglers, popcorn by the bucketful, crosscurrents of flirtation, now and then somebody actually doing some bowling. But this crowd here, no, these customers are only *pretending to bowl*. Stepping through spare-conversion systems the way movie actors pretend to dance. Busy lighting each other's cigarettes, writing down phone numbers—huh, who, me? oh just a carefree hour or two at the lanes, officer, surely you don't think we're up to any monkey business . . .

"Wait. We're not gonna roll a couple frames at least? Why am I carrying this ball? Where are we going?"

"You'll see."

On into a dimmer region of pool tables, pinball machines, and Skee-Ball setups, where it's currently semifinals week for the Northwest Milwaukee Skee-Ball League, defending champs of the Ladies' division, which dates from 1929, when the regulation lane was shortened to fourteen feet to accommodate the ever-growing number of talented and serious *gal devotees of the hardwood sphere*, as they're known in the sports pages. It also doesn't hurt that the local league has chosen an alluring uniform including two-color box-pleat skirts, magenta and green, so that any motion beyond a simple shimmy produces a color spectacle not easy to ignore.

Down some stairs, arriving presently at a jukebox going full blast and a dance floor full of Lindy-hopping youth. Hicks slowly recognizes an American swingtime version, at the moment getting some attention in Milwaukee, of the German street anthem known overseas as the "Horst Wessel Song,"

> Hold-yer flag up high, yeahh,
> Let's swing it, for the Naah-zis—
> Tight'n-up those ranks,
> You troopers out tonite—some
>
>   lid-dle
>
> Com-mie rats! won't
> Feel so, hotsy tot-sy—

Cause Brownshi-irts don't,
Go down, with-
            -out—a fight! Some
                        lid-dle
Com-mie rats—

and so forth, as meantime a gent with a swastika armband moves in on Hicks for a swift-finger once-over—finds the little snub-nose, lifts it smoothly away. "Hey," Hicks points out.

"Only temporary— Oh, izzat you? Hicksie?"

"Ooly Schaufl, holy smokes, how long's it been."

"Going by Ulrich these days. Heard about your P.I. license, Steamy Detective himself here, salary, commission, unlimited ammunition. Whoo-ee!"

"Looks better in the movies, less fun than you'd think."

"Don't start tellin me how you miss all that headbustin, I sure's heck don't."

"Good old days." They eyeball each other.

"Well, old, anyway."

"Not that I'm headed for some retired torpedoes' home in Oshkosh, um, Ulrich, I'm as bad as I ever was, you need anybody leaned on, you know you can always—"

"I'm not sure . . . maybe it's only since the private dick license, you seem more respectable somehow."

"Ouch. Call me anything but that."

His old mentor. Whaddaya know. They were briefly at North Division High together, Ooly was the older kid, too old in fact for high school anymore, too smart to be taking years over again, so it must've been something else.

"Somethin about violent criminals in the family, hope that's OK with you."

"Welcome to the delinquent bin, stranger. You ought to fit in fine."

Ooly went on to a brief yard apprenticeship up at Waupun before finding himself launched bang into the Roaring Twenties, the appeal of pure action never more keenly felt, the newly rich everywhere, young, beautiful,

Republican, throwing parties in lakeside houses which in more tropical surroundings you could've mistaken for hotels all jittery with cocaine, whoopee and swing that went on for days, except possibly at Marquette during Lent.

"Kids, all of 'em, dimwits in plus fours, flappers of both sexes, no idea of what was lying in wait, empty-headed and innocent and about to be jumped by the forces of Red revolution—wasn't it a man's duty to resist? Ain't it why we were all out there on the fence line?"

"C'mon, it was only plant owners nervous about their property, working stiffs looking for better pay, and hell, who ain't?"

Look of concern, "You didn't go Bolshevik on us, I hope, a Commie flatfoot?"

"How about your pal Hitler, you're handing your life over to this li'l comedian now?"

"Hey, just a friendly brat-and-beer get-together—we're National Socialists, ain't it? So—we're socializing. Try it, you might have fun."

"The Nazz-eyes? Sure, I'll be in touch with ya about that one . . ."

"Enjoy it while you can, pal. Don't wait too long. Leavin th' station, now's the time to climb on board, later maybe it won't be so easy . . ."

He is interrupted by a party of wholesome types in suits just off the rack.

"Hold it, boys and girls, pursuant to federal law we have confirmed the presence of alcohol in the building, soon as local police arrive you'll all be under arrest, sorry about that, till then behave yourselves, don't go anywhere, and remember, compliance is the price of liberty."

"*Heiliger Bimbam*," exclaims Ulrich. "Federals been in every night this week."

"Sure tops off the evening, don't it."

"Looks like 'at li'l Vic Durbow and his posse of Dry irregulars again, oh and Hicks, now that I recall, you and him have some history, don't you—" Ulrich now considerately tossing Hicks's heater back to him.

Catching it, "Thanks. They would've took that out of my paycheck," as house flappers and lounge lizards and Skee-Ball leaguers of both sexes make anxiously for the *Ausgang*, hired urchins meanwhile filtering everywhere handing out business cards with phone numbers of twenty-four-hour bail bondsmen.

"If dog pounds had psycho wards, that's where most of these jokers would be recruited out of."

The Dry agent in charge, Vic Durbow, hat brim too wide for his head keeping his eyes in shadow, leaving exposed an upper lip set in a permanent sneer, is known far and wide to be on the take from bootleggers he then turns around and collars anyway, which some call betrayal, though Vic prefers "moral integrity." When he runs out of beer barrels to smash, Vic will settle for busting up anything he can find, leaving raid sites around town littered with free-lunch debris, petals fallen from corsages, fragments of glassware and plates, pieces of furniture. Vic's trademark routine is to throw pool balls at speakeasy mirrors, not off-axis or anything, but straight at his own image.

Hicks's brisk to chilly relations with the federal level date in fact from pretty much his first encounter with Agent Durbow, who had just descended on some Old-Country Germans with a busy kitchen sink. Hicks has known Mr. and Mrs. Dinkelsbühler since childhood. They're already being tapped by the Guardalabenes for $20 a week, and now here comes this federal kiddy, new in town, with his own greasy mitt shamelessly presented.

Hicks had been asking around the Ward to see if the fee situation for Mr. and Mrs. Dinkelsbühler couldn't be adjusted, and on his way out of this particular gin mill was nearly beaned by one of Vic's pool balls whirring by a 64th of an inch from his left earlobe.

"Stee-rike! Hit the nigger in the head and win a free cigar!" Catching sight of Hicks, "You enjoyin the show, Buttercup?" Same look of strenuous pleasure Hicks has often noted on the faces of company goons.

"Sometimes," Hicks with a sociable nod, "just a couple of deep breaths can help."

"Private party here," Vic reaching into his coat, "best you vamoose." But Hicks has already located among the bar debris a solid oak bung starter, with which he now zeroes in, humming "On, Wisconsin!" a little off-key, and down goes Agent Durbow before any gatplay can really figure into the fun. This was still back in Hicks's lumber-assisted period, when subdural hematomas were considered of little more account than a case of the sniffles.

"Always comes back to beer," advises another prohi, drawing himself a free glassful from one of the few unmolested kegs remaining, "somehow, ain't it, unending damn Great Lakes of it, beer fraud, beer vendettas, beer matrimonials. Beer clandestine, beer undeclared, beer in name only. And the kicker is, is most of it's head, nothing more to it than foam. Kicking down the door, shoot-outs in the streets, indiscriminate pineappling, blood, wreckage, innocent lives lost, honest fortunes pissed away, all for millions of cubic feet of nothing but bitter-tasting bubbles." Raising his glass, *"Auf deine Gesundheit*, so forth."

DURING THE MERRYMAKING at New Nuremberg Lanes, Hicks picked up the impression, just from fast looks flickering between Uncle Lefty and elements of the federal assault, that these are guys who all know each other. As diplomatically as he can he brings the matter up over the next casserole, to which something new has been added though Lefty is being so coy about what it is that Hicks is reluctant to ask. This seems to amuse Lefty or at least ease him into a mood where he doesn't mind sharing his history with the federals after that bomb in the station house went off back in 1917, and the worst that could happen happened, leaving Milwaukee PD to drift like a doper in a doped-up twilight.

Under the Curse of the Dago Bowling Ball, rolling forever down the alleys of fate, doomed to less time colliding with maple than off in the gutters, at best unlikely to pick up even easy spares, Detlef found himself reaching beyond the station house walls that had proved so frail, and out to higher levels of police, state and after a while federal, as Prohibition deepened, as the gunfire down in Chicago reached peaks unheard-of, as even more G-boys came pouring into SMEGMA (Semi-Military Entity Greater Milwaukee Area), which by then had become a staging ground for frontline operations in Chicago. Uncle Lefty found himself after and even sometimes before working hours hobnobbing more and more with the federals . . .

"Any thought of hiring on?" Hicks settling into an all-purpose sympathetic squint.

"Never came up. Different budget line, they wanted information more than extra gunhands. Now it seems they want to talk to you, Hicks."

"They're making an appointment? Polite bunch of coppers, ain't it."

"Low visibility. Any visit they make right now will look bad."

"Bad for them, worse for me, as Jack Zuta might say. If he was still around to say it. I guess they want me to hop the el in to Chicago."

"Actually they'd prefer Milwaukee."

"Onk, there's no such thing as a B of I office in Milwaukee, not since the good old days."

"No, but they're planning to reopen for business soon, same site, maybe you noticed that new construction going on over at the courthouse."

"That's them? Michigan Avenue side in back?"

"Five stories, all their own."

"Anything to do with the Big Guy being in the pokey?"

"How am I supposed to know?"

"Figured you all for ace buddies."

"I hear things. Sometimes I pass it on, sometimes I don't."

"Like what else?"

"They're trying to hang the Stuffy Keegan bomb on you."

"Me?" Half a beat, "They?"

"*Mein kleiner Neffe*, even downtown you are on a seriously short list of reasonable patsies to pin it on. Listen. Uncle on the job or whatever, city cops can be stupid, overweight, and corrupt as they come, but we're still dangerous, there's only so far you can take liberties with the wise remarks and so on, before it's time to seek help at higher levels of enforcement."

"This is also copasetic with your pals out at Nuremberg Lanes?"

"Someday we'll have a nice long discussion about that. Use the entrance on Michigan. Mornings would be best."

11

On days of low winter light the federal courthouse can take on a sinister look, a setting for a story best not told at bedtime, the jagged profile of an evil castle against pale light reflected off the Lake, bell tower, archways, gargoyles, haunted shadows, Halloween all year long. Or as some like to think of it, Richardsonian Romanesque. Heavy icicles all along the overhangs, waiting to let loose and pierce your skull, with no safety hat on the market known to be of any help.

Inside, today, the place is a wreck. Smells like sizing and paint not yet dry, sawdust, solvents, joint compound, soldering smoke, sanding, ozone from arc welding. Riveting, hammering, hollering in German and Polish as well as less familiar tongues. A maze of interior renovation, with not always helpful signs tacked up on the new partition walls.

Hicks is never too comfortable talking directly to any level of cop, even what starts out as a friendly chat having a way no more than a couple smokes later of him ending up inside looking out. Though he wouldn't call it a full-scale attack of the Fee Bee jeebies, what gets him especially nervous about this newer type of federals is that nobody knows yet exactly how bad they can be.

Today's unknown quantity, Assistant Special Agent in Charge T. P. O'Grizbee, occupies a desk in a surprisingly tidy office suite, given the chaotic surroundings. Everybody pretending all this is is just another workday office, except for whatever else it is that's really going on. All the correct elements are in place, steno girls carrying steno pads, gossiping around the bubbler, bells and clatter from the typing pool, updates thumping in and whizzing out by pneumatic tube, middle management yelling into at least two telephones at once, office aromas of coffee percolating, hair pomade, and typewriter-ribbon ink blended with a perfume-maker's care, everybody looking like actors in a show that's run long enough by now for each to be comfortable in their roles. Plus, as any P.I. might add, that feeling that close by, just outside of sight, hearing, and the bounds of etiquette, at least one supply-room quickie is in progress.

"They tell me you gents are opening up shop again in M'waukee. Nice to be back in the big time, we were startin to feel neglected."

"Milwaukee's always on our map, Mr. McTaggart, more Germans than you can wave a knockwurst at, and Germans, especially of the Nazi persuasion, will bring our fellows to town sure as beer'll bring the prohis."

"In the present matter," adds a sidekick, "if it wasn't for this Nazi angle we'd've been happier leaving it to your local MPD. But as you seem to be one of the last to have spoken with Mr. Keegan—"

"This is about Stuffy?"

"His disappearance. In particular what part Nazis, foreign and domestic, might've played."

"He was pretty desperate to skip town. Seemed like somebody could've been after him. What for, he didn't say."

"Maybe he saw something, maybe he doesn't know what he saw. Knows enough not to talk but not exactly what he shouldn't be talking about. Or who to. Which makes him dangerous, putting forces he never knew existed to the trouble of setting things right again."

"And it's big enough you think that somebody might want to shut him up about it permanently?"

"There's also the matter of something that showed up out in the harbor that same night, believed to be a rogue Austro-Hungarian U-boat that refused to surrender, making it more than just a submarine but also an outward and visible expression of paths not taken, personal and historical—would that about sum it up?"

"Sure, if I knew what that's supposed to mean."

"Just as well you don't. Espionage Act and all . . . What I can tell you is that deep in our archives, in a highly secret vault whose location I can't divulge, are several combination safes' worth of Anecdotal Field Reports, sightings of unconventional vehicles undersea and airborne as well, witnesses ranging from the usual barking and drooling to senior officers who wouldn't care to jeopardize their pensions by testifying to anything that isn't there, including it seems this same Austro-Hungarian submarine . . ." pretending to consult a file, "U-13. Built in sections at Budapest, assembled at Fiume and the Imperial naval arsenal at Pola, making it both Hungarian and Austrian. Regardless of which, supposed to've been scuttled, scrapped, or handed over after the War, in accordance with the treaties of Saint-Germain-en-Laye, Articles 136 and 138, and Trianon, Article 122."

"But . . ."

"It wasn't. Officially there never even was a U-l3, skips directly from 12 to 14, like the thirteenth floor in a skyscraper. Our information is that you actually witnessed its arrival in Milwaukee."

"Don't know. Saw something. Lights under the ice. Could've been a sub, I guess."

"We have a statement from a minor, one Floyd Francis Wheeler, known informally as Skeet."

"Oh come on, I hope you birds ain't after Skeet, he's just a kid."

"Cigarette taxes, assorted U.S. code violations plus Federal Radio Commission General Order 84, if you're familiar—"

"Keep a copy handy at all times, right next to the fan magazines."

"Your young friends have been conspiring to operate a shortwave transmitter, possibly dangerous, certainly illegal."

"Kids with a radio hobby, so what?"

"An alarmingly high percentage of the traffic is encrypted, with a potential for altering events far removed in time and space from the likes of—" gesturing around the beaverboard interior.

"Uh, huh, just a couple of working stiffs, you and me, ain't it."

A passing smile, in which any note of cordiality would be hard to locate. "And should you be telling me stuff like this?"

"Falls within your need to know, if you're going to be working on the case."

"Who said I was—"

"You speak the German tongue, we're told."

"Picked up a word or two, who don't, beer-barrelin around M'waukee?"

"Anything else? Polish, Italian, Hungarian?"

"Only enough to get into a fight. Why? Sounds like out-of-town work, which I don't—"

"Oh, quite far out of town in fact."

Now, most of the time gastric distress and Hicks are strangers. Alka-Seltzer is not about to name him Customer of the Year. But there are exceptions, brought about by even the hint of an out-of-town ticket, when the best he can manage is to sit very still with a deaf-n-dumb expression on his kisser.

"Boynton Crosstown at the U-Ops has every confidence."

"Uh-oh, now I *am* worried. Appreciate the job offer if that's what this is, but maybe somebody missed the patch of troublesome history between me and you folks's shop—"

"We're not the prohis. All that foolishness we're ready to overlook. You'll find we're easygoing, bighearted 'mugs,' in a funny kind of way. All warrants will be suspended, all charges dropped, you'll be as pure as Ivory soap."

"Let's see, that's ninety-nine and 44 one-hundredths percent, so a hundred take away 44, that still leaves . . . wait . . ."

"They don't have Original Sin in Milwaukee?"

"South side, maybe . . ."

"Truth is," the federal as if sharing a confidence, "it's your job history. All those labor radicals you sent to the accident ward. Somebody who's anti-Red but not a Nazi either."

"Plenty of them to pick and choose from, I'd of thought, and anyhow I'm semiretired these days, haven't busted a Bolshevik head in can't remember how long but thanks anyhow, nothin personal," heading amiably for the door, "just a working flatfoot, see, makin this a definite Pasadena—"

"We'd much prefer that you cooperate, though you're always welcome down at our little country jailhouse in Atlanta G-A, plenty of southern hospitality to enjoy, why, who knows, you could end up cellmates with the Big Fellow himself."

"And you'd be runnin me in for what again?"

"Too technical to explain, think of it as Aggravated Mopery."

"Wrong tough guy. Try Primo Carnera."

"Your country calls."

"Line's busy."

"I'm afraid it isn't optional," explains T. P. O'Grizbee. "Like it says on the subpoena we haven't served you yet, laying aside all and singular your business and excuses. A federal rap, not to be shrugged off. Potential wrongdoers might keep in mind as yet little-known lockups such as Alcatraz Island, always looming out there, fogbound and sinister, and the unwelcome fates which might transpire therewithin. The Drys can seem like the violent ward at Winnebago sometimes, but this is the next wave of Feds you're talking to. We haven't even begun to show how dangerous we can be, and the funny thing? Is, is we could be running the country any day now and you'll all have to swear loyalty to us because by then we'll be in the next war fighting for our lives, and maybe that'll be all you've got." Taking off his horn-rim specs briefly to drill Hicks with a rhetorical eye-to-eye. "It's your wife and kids too."

"Single. Too young for the last one, always felt lousy about that, next one I'll join up and get killed in it, promise."

"A bonus marcher in our midst," mutters the G-man, "how entertaining . . . Oh and before you go—please. Compliments of the Bureau."

Since about 1930, immigrants arriving at Ellis Island have been receiving boxes of Jell-O plus a Jell-O mold in the shape of some famous U.S. landmark as part of their welcome-to-the-U.S. package. This one they're handing Hicks happens to be the Statue of Liberty. Plus a handy kitchen-size pamphlet full of creative Jell-O recipes.

"So I'm an immigrant now?"

"Maybe not to the U.S. as you know it. Maybe to the future U.S. we in the Bureau expect to see before long."

"And you're going to explain the difference to me."

"No. Maybe if you ever decided to hire on with us, your own free will, general makeover, new name, new identity papers, oath of loyalty, so forth. Enough idea of who you're working for as we think it's safe for you to have."

A Statue of Liberty made of Jell-O. Where do you start eating it? The head? The torch?

12

"I could use some advice, Boynt."

"Uh huh, and any chance you'll be snapping out of this anytime soon?"

"I'm getting a hard sales pitch for somethin I don't even know what it is."

"Of course they're trying to turn you. Back to what you never stopped being. They know all there is to about you, more than you ever knew. You think you're reformed now. Not just a normal tough guy but a saintly one."

"No use tryin to talk me back down into it either, Boynt."

"Oriental Attitude, discipline, serenity, call it what you like, wallow as deep in it as you can get, but he's still in there, Hicks, still the same dirt-stupid gorilla always ready to take short pay for beating up whoever he's told to. You think you've gotten past it, but those we all report to, they know better, they know that once you're down here with us, you'll never change, there'll be no getting rid of that inner torpedo. Whenever they need him, they will know how to call him out to do their bidding."

"They."

"The federals who had you in are likely just a front, OK? It's the outfit that's behind them, a nationwide syndicate of financial tycoons, all organized in constant touch against the forces of evil, namely everything to the left of Herbert Hoover. Worried about the next election, worried this latest Roosevelt if he gets in might decide to step out on his own, and even if he does revert to type after all, it might not be in time to stop the Red apocalypse that's got them spooked out of what they think of as their wits. And when big shots get nervous? Well. Better if the rest of us arrange to be someplace else. Which is why—"

"Oh, boy. The cheese heiress ticket again."

"Quick as ever on the uptake, I always admired that about you."

"Boynt. No. We had a deal, you said, I heard you say it, no more out-of-town jobs from now on, nothing further than half a pack of smokes down the Dubuque, Madison & Waukesha."

"Don't think this is easy for me, I admit once long ago in an absentminded moment I might've said something about not sending you out of town again, but this probably won't take you much past Chicago, and what's a hundred miles to the streamlined velocities of the 1930s?"

"Sure there isn't some way we could just do this all out of the office? Shortwave radio or something?"

"Too slow."

"Radio waves, what's faster'n that?"

"A live op who's there already, on the spot."

"Not me, remember I'm just the strong-arm gorilla, I don't do runaway heiress tickets, that's for new hires, kids with the energy and enthusiasm, talk to Zbig Dubinsky soon as he's out of observation at County General, ain't like I don't have the time in, Boynt."

"Too bad you never got around to the Civic Opera before they shut down. Deep lessons in it for the working gumshoe. For instance, you know how puzzled civilians always get when some frail little tubercular seamstress turns out to be a good-size specimen healthy enough to belt out her numbers to the back rows of the cheapest balcony seats in town and beyond? Well, which is she, they keep wondering. Answer is, is she's both—but neither as important as what she really is, which is the love of the tenor's life—and he's not necessarily any Valentino either. Educational point here is you never know who's apt to be smitten gaga by whom, which guarantees plenty of job security for everybody in the business."

"Boynt, how often do I say it, she don't remember me, no idea what I even look like—"

"That'll help, just keep that pan as dumb and honest as it is, it'll be like picking up an easy spare. All else fails, go in there and make with the clodhoppers, who knows, she might not even yell for help. Here, let's just . . ." Boynt rolling over to the window, opening it, reaching outside into the freezing night and retrieving two heavy warped icicles, each with a vivid emerald bottle of Canadian IPA frozen into it.

"Back when you hired on, only a sap would believe there was anyplace to be promoted to around here, but modern bureaucracy must have a soft spot for saps, like God does for drunks, because now, and I'm sure you read the memo, the back office is creating a new mid-level job and calling it 'case director,' and planning to promote a few of you up to that. You'll have your own office—each get to run your own string of field agents . . ."

"Soon as I get back in from out of town, and in one piece, natch."

"Upper management believes we should begin cultivating the luxury market, taking clients only in the upper brackets. Let all those deadbeats you know so well just drop off the edge, once prosperity returns we'll have position, see. The U-Ops is headed uptown but definitely, which incidentally means all of us presenting more of a quality appearance."

"You're trying to tell me something."

"Nothing against the suit, Hicks, the cigarette burns, the multiple reweaving, buttons that don't match up with buttonholes, personally I think all that adds character, a just-folks image that may've worked fine once among the less sophisticated, but the more we expect to be face-to-face with the well-to-do, you get it? Hiring gorillas who'll take short money to get beatings they probably deserve, that's so out-of-date now—these days they're looking more for William Powell, some brainwork, some class, which for one thing will mean a higher price tag suit, trust my sense of style here, the Prince of Wales and I both subscribe to the same fashion magazines—and now as to the shoes . . ."

And so forth—Hicks figures a real bottle of beer is worth sitting through ten or fifteen minutes of this, though any longer might have to be negotiated.

". . . as the P.I. field in general begins to shift from skips and small-time offenses into more of an espionage racket, along with that comes the need for a snappier getup, European Fascist uniforms at the moment, as you may have noticed from the newsreels, being widely admired and commented on."

"Where do I find the money to afford anything ritzier than what I got on?"

"The national office. Next paycheck everybody'll be seeing a nice WUGA."

"That's, uh..."

"Wardrobe Up-Grade Allowance? There was a memo."

"How much?"

"Sliding scale. You, now—if we could only be sure you wouldn't just go blow it in some juke joint—why your WUGA could be worth up to, oh, 20, 25 bucks."

"What your wife's always tellin me, Boynt, except she sez closer to 50?"

"Uh-huh, well, whatever you spend it on, don't forget neckties and pocket handkerchiefs. Heart and soul of the business, if you really want to know..."

"Will I have to start drinking Martinis?"

"Stick with beer for now, and any plans to pose as some uptown society sleuth, let's count on at least a year's remedial work first."

"Hey, I've got acting skills, that Duchess of Uckfield ticket, how about that?"

"That was back a while, maybe you got away with it then but we're living in bleaker times now. Better just be yourself—with you, not the perfect option, I agree..."

Hicks looks in his shirt pocket, finds an empty cigarette pack, reaches a loosie from the shoebox-full that Boynt keeps on his desk, goes in another pocket, takes a penny and carefully places it in front of Boynt. "There's got to be even sorrier cases than me who've been involved with ol' Daphne, big-business melodramas of the Airmont family I was never told nothin about, plus which," lighting up, inhaling, coughing dramatically, "any statutes must've run by now, am I leaving anything out, oh and why is it again you're picking on me with this?"

"Some husband or wife gets bumped, who's the first one anybody looks at? Homicide Bureau ABCs."

"Not sure I see the connection."

"Better that way." A little wistful. "You'll be happy to hear in any case that we've set up a get-together for you and the family lawyers. Even thought maybe I'd tag along."

"Just to add that uptown touch, thanks, Boynt."

THE MAGAZINE SELECTION in the outer waiting area at Godwin Zipf includes *Popular Litigation, Modern Psychopathy,* and *Steamy Detective,* deep in whose cover story it's not till Boynt reaches and shakes him does Hicks realize he's been immersed for a while. "Oh."

"They say sometime this week."

"On the way, Boss."

"Not as high-caliber around here as it looks," a front office type answering to Peckenway greets them smoothly, "more respect than revenue. If you need an attorney for the damned, that's still Brother Darrow—we're more like attorneys for the gol-durned, the gin mill across the street that picks up the overflow."

"And," Boynt's idea of suave, "runaway heiress work . . ."

"Mrs. Airmont would like her daughter back with as little public attention as possible, and without the clarinet player."

"—and how much thought has she given," wonders Boynt, as if he's forgotten he's talking out loud, "to what she's willing to pay him to dump Daphne?"

"That'll be another department, Special Arrangements, just down the hall, six attorneys, each a potential junior partner, no waiting."

"Back in a flash."

After an avuncular, though few would go so far as to say kindly, once-over, "According to our files, Mr. McTaggart, you and Miss Airmont have some previous relationship."

"One long-ago boat ride, couple hours' work—an impulse! Which happened years ago! I don't even get a statute of limitations here?"

"Are you aware of the American Indian belief, referenced in depositions filed on Miss Airmont's behalf, that once you save somebody's life, you're responsible for them in perpetuity?"

"No. No. I didn't save her life. Which first," Hicks explains, "means she had to be in some danger, which she never was, see, it was all timing, location—"

"Yes, turning briefly," paper-shuffling, "to the words of the young woman herself—'It was a crucially decisive intervention. The few hours' time it bought me then have since represented all the difference between growing to normal adult maturity and being condemned to a lifetime of infantilized misery.'"

"Funny, she sounds just like a lawyer."

"Given that ear for nuance, you may also appreciate the distinction between saving somebody's life and changing the course of it, which considering also that Wisconsin law doesn't apply on Ojibwe territory could be argued in court forever," a shrug from which some private merriment may not be entirely absent.

Nodding, eyes held amiably wide, "Maybe you know what that means, but don't bother to explain. Did Mr. Crosstown mention that my specialty usually is considered more along the lines of the muscle category?"

"Making you just the man for the job. Miss Airmont can become on occasion violently uncooperative, even with those concerned only for her mental well-being."

"I think it's called resisting arrest."

"You'd approve of that, I expect."

"A dame with some moxie instead of one more baby-talking lulu. Hmm, well, let me think that one over."

Boynt comes back from down the hall looking strangely feverish, as if he's fallen off a wagon too recently hammered together to have a name yet.

"How much?" Hicks asks once they're outside.

"Hefty to whopping. You'll see."

13

Hicks has always preferred not to work for anybody too upper-class if he can trade tickets with one of the other ops, who're usually only too happy to. Despite which he now finds himself up here on Prospect Avenue with the aristocracy, looking around for moats and drawbridges and so forth, though the Airmont mansion turns out to be a notch more modest, turn-of-the-century millwork, unblocked view of the Lake, Menomonee Valley brick kept clear of downtown industrial gray, fresh as a dairymaid's morning delivery.

Hicks gets off the streetcar a couple of stops early and walks in by way of the Airmont driveway, appearing on city maps under a street name of its own, where he finds a new Cadillac Sport Phaeton with the hood still warm, plus a Bentley bobtail cold to the touch as daytime Milwaukee, throwing him an idea of what he's likely to find inside.

Once past a couple-three Waupun alumni posing as residential security, he's stashed in something they call the library, though there aren't that many books or even magazines around. Tries to keep his hands in his pockets and remember where his elbows are.

Social chitchat around here, as he learns from falling into conversation with a number of eccentric Airmont cousins wandering around without much to do, seems very focused on cheese, in particular the recent Bruno Airmont Dairy Metaphysics Symposium held annually at the Department of Cheese Studies at the UW branch in Sheboygan, this year featuring the deep and perennial question, "Does cheese, considered as a living entity, also possess consciousness?"

"Cheese, oh to be sure, cheese is alive. Self-aware, actually, maybe not exactly the way we are, but still more than some clever simulation. We're at a pivot point here in the history of food science, a strange new form of life that was deliberately invented, like Doctor Frankenstein or something—"

"Cheese—wait, cheese . . . has feelings, you say? You mean like . . . emotions?"

"Long-time spiritual truth in Wisconsin. Thousands of secretly devout cheezatarians . . ."

"Secretly?"

"Only waiting for our moment. We have to be careful, don't we . . . wouldn't want to go through all that Christians-and-Romans business again, would we?"

"Wisconsin is possessed by some vast earth-scented spirit of Bovinity, docile herds of cows by the untold thousands all across the state every day at the same hour lining up shed-side in patient queues waiting to be milked, while microbial cultures, silent yet conscious, working below the level of human attention, go on bringing a strange shadowy inertia into human character . . ."

"And no wonder the Japanese hate us, no dairy element to speak of in their diet, they see us as a bovine race, lacking all martial spirit."

"What you could call a negative attitude toward cheese in particular."

"How the heck do we create a market for dairy products in Japan short of invading and occupying the country outright? Taking away their tea or sake or whatever it is they drink and forcing them to drink milk like normal human beings?"

From which Hicks after a while politely detaches, to have a look at a number of framed four-color posters advertising the once infamous food product known as Radio-Cheez, the basis of Bruno Airmont's fortune, briefly competitive with the Kraft classic Velveeta, as well as Pabst-ett, the Pabst brewery's attempt to make up for loss of beer revenue. Radio-Cheez was designed to stay fresh forever, in or out of the icebox, thanks to a secret, indeed obsessionally proprietary, *radioactive ingredient*.

Hicks has paused in front of one of these chromos showing a wholesome American married couple, posed in a subpornographic embrace in a kitchen where the only food seems to be Radio-Cheez both packaged and in use, with speech balloons reading "Oh honey, it's all been so REVITALIZED around here thanks to Radio-Cheez!" with the husband replying urbanely, "Not too bad yourself!" The wife, though maybe not typical of Milwaukee housewives, is in fact pretty cute, done up here in some sort of screen-siren rig, under a platinum hairdo.

In this fictional household, radioactive cheese seems key to romance, it being radium's grand hour of popularity, when it's still medical wisdom to seek as many ways as possible to introduce radiation into the human body—radioactive mineral water, patent radium elixirs and aphrodisiacs, radium suppositories—despite the appearance five or six years earlier of poisoning symptoms down in nearby Ottawa, Illinois, where hundreds of "Radium Girls" were employed in painting numbers on glow-in-the-dark clock dials, licking their brushes every so often to keep them finely pointed.

For Radio-Cheez, all too soon, the honeymoon was over, federal Food and Drug killjoys declaring it "harmful to human health" somehow.

"New one on me, folks," Bruno gesturing affably as he worked the crowds outside the federal courthouse at his first, though not to be his last, indictment, flash powder going off, local press screaming questions nobody can hear, protesters trying to hit him on the head with picket signs reading CHEEZ IT, THE COPS! and IRRADIATE BRUNO.

Reports furthermore beginning to come in from grocery stores all across the U.S.A. of Radio-Cheez *shelf incidents*, getting warmer and warmer till eventually exploding, sending once loyal customers running in blind panic down to nearby rivers to throw in all their as yet unexploded jars of the product, which were then carried away buoyant and glowing downstream, sometimes hundreds, even thousands of miles to coastal harbors and ports before detonating against the hulls of ships at anchor, any found still upstream being promptly labeled *enemy mines*, with duly sworn sharpshooters ordered to fire at them from a safe distance. Fish in the rivers and harbors were briefly puzzled by the bright new scatter of food potential, until deciding, all together the way fish do, that they didn't care much for Radio-Cheez either.

None of which disarranged by so much as an eyelash the public gaze of Bruno Airmont, already becoming known in the industry as the Al Capone of Cheese, who without mentioning it to anybody, including his family, has been carefully planning an unannounced exit to legal safety elsewhere, which at last, one night in the deep hours reserved for petty theft and romantic misjudgment, became the next morning's headline—growing less newsworthy as the weeks rolled by and the radio jokes moved on, and Radio-Cheez dwindled to a strange afterlife among those who still claimed health benefits from the mysterious rays it continued to emit.

When Bruno skedaddled off the civilized map for parts unknown, Daphne Airmont was just at that point of later girlhood when an understanding Pop might've come in handy, instead of leaving her stuck with a stag line of know-nothings and pikers out the door and down the block . . .

From motives which did not include sentiment, she took a long, unauthorized look over and through the paperwork Bruno had left behind, which was plenty, a mountain of dummy corporation records, lawsuit summaries, dishonored checks, rap sheets and police reports, not the sort of homework any dog in their right mind would be tempted to eat.

Here began a sort of higher education. Since the end of the War the center of gravity of the Cheese Universe has apparently been shifting, to some observers at alarming speed, in the direction of Chicago, where Kraft, having by now captured 40 percent of the U.S. market, looms unavoidably as the chief factor to be dealt with. Beginning with its acquisition in 1927 of Velveeta, whose introduction (apart from its role as a Radio-Cheez competitor) has proved not unpivotal, a regional-scale roll-up has been in progress, more modest cheese operations all over Wisconsin and beyond quietly being absorbed one by one. There have of course always been price-fixing scandals since at least back in the last century, from involvement in which even the Wisconsin Cheese Exchange, located deep in Sheboygan County, hasn't been entirely free. But nothing like this.

The year 1930 happened to be the 1776 of the cheese business. The

British company Lever Brothers merged with the Dutch cartel known as the Margarine Union to form Unilever. After the merger of National Dairy Products with Kraft everything avalanched, faster than anybody was ready for, climaxing in the Cheese Corridor Incursion, a wildcat operation denounced at the time variously as Bolshevik, cartel, or Capone-related though in fact nobody knew where it came from, a major sector of Wisconsin decheesed in the blink of an eye, entire cheese inventories hijacked right out the gates of more than one cheeseworks, from Sheboygan on west, one after the other, a coordinated rolling knock-over, truckloads of case-hardened palookas, many said to be from Illinois, trooping in and out of plants big and small, tossing provolones back and forth like footballs, rolling along the ground giant waxed wheels of domestic Parmesan, no cash taken, no payrolls, only physical cheese, Colby longhorns, bricks of Brick wrapped in tinfoil and carried away by the hodful, storming on down the Cheese Corridor in a bold sweep already "legend-dairy," as newspaper extras were proclaiming before it was even over with. What didn't get gobbled down on the spot or stashed for further aging in caves at secret locations was quickly distributed among lunch wagons, soup kitchens, one-arm joints throughout the upper Midwest, effectively down the hatches of the hungry inside of forty-eight hours.

Some believe it was masterminded by Bruno Airmont, even though he was the loudest complaining—that it could've been intended as an early warning to dairy folk who were thinking about joining in any mass effort to redefine the price structure. In any event, Bruno, bewildered as anybody, emerged as the last man, if not standing, at least able to stumblebum around, somehow finding himself in supreme command of a darker project he may never have learned the true depth of.

The world of cheez and its ways, already perplexing, had turned suddenly opaque as well for Daphne, who found sometimes she had trouble keeping a handle on it all. If Bruno really was, or maybe still is, the Al Capone of Cheese, didn't that suggest there also had to be somewhere a Cheese Outfit that could be running at any scale from statewide on up, blessed with supernaturally accurate bookkeeping, short on mercy, located either nowhere or anyplace it liked—and why stop there?

Whatever levels Bruno might be reporting to, Daphne gathered from notes scribbled to himself, he was already too high up for personal comfort. Found himself thinking of all the public toilet walls across the Midwest and the names he was being called, the fates that ungifted restroom cartoonists were imagining for him. Starting to worry about marksmen out there waiting for him to wander into their sights.

SOONER OR LATER the kingpins had to meet—as things fell out, at Al Capone's own Midnight Frolics cabaret, on East 22nd in Chicago. Bruno at this point in the evening was entering a haze of indifference as to the exact ingredients of what he might be drinking, as long as it did the job.

"Yeah! Yeah I'm the Al Capone of Cheese, see? Il Al Capone di Formaggio."

"Pleasure to meet you—in fact I happen to *be* Al Capone."

"Hep to that, my paisan! And what is it *you're* the Al Capone of again?"

Al Capone after a pause only shrugged, laughing nervously, not always regarded as a good sign by those familiar with him and his impulses.

Despite this uneasy beginning, the two seemed to hit it off. Bruno began to feel a perverse kind of protective aura. Soon he was making with the cheese quips. "Mother of Mercy, is this the end of Ricotta?" and "You don't like it, eh va' fondue," and so forth.

"Bruno, you card." The Big Fella meant the Joker, but Bruno may've been thinking of an older deck, an older card, numbered XIII, the one nobody likes to see turn up, especially considering how mysteriously rival figures in the Velveeta/Radio-Cheez/Pabst-ett theater of combat were beginning to disappear from the cheezscape.

"How many'd you lose?" Al Capone, as the story goes, once asked Bruno, who in his innocence thought Big Al was talking about dollars.

"Oh," Bruno pondered, "um . . ."

"Now you're the boss," advised the celebrated bootlegger, "don't think you can relax. 'Cause now there's even more people out to get you, see, Valentine's Day comes more than once a year, any minute can be your last, you need to be more alert than ever, capeesh? Sleep especially. How you been sleeping lately, goombah—things OK with that?"

G. Rodney Flaunch, a onetime male flapper somehow delivered into premature middle age, seems unable to maintain a direct gaze with anybody, preferring to glower off into space, throwing the word "fiancé" around a lot, embarrassingly open about the scale on which he hopes to profit. "A million and a half, that's my magic number, I'm not greedy, only asking a fair return for the work I've put in . . ."

According to Rodney, everyone up here on Prospect despises him while secretly admiring his courage in daring to actively court the daughter of the Al Capone of Cheese, honorific or whatever.

"Step easy, G. Rod," fellow loophounds caution, "you know what they can do to you."

"No risk, no reward," Rodney far more breezy about it than the situation may actually call for.

"This is the Al Capone of Cheez, Rodney. He runs empires. A byword of terror in milk sheds throughout the land. Public enemies shiver with fear. How much trouble could one cheap adventurer give him?"

"A million and a half," Rodney sincerely offended, "is not cheap!"

"You could be going after twice that."

"Oh?"

"Pikers like you never get it right. First thing you should've done was hire a manager."

So as if contempt from the family of Rodney's intended bride isn't enough, there's a certain coolness to be put up with from that old gang of his as well.

"Others in the family stand to lose carloads more than my insignificant sum," he explains to Hicks. "We're all chipping in, each according to their means, to foot the bill, whatever it amounts to, to get our Daphne back safe and sound." With a meaningful wiggle of the eyebrows meant to suggest a per diem plus expenses lavish beyond the dreams of small-timers such as Hicks.

"Wait, but . . . you yourself . . ." Hicks pretending to grope for tactful language.

"I know—fine one to moralize, you're going to say, but that's all over with now, isn't it, the former scheming heel known as G. Rodney Flaunch is no more, I swear, he's betrayed his last milkmaid."

"Do tell."

"What's a million and a half, I'd gladly forgo it all if only she'd come back to me," and so forth. Those who don't mind hiring a private dick now and then have been refining these arts of sincerity since Pinkerton was a pup, though sometimes it only turns out to be professional courtesy among fellow con artists. Nothing around here of course but gentlemen, so Hicks doesn't ask to see anything in writing.

"And how much appreciation do you think I get from this careless, hate-driven family? They sell each other used cars they know will catch fire at awkward moments, lure and get lured again and again into indiscretion and blackmail and who's always the fixer running around cleaning up after everybody? Dear old Rodney the family lowlife. When he isn't being delegated to deal with private coppers and other scum."

"How lousy for you, and yet . . ."

"Out, out with it, please," Rodney throbbing with resentment.

"Only thinking, what if it really is, well . . . something emotional. Sometimes," pushing it, "it's love, is all it turns out to be."

"Love." Rodney is squinting at him in a way that reminds him somehow of Boynt. "Let's not forget simple insanity either, then, shall we. Nothing to concern yourself with in any case, your role is limited to finding her and convincing her to come back."

"For a sum any self-respecting chicken would turn up their beak at—"

"I didn't say that."

"Somebody did."

"For just another crook with a license you're sure a touchy customer."

"And yet maybe you people need us as much as you do psychiatrists and bookkeepers, and better hope we never get together in a union either, John D., 'cause even one wildcat strike and it'll all be over for the whole truckload of ya. Now here," reaching for his briefcase, pulling out paperwork of various shades and sizes, "is where I'm supposed to remind you about this concentric zone system we use at the U-Ops—anywhere outside a hundred-mile radius of Milwaukee City Hall, which would include parts of Chicago, we'll need to charge you some extra. Plus insurance billed weekly in advance, oh and there's the hazardous-duty bonus? if somebody turns out to be packing a firearm, for example..."

Hicks is nodded on into a sub-parlor less vast but not quite intimate, tricked out with a cocktail bar, radio-Victrola console, telephones in gold-accented mother-of-pearl, modern art on the walls where the dames though possibly nude are lopsided in ways not easy to make sense of... plus what seems to be an excessive number of electric lamps, floor and table models, far too many for a room even this size. Some are unusual-looking, to say the least, and few if any in what you'd consider good taste—a disembodied nose with a light bulb in each nostril, a grinning Negro with a watermelon he is *strangely leering* at, assorted celebrities of politics, show business, and the criminal underworld misbehaving in ways somebody in the Airmont house must've found entertaining.

Mrs. Vivacia Airmont sweeps in, pretending to ignore Rodney and laying a hand noticeable for its lack of body temperature on Hicks's sleeve, the one without the French reweave. "The latest we've heard of my daughter, she's in Chicago with this Hop Wingdale person and the dance band he plays in, the Klezmopolitans, about to go off to New York and then overseas on tour and for all I know irrevocably 'gone hepcat,' all night in the black-and-tans breathing that mentholated smoke, running tabs that always end up being sent to *me*, sums the plutocrat of your choice couldn't help raising an eyebrow at, and the press coverage!—class traitor, baby gun moll, this and worse, no delusions herself about what she's become, and only a rough idea how it happened. She's lost her grip but she's still my daughter, for heaven's sake, she needs to be rescued from that milieu."

"Our sympathy, we'll sure do what we can, which ought to be plenty..."

"I only wish she'd come back home, and if she's still skating by on looks, well good for her and let's hope she's also been investing wisely—California real estate, for example, these Arabian oil wells one keeps hearing about... but don't mind me, getting sentimental these days... yes, li'l Daffodil," slipping into a sort of ballad tempo, "I'm beaming my thoughts to you by telepathy, wherever you are, how near yet oh so far... And you know what she answers? 'Uh-huh, spare us those tears, Mother, God bless 'em, but gimme knockout drops any day.'"

This sort of thing in a movie would have Hicks reaching for the Kleenex, but out here in the daylight of normal civilian hypocrisy and fraud, having by now gained a dim idea of when and when not to dummy up, he finds it more helpful, as the Gumshoe's Manual advises time and again, to try and appear professional, already knowing it's no use, he's in the soup once again and his job will be to get in the way of and absorb any violence that might arise, as if there's some Private Dick Oath like the one doctors take, with a no-harm clause, which there isn't.

14

Hicks just stepped into it without much thinking ahead. Having obtained by way of his Uncle Detlef master keys for most of the high-performance smuggling craft captured in local waters by the Drys and kept down at a lakeside boat pound they rented from the MPD, now and then Hicks liked to take one of these 12-cylinder whizbangs out for a cruise, usually down to an unincorporated patch of riot and sin north of Chicago known as No Man's Land, right in the heart of the hoity-toity North Shore. Tonight with a storm heading in from somewhere out on the prairie, winter surf, the mournful high-low booming of more than one foghorn up and down the Coast, shifty air pressure, chances of rain, a longtime pal of Uncle Lefty's, casting off lines, gives Hicks a meaningful headshake. "Don't much like the looks of that sky. Already seeing some swells, might keep an eye out for local fogbanks too . . ."

No Man's Land lies between Wilmette and Kenilworth, right up against the Lake. There were grand plans once upon a time. They were going to call it Plaza del Lago, and "Spanish Court" would be one of the first drive-in "shopping plazas" in the U.S.A. . . . But the timing was terrible, before anybody knew it the Depression had come swooping in to claim one more hopeful project, and the Plaza slid into an underlit honkytonk with its archways in permanent shadow. Nowadays among the derelict Spanish-style architecture there's still a movie house, and Dopplinger's Chinese Amusements, a Keno salon whose bar Hicks at the time was a semiregular at, just across the shore road from the Lake, close enough that you could hear waves coming in, with permanently flickering electric light owing to a tangled history with Commonwealth Edison plus the fiercely independent power plant in Winnetka, and of course the Outfit, who were tapping off a percentage of everything that went in and out of No Man's Land, every glass of beer, sack of movie popcorn, tip given, tip taken, not to mention the Chinese machines, the horse games, the slots, working ladies full- or part-time or semipro, including adventurous local housewives, and of course every tiny fraction of an amp of electric current, which kept sending foolhardy amateurs up the power poles trying to bootleg more juice in off of the ComEd line along Sheridan Road, too often ending in ambulance sirens and sorrowful headlines.

New Trier kids work in the movie house as ushers and usherettes and popcorn slingers for 25¢ an hour, minus the rake-off to Red Barker, currently running the ushers' union off and on between episodes of jail time state and local and keeping an eye open in the back of his head for unwelcome attention from Large Alphonse, who cannot be said to wish him well.

"This Lois the usherette you're inquiring after?" Sheldon the apron on duty tonight sliding an Old Log Cabin Presbyterian in front of Hicks, "since when, mind me asking, did you start chasin jailbait, Hicks, that ol' middle-age hankering creepin up on you, pal? Not too happy a prognosis for none of you degenerates, better you nix that jive while you still can."

"Lucky for us both, Sheldon, my interest right now ain't so much in Lois herself as her circle of friends, including the customer who just walked in."

"And a pleasant good evening to you, Hicksie, what's up, you're supposed to be dead."

Giancarlo Foditto, or Dippy Chazz, as he's known in the lounges of the underworld, has made no secret of his deep yen for Lois, which he can't explain, much less control. Chazz is a gangland kiddy of the more amiable sort who all his life has wanted to be taken for menacing, trying to wear the snappiest cut and shade of suit, the most sinister model of snap-brim, yet always coming across harmless and vulnerable as a fairground balloon, having somehow hypnotized the whole International Brotherhood of Tough Guys into respecting his need to stay unpopped as long as possible. Anybody so much as lays a finger invites correction.

"I'll take your word for it, Dipster. Haven't seen you around much either, come to think of it."

"Business activities, tryin to stay low."

"How much you owe them this time?"

"Ain't money." A tremulous silence. "If it was money—"

"—you'd already be out with the tambourine and I'd be out the door."

Dippy Chazz's usual Wisconsin Old Fashioned shows up, Korbel brandy, 7UP lithiated lemon soda, and, sharing the toothpick with a cherry, a pickled Brussels sprout.

"Ciao, Caramello." It's Lois, the usherette of interest, blonde, curvaceous, without flaw, precisely fine-tuned as to the exact makeup that goes with the undependable light in here. As if aware of its effect on Chazz, she hasn't changed out of her usherette outfit either—that, that *green stripe* down the trouser leg—mm, hmm! Accompanied by a redhead tonight just as attention-getting.

"*Amore mio*," helplessly murmurs Dippy Chazz.

"Ooh yes, just a li'l sip, puh-leeze?" from a narrow velvet case producing a custom gold-plated soda straw with a noticeable *L* engraved on it. Snuggling in, she gets to work on the Wisconsin favorite, unlipping her straw long enough to remember, "Oh, Giancarlo? some funny men came around this morning, to our li'l playroom?"

"*Porca miseria*," turning his head so fast his hat slides off of it, "and they followed you here, right?"

"Hm? Oh, no forget it, not my type, I like 'em suave and Continental and— Chazzy? Sugarcube? Where the hell'd he go?"

"Seven-teen'll getcha twen-ty, yes," Sheldon murmuring to the tune of "Shadow Waltz," "it will . . ."

Lois fishing around for her car keys. "See if I can catch up with him, you mind, Daphne?"

"Oh no, not at all," her friend smiling and glaring at the same time. "Thought we were going on down to Chicago tonight."

"You'll be OK here."

"Till I'm not OK, Lo-life."

"Giancarlo's friend here, what was your name again, he'll keep an eye on you I'm sure. Hicks? Meet Daphne. Back in a breeze, children."

Hicks and Daphne have a quick look at each other.

She's not exactly screaming "Help me!" but then she doesn't have to. Natural redhead, captivating set of pins, a way of letting you know you're getting the O-O but gO-Od. Hicks doesn't devote much thought, he just steps in.

"OK, um, Daphne, anything here I should know about?"

"Sure. Those two gorillas that just came in the door?"

So there are, sporting vaguely medical whites, looking a bit cross, as if they were expecting a quieter evening.

"They're after you? Better come on, then."

"Oh, brother!" comments April when she hears the story later. "Just like that, natch, 'Better come on, then.' Leave the thinking to Officer Johnson, as always."

"Two on one, come on, Angel, fair's fair, ain't it."

"Maybe you also recognized her from the society section, thought you'd promote a quick fetch-and-return fee."

Out the back way, full speed. "Abyssinia, Sheldon."

"OK and whose tab? Yours or Miss Airmont's?"

"Miss who?"

"Madcap Subdeb Cheese Heiress all over the papers for years now? how jay it's getting around this joint anymore."

At the moment Daphne happens to be on the run from Winnetka Shores Psychopathic, a ritzy banana plantation in the neighborhood, overseen by a Dr. Swampscott Vobe, M.D. Known for a susceptibility to anything newfangled, Dr. Vobe has somehow gotten it into his head that the patients at WSP are all available to him as lab material to try out his therapy ideas on, free of charge. Drugs, electricity, rays. Dr. Vobe is specially interested in rays.

"Come on in and have a look, just looking can't hurt, can it?" There's a chemical hospital smell, lights blinking across the panels of mysterious electrical equipment, an oppressive throb of insincerity. "You'll like it here, nothing unpleasant, brief sessions under the rays, a few injections . . . Oh and we'll need a quick signature and a set of fingerprints—"

"You bet, only be a minute," Daphne amiably, head-feinting one way then taking off in another, pursued, after a moment to confer, by the two heavies in loony-bin garb who by luck both turn out to be slower than Daphne by the step-and-a-half she needs, so that by the time they're up to speed, she's already on the running board of Lois's snappy yellow Kissel Speedster and accelerating away.

"Sure, it could've been more romantic," Hicks admits later to April, "but there was this crosswind situation, a sky nobody could see let alone read, kind of night when gales come down out of nowhere."

They proceed at a brisk pace past the shadowed Spanish melancholy of the abandoned Plaza del Lago, maintaining in the dark its vigil for the return of Prosperity. Down to lakeside. Hicks hands Daphne aboard the speedboat he came in on, and off they go.

Later, out on the Lake, rooster tail luminous behind them, "I like this mahogany detailing. Honduran, isn't it, not the cheap African stuff you find in Chris-Crafts."

"Don't tell Al Capone, he has a whole fleet."

"Not that I'd dream of calling the Big Fellow a cheapskate, understand."

Breezy chitchat. Hicks wonders how she knows so much about rum-runner design.

"You know, Miss Airmont, you could've said something. Snazzy red-head, how's anybody supposed to react?"

"Thanks. Maybe just once I'd like to be rescued for myself, not for my hair."

"This is what we're doing? I'm rescuing you?"

"The Indians have a belief . . ."

"Sure, just gimme a second here," Hicks sashaying them around a buoy rearing up out of the fog.

"You can't go rescuing somebody and then just forget it—Ojibwe belief is, interfere with somebody's life and you're responsible for them forever—"

Opportunities for light conversation after that deteriorated along with the weather.

"See if I have all this straight," April with an unnatural calm he recognizes, "you're barrel-assing up the Lake with this very underage baby vamp, invisible state lines everyplace, cross any of which and it's a federal rap, white slave laws and worse, when did you get so adventurous?"

"Last thing on my mind."

"That I can believe."

"All over with long before I met you, Angel."

"How long?"

"Oh, long . . . long."

"Happy we cleared that one up, Lunchmeat, and I'll sure do the same for you sometime."

"You have this confused with one of those type of movies you dames go to."

"Lowlife and high-society party girl, is it so improbable?"

"Just a lift for a lady on the run, quick trip, no romance. Sorry." Aware as he says it of how often he's likely to have to again.

November gales out here being respected for their violence and deadliness, having over the years carried off Lake navigation of all tonnages, sending to the bottom lumber schooners and daysailers, working steamers and pleasure yachts, sparing nobody, arriving without warning, proceeding without mercy, not leaving till they decide to. Tonight's is turning out to be one of those.

"Trouble, captain?"

"With this on-and-off fog situation I'm not sure exactly where we are anymore."

Daphne thinks they're pretty close to an Ojibwe reservation, maybe not exactly one on the map, "Where I know some people."

"High-ticket head case with pals among the Chippewa," muttering to himself. "Check 'n' double check. But—"

"Some of us," she explains, "get to go to finishing schools over in Europe someplace, others have to learn to enjoy a lifetime of getting bounced around by adults who in general have no idea of what they're doing, tough on the nervous system but a great way to expand your social horizons and of course always better if you're the bouncer not the bouncee, ain't that so, and here's the rez by the way, you could just drop me off if you wouldn't mind."

"Not at all. What I do mind now and then is gettin Lindy-hopped around."

"You're sure sensitive, for a side of beef."

Without knowing exactly how, even after looking it up on nautical charts afterward, Hicks seems to have run Daphne a good way up what's known here as the Shipwreck Coast, as far as a *secret Indian reservation*, mentioned only once in a rider to a phantom treaty kept in a deep vault under a distant mountain belonging to the U.S. Interior Department and unrevealed even to those guarding it. Like rezzes elsewhere in the state more familiar and earthly, there's no Wisconsin statutes in effect here, either. "Where white man's law is null and void," as Boynt likes to put it, "and savage ways prevail."

BY STRANGE CHIPPEWA telepathy a small committee has gathered dockside in the fog and drizzle to welcome Daphne. A gent in a Cubs baseball cap, with a bargain cigarette hanging off his lip and a night shift someplace nearby to get back to, hands her ashore.

In travels around workday Wisconsin Hicks has come into eye contact with a native Indian or two, without ever learning much. The gazes he's getting now sort out the way they usually do, into wary, unfriendly, too ancient to decipher, too claimed in the present tense by details like the motorboat and the girl. Everybody's smoking cigarettes in the ten-cent, or with no taxes around here maybe closer to five-cent, range. Woodsmoke comes seeping out of galvanized flue pipes, mixing with the damp fog now rolling in, and a fishing-boat smell. From up the Coast comes the half-earthly two-note bellow of a foghorn. Kewaunee, most likely. Maybe Two Rivers. Thunder west of here, something on the way.

"Thanks, you just saved me from life in the nuthouse." Kissing him formally on the cheek.

"Step easy, there, Daphne."

"Abyssinia yerself, Life Saver, and get back OK," or something like it, already walking away, calling against the wind, trying to be tough, if she's nervous at all being carried through by grace Hicks can sense but she may not.

All Hicks has ever had for grace is reflexes, which he depended on all that long night ride, pretty much running on fumes by the time he got back to the MPD moorage. Only days—all right, hours—later did sexual regrets begin to arrive, deep as a two-note foghorn—"Tough... Luck! Too... Bad!" like suppose she'd been legal age all along! Maybe they could have found a quiet inlet, rode out the storm, done some kidding around, "So forth."

"And you never saw her again, got her phone number..."

"That's right, hammer it in."

"Can't help remembering ourselves, that one time, in that boat..."

"Remember it well, Upper Nemahbin Lake, same summer Jack Zuta got the bump, li'l Evinrude outboard. But this other boat Daphne was in was a rumrunner, doing up to 80 knots, 15-foot waves, winter gales rollin in, hell, 20-foot, and enough else to worry about."

"Not a night for romance, you're saying."

"You do understand."

"The hell I do." Reaching for the smokes.

ONLY WEEKS LATER did Hicks run into somebody from that night, up in the Ward, at his hatmaker Vito Cubanelli.

"You again!" Vito busy with tollikers and curling shackles and a steam nozzle, shaping the brim of a derby, "some picky character walks in off the street, wants left and right sides different, sort of like tilting your hat without tilting your hat, three different diameters, and people wonder we go crazy."

"And here I thought it was mercury fumes."

Vito does a lot of his own felting, dealing direct with Indians who are apt to show up here at all hours with a rumble seat full of beaver hides, come in, drink some home brew, clown around, Vito buys in volume, gets a discount, all is copasetic.

"*Cazzo*, get a load of this topper, all you gotta do is step out the door. Hopeless."

"There's a lot of activity on the job," Hicks explains, "... what a hat goes through out there a dozen times a day, sat on, hit with snowballs, set on fire, checked in and out of a number of different classes of joint by careless tomatoes with long, sharp nails—"

"Don't forget natural disasters, good morning, Jimmy," to a hide seller who just stepped in, whose Ojibwe name means He Who Watches in Secret, but who goes by Jimmy when he's in town.

Catching sight of Hicks, "Hey, it's 'at speedboat captain again, ain't it."

Nodding, "Well. How's the Airmont broad been keepin?"

"Only what I see in the papers."

"If I'm not bein too nosy, how'd she ever get connected up with you folks?"

"You know how once you're bit by a werewolf, you turn into one yourself?"

"You tellin me ol' Daphne—"

"No, no, Ojibwe, see, instead of the werewolf, we have the Windigo. Maybe human, maybe not, nobody ever likes to look too close . . . turns out to have a human flesh habit for one thing, which fifty, sixty years ago began to create a dilemma for the white man, whose normal policy up till then had been whenever possible just shoot the Indian, except that Wisconsin back at that moment happens to be going through one of these bleeding-heart reform situations, loony bins state and county being constructed by the dozen at public expense, taking the 'humane' approach that whenever any member of any tribe even so much as thinks about nibbling on a gingerbread man, this should right away be labeled early-onset cannibalistic 'Windigo Psychosis' and the offending redskin locked up for mental treatment and preferably for good."

"And . . . Miss Airmont . . ."

"Oh. Apparently in one of these childhood loony bins she was in and out of, Daphne crossed paths with some Ojibwe Dawn Society brother being railroaded in on just such a phony cannibal rap. One thing must've led to another and first chance she got she was off on her Spirit Quest, somebody runs her out into the deep North Woods, leaves her there to do what she has to to make her way back, in hopes that somewhere in the logistics of return, she'll pick up a spirit guide."

"And . . ." Hicks flashing back to those first few minutes after he'd set her back on land, stepping off the rumrunner's special and already on her way to becoming the darling of scandal sheets including *Modern Peeper*, *Yikes!*, and *Lowlife Gazette*, featuring photos of her sporting a range of lurid getups and a loose smile she may not by that time of the evening have been in full control of, surrounded by a prize selection of merry loophounds gazing at her like chorus boys in a musical number, under headlines like DAIRY DEB SIN SPREE.

"You know you saved her life, bringing her up to the rez when you did."

"This again, thanks, heard it before, just giving a hitchhiker a lift was all."

"Fact remains that once you put so much as a toe into the flow that is the life journey of another . . ."

"Wait, you're tellin me, one helpful act—not even that, just *trying to be polite*—has dumped me into a washday radio drama that can go on now for, what, years?"

"Back in Pozzuoli we have this all the time," Vito puts in, "it's called *la vendetta*, what's the commotion?"

"And if I say thanks but no thanks, what happens, I get an arrow through my head?"

"You don't have to be all that way about it either, white man."

15

For days now Hicks has been noticing, even in the daylight and out on the street, the return, from somewhere back in deeper Prohibition times, all across his body and over his face, light as delusional bugs, the ghostly crawl of professional finger-eye coordination, somewhere above and in the distance, tightening in on whatever is centered in its crosshairs, which at the moment happens to be Hicks's head.

To a concertina rendition of "Hark! The Herald Angels Sing" half a block away, Hicks is handed a parcel wrapped in festive red-and-green paper whose design features Xmas trees, reindeer, candy canes, so forth. Ribbon tied in a big bow. Something to do with Christmas.

"This is for you."

"Not me."

Shrug. "We're only the delivery guys."

Hicks takes a close, doubtful look. "Which would be . . ."

"We're Santa's elves."

"Uh huh, but . . ."

"You know Billie the Brownie down at Schuster's, right? OK, we're relatives."

"Cousins."

"They made him up, he's a make-believe department store critter—"

"Skeptical, ain't you?"

"Billie the Brownie *is* real, you never heard him on the radio?"

"WTMJ, weekdays at five."

"Sure, the person who plays Billie on the radio is real but . . . maybe not Billie himself, not in . . . the same way that, oh, Walter Winchell is, for example."

"Walter Winchell is real?"

It isn't that Hicks enjoys mutually blank staring, though now and then he'll find himself provoking some, like calling a time-out in a game, hoping to pick up a few meaningful seconds. Which doesn't seem to be happening here.

"And . . . now we suppose you'll tell us Amos 'n' Andy aren't really Negroes either."

"Both white guys, sorry, didn't you see the movie?"

"*Check and Double Check*, sure, two white guys in blackface."

"Well, that was them. Can't believe I'm the one you heard it from first."

"And, and . . . Heinie und His Grenadiers, how about them, they're not really Germans?"

"Standard-issue Americans, the whole gang, sorry."

Here they are standing in the middle of downtown Milwaukee, holiday shoppers hurrying to and fro, having this discussion.

"Sorry, but somehow you boys don't look like elves."

"We're not short enough?"

"Ears, he probably wants pointed ears."

"That'd help, yeah, and aren't you supposed to be in some kind of elf outfits or somethin too, you know, those hats you guys wear . . ."

"Only during working hours, at the moment we're still off the clock, this isn't official elf business."

"Not like he needs to know, Sven."

"Oops."

"Could you give me some idea who this is from, at least?"

"Not unless you're authorized to see the work order, which could put the Saint in something of a mood, just when he needs his wits about him, big delivery schedule coming up and so forth . . ."

"Wait, the name here, this isn't me, this is for somebody else, you got the wrong—"

"Got to breeze, children all over the world to deal with, you understand."

"You have a real Merry Xmas now, Mister Schultz."

And like that, considering the tool kit of tricks available to elves, both of them have vanished. Hicks has begun to get funny looks from passersby. The package, however, is still there in his hands. Seems heavy for its size, which could always mean something interesting, maybe even a gold ingot or something. 'Course there's interesting and there's—

"Well, howdy there, Capitalist Scum, funny running into you again."

Damn if it ain't the same sawed-off Bolshevik striker Hicks didn't manage to kill that fateful night not so long ago—

"Sure . . . been a while, never did catch your name . . ."

"Four-Eyes is good enough, don't mean we're part of each other's social life now."

As things fall out it only looks like Hicks saved Four-Eyes's life back then—in fact now it's Four-Eyes who's about to save his.

"None of my business what's in that package they just handed you there, but over on my side of the Beerline those two guys are well-known as the worst kind of bad news, and the sooner you deep-six that thing the better for everybody."

"Really, you think?"

"Chump, everybody can hear it ticking from down the block. Happiest holiday wishes, if you should live so long."

"Sure, and a Merry Christmas right back atcha."

Carrying the package like he would any normal object, Hicks heads for Wisebroad's Shoes, a short walk away, through iced-in weekday gloom, dodging streetcars with snowplows bolted onto their front ends and window-shoppers throwing him troubled gazes, past Depression-Christmas vaudeville houses less brightly lit, reduced prices matinee and evening, according to industry folklore this being among the worst weeks in show business, and since it's a week in Milwaukee besides, twice as bad as that, maybe more.

Whenever he's out in the street and not sure what to do, being superstitious as anybody, Hicks has fallen into the habit of stepping over and onto the nearest penny scale and reading his fortune.

Today he gets the traditional ticket, weight on one side and fortune on the other—"Need to lose some extra weight, pal, and sooner'd be better than later. Good luck."

By now Hicks is used to this sort of thing, a network of penny scales all over town plus Chicago that can recognize him personally even blocks away. Must be done with radio waves somehow. He keeps meaning to ask Skeet and his pals . . .

Let's see, it said extra weight . . . hmm . . . could that mean . . . He finds and fishes out another penny and drops it. The ticket reads "What'd I just say? You're carrying TOO MUCH EXTRA WEIGHT, Einstein, get me? Think about it and don't take too long."

A wave of leather and shoe-polish aroma billows out to greet him as he comes through the door of Wisebroad's. Everybody's in their socks, as if business is so slow they're reduced to measuring each other's feet. Al, Benny, Chuck, DeQuincy, and Edgeworth aren't their real names but actually code words based on shoe widths—with a Depression on, salesman-to-salesman talk tends to be guarded, like "Anybody seen Benny?" can mean "We don't have this in a B width, what can we switch it for?"

"Season's greetings, Zoomer," Hicks's handle around here, short for Halls of Montezuma, a way of saying "Shoe's a triple-E."

"How's 'em wingtips workin out?"

"Big hit at the country club. Mind if I give somethin a quick once-over on your X-ray machine there?"

"Long as somebody remembers to call the bomb squad."

"Thanks." Hicks bringing out a fin as several hands reach simultaneously. "Wait, let me look and see if I've got it in singles."

One of many interesting facts about Milwaukee is that along with the Harley-Davidson motorcycle and the QWERTY typewriter keyboard layout, it's also the birthplace of the shoe-store X-ray machine.

"Not only hometown as they come," Benny sweeping a gesture of respect, "but still under warranty too."

"More of a Brannock Device fella myself," remarks Edgeworth, "X-rays being fine, far as they go, except they don't pick up fat, and fat's the key, see, true fit is always a function of how fat the foot," and so forth.

They gather around to eyeball the ghostly image.

"Any idea what that is?"

"Don't look like much of anything, you ask me."

"Yeah, well, it's ticking, I can tell you that."

"Just your imagination."

"I think it could be a clock . . . maybe a pocket watch. Aren't those numbers there, look."

"Could almost be somebody's face, see, that's the nose there and—"

Despite a certain blurriness, Hicks realizes it is inescapably a face, not unchanging and lifeless, like you'd get from a severed head for example, but instead *gazing back* with its eyes wide open and holding a gleam of recognition, a face he's supposed to know but doesn't, or at least can't name. Mouth about to open and tell him something he should've known before this. The window he never wanted to have to look through, the bar he used to know enough not to set foot inside of.

"Um, and how long do we plan to keep pumping X-ray energy through this object of unknown design?" inquires DeQuincy.

Edgeworth gives it a squint. "I'd call it in to the MPD, if you haven't already." They all exchange looks back and forth for what seems a while.

The Milwaukee PD bomb squad, given the history here, is possibly not the unit to be expecting much help from, even with boilerplated trucks these days, plenty of mattresses and so forth. Sometimes they don't even return phone calls. "And heaven help you if it's a false alarm, then they send you a bill, then bill collectors packing service .38s, everybody meantime pissing and moaning about taxpayer money."

"Here, now put it up alongside your head, get your ear right down next to it, and—"

"Aghh!" DeQuincy recoiling in terror. "Not just ticking, now it's playing . . . tunes, some . . . horrible Christmas medley. Just get it out of here once, if you wouldn't mind?"

"Traditionally," Edgeworth can't help pointing out, "time bombs get set to some exact hour, right now it's about a quarter to, gives you enough time if you care to to go deep-six this down in the Lake, which you recall is only a block or two out the door and to your right."

"If you hear anything really loud out here . . ."

DeQuincy smiles briefly, narrowing his eyes, "Sure thing, Zoomer. Next of kin still at the same phone number?"

Dum dee um dum, tickticktick . . . Threading through the midday traffic, pedestrians in the classic Milwaukee stupor, Hicks, trying not to show too much of a problem with his nonchalance, makes it down to the Lake and not a minute too soon.

Not to blame the Depression or anything, but there seem to be a considerable number of fish-happy unemployed to be found today out here on the frozen expanse, with sleds, tip-ups, bikes pedal- and motor-driven, shelters more and less elaborate. Small fires going, coffee percolating, kerosene lamps cutting some of the gloom, portable radios at low volume, possibly on some theory that music will hypnotize fish up through the ice. Pinochle and Sheepshead games in progress as well as a curling tournament, what curlers call a bonspiel.

As luck would have it, an ice fisherman happens to've just augered a hole. "Mind if I—" Hicks sliding the festive holiday parcel in, stomping it under the ice as far as he can, "thanks, you're a real sport," turning and heading for shore, motioning everybody to keep clear, whereupon—

KA-BOOM. And then some. Addressing every bone in Hicks's body, including the one just under his hat. A colorful and earsplitting fountain of ice, blood, silt, factory waste, and pieces of perch, pike, whitefish, and two or three varieties of trout meanwhile hurtling skyward, the echo racketing away to cover most of Milwaukee, then returning in a downpour of Friday-night supper ingredients which a sudden crowd have showed up with buckets, bags, and hats to collect.

The guy with the auger isn't too happy. "Dammit, you dynamite hounds," he screams, "this is sinful, don't you know the Angler's Creed forbids this kind of thing?"

"Missouri Synod Lutheran, myself," Hicks in a shaky voice he almost doesn't recognize.

About now a beat cop and old friend of Uncle Lefty's shows up, "Have to ticket you for crossing against the light back there, Hicks, sorry but it's a dollar fine."

"Price is right considering it just bought me my life."

"You must be getting up in the bucks, this side of town the going rate's closer to 39¢."

After a while, The crowd drifts away leaving soiled and shattered ice, a patch of water already begun to ice over again, and, not too many hours away, frozen Milwaukee sunset, and the night ahead.

"**Aren't we the night owl.**" April blinking, truculent, not fully awake. Of course it's her door Hicks would be showing up at.

"Thought you might still be awake."

"If you want to call it that."

"Tell him to use the bedroom window, nice snowdrift back there, only a short drop."

"Maybe you didn't notice, but it's half past ungodly."

Stares at the back of his empty wrist for a while. "Huh. Somebody must've lifted my watch."

"You look a li'l more dilapidated than usual, Cupcake, if I may say."

"Speaks are all closed by now, force of habit, wasn't thinking, sorry . . ."

"No, wait, Hicks, come back, only talking in my sleep . . . Hicks?"

"I must be getting, what is it, sensitive? No, wait, sentimental?"

"Sure . . . and remind me, what are you doing here again?"

"Thanks, maybe I will just for a minute," Hicks beating the evening snowfall from his hat, stepping cautiously in over the doorsill, as if something might be waiting in the room tonight to jump him, as beat up in spirit as April has seen him, even from the worst nights of mob warfare in Chicago not all that long ago.

Somewhere off in the house, upstairs or maybe down, Christmas carols over somebody's radio, somebody else picking a blues line on a guitar. From outside now and then come sounds of late river traffic. The new foghorn down on the breakwater.

"You're shaking, what happened, you forgot your earmuffs again? We're out of beer if you were planning to cry into some, but there could be a bottle of Mistletoe gin around someplace . . ."

"Wouldn't mind."

"Dig in."

"Thanks," going on to try and what the insurance forms like to call "explain." She listens, eyes never leaving his face.

"Elves." Putting on a tough-girl scowl, pretending to adjust the angle of Hicks's head. "And you bought that?"

"Well, they were the right size, and they seemed pretty sure."

A pause to consider a number of comebacks.

"We may have discussed this before, but at the risk of seeming to nag, did you ever think about some line of work maybe a little less, oh, unhealthy..."

"Sure, even thought about the Milwaukee PD for a while, till Uncle Lefty set me straight."

"Not enough bad habits for them? Too un-stupid, what?"

"Too many Italians in my social life, I guess. Nothing personal. Ever since that spaghetti special went off in the station house even some harmless case like me swinging traffic at a bankruptcy sale is suddenly too dangerous for the likes of the MPD."

"Don't suppose a friendly heart-to-heart with the bomb squad—"

"Not when they're about to run me in for Stuffy Keegan's truck."

Her eyelids narrowing that telltale 64th of an inch while her brain races on, "Maybe my Uncle Cici can talk to somebody," this particular uncle being none other than Francesco "Finger of Death" Sfuzzino, locally year after year coming in at the top of everybody's most-frightened-of list. "Anything for you, my lit-tle breath of spring, you only need to ask, each time it's like 'O mio babbino caro' all over again, ain't it, only different."

While April is thinking of some other song, most likely Annette Hanshaw singing "Those Little White Lies."

"Damn but you're a sweetheart." Hicks means it.

"Then again," short nod, shorter smile, "gotta remember this'd be the Bay View or north Italian branch of the family. Bacciagaluppi, snooty bunch, little dim, detached. Sicilian side might be more accommodating."

"Except that..."

"Exactly."

Stories have begun to drift in of couples teaming up, jumping boxcars and thumbing rides together, even waiting faithful long weeks for each other's release from the county lockup. Working-stiff gear, hair cropped or bobbed, chain-smoking, tough yet elegant. Nobody wants to go through trouble alone, yet how can Hicks even ask, never mind expect, that much from any dame, even one he can see himself going sentimental, if not already borderline daffy about?

Jumping catfish. What kind of a mid-career outlook is this? Poverty and longing. Not that he's any special fan of the single life, understand, and it isn't their fault if women are as superficial, untrustworthy, and unwilling to stick around when the going gets the least bit tough as he has found them in general to be.

"OK," April considering which of a number of blunt weapons in her handbag to bring out, "but aside from that?" The counterargument, obvious to anybody but a beefbrain like Hicks, being that in times like these to stay at anybody's side for longer than five minutes could qualify as at least potential lifetime partner material.

Last thing Hicks would want to admit hoping for, that he and April could've been another one of these couples hitchhiking together through the Depression, teamed up against each day and its troubles, each dusk out on some country road, thumbs at the ready, heading for who knows what waiting deeper for them in the night. Some dame, someday. So far he hasn't got around to sharing any of this with April, who could easily react along the lines of "Oh no, another one of these fragile types pussyfooting into my life, just when I have you figured for some lone warrior out on the edge of a cliff someplace, don't need a thing from anybody, all the while turns out you're just one more sentimental sap, well, unobservant me."

Uncle Lefty notices it's been taking Hicks a while to hold flame and cigarette together long enough to light up.

"Heard about your surprise package."

Regarding his hand thoughtfully. "Should've been over this a little quicker."

"Try fifteen years. Maybe now you begin to understand a thing or two, maybe lay off of the bocce ball jokes."

Shaky as Hicks may be feeling, a man still has to climb back aboard the critter that threw him. Investigate.

Before the echoes have died away, Lino Trapanese is on the phone. "Case you were wondering, it ain't who you're thinking."

"He tell you that himself?"

"'Hope Twinkletoes ain't taking it too personally,' is how he put it. Plus best regards and sincere wishes for a speedy recovery of your nervous system."

"Al Capone would've sent flowers at least."

"Strange, almost like Don Peppino's been in a long discussion about this with somebody."

Which it has already occurred to Hicks might've been April, but so what? "Looking at the list of people I've gotten on the wrong side of . . ."

"Of course I don't speak for the whole *consorzio*, but . . ." Hicks can hear the shrug even over the phone. "Somebody could be getting you mixed up with somebody else, you know. It happens. Tradition in Milwaukee."

"Those elves called me Schultz, we know anybody by that name?"

"Sure narrows it down, don't it?"

MICHELE "KELLY" STECCHINO, an old-time Third Ward hardhead dating back to the Vito Guardalabene era, turned anarchist in his retirement years and highly regarded locally these days as a bombsmith, occupies an oversize Polish flat, reached via a pathway lined with Chicago Hardy fig trees, scungilli shells, lawn statuary on assorted Italian themes, including Benito Mussolini. Stained glass windows a little more bloody and religious than commonly found in Milwaukee.

Cooking "soup," the idea is to take dynamite sticks, break them into pieces and place in boiling water, and skim off the nitroglycerin that forms on the top. Serve at appropriate times and places. Singing "treb-bi, la zup-pa" to the tune of "Vesti la giubba," fussing at the stove, Kelly even has one of those tall chef's hats that he likes to wear while he's working, in the belief it will keep him safe from unexpected explosions. "Ba-ccia, galup-pa . . ."

Hicks contributes a few contrapuntal bars of "Dinah, is there anything finer," which is what you might sing if you want to kid a box-blower, though the practice is generally not recommended.

Kelly directs a glance you could call discouraging. "Ten Our Fathers, ten Hail Marys, and a good Act of Contrition. Fumes are givin me a headache here, reach me that Alka-Seltzer bottle, could you, and was there anything else today," slowly rocking the hand he doesn't shoot with, meaning please don't waste his time.

"What'd I do now?"

"You're not supposed to know this address."

"I wouldn't risk offending you today if it wasn't serious."

"Downtown bomb squad's already been by, case you were wondering. Italophobic, you people, ain'tchyiz?"

They exchange a look. Hicks tries to be nonchalant. "Usual MPD bomb equals Italian malarkey."

"In the business, we understand that an explosion, not always but sometimes, is actually somebody with something to say. Like, a voice, with a message we aren't receiving so much as overhearing."

"This pair of elves who delivered it might've thought I was somebody else."

"Even if it wasn't meant for you personally that don't mean you ain't in some trouble, which if you're not too big of a *minghiun* you can see how much you're in right now?"

Well, here it is again, sure took his time about it.

"You know who's pickin up her IOUs, Hicksie. You've had a look at the rundown on his career, maybe you're overdue for a vacation, and I don't mean no weekend down to Edgewater Beach."

"Quit fooling." Somehow Hicks knows where he's talking about.

"Give it some thought, it's paradise over there, of course anything after Milwaukee would be—we get you plenty-a nice discounts—dames, coke fa you nose, bowlin alley, whatever you American boys go for, make you feel right at home."

"It's a Fascist dictatorship, *Professore*."

"Don't tell them around Palermo. What makes you private dicks any different?"

"Oh, swell, P.I.s are Fascists now?"

"Study your history, *gabadost*, you started off, mosta yiz, breakin up strikes, didn't ya, same as Mussolini's boys."

"That don't . . ." then stopping to think about it.

"Goon-squad work, stay in it long enough, you should know what happens."

"I'm out of that now."

"Yeah and once a torpedo, always a torpedo, ain't it."

"Just a hayseed flatfoot, Vuscenza."

"Wouldn't want to be sending you to your doom, see."

"Appreciate that. But say you did . . ."

Afternoon has been steadily on the creep. "Dark already, time to go turn on the scungilli," each of the conch shells decoratively lining the front path being illuminated from within by its own tiny electric lamp. Kelly flips one switch and it's all lit up around here like Dearborn and Randolph. More dazzling as the night advances.

THE NAZIS ARE even less easy to get a story out of. Too many of them would be happy to take credit for a bomb of any size, even those who wouldn't know one end of a firecracker from the other.

Ooly Schaufl seems sympathetic enough but isn't too forthcoming. "Nobody our side of the Alps. Don't know, somehow it don't feel local. Somethin's on the way around here, bigger than a gang war."

"OK, without putting my nose in too far, on the off chance these two whizbangs are related . . . any thoughts about Stuffy Keegan? Like where is he and so forth."

"No."

"Is that no you don't know where he is, or no, Hicks, I'm keepin shtum?"

"If I told you where, you'd ask why. If I told you why, you'd say, I don't know what that is, explain it to me. By then I couldn't explain much of anything 'cause I'd be dead."

"Helpful for sure. All I wanted to know was—"

"Hicksie, maybe everybody knows, maybe you're the only dummkopf from here to Peoria who *don't* know. Maybe there's things't'll never be spoken out loud. Maybe this is bigger than the Saint Valentine's, bigger than the Lindbergh baby. You're the one with the license, so go ahead—private investigate your keester off, good luck, maybe you'll even find something, but leave me out, OK, I don't see it'll do me much good to know or not know."

Lew Basnight isn't much more help.

"I may not know exactly who it is, but maybe I have a number of ideas about who it isn't, a list you've already been through as thoroughly as anybody. What we're after is an Overlooked Negative, an all but forbidden topic anymore, a whole chapter about which, in fact, like certain books of the Bible, was deliberately left out when the Gumshoe's Manual was put together."

"Sure, Lew, you mind running me through that again?"

"I might if I could remember what it was I said, but I may in fact not be the wised-up old-timer you seem to be taking me for."

"Lew, don't disillusion me, you were always what I was hoping to be someday."

"You don't know how sad it makes me to hear that. Ain't that easy for tough guys. I may not look like it, but I was a tough customer once. Civilized appearance was only one of my secret weapons. I can quote you a list of well-known hired artillery who underestimated me, much to their subsequent dismay."

"Your name still strikes fear. I use it instead of flashing my license."

"You don't have to grovel."

16

The day has darkened, the shop is quiet, the evening trimotor hop over to Grand Rapids will be taking off soon, everybody's knocked off work except for Hicks and Boynt, Boynt's shoes restless on the rug, last light of day severely raking over the prairie down across the town, bouncing off the Lake, rebounding off the ceiling, desktop, Boynt's eyeglasses.

"If it was me I'd've pulled you long ago, but it's Home Office that have the say-so here, all you need to know is it's a numbered account, one of the Loop banks that's still solvent, checks all clearing just swell, thanks, and look for a letter of credit waiting for you in New York, at the Gould Fisk Fidelity Bank and Trust, not too far from Pennsylvania Station—"

"Boynt. Is that New York I just heard?"

"Let me guess, you're wondering why are we sending you eight hundred miles out of town? go ahead and think what you like. None of my business anymore, maybe Don Peppino and that crowd down in Little Cosenza bought me off, maybe somebody believes you're worth travel expenses, even if it's only 50 smackers."

"You say 50?" Wait. "Boynt, now that's 50 one-way, but . . . how about—"

"Let's take it one direction at a time, ain't it," handing over an envelope with a train ticket inside. "Union Station, tomorrow noon sharp, don't be late. Pack light."

"We'll be years squarin this one, Boynt."

A look Boynt has only thrown him a couple of times, and those, while memorable, not in any way you'd call sentimental. "Focus your attention and consider how maybe we're doing you an act of uncompensated kindness here, what our friends of the Jewish faith call a mitzvah. Don't bother to thank me or anything.

"It's the elf bomb, sure it is. Home Office are assuming you were meant to be a sort of human version of Stuffy's truck. What the bomb rollers wanted from Stuffy they also wanted from you, maybe nothing more complicated than silence, and if you hadn't been in to talk to the Fee Bees you'd've probably got off just as easy as Stuffy."

"Somebody knows this for a fact?"

"Let's say somebody saw you at the federal courthouse the other day. Going in around the back way, with all the construction and Keep Out signs. Wondering who you were there to see. Maybe, all I'm saying, what you really needed was to keep away from the Feds."

"Sure. How about somebody gettin them to keep away from me . . ."

"Exactly what's got everybody at Home Office nervous. The best solution they can see is for you to pull a fade like Stuffy did."

"Fade, fade is good, I know how to do that, but why does it have to be New York?"

"You'll see. Have fun, take in a show. Back before you know it."

SKEET ON THE other hand has had too many goodbyes in his life to allow himself much reaction to this one.

"Stay in touch with the shop, OK, they can reach me if they have to," hoping this isn't just wishful thinking.

"Here, Hicksie, this is for you."

A U.S. half-dollar, with the heads side showing a willowy package in a flimsy getup, representing Liberty, out for a stroll at what seems to be around dawn, because the sun is located very low in the design, in fact below the hemline of Liberty's gown, inspiring some out there who can afford to to carefully engrave on the solar disk a face gazing with a lewd grin underneath the skirts of our national allegory. Skeet has been carrying this piece of folk art around since Hicks has known him.

"Thanks, Skeeter, but I can't accept this, licenses have been pulled for less, and besides, it's your good luck piece."

"Well, I can't be lugging it around town all the time either, can I."

Having run errands for any number of bush-league plutes, Hicks and Skeet both know the weight of a 50¢ tip.

"Only a quick out and in, honest."

"If I tell you somethin will you promise not to take it personally?"

"Since you put it that way, no."

"Thought I'd have a look at Stuffy's case myself."

"There's apt to be some dangerous customers mixed up in this, kid—"

"It's OK, I'm a creature of the streets, all gatted up, don't trust nobody—"

"Both sides of the law comin at you all directions, including coppers local and on up who ain't above faking a birth certificate, trying you as an adult and railroadin you into Waupun onto some indeterminate taxi ride—"

"You always did know how to give a pep talk, Hicksie. Bon voyage."

And just to slap the Good Housekeeping Seal onto everything, here's Lino Trapanese again. Hicks is just about to step into the Meal A Minute for a three-decker when a Packard Custom Eight limousine pulls up over the curb and onto the sidewalk inches in front of him. No chrome, no wax job, no shine, flat black all over. A window rolls down an inch and here's Lino glittering through the slot. A door swings silently open and Hicks gets in.

"Somebody would like me to mention how very grateful they are to you, Hicks, this step you've agreed to take. How very, very grateful."

Hicks looks around for the satchel full of cash that would normally come along with talk like this. "Something here, or not here, you're supposed to explain to me, Lino?"

"You can trust my sacred word, their gratitude amounts to more than any bag can hold."

"A head start out of town."

"A word to the weisenheimer, is how they put it."

"Somethin fishy going on, Lino, nobody wants to spill the straight story, you can call it honorable if you want, but I call it spinach. Don't try to tell me omertà, I know what dummied-up Italian looks like and this ain't it. Cokeheads getting the third degree have more of a grip on their nerves than any of you mugs do lately."

"Hicks, now—" reaching playfully into his suit for a roscoe he may not be carrying, "y' just better watch 'at stuff, once."

"Maybe those elves weren't hired by anybody you associate with, so you keep sayin, which case whoever it was might be makin you folks as nervous as they're makin me. It's OK, Lino, no dishonor."

"What have you got to tell us," chuckling more in disbelief than amusement, "about dishonor? Lissen-a me now. Down in the deep Mezzogiorno, there grows a grape so harsh and bitter you'd never make wine from it alone—but when you blend it with other grapes, sometimes only a couple percent, suddenly a miracle, mmmwa! *che figata*, you capeesh-a da jive?"

"Only a beer drinker, Lino, but I'll keep it in mind."

"You want to know more, go ask your pal Dippy Chazz."

Sure, and *auguri* with that one, Chazz's phone line has been disconnected for a week, as Lino, from a quick look at his kisser, is also aware, and Chazz according to what Hicks can find out fled into exile, out beyond the pickle patches, someplace quite unconnected with local geography.

Hicks considers a diplomatic reproof but settles for "Chazzy's *umbatz*, nuttier than a Giant Bar."

HICKS AND APRIL rendezvous aboard the southbound SS *Christopher Columbus*, once queen of the '93 Chicago Fair and about to be queen dowager of the new fair coming up, a festive pile of decks like an electric birthday cake, all raring to go as the next century of progress and miles o' smiles, as it sez in the ads.

The shoreline rolls by, some cumulus in the west backlit by the setting sun, spirits, mixers, and chasers flow, and the dance orchestration includes both a full-keyboard accordion and a Chemnitzer concertina, which means every once in a while, between the slow dreamy numbers and the upbeat jingles about how great everything is these days, there'll be polkas. Just in case anybody was thinking of wandering off and jumping overboard.

"Enjoy it while you can, Chuckles."

"Because . . ."

April, hands to hips, eyebrows all zigzag, won't look at him.

"Unless maybe it's all sealed and done already."

"Oh, you damned ox," and she's crying all over his shirt just back from the Chinese place.

"You could have said something, even if I already knew."

"You? Who would tell *you* anything?" She has fished out one of his shirttails and is blotting her nose, with a ladylike sniffle, all over it.

"Your line," after a while, "is, 'D and D, Hicks, took the oath, can't say any more, please don't hate me'—"

"I know my line, Fathead— oh, are we on the air?"

A moon of the sort more commonly observed in Iowa has just risen, and the plaintive squeezeboxes are now joined by electric uke, reeds, French horns, a jazz drummer on temporary booby-hatch leave. April and Hicks are dancing. "Someday," he whispers, "it'll be the right joint, and a full-size band, maybe even a moon like this one, and we'll dance like those Castles do, long as you like, I promise."

"Meaning you'd have to never let go of me, yeah, just dream on, you big chump."

The charmed old vessel steams gently along the wreck-strewn coastline of Wisconsin. Children on shore drifting asleep beneath the roofs passing in the moonlight, distant polka and Lindy-hop music stealing into their early dreams, plus the occasional ballad such as the one Hicks is crooning into April's ear.

> Ubiquitous . . . you're out, ev-
> -v'rywhere, you're
> ubiquitous . . . like the
> airwaves, through the air, it's
> iniquitous . . . that you
> never-seem to care, how
> ridiculous-ly I'm yearning, in-
> -to what a sap I'm turning . . .

                                        you're-here-and,
then you're there,
Though the guy's not always me,
I try-to-act debonair,
Like I know I'm s'posed to be—how
I-wish-you'd, c'mere and, kiss-me-quick,
                                      Till-we're-both-of-us
brainless, as-a-brick,
Though it's got kinda thick-with-dust,
once it sure did the trick with us,
'n' you, you've gone all . . . u-biquitous . . .

"Listen to me, *gabadost*, and I'm not kidding."

He guesses she isn't.

"You noticed this?" Who hasn't? the sparkler on her finger looks like you'd expect to find one or more Black Hawks skating around on it, announcing that April has become the all but kept tomato of Don Peppino Infernacci the bad and big. "He's Calabrese, 'Ndrangheta 200 proof, he'd rather kill you than work things out, and just when I start asking myself what'd I get into, here he comes again with that down-home *nun sò che*, or maybe I feel sorry for him 'cause his wife is such a tramp, runs around after anything . . ."

"My kinda woman, how come you haven't tried to fix us up yet? We could all get together and play bridge, and maybe she'll be packing too."

April turns her face away like he just reached for it or something. "Thanks."

"Now what'd I say?"

"Oh, don't mind me, just go on ahead with the happy patter, you Einsteins, what is it with you? Heads in the fog, never know how much trouble you're in."

"How many Einsteins would that be again?"

"I'm such straight-up trouble, Hicks." The eye-to-eye she's waited till now to hit him with doesn't go out over the air either.

Hicks with a tremble in his voice she has never yet mistaken for anything but strategic, "Maybe I always knew about"—almost naming Don Peppino—"*that* . . . and maybe I don't care?"

Sure. But, *"That* could change quick enough, ya ten-minute egg, you. I keep hoping ... if we could just get past it this one time, who knows, I mean if there is a next time—"

"If" is seldom a good sign. Pretending he didn't hear, "Careful with that 'we,' Angel."

"Oh, I know how to be careful. I wish you did."

No goodbye night together in Chicago. Hicks would be sorely disappointed, if there hadn't been so many lesser occasions already.

"So—family business, huh. Thought your uncle was retired from all that."

"That's Uncle Luca, this is Uncle Ruggiero." April never runs out of uncles, kind of endearing, long as he remembers not to take it personally. Would loving her mean loving someone who has committed routine betrayals and will again, yet never admit it, let alone allow anybody to bend a sympathetic ear?

THE MAIN CONCOURSE at Union Station is nothing you'd want to stare upward into for too long—115-foot-high semicylindrical barrel-vaulted overhead, skylights running along its length, open trusswork girders. Best to have some compelling business down here on the ground.

Rain in Chicago today, a downbeat hush. Yard bulls in slickers moving among the gaunt steel monsters, rain-brightened rails, treacherous footing. Taxi-war veterans, Yellow, Checker, and Parmelee, all at curbside, exhaust brightening visibly into the air like the breath of coach horses not that many winters ago. Grease, steam, overheated journal boxes, some send-off except that whaddaya know, here's April again, up early, for her, wearing a pale peach fedora with a brim swept alluringly, a careful soft dent in the crown. Greeting him a little too fast, with a touch of what a fight announcer might call pugnacity, making an effort to dial down the emotion. Confirming, if it wasn't clear to Hicks already, that her story about being in town to visit yet another branch of the family is hooey.

Buttoning her lip, she settles poised against him with dance-floor hands where they're supposed to be, her perfume, Shalimar as usual, even an hour into drydown locally overriding the cigar and coal smoke of the echo-filled concourse, and here they are, dancing together to a tune only they among the hundreds streaming by can hear, in and out of the towering, vaulted volume of rainlight and public-toilet acoustics, clasped in that always just about to be no longer reliable routine they find themselves sliding into whenever things look like ambling off into the swamplands of sincerity. Orchestral backup as usual remaining discreetly invisible . . .

Somewhere below the Chicago streets, all but trainside, a sulfurous note from the coal smoke in the air, in some little last-chance joint that isn't the Fred Harvey's upstairs, April even gets a chance to reprise "Midnight in Milwaukee," and in her glottal attack, for example, on phrases like "Any town but this one," her voice breaks a little, as if she's actually getting emotional about the lyric. Fact, this is one of those times it's almost more than either of them can take.

"You know as long as there's no more surprises waiting down the line—"

She has been rolling up his necktie against just such a declaration, and now stuffs it quickly into his mouth, inquiring with her eyebrows if he understands. Nodding, Hicks opens his mouth and lets the damp tie unroll back down over his shirt.

"Schuster's, on sale, 39¢, but I still try not to drool on it too much. You know, sentimental." Hicks with a hesitation step and turn that gives them no choice but to kiss goodbye, at length and both sincere as they'll ever get, beside the Broadway Limited cranked up to go, and for a minute it's unclear which of them is staying and which leaving.

"Keep out of trouble, genius."

"Don't let's hear nothin good about you, hot stuff."

Up ahead somewhere the engine makes with some loud escapes of steam, wheels still wet from out in the trainyard taking a few seconds to gain purchase, till the looming mindless iron critter begins to move. And as Annette Hanshaw might kiss it off, "That's all."

17

Streamlining on into afternoon deepening to blue evening, through Depression Pittsburgh, a ghost city, fires at the iron- and steelworks banked, massive structures unlit, though not unoccupied.

Later on, up in the mountains, between Pittsburgh and Altoona, entering deeper into the night run, having left behind and below what neon still shone, the Hoovervilles, the ghost-city light, hobo gatherings around trackside trash fires, stray auto headlights gliding briefly alongside the tracks, some fractional moonlight through the windows plus a few dim electric lamps in the observation car, deserted at this hour except for Hicks.

"You OK in here?" It's a Pullman porter, whose name, as he's quick to point out, isn't George but McKinley. "We're running underweight tonight, there's empty berths back there if you want to grab some shut-eye."

"Thanks, I'm fine catnappin in here, if it's OK."

McKinley Gibbs turns out to be running a sideline in race records, and before long is showing Hicks a good-size stack of platters carefully interleaved with newspapers he's also bringing on to points east.

"Interest you in a *Defender* here, makes a good Hoover blanket too."

"Sure, thanks, but mind if I ask, what's with all this 'Turn Lincoln's face to the wall' and so forth?"

"Hate to be the one to tell you the sad tale, but everybody knows by now what Hoover is, and it ain't no Lincoln."

"But he's an engineer, ain't he, a management expert, solved the hunger in Europe, anybody knows how to fix the economy it ought to be him. Besides which, come on, all those loudmouth Democrats down yonder there?"

"Who'll keep doing what they want regardless of which of these two rich white guys gets in the White, did I say White House . . . Some choice, ain't it."

"Some've been calling Roosevelt a traitor to his class."

"Makes him worth a look at least. But he needs the Solid South. Whoops," as a shellac disc comes sliding out of the folded *Defender* and he dives to catch it.

"Got some Hits of the Week, Fletcher Henderson band, Coleman Hawkins, Benny Moten, that young Basie?" so forth. "That's if you dig it of course—here, Jabbo Smith and his Rhythm Aces, one of your local Milwaukee horns, there's people say he's better than Louis Armstrong, whole lot of these Paramount platters here, straight out of Grafton, practically your hometown, just up the road, give you the factory price . . ."

"Blind Blake, 'Police Dog Blues,' mind if we . . ."

McKinley brings it over to the club-car Victrola, puts it on. Before bar three Hicks is about to topple into a romantic nostalgia episode. "I've heard this. Not on a record, not in a club, but . . ."

Down some long hallway someplace deep in April's place on Brewer's Hill, maybe upstairs, maybe down . . . no fixed hour, some nights not at all.

Hicks has been around enough close-up card-trick artists to know when he's having a card forced on him, and yet here he finds himself with a record he didn't mean to buy. No label, pure black geometry.

It's April. Natch. First time he's ever heard her on shellac. Her voice is different—electrical as a thunderstorm, yet somehow reluctant . . . Orchestral backup seems to be a little more grand-scale than usual—strings, a Latin percussion section.

If I Tell You (Bolero)

If I tell . . . you, if I
tell you, what it's, all a-bout . . .
Somebody better sell, you,

a tick-ket on the next-train out,
forever—
                      Leave
me to my real times, just
be off and away . . .
don't even think of me at mealtimes,
waitin for that souf-flé . . .
To fall— Just
remem-ber when you asked me,
Asked me what's it all about,
I coulda let-it sail
past me, but
was-there really a-ny doubt,
that someday,
darlin I'd fum-ble, and you'd
have-to-be dumb not to tumble, so unbel-
-lievable with you, but
less, com, -pli, -cate, -ed, with, out . . .
                                  oh, dim-
-wit of my dreams, yeah,
strange-as-it seems, that's
what it's about . . .
all about, my ba-by—
all about . . .

    Plays it over a couple more times, nods out, wakes up to find the turntable of the Victrola still and empty, and no promise of a restful evening. A quick pass up and down the train looking for the disc and the shellac merchant who sold it to him, but nobody up at this hour has heard anything, though maybe once there might've been a McKinley Somebody or other, except he's long retired, some say to California.

    Horseshoe Curve, Gallitzin Tunnel, track unwinding back into the dark, sleep it seems nowhere in the cards. The rhythm of the rails does nothing for Hicks the rest of the night but repeat *wottachump, wottachump, wottachump* till dawn, which arrives sometime between Harrisburg and Paoli.

18

Hicks figures he'd better do a courtesy drop-by at the New York branch of U-Ops, which he finds slightly west of Broadway beneath a neon sign featuring a pair of eyeballs electrically switching back and forth between bloodshot vein-crazed and lens-blank pop-bottle green.

"Boynt wired, said you'd be by." Connie McSpool is a former city cop obliged to retire early after his enthusiasm with the dizzy-stick finally disheveled a hairdo too well-connected to be squared that easily.

"You just missed Judge Crater, he was in here looking for you." Even if as a radio gag the Crater disappearance has pretty much had its day, people still can't let go of it. Everybody knows the story, or thinks they do—after dinner in midtown Manhattan with a girlfriend and a lawyer he knows, the Judge, in cheerful enough spirits, gets into a taxi and rides away, never to be seen again by mortal eye.

"Still an active ticket around here, I see."

"No kiddin, Crater was pals with Arnold Rothstein and Legs Diamond, both as you'll recall recent recipients of the bump, and it's not only the crime syndicates, not just Tammany Hall, but worst and least merciful . . ." lowering his voice. A moment's respectful hush. "New York real estate."

Going on to explain how Judge Crater, acting as receiver in a bankruptcy, acquires a piece of property for chicken feed, the city then pays millions to get it back, the Judge, having just shelled out 20 Gs for his judge appointment and maybe looking for a quick offset, thinks his piece of the profits should be more generous. "There's a dispute, bang bang, decision made. Zzt, there and gone. All that cement you notice they been pouring up around 181st, anchoring for the new bridge over to Jersey? he's more likely under that."

Hicks's eyes must've unnarrowed for a second.

"What—they never heard of that in Milwaukee?"

"Oh, well, sure, but usually we get into an argument about which brand to use, Portland sets faster, Rosendale lasts longer, on into the late-night hours, neighbors complain, by that point the stiff's already been ditched in the Lake anyway . . ."

"Don't fall for the rube act," Connie advises, "this gent is straight out of Chicago, where he dodges more bullets per work shift than all the donuts the lot of ye's eaten in yer careers."

"Milwaukee, where is that again . . ."

"Just down the road from Racine, where Danish pastries were invented."

"Known for beer, bowling, and Daphne Airmont. Oops—"

"Sorry, Hicks."

"How's that?"

"You just missed her, she's off on that midnight liner for overseas. Maybe you're getting a lucky break."

"Some tickets are jinxed. Every time the name Daphne Airmont gets typed into one, somebody sooner or later has to go wake up a doctor."

"By which point the paperwork mysteriously got lost someplace everybody forgot to look."

"Which always turns out to connect back somehow to that Big Al of Cheese himself in exile, natch, keeping an eye on his li'l girl. Oh—sorry, Hicks. Not tryin to talk you outa nothin here."

Overseas. That ought to be as far as it goes. The U-Ops wouldn't be crazy enough to, or put it another way . . .

NOT THAT HICKS has spent that much time in and out of banks, but there's something weirdly off about Gould Fisk Fidelity and Trust. It doesn't smell like a bank, for one thing. No clean paper and ink smell, but enough inexpensive cigar smoke. More like a speak with its own distillery located somewhere on the premises. He is immediately escorted to a desk in back with a quick exit to the street, where a shifty junior officer avoiding eye contact slides over an envelope holding an advance on two weeks' pay plus expenses, plus—

"*Oh* no, wait a minute—" There seems to be a steamer ticket and a brand-new passport too. "No, I wasn't supposed to—"

"Not to worry, we do this all the time. Like they sing it on the radio, 'At Gould Fisk, it's worth the risk.'"

This shouldn't be happening, but is. Out the back exit and into the street Hicks finds a phone booth, tries to call Boynt at the Milwaukee U-Ops.

"Didn't expect to hear from you so soon, no difficulties with the boat ticket, I hope?"

"Now you mention it—boat ticket, yeah, feels like being under a sort of handicap here, not having the whole story, Boynt?"

"Only a harmless episode of international transnavigation . . ."

"Saw you play the Majestic once, Mr. Fields, fun-filled evening for sure, but could you put Boynt back on?"

"Have we been keeping something from you? Answer is yes, moron, of course we have, and was there anything brzzghhllkk-kk-kk—"

"Hello? Hello, Boynt, there's some noise on the line—"

"Ghzzmm ngngngng zzzngtt—" The line goes dead. No operator to apologize, no background hum, nothing. In his idiocy Hicks keeps trying. Broken connections, runarounds, wrong numbers, busy signals, hung up on, told not to call anymore, telephonically 86'd, till finally after a while the coins don't even register when he drops them in.

He goes to a Western Union office and wires Milwaukee—60¢, means he'll have to skip lunch, YOU CRAZY NO DICE WIRE FARE HOME SOONEST, leaving him two words under the limit, the two words that come to mind not being allowed, and stranded on the "beach" in front of the Palace Theatre along with jugglers, ventriloquists with dummies, ukulele virtuosos, casualties of acts no longer sure, in these final days of vaudeville, of being hired anywhere, not even along the death trail stretching southwest through farm towns, broken country, and deserts toward L.A. like a panhandler's arm seeking the tiniest handout of mercy from the source of its sorrows.

Hicks ends up later that night with Connie McSpool and a few of the boys, at Club Afterbeat up in Harlem, where there's a radio show in progress.

> Whoopin and troopin,
> Doin' th' Heav-y-side Bounce,
> Swingin and sportin,
> Snortin up, ounce af-
> -ter ounce . . .
>   c'mon and
> let's . . .
>   go . . .
> truc-kin on down-that floor . . . all
> night-till
>   quarter to five, 'n' then
> th' cops're arrivin, 's when
> we're jivin on out, the back door,
>   until
> th' very-next evening—just, as, th'
> sun, goes, down—
> once again . . . o-
> -ver-the-ra-di-yo,
> *here* comes that *far*-away beat,
> Street by street—
>   it started
> down-by-the levee-side,
>   Hmm!
> soon it will be at your,
> ev'ry side!
>   Uh huh,
> Right up there where it counts,
> Just, waitin to pounce,
> It's that Heavysi-i-ide Bounce!

"Yes it's time for Rex and Rhonda, the Civilized World's Most Sophisticated Couple, and 'Speak of the Week.'" In which the two R's broadcast remote from a different Manhattan nightspot every Saturday on into Sunday, and it's really a show for everybody who's stuck at home Saturday nights beside the radio, while the rest of the world's out making whoopee—for those of us who like to hear about it even if we don't get to do it, here week by week are the friendly bars of our dreams, a welcoming communion of regulars, romantic strangers, and traveling rogues who breeze in past the bouncers, cause some commotion, then vanish back into the unlit ether, bartenders reliable as the law of gravity, one of the more appreciated side effects of Prohibition being what a bartender *doesn't* do, and with how much finesse, sometimes genius, he doesn't do it. You lean forward, radioside, you have your own supply of hooch, perhaps, as this is a drink-along show . . .

"And a Happy After Hours to radio sophisticates everywhere . . . Have you noticed, Rex, how the closer we get to Repeal, the less and less drinkable becomes the sort of thing they're putting in bottles these days, it's a disgrace, and we do hope you won't be running across any of the shipment *we* got needled by this week . . ."

"Ever so true, yet what li'l Rhondayvoo here neglects to mention is how she in particular, with her willingness to drink anything she doesn't have to pay for, has been doing her best, every night for the duration, to give alcohol a bad name—"

"Mmm, but Rex, darling, those who actually listen to what I say know what a gay old personality I can be, and those who don't like it, well, do feel welcome to your choice of impolite suggestions, a sophisticate like you has surely heard them all—"

Continuing to bicker, at first charmingly, but then with more of an edge. Are they "fighting," really, or only pretending to? Depends on how much radio listening you do. Audiences go for this, while at the same time secretly hoping that one day one of the two R's will go so far as to murder the other, ideally while on the air . . .

"But somebody," Hicks meanwhile has been trying to explain, "wants me 86'd clear out of the U.S.A."

"Their money's good," shrugs Connie McSpool, "which if that's not the problem then why worry? Horrors of the Deep, forget it, there's plenty of shipboard activities to keep you busy, gambling casinos, glamorous tomatoes aplenty, why sure and you'll be back on dry land again before you know it."

"Yeah, but meantime instead maybe if I could just donate this boat ticket here to one of your cop benevolent funds—"

"Cash only, lad, sorry. Tradition and all."

"It's the bum's rush."

"I know. We just got a memo from the Home Office to that effect, requesting our assistance if needed."

"Con, you wouldn't."

"Me, no I wouldn't, but there's plenty on the payroll these days who would, and I can't speak for everybody, can I?"

19

About all Hicks can recall is having what he thought was an innocent beer, which in fact turned out to've been visited by a needle full of something in the chloral hydrate family, sending him off to dreamland before he could remember how to find a coaster to set his glass on. Next thing he knows he's out someplace draped over what seems to be . . . something big, steel . . . moving around under his feet, smells like salt water, Diesel fuel no wait, nngghhh no, can't be can it . . .

Sure can. Turns out to be the ocean liner *Stupendica*, by now someplace well out to sea. He risks a nauseated, desperate look aft, as if there still might be land in sight, which there doesn't seem to be.

"Little green around the gills, there." Looks like a seagoing-type tomato, a species he doesn't recall running across that often, smoking a Melachrino in a jade holder, doll hat in pale mauve perched over one ear, hair styled in one of those varsity bobs, curl dipping in at the eye kind of thing. In Wisconsin they'd say either too young or too East Coast.

Somehow Hicks seems to be still wearing his hat, whose brim he now gives a touch. "Swell, thanks, how about yourself?"

"Oh I never get seasick, this is only research, you know, working the rail, learning to tell the sports from the stiffs, the stomach never lies."

Glow Tripforth del Vasto is here on assignment for *Hep Debutante* magazine, sending in a series of articles on how to be a Jazz Age adventuress on a Depression budget.

"Stick around, I may need some advice."

"Ooh! poor thing, asleep on your feet, maybe you'd be safer in your cabin, do you think you can make it there all right?"

"My . . ."

Hmm, forgotten his cabin number too . . . Sparks of interest, all right. Some girls go for a man in uniform, but give Glow an amnesia case anytime. No ex-wives or old flames to brood about, can't get much more romantic than that.

"All's I know is is it ain't Harlem, which last I knew it was."

"But you do . . . remember *who you* are, right?"

"Who I . . . am . . . sure, just gimme a minute."

Next thing they're on an upper deck someplace, accompanied by a junior purser. Glow is puzzled. "You're sure this is it."

"Right here on the ticket, Miss."

"Well. My antennas need tuning, all right. I had him figured for tourist third, tops."

In the cabin, Hicks finds a steward named Clifton busy light-fingering his way like a working Parisienne on her lunch break through steamer trunks full of uptown wardrobe choices, growing more excited as he proceeds.

"Mind my asking," Hicks not wishing to spoil anybody's fun, "all the high-priced dry goods around here, somebody else's cabin, maybe? Edward, Prince of Wales, one of them?"

Up goes an eyebrow. Nothing in the ship's records to suggest the cabin's assigned to anybody but Hicks. "Here, how about this one?" suggests Clifton, "Midnight aubergine and electric kumquat . . . not perhaps as understated a look as one might wish." Though in fact, as the Gumshoe's Manual points out, quite useful if you want eyewitnesses to be focused more on the suit than the mug happens to be in it.

Idly curious, Hicks grabs a handful of the getup and tries to wrinkle it. No go, it just bounces back good as new. You could sleep in this number night after night, still be ready to walk right into the ritzy gathering of your choice, nobody'd even blink . . . Shrugging into the jacket for a second, "Fits like a glove, ain't it." Well, a catcher's mitt anyway.

"And maybe . . . this tie? couple shirts . . ." meantime making furtive Ronald Colman faces at himself in the mirror, "snappy hat here . . . how about it, Clifton, how's this look to you?"

"Clark Gable green with envy, sir."

"Not too cowboy-style around the brim, you think?"

"Um, sorry, boys, don't mean to interrupt—"

Clifton catching sight of Glow, "Welcome aboard, Señora del Vasto, unless this is her kid sister, of course."

"Lovely to see you as always, Clifton, once again by strange coincidence in the old familiar pickle, can you guess?"

"Your—"

"Yes! my ex- or as he likes to think of it current husband Porfirio, up to his usual melodrama, somehow finding out whenever I book passage and arranging to be on the same boat. Only trying to keep me out of trouble, as he calls it, just when I'm trying to get into some. The latest just in is now the big sap wants to give me an autogyro, all set to fly, supposedly waiting for me on the dock at Tangier."

"One of those rigs," Hicks recalls, "I keep seeing in *Popular Mechanics*."

"Just so. A Spanish invention. Spain and the autogyro are linked intimately, Porfi would say romantically . . ."

TONIGHT THE SALOON DECK is swarming with grinning stewards, uniformed juveniles years corrupted, American sorority girls, exiled royalty, chorus cuties trucking across at all angles shaking ostrich-feather fans in footlight colors, postwar liner travel in full swing. "Icebergs? enemy torpedoes? Phooey! if that's the worst that could happen, then it's happened already, hasn't it, and anything else is only an amateur act. Long as we're alive, let's live."

"*Gaudeamus igitur* to that, Jack!"

Champagne Cocktails, Sidecars, French 75s, Jack Roses, and Ward Eights flow without interruption. Staircases grand and otherwise being left unpatrolled by ship's security, allow different classes of passenger all to shuffle together.

Up in the first class saloon, seated beneath a mural big as a billboard showing the *Stupendica* herself driving gallantly head-on through a Force 3 weather event, Hicks discovers Royal Navy Lieutenant-Commander Alf Quarrender, retired, and his wife Philippa, neither quite old enough for the story they're peddling—off on an extended world tour, gathering impressions wherever they go. With the States, sorry to say, not figuring as much of a high point.

"You've in so many ways such a lovely country, it's a pity one can't find a proper Sticky Toffee Pudding in it anywhere."

"Sorry, 'a proper . . . '?"

"That's it! That's the tone exactly! One tries ever so hard to make them understand, 'Sticky—Toffee—Pud-ding? surely you've heard of it?' 'You bet, lady!' And then they bring you in one more horrible, inedible simulation."

"The nation which cannot produce a plausible SticToPud," summarizes Alf, "is a nation whose soul is in peril. Now Germany, although the true SticToPud per se may not exist there either—yet, if a bloke *fancied* one, well . . . *achtung*, you know. Waiting for you at breakfast the very next morning, and impossible to tell from the real thing."

"Next time you're in Chicago," Hicks amiably, "you might want to try a chop house called St. Hubert's, specializes in genuine English food."

"Actually yes, we did of course, all but one's first stop in Chicago, but regrettably with no better than indifferent luck, though I do recall ever such a nice chat there with a Mr. Guzik."

"Greasy Thumb Guzik? Sounds like the place, all right. But, um . . ."

"Busy chap, corner table, constant procession to and from, not entirely respectable-looking, all seemed to be carrying paper bags of one sort or another."

"He's Al Capone's chief financial adviser."

"How marvelous and apparently quite thick as well with your Mr. Dawes, savior of the German economy."

"This joint is right next door to the Union League Club, see, big Republican hangout, paths've been known to cross."

"But Al Capone, I say— Republicans and gangsters? How can such things be?"

Hicks blinks once, maybe twice.

"Though he seemed rather a modest retiring sort, Mr. Guzik did happen to mention his role in helping with what we now know as the Dawes Plan."

Hicks dimly recalls something about German inflation right after the War, wheelbarrows full of unspendable billions of marks in paper money, a crisis Charles Dawes was widely credited with resolving.

"Your Guzik chap's a financial genius, apparently only took a minute to suggest that Mr. Dawes make them a good-size loan against his own bank, thus in an instant clearing up a number of complications all round. Rescued Germany absolutely, put them back in the game, setting the stage indeed for the New Germany we're now witnessing."

"There's that ol' Greasy Thumb for ya."

"We should never have fought them in the first place," opines Alf, "certainly never demanded reparations on that scale. The only good to come of it's that now with the old lot on their way out, there's a second chance, not only for Germany but for all civilization."

Hicks eyes the couple uneasily. Though they might really be no more than innocent retirees out to see the world, there's also about them an air of international monkey business, maybe even some kind of *espionage racket*, hard at work. Plus that familiar feeling that at any moment the name of a certain German Political Celebrity is about to come up, which indeed it does, only to sink, to Hicks's relief, back into the general effervescence.

"The whole idea, then as now, being to keep the bolshies behind the fence." Alf expects a "Great Simplification" quite soon, "Matters will then all be ever so much easier. Not like the last show. This time around, thanks to improvements in radio, internal combustion, aeronautics, no time zone will be spared, no more of those strangely named distant purgatories . . ."

"And with each day brought so much more into doubt than the one before," adds Philippa, "imagine how enormously simplified romance will become, scarcely time for it, anyway, once is enough, isn't it, and tralala on to the next." A strange hectic glee taking hold of her for a second or two. Hicks thinks he sees goose bumps.

"Look, folks, do you mind if I ask you something?"

"Anything, my darling, name it."

"Don't take this the wrong way but . . . Would either of you have any idea . . . how I got here?"

"Ah. Well . . . you see . . . when a Mum and a Dad love each other very much—"

"Now, none of that, Pip Emma, you damned flirt," Alf waving a finger, "stop it at once, I say—"

"What I mean is here on this boat, see, I don't remember ever . . . really . . . coming on board?"

"I shouldn't wonder, you were altogether blotto."

"Mickey on the menu. Anything else?"

"Some sort of American government vessel, chasing after us, at flank speed."

"Bureau of Prohibition?"

"Declined to identify themselves," Alf recalls, "behaved as if they didn't have to, no hull number, nothing at the jackstaff, put a shot across our bow, actually," whereupon the *Stupendica* had dutifully matched course and speed with the pugnacious little cutter, which sent over a line, and soon after that Hicks, winched across in a canvas sling, above a furious aftward rush of ocean whitecaps . . .

"HOW'S THE AMNESIA, forgotten anything interesting lately?"

The del Vasto broad again. Carrying a Jack Rose the size of a birdbath.

"Yeah, what's the legal age for one of these? I believe it's proper etiquette for the gentleman to go first?" Grabbing her glass and swilling down about half what's in it, "hmm, old enough maybe, too soon to tell, let's just . . ."

"How about leaving me some, all right? You're . . . how old again, thirty? Older? You don't know how young I can play," Glow warns him. "Or the trouble it's likely to get you into."

Nothing personal, as Hicks will discover. Glow has a way of flirting with everybody on the ship, pursers and underpursers, bridge officers and suspected stowaways. She seems to have Hicks tagged as the philosophical type, at least he can't make out much of her conversation. "And while he was down there, he bit my ankle. Rather like human existence, wouldn't you say."

"Y— well, no. Sure. Um—"

"Leave the deep thinking to others and get on with the action, that about cover it?"

"Action, well, I try to avoid that too, when I can."

"Oh, dear."

"Don't worry, it doesn't always avoid me."

"I may need protection," taking him by the necktie and pulling him closer, expressing herself meantime by way of hips and legs, like a tango partner.

"Things been a little slow, Gingersnap, back where is it you're from again?"

"Slow as it gets, any thoughts occur to you?"

Despite a lifetime of easy-to-grasp lessons about getting mixed up with anybody he just met while still recovering from a mickey of unknown recipe, Hicks finds himself hopefully admitting, "Well, standing up in a hammock was one I always wanted to try."

"Sailors everywhere on this tub, where there's sailors there've got to be hammocks, wouldn't you think?"

And so forth. Things are rolling along just jake till here in off one of the less familiar decks comes breezing the Latin lover no Anglo wants to see inside manhandling range of any dame in whom he may have taken an interest, however faint—Glow's ex- or possibly current husband, Porfirio del Vasto, smooth as a ten-cent panatela, in a white dinner jacket and one of those halos of entitlement to behave as unpleasantly as he likes. A slick customer. Ramon Novarro could learn makeup tips. "And jealous?" according to Glow, "he should run a correspondence school. Advertise on the radio. A professor of jealousy."

One of the side effects of private op work is you do see a lot of jealousy. Previously inattentive husbands are suddenly underfoot all the time, taking chances with their personal safety that would make Harold Lloyd think twice. Telephones and binoculars become everyday attachments to ears and eyes, and "As long as none of it's happening to you," the Gumshoe's Manual advises, "it's funny—but then, when it does happen to you, you wonder why you ever thought it was funny."

The unspoken kiss-off, which the Manual doesn't include but experience in the field confirms, being that after a while, if you should live so long, it gets funny again. The tricky part is recognizing when each of these happens. Too many colleagues you would've thought experienced enough have ended up in Forest Home or Pilgrim's Rest from not judging the timing accurately enough.

"Couple of foxtrots," Hicks meantime is busy protesting, "a Lindy hop for instruction-purposes only, maybe a waltz, but no funny business, solemn promise—I could lose my license."

"How much?"

"Beg pardon?"

"I provide a substantial source of income for a population of gigolos, seducers, and impulsive youths smitten by my wife. Fortunately, it is but petty cash to me. La Gloriosa refuses to accept a centavo," now producing from some inside pocket a respectable wad of U.S. currency, "though the same can seldom be said of those who profess to have fallen under her spell."

"Best not be waving that stuff around too much, folks could get the wrong idea."

"If cash offends you, we could arrange for compensation in lieu, coupons, vouchers . . . if you're interested I could get you a nice price on an autogyro. Tip-top condition, barely flown."

"Matter of fact, Señora del Vasto did mention that you're planning to, uh, offer her one of those?"

"To be precise, not give but sell, and meaningfully below cost, I can show you the invoicing. The only thing I ever tried to give her once was a castle. In Spain. Well, twice in fact, first time it only embarrassed her, next time, I admit, was a terrible mistake. She may have laughed briefly yet scornfully . . . 'How can you expect any woman to be stupid enough to fall for that? Even once? What kind of amateur do you take me for?' I thought it was a serious question. 'A gifted amateur,' I suggested. Not what she wanted to hear."

"Maybe you'll have better luck with the gyro."

"I sense a certain reluctance to bargain. If you're unwilling to be bought off, I might begin to believe you really are in love with her, may even somehow be making a serious claim, in which case I should have to kill you."

"Oh. Sure, well . . . mind my asking, does . . . that happen a lot, in your, um . . ."

"My accountants assure me it's a legal business expense. Usually written off under 'Postnuptial Miscellaneous.'"

By now they have strolled out on deck, into Atlantic moonlight. Hicks feels strangely sophisticated. Most matrimonials, the husbands he runs into are nervous wrecks, not so much love-happy as preoccupied with making sure the wife knows how much he's paying the U-Ops Agency, and somehow always expecting Hicks to be the one to tell her the amount.

Playboying his way around the hemispheres, Porfirio now confides with a sinister amiability perfected over the years, he's grown a little blasé about the sultry señorita package. "A man's eye is inevitably drawn elsewhere. These days, I'm sure you've seen them out on the dance floors, an 'American type,' not too much makeup, hair kept a little longer than bob length, as if reluctant to let go of girlhood—athletic grace, straight talking, somehow immune to or unable to reach a fully adult stage . . . the current expression is I believe 'wholesome' . . ." Who but Glow would he be going on this way about? They happen to be passing a bar with a couple of empty spaces. Against his better judgment, Hicks accepts Porfirio's offer of a drink, and next thing he knows he's hearing, "¡Ay, ay, Porfirio infeliz! how was it possible not to fall into unqualified surrender at the mere first glimpse? Call it obsession but it is in fact a duty, an all but sacred obligation to remain faithful to the moment of love at first sight, for who knows how many years to follow, keeping it uncorrupted, not allowing a day to pass without in some way returning to it—The Moment. El Momento, you might say."

"Sure—used to smoke them all the time, before I moved on to nickel cigars."

"I love her!" the disoriented Spaniard raves on. Known to happen of course, even in matrimonials. But given the man is a smooth talker by profession, how sympathetically should Hicks be listening to this? "Not to get metaphysical, but she is an angel, you see, being an angel is a fate she moves toward blindly, believing herself no more than a gold digger like everyone else."

Shifting uncomfortably, "Hot tomato with a soul, not for everybody o'course but if that's your pipeful, Jack, just keep puffin away, peace be with you and however the rest of that goes."

Porfirio brings out a gold case full of Kyriazi Frères, Hicks takes one and lights up, grabbing another to put behind his ear. "For later."

"An optimistic thought, 'later.'" A pause to inhale. "I assume you're taking precautions."

"Against . . . ?"

"There's a betting book already open on you. The smart-money narrative has it that you are an American gangster, being deported to somewhere in Eastern Europe. Traveling in the custody of Lieutenant-Commander and Mrs. Quarrender, of the British Intelligence, currently under contract to forces unnamed to provide secure shipment and delivery."

"The British what was that again?"

"It's an open secret. You might want to have a word with them. Try not to bring my name up if you can help it."

20

"He looks so innocent, Alf. One can trust him, surely." The Quarrenders tap a shuttlecock-weight glance back and forth. "See here then McTaggart, you can keep a secret can't you, hmm no I thought not."

"You mustn't mind him, he's only taking the piss again, pay no attention, I never do."

"He may as well know," Alf continues. "McTaggart, you're familiar we assume with MI3b. Among ourselves we call it F.'s shop, after the way Mansfield Smith-Cumming of MI6 signed himself 'C.' Our bloke? F. Quite unremarkable in person, to look at him you wouldn't think he'd a brain in his head. But that's him, the big boss calling the shots. Barking mad, of course."

A look from Philippa. "Alphabet Soup, you are once again committing felonious indiscretion, do take more care in your speech or one shall have to liquidate—who knows, even further than that, glaciate you."

Whereupon at length it comes out. Seems Alf and Pips have been out on a worldwide scouting expedition to find recruits for the Secret Intelligence, and are currently on their way back from the U.S., where a number of code breakers have recently found themselves at loose ends after the Black Chamber was shut down, on Halloween of 1929, just after the stock market crashed, by Republican bigwig and Secretary of State Henry "Gentlemen Don't Read Each Other's Mail" Stimson.

"Finding many new hires?"

"A dim outlook, given the budget we've been authorized. Plus the competition from Germany, Russia, Japan, and so on. Wouldn't be interested, would you, McTaggart? Nice espionage career? Pay is terrible to begin with, all somewhat boracic around the MI these days, you know, but one does get to mingle on an everyday basis with persons of consequence."

As adventuresome younger children of merchant families were once sent eastward to make their fortunes, so nowadays children of civil service families are sent out to gather not riches, but negotiable intelligence, military and political. "Used to be a gentleman's game. Started to go haywire I suspect as early as the first Reform Act, less and less per annum to qualify sort of thing, till we're all taking in each other's washing, and any angels who might be watching over us apt to be as down on their luck and knowing no more than we do."

"And now, as we've been frank and open with you, McTaggart, perhaps in your turn you might—"

"Frank and open," mutters Hicks. "How come everybody thinks I'm being deported and you two have got me somehow in custody? When you guys know I'm only a private op."

"Well, one hopes that's all you are, of course."

"Routine ticket, only over here for as long as it takes, till everything's back to normal."

"Oh, dear," Pips making with an eyebrow, "do you really not know? 'Normal'? Things will never go back to the way they were, it'll all just keep getting more, what the Chinese call, 'interesting.'"

"Take up shooting," advises Alf. "Trapshooting off the fantail every day here, you know. There'll be plenty of live targets soon enough," adding once Hicks is out of earshot, "Man's an idiot."

Pips isn't so sure. In their early careers both of them were seconded to the Royal Academy of Dramatic Art for instruction in how to appear, if not innocent, because who actually is, then at least thoroughly unacquainted with Secret Services either side of the Atlantic. If Hicks's ignorance here is pretended, then he has been trained by levels of theatrical genius quite unreachable even by Brits.

"It's this del Vasto person he's been talking to," declares Philippa, "a millionaire with no visible day job? Violating the A. J. Raffles principle that a successful jewel thief needs a legitimate cover, such as star cricketer, to divert attention from what he's really up to, sharing with cricket bowlers especially a kitful of deceptive skills, as we know from the film."

"Ronald Colman wearing a blazer on the pitch," Alf mutters, "not cricket really."

Alf and Pips have had a careful eye for a while on Porfirio, having spotted the gag right away—provoking amusement or class resentment to direct attention away from the brush passes, handoffs, and drops of his real trade.

"Either a jewel thief or a spy. Travels everywhere and never has to bring out a sixpence. Handed thousands of miles of free globe-trotting per year, unconditionally and off the books, like a maharaja in the newsreels—one by one they come creeping up to him with their gifts of translocation and velocity, pilots, travel agents, airline executives, only time he ever slows down is to collect a freebie or sell one off. Meantime down inside a vault under some Alp, his secret bank accounts continue to grow."

"And then there's the wife," Philippa archly.

"Ex-wife, according to her. You think she's in on it?"

A don't-waste-my-time smile. "Not Hicks's innocence I'm concerned about, it's hers. He could corrupt the girl so easily."

"Now, Pip Emma . . ." warns Alf.

"Someone has to tell him, he's a loaded weapon, not that you'd be the expert on that, of course."

Pips being actually herself the hired gun around here, "Brought us through some unhopeful innings indeed, remember in Dar that time, thank goodness for the extra Webley in your pocket—"

"Oh, Alfalfa," eye-rolling innocence, "it was KL, and I scarcely knew which end of it to point."

Raising his gin and It, "Sticky days, my conference pear . . . you see," as he later explains to Hicks, "on any given yearly audit, it was Pips who handled most of the *Boy's Own* activities whilst I was only the Room 40 O.B. crypto whiz confined in that crowded little sweatshop where we were all breathing each other's tobacco smoke . . ."

"Don't listen to him, he loved it in there, he wouldn't know what to do with himself outdoors."

"Never thought I'd miss minesweeper duty that much."

"All you had to do was drop a hint, they'd've been happy to redeploy you."

They're down in the casino decks, more extensive than you'd expect, just because a liner's designed for speed doesn't mean there won't be time for cutthroat baccarat or lightning roulette, or certainly a go at the high-velocity fruit machines, though as for emotions and high drama, Hicks has seen more vivacity in old-time Wentworth Avenue opium joints during the graveyard shift.

The bar turns out to be strangely vertical, reaching down all the way to the orlop deck refrigeration spaces where the beer and champagne are kept, having over several voyages become an informal skip-tracing bureau, for not only are there more passengers aboard the *Stupendica* than at first appeared, but their numbers also have been *strangely increasing* day by day, despite no ports of call so far having been stopped at, and the overflow tends to congregate here.

Passageways long after hours clamor with what sounds like an immense unsleeping crowd, not to be explained away by corridor acoustics or the unceasing friction of the sea.

"Not too many of them exactly visible," Alf speculates, "yet still wandering the ship at will, in and out of spaces both authorized and forbidden."

"He's embarrassed to say it out loud," Pips with an upward roll of the eyeballs.

"This wasn't always a passenger liner," Alf doesn't exactly explain, "converted during the War to a hospital ship . . . Still populated by casualties physical and psychical and those in whose care they were conveyed . . . unquiet stowaways with broken odds and ends of unfinished business from the War, common to all being a hope no longer quite sure and certain that injustices would be addressed and all come right in the end."

SUMMERS WHEN HE was a kid visiting his mother's side of the family in Wonewoc, Wisconsin, out in the Driftless about twenty miles from Baraboo, "There was this what they called spiritualist camp," Hicks remembers, "séances and so forth going on all the time."

Hicks and his friends used to hang around Wonewoc hoping to see ghosts or other supernatural visitors, unaccountable lights up on Spook Hill after dark, sounds of warning, of lament, which couldn't be explained away as owls or the wind. Shapes which did not respond when addressed.

"And one of your relations," Alf guesses, "possibly a great-aunt, was in touch with other forces."

"Cousin Begonia," Hicks amiably, "once removed. At the time it all seemed normal. For Wonewoc anyway."

"And the séances?"

"Once or twice. Nothing much happened. Lights out, everybody quiet, it was like listening to the radio."

"Parlor tricks," footnotes Philippa.

"Many are the misguided," Alf putting a hand on hers, "who need to believe that's all it is, poor old dear, seen it a hundred times, hasn't she, but can't admit it."

While not a dues-paying member of the Society for Psychical Research, Alf is more sensitized in these matters than Philippa, who attends impatiently to her fingernails or hums music hall tunes whenever Alf reports a sighting of uncertain luminosity, or a wordless voice that might be more than wind strumming the guy wires of the radio masts.

"It's a strange time we're in just now," Alf reflects, "one of those queer little passageways behind the scenery, where popes make arrangements with Fascists and the needs of cold capitalist reality and those of adjoining ghost worlds come into rude contact . . . many have been quick to blame it on the War, on the insupportable weight of so many dead, so many wrongs still unresolved."

Which now may have come to include recent paranoid suspicions the liner is being tracked by a mysterious submarine. Some see it, some don't.

"There, look, see that? It's a periscope, I tell you!"

"More like a whale spouting, if anything."

"Report to sick bay, you're only seeing things."

At sunset, light coming in at a shallow angle, the view back along the wake is apt to include all manner of shapes, there for a brief flash and then gone.

"They're looking for you in the Marconi saloon, by the way."

Sounds to Hicks like a Third Ward speakeasy but turns out to be the radio gang's recreational lounge, up at shelter-deck level, along with a fairly constant flow of field-tripping sorority girls in and out of the first-class dining saloons.

"Oh Phoebe, you're such a spinthromaniac."

"What kind of maniac did you just call me?"

"Spinthro, Sweetie, it means crazy about Sparks."

"Oo! You—" and before anybody can step in, not that Hicks would, being content to look on, the two co-ed cuties are going round and round. Hair gets pulled, clothes ripped, faces slapped, the usual entertainment. It isn't long before chaperones hired for their refereeing skills have plunged bravely between and separated the opponents.

"McTaggart?"

"Uh, this go on much around here?"

"Ever since we sailed. Come on in the shack. Maybe you heard there's a submarine been following us."

"News to me." Which it isn't. Suspicions beginning to creep.

"You seem to have friends aboard." Handing Hicks a pair of earphones, "OK if we listen too?"

"Hicksie, that you? It's me, Stuffy. Stuffy Keegan."

"Long time, Stuffy. Don't sound like you."

"You neither, come to think of it. Case you're wondering, that's me, I should say us, in the U-13, off your starboard quarter. Funny running into each other again out on the high seas like this, ain't it."

"You hear somebody laughin it must be we're all in the loony bin. First I get railroaded back to New York, next thing somebody slips me a mickey, and I wake up on this tub. Sooner or later they're gonna offload me in Europe someplace and that's all I can find out."

"We're headed in to home port in the Adriatic Sea, if that helps any."

"You guys wouldn't be planning to . . ."

"Not us, nothin on board to do it with anymore." Explaining that around the time the War ended, the Skipper got, maybe not religion, but something along those lines. "Some Allied commission ordered him to bring the boat in to be scrapped and he decided not to. Went on the run, got her refitted for peacetime instead, deep-sixed all the torpedoes, torpedo tubes, guns, ammo, leavin plenty of room inside, free to start a new career running only nonbelligerent chores."

"Meaning, remind me again . . ."

"Well, most of it, coppers like yourself would call us smugglers, though we like to say 'outlaws of the Deep.'"

"There you go."

"Free trade—see, back in Milwaukee, freedom, nobody thought much about it, we just figured hey, a free country ain't it and left it at that. But—" this being about the point Hicks begins to feel warning signs from his feet—"the real thing, what if that's only when they're comin after you for somethin? But they haven't caught you yet. So for a while, as long as you can stay on the run, that's the only time you're really free?"

"Uh-huh well Stuffy like they say there in the submarine racket, too deep for me."

A stretch of atmospheric crackling easy to confuse with loss of signal. From the dining saloon across the way, sounds of crockery, glassware, festivity.

"Let's talk it over sometime," Stuffy suggests. "Better if there's beer on the table. You ever get to Fiume, that's our home port these days, there's some swell beer joints, it's the Milwaukee of the Adriatic."

"Sure, fair enough. Lookin forward, Stuffy."

MEANTIME THERE REMAIN the more immediate and less certain emotions of Porfirio del Vasto to worry about.

"Look, Clifton, you've dealt with him before."

"Off and on since the War."

"And how many admirers of his ex- or do I mean current missus has he given the bump to?"

"How many in person? . . . not counting all the duels, hmm . . . a dozen?"

"Duels."

"Pistols. Antique set of Wogdons. Perfect record, goes without saying, though Don Porfirio prefers to think of himself as a lucky amateur. The simple appearance of his name on a passenger list is enough to transform the most cheerful vessel afloat into a Liner of Doom . . . alcohol consumption rises drastically, stylish black frocks come out of steamer trunks to be ironed and ready, given the high expectation of more than one burial at sea."

"I think he might have me on one of his lists. He's got an idea somehow that me and that Glow've been kidding around."

"With you, not likely. Dancing all night in public? How would you have found the time?"

"There you go. Do me a favor and mention that to him next time you get a chance."

"Soupe de canard, as they say on the Île-de-France."

Hicks signals for another Jack Rose, drinkers of which seem to make up a good percentage of the passenger list. Part of the appeal is watching a steward try to bring one across a deck forever in motion without spilling any from the glass it comes in, a shallow cone set on a long stem and filled to the brim. Instead of Stateside applejack they're using calvados, and making the cocktail in bulk early each morning so that it can be delivered out of a convenient spigot arrangement. At this rate Hicks will be a screaming dipso before he ever sets foot on land again.

AFTER LURKING IN doorways in Milwaukee observing pickpockets at all levels of skill, Hicks figures he has a pretty good eye for the profession by now, but this Porfirio is something to watch. First time Hicks tries to chisel a smoke, *"Cómo no, mi amigo,* allow me a moment," scanning the deck traffic for a likely target, eventually lifting from a passing inner pocket a cigarette case, taking out a cigarette for Hicks and another for himself, substituting two different and cheaper brands, returning the case, meanwhile lighting up, and nobody the wiser.

"Oh, who doesn't love a jewel thief, good-hearted outlaw preying only on greedy plutes who can afford to lose a sparkler or two. Hardly ever collared for it, filed under Annoyance more than Threat."

"Harsh words, though deserved. It's why I should really quit the game—too safe, too low-energy, I need a more elevated level of risk."

"Uh, huh. And how's that going for you?"

"Hmm?"

"World Depression, so forth?"

"Could not be more lively. We are currently in a golden age of jewel theft. Theatrical skills, physical timing, stage magic, acting, improvisation, all the tool kit of gemstone redistribution, called upon as never before. I can't complain, although I imagine I do, perhaps more than I'm aware."

A little disingenuous. In fact he hasn't quit at all, and uses the revenue from his light-fingered activities to finance a diverse portfolio of projects, among them currently the used autogyro business. Amateurs who thought they'd be up flying everywhere on the cheap are discovering it requires more from them in the way of dedication than they can provide. Not to mention the infernal noise. Hence suddenly a sizable inventory of pre-owned autogyros there to be picked up for eight bars of "I Got Rhythm" with or without ukelele accompaniment.

BY THE TIME Hicks and Glow might've been ready to rendezvous under a suitable phase of the moon with a studio orchestra somewhere in the background, the weather has in fact turned from unpleasant to quite unpleasant indeed, not exactly Oconomowoc Lake in the summertime, the ship beginning tonight in fact to take some 20- to 30-degree rolls, waves rearing up and crashing all over the weather decks, which not unexpectedly are now forbidden to passengers.

Glow, tonight sporting a metal-gray Fortuny Delphos gown, a glamorous finely pleated hand-me-down that more than once has been pulled whispering through the circumference of a wedding ring, her own or somebody's, seems strangely energized by all this.

"And isn't that just the appeal, tough guy? Somebody doesn't want us to be somewhere. So we sneak out together to a forbidden liaison, helpless before the towering waves of our passion."

"Jake with me," though it's setups like this, actually, that the Gumshoe's Manual tends most earnestly to caution against, often adding, more than once in fact, that the generally accepted procedure here is to just breeze, with no second thoughts.

Then again, alone out here on the ocean with tomato quality like this and so forth . . . c'mon.

Of course into the churning seascape of possibilities, as if on cue, comes striding who but Porfirio, with a betrayed pout on his face.

"After I bared my soul to you, after you gave me your word you'd stay away from her . . ."

"It isn't what it looks like—"

. . . whereupon Porfirio hauls out a high-caliber cannon and blasts Hicks backwards over the lifelines and into the sea, and forgets to call "Man overboard."

Well, no, actually Porfirio now seems to be pushing a *wad of cash* into Hicks's pocket. "By way of apology. Far below the customary rate, if that helps any."

If what Hicks sees in Porfirio's eyes isn't exactly uneasiness, it's at least some recognition that gunplay might not be the best option here.

"Apologizing for not shooting at me?"

"For not taking you seriously. It was the dancing that had me confused. She's still too young for gigolos just yet, but somehow—"

"That's what you had me figured for. Don't worry, hey. The hand I kiss at the end of a number has often enough been known to have a double sawbuck wadded up in it, which she usually gets back in free drinks by the end of the evening anyway, so everybody ends up happy. Wish I could say the same for you."

"Me? *Felíz como lombriz*, why, do I appear melancholy somehow?"

"Idiotic would be closer," Glow sez.

"A matter between men, *mi vida*, you still have much to discover," a rapid side-glance at Hicks, "about what a *tipo fácil* I can be."

First port of call is Tangier. Porfirio and Glow debark together, and sure enough, there waiting on the pier is the autogyro.

"Fresh from the assembly line, stock model Pitcairn, Wright engine, just out of final inspection. Can't have been flown much more than 10 kilometers, all yours now, soul of my heart."

Stolen from some scatterbrained millionaire, fallen off a truck, anybody's guess.

"Lists for $6,750 new. Call it six even, we'll throw in a two-year maintenance plan, parts and labor exclusive of rotor drive and transmission..."

There remains the question of how she'll come up with the monthly payments in Swiss francs, which Porfirio insists on as part of the deal, foreseeing up to a year of dreary small-scale swindles in neighborhoods normally better avoided, sweet-talking after-hours working stiffs out of pocket money they'll always have better uses for, pretending to herself it's no worse than B-girl work, at least she's not selling anybody rotgut, which possibly amounts in the long term to a net salvation of stomachs...

Yet it's always a source of personal humiliation that from time to time she's obliged to put in actual working time as the cut-rate adventuress she pretends to be in her magazine articles, running tabs in saloons everywhere from grand hotels to waterfront dives, not just ambi- but multidextrous, keeping three, sometimes four routines going at any given time, while softly—with luck, attractively—humming the divorcée blues.

Worse, she's begun sometimes to find the humiliation not so bad, almost healthy, among the earliest signs of what's already taking hold of her. People assume she's a masochist of some kind.

"In the sense," she supposes, "that Pollyanna is a masochist, along with racetrack touts, stock market analysts, from any of whom a happy attitude is required despite evidence otherwise."

Presently here are the del Vastos, up in the autogyro, out for a test spin, breezing by, waving, bound for the Rock of Gibraltar, a brief though dramatic landing on top. Later the same evening, a quiet knock, TAPtaptap, on a window far above street level. Glow responds, of course, who would it be but Porfirio, anchored swaying against the night.

"Yes, once again it is I, the Saint Nicholas of love, gently landed on your unforgivingly angled rooftop..."

"Yes, Porfirio, and Feliz Navidad back to you of course *pero qué carajo* this time of night..."

"Only, *mi vida*, that being together with you in the sky today it slipped my mind to mention how critical is the ratio between engine speed and rotor tachometer reading, which must be held at 12 or 12 and a half to one—"

"And you wouldn't have gotten to sleep all night and been too tired tomorrow to remember to tell me then, how thoughtful, Porfirio."

"Many have been ejected from the Brotherhood of International Gyro Brokers And Dealers for infractions far less serious . . ."

"I suppose I should at least invite you in for mint tea. That machine is securely parked, I hope. Not about to slide off the roof or anything."

21

The train stops at Belgrade for about an hour. Hicks, nodding in and out of slumber, is aware that at some point Alf and Pips, after an unexpected wire from London, "Uncle Bostwick having another episode. Please do try to pop round forthwith. Regards from all," have taken their leave, promising to reconnect soon in Budapest, handing him a nickel-plated policeman's whistle, "Just give us a blast on the old Acme Thunderer here, we'll be with you straightaway."

"If you're close enough to hear it, you mean."

"No matter how far apart we are."

"A long-distance whistle? How's that work? Radio?"

"Apports. Ask anyone when you get to Budapest, they'll explain."

Out the door, onto the platform, off into early Yugoslavian night, as a new and slippery customer arrives to replace them, introducing himself as Egon Praediger, International Criminal Police Commission, flipping open a leather ID holder, "We happen to be headquartered in Vienna, though our remit covers the Continent."

"Those Interpol guys." A European inter-cop concept Hicks now dimly recalls Boynt Crosstown being a big admirer of. There may have been a memo way back when, maybe even two.

Hicks figures this Viennese flatfoot for around inspector level—a shade too nervous for the suave cop-about-town impression he's trying for, haircut marcelled to an eight-ball shine, bespoke suit, three buttons, side vents, soft shoulder, lowered lapel notch, lapels visibly spangled in white which doesn't seem to be dandruff.

"Knize, the single oasis in the sartorial wasteland between Naples and London, unless you count the newer German military uniforms which begin to show some glimmerings of promise." Out with a jarful of cocaine crystals, producing a miniature hand-cranked grinder and sifting a cone of white powder which he then carefully formats into a number of nose-appropriate lines, a routine known around Chicago as "hitching up the reindeer." "Sometimes about now, a *schnupf* at the right moment can help us to refocus and not go wandering off down the dead ends of the afternoon . . ."

"Ask you something there, Egon—does U-Ops know about me getting shanghaied and so forth?"

"They're the ones who set it up."

Oh, boy. "And it's jake with them you tellin me about it?"

"Can't see much harm." Meaning what are you going to do about it, chump?

"Wait a minute," sometimes with unfamiliar coppers, a gumshoe needs to carefully review who expects what in the way of coordination, "nothin personal, just like to know how it all shakes out, who's workin for who again here exactly and so forth?"

One of those mid-European eyebrow gestures. "Actually, ICPC have a reciprocity arrangement with your U-Ops, free access to the services of any field operative anywhere in the world. And to be honest, just at the moment we could use some of that famous American 'moxie'—"

"Who, me? I'm already over here on another ticket, what happens with that?"

"A runaway cheese heiress you have been assigned to locate and return to the U.S. whose father"—ominous pause—"Bruno . . . Air-mont," the way Dracula pronounces the name Van Helsing, "happens at the moment to be our most sought-after public enemy."

"Sure, big around Milwaukee once upon a time, Al Capone of Cheese, dropped out of sight a while back, foreign jail, some say a remote tropical island?"

"He's out and about and quite among us I fear. His dossier has continued to thicken, criminal activities including murder, tax evasion in a number of countries, Cheese Fraud routinely committed by a counterfeit cheese operation Continent-wide, plus any number of offshore affiliates—"

"Egon. Wait. C'mon . . . counterfeit cheese?"

"Oh *ja*, far worse than most civilians realize. Half the time don't know what they're eating anyway. Nor have the least idea how difficult the International Cheese Syndicate can become. The Roquefort police, the Gorgonzola *squadri*, even Switzerland—harmless by comparison. InChSyn are the mad dog of Cheese Enforcement, authorized to conduct special operations, come in through windows, breach walls, deploy explosives . . .

"Cheese Fraud being a metaphor of course, a screen, a front for something more geopolitical, some grand face-off between the cheese-based or colonialist powers, basically northwest Europe, and the vast teeming cheeselessness of Asia, their widely known reluctance to have much to do with cheese, given a long history of keeping cattle more for farmwork than for dairy products, millions of Orientals over the generations have grown unfamiliar with cheese, what little they do run across giving them indigestion, putting Asia out of the picture as a major cheese market . . ."

Praediger's upper lip by now is shining from a nasal flow more or less constant. Trying to ignore crazed eyeballs, too much white showing compared to iris, sure signs of either a hophead or a candidate for Winnebago, Hicks pretends they're having a reasonable discussion.

"See, there's nothing on my work order," he tries to point out, "says anything about no Bruno or nothin, we'd have to start a new ticket for that, which would need Home Office approval, which somebody could put in a request chit for, back to Chicago, if they don't mind springing for overseas cable rates—"

Laughing dismissively, a reckless glaze creeping over his eyeballs, Praediger hands over a weighty file. "Just a summary, understand, full documentation would require an extra railway carriage at least."

TURNS OUT BRUNO has been over here in Central Europe for some time now, headquartered in Geneva, where as the Al Capone of Cheese he swiftly reached an arrangement with the InChSyn about the time the Swiss Cheese Union took its fateful step of declaring fondue the national dish. Dispatching international flying squads, said to be packing automatic *snub-nose crossbows*, to implement and if necessary enforce rind inspections, requiring that the word "Switzerland" appear repeatedly at a frequency and in a typeface and shade of red which had to be exactly right, or risk consequences grim indeed . . . though undeterred as always, counterfeiters, Bruno among them, nevertheless abounded. It was like Prohibition all over again, only different.

"Meanwhile, as you pursue the elusive Miss Airmont, we keep the shadow on you day and night, hoping that Bruno at a moment of diminished attention will make some fateful lunge and be drawn out of his safe perimeter, even for a fraction of a second, whereupon we are prepared to step in and apprehend."

"And maybe you can tell me, is Daphne in on this too?"

"Is it of some concern to you?"

"If she's helping to bring down the law on her own father—"

"In your investigations you cannot have failed to notice how often fathers and daughters are run by strange emotions, which, although occasionally dangerous, do continue to guarantee job security for us all."

"OK, just gonna look in the Manual here for a minute . . . right, the next question I'm spoze to ask is, is who are *you* reporting to, who is it that's sending me off onto one more miserable damn hopeless ticket I never heard of, here?"

Praediger doesn't answer, his eyes are open but his attention seems to be elsewhere. Just about the time Hicks has decided to give him a poke he begins to speak.

"This is the ball bearing on which everything since 1919 has gone pivoting, this year is when it all begins to come apart. Europe trembles, not only with fear but with desire. Desire for what has almost arrived, deepening over us, a long erotic buildup before the shuddering instant of clarity, a violent collapse of civil order which will spread from a radiant point in or near Vienna, rapidly and without limit in every direction, and so across the continents, trackless forests and unvisited lakes, plaintext suburbs and cryptic native quarters, battlefields historic and potential, prairie drifted over the horizon with enough edible prey to solve the Meat Question forever . . ." by now having lapsed into some prophetic trance, at which the best Hicks can do is stare politely and wait for it to all go away, wondering how he's supposed to deal with this—pretend to understand what the bughouse Austrian is talking about. Humor him? Do a sociable noseful just to keep the conversation going?

Hmm. Well, maybe . . .

"So . . . you're bringing me in to Vienna?"

"We are continuing on to Budapest."

"I thought Vienna was you folks' version of downtown."

"Another 'tale of two cities,' Vienna solemn and psychoanalytic, while just down the river in Budapest carouses a psychical Mardi Gras in every shade of the supernatural no matter how lurid. *Dieser Stadt*," a shiver perhaps not altogether unconnected with sleigh-riding activities, "*ist mir sehr unheimlich*. You would say, it gives me the creeps. Vienna is perhaps not for everyone, but Budapest—*iih*! Budapest just at the moment is the metropolis and beating heart of asport/apport activities, where objects precious and ordinary, exquisite and kitsch, big and small, have been mysteriously vanishing on the order of dozens per day, creating hours of overtime not only for the Budapest police but for us at the Inter-police Commission in Vienna as well.

"The chief beneficiaries according to the Evidenzbüro are a syndicate of fences closely associated with Bruno Airmont." Handing over a folder with a couple of mug shots.

"Who's this?"

"Bruno's deputy, Ace Lomax, wants and warrants out on him internationally for years now, a miracle of lubrication, no matter how tightly we think we've got hold of him, somehow he always slips away. We have found it necessary to seek help in Budapest, and come to arrangements with the noted apportist Dr. Zoltán von Kiss. Obviously the Directorate cannot officially admit any connection with apports and the paranormal, preferring in fact to deny all acquaintance with Dr. von Kiss, despite his reputation throughout Central Europe."

"Hep to that, Milwaukee PD has the same problem, psychics make 'em all jumpy."

"Dr. von Kiss will be meeting us at the East Station. He is actively engaged on a daily basis with criminal elements in Budapest, especially receivers of stolen goods, and through them, from time to time, with Mr. Lomax. Which should allow you to keep a close eye without raising too much suspicion."

"That's not what I'm supposed to be doing over here, you can check with U-Ops—"

"We did. Ace Lomax is your new assignment. The paperwork will arrive in a few days."

"If somebody's dog don't eat it first. And if I decide to skip on you? That could happen too."

"Where would you go? We would arrest you before you could get anywhere. Here's the warrant, all filled in, approved, signed and stamped, Unlawful Flight to Avoid Employment." Out with another mug shot, which he attaches to the warrant.

"Wait. That's me?"

"Belinograph, all the way from Chicago. Pretty close likeness, isn't it, allowing maybe for some facial wear and tear since the long-ago day it first went into your file."

"I look like such a kid, what happened?"

"Something about this troubles you, I can tell."

"Well, there used to be more time to make a getaway. Now they're flashing everybody's mug shot all around the world in the blink of an eye, pretty soon there's no place to run to anymore. Aside from that, no, nothin too bothersome."

"Meanwhile please accept this gift from the ICPC—"

Setting it carefully in easy reach. Well. What's this then. Black, quietly gleaming, shape like a 1911 Colt automatic but smaller, lighter, the little guy in a saloon fight who eventually mops up the floor with everybody.

"Mr. McTaggart, may we introduce the Walther PPK. Newest model, fits unobtrusively in the pocket of the most respectable civilian suit, even what you have on. As popular on this side of the law as the Mauser Bolo is on the other. Already billed to U-Ops corporate overhead and registered in your name. Legally yours, take it away."

"Quick work."

"All done before you even left the States."

Takes a minute for this to register. By the time it does, Praediger, nose merrily aglow, is on about the PPK vis-à-vis the Versailles-compliant Mauser C96, known as the Bolo because it's said to be a big favorite with Bolsheviks, "providing a fine example of the LOUIE, or Law of Unintended Effects, five and a half inches having been too long a barrel for the victorious Entente, who decreed that the C96 must have an *inch and a half* of its barrel chopped off before they'd feel safe in their peacetime beds, but then ha-HA! in kicks the LOUIE, as criminals everywhere begin to realize owing to the shorter barrel how concealable under any number of getups the Bolo has turned out to be, finding its way into places where its earlier full length never would have allowed it . . ." another jingle-bells excursion out onto the ski slopes of commentary. Hicks chisels a Régie from a passing train attendant, lights up, and pretends to be listening. But his mood is troubled.

22

The Oktogon is jumping. A good percentage of the foot traffic in this part of Budapest look to be young women, turned out far more snazzily than anybody working West Wells Street, or the Loop for that matter.

Zoltán von Kiss is sporting a suit of summer-weight fresco in a citric shade sometimes observed on swing musicians. A quick once-over further reveals that the suit, though appearing slept in for a number of nights in a row and uneasily at that, has working buttons and buttonholes on the sleeves, suggesting that it may have been run up just for him, someplace exclusive.

"Ebenstein's," von Kiss notices him looking, "actually, best in town, I'd be delighted to introduce you." His gaze remaining for an extra few seconds on Hicks's own purple-and-orange check turnout.

"OK with this one I've got on, no place in my bag for another suit anyway, but thanks, Doc."

"Call me Zoli, everyone does, you can ignore the 'von' part, it's political."

They are approached by a young woman on a Moto Guzzi motorcycle with an uninhibited exhaust.

"I kiss your hand," murmurs Zoltán, "and while I've got it," pretending to scrutinize her palm, "you will meet a tough and indeed hardboiled, if that's your type, American who— well look at this, he's been sitting right here all this time."

"Terike," nodding to Hicks, flashing him a look familiar since back in high school—they warned me about you, I shouldn't be anywhere near you, even outdoors in a brightly lit crowd.

Along with pickup and delivery citywide, Terike does occasional apport work, "Glamorous Assistant basically, though no easier on the nerves than a magic or knife-throwing act." No idea what will come through one minute to the next, from top notes of some perfume nobody can afford to a grand piano falling from an upper story. A girl has to stay on the alert, ready to take cover. Some knowledge of emergency nursing is also helpful. "At least the pay is good. Which reminds me, Zoli . . ."

Zoltán reaches into some tailor-made inner pocket and comes out with a discreetly stuffed envelope and hands it over. Arranging for Hicks and the tabletop to be in the way of any third-party curiosity. Terike throttles up and rolls on her way, waving to Hicks, calling, "*Szia!*"

"Hope so," sez Hicks.

"Hungarian for so long," Zoltán explains.

ZOLI WORKS OUT of a modern-style office building, convenient to the East Station, sharing a floor with Anglo-Danubian Casualty and Theft, specialists in the newly emerging field of apport insurance, whose advertising can be seen on a number of streetcars around town—a poster showing a top hat brimming with diamond jewelry making a swift escape into the sky, apparently under its own power, while far below on a hotel terrace crowded with elegant dancers a hatless, gemless couple gaze up after it in dismay. "We should've insured with Anglo-Danubian!"

"Sad spectacle, isn't it, once an echt working apportist, lately more of a psychic celebrity detective pursuing a life enviable at least from a distance." Police departments and Foreign Offices bidding for his services, women amateur and professional throwing themselves in his direction, newsreel and magazine photographers his natural element, flash powder and neon his everyday light.

"What I took at first for amazement and respect turned out to be little more than applause for the hired entertainment. You mustn't imagine I enjoy all this attention."

"Coulda fooled me, Zoli."

"Oh . . . champagne, limousines, women who enjoy a good time, of course—but really, what need has a spiritual person for any of that?"

"Dunno, let me give it some thought . . ."

"You are a practical people, Americans, everyone is either some kind of inventor or at least a gifted repairman. I myself have grown to rely too much on the passionate mindlessness which creeps over me just as an apport is about to arrive or depart. I am painfully aware of how much more exposure I need to the secular, material world."

"And you figure Americans are just the ticket. Are you telling me this stuff is all a variety-house routine, that it doesn't . . . really happen?"

Beaming playfully, "You will want proof, some trivial example"—producing out of as far as Hicks can see nowhere a small single-action revolver, offering it butt-first, tapping himself on the forehead—"go ahead, point-blank, as many shots as you like . . ."

"Are you crazy, get that goldurn thing away from me—" looking nervously around for something to dive underneath.

"Won't matter, every round will just asport away to someplace harmless. These days I don't get shot at as much as I used to, now and then some ambitious party still thinks they'll get in a lucky shot a split-second before I can make it de-manifest."

"Must put a nice edge on your day. You'd sure have fun in Chicago."

The gun abruptly vanishing, "And yet, trust me, I'm a mind reader, you're asking yourself, did that really just apport in and out of the unknown, or was it all a cheap stage act, a French drop performed at lightning speed, a moment of trick cinema, here one frame, gone the next."

"I give up," sez Hicks, "which is it?"

"If I knew, which I don't, I couldn't tell you, it'd be bad for business. Perhaps tomorrow night you'll have a better chance to judge."

"Howzat again?"

"Our first assignment—"

"Our, that'd be . . . me and you."

"—will be to locate and restore to its owner a somewhat tasteless table lamp, indeed among lamp collectors considered the crown jewel of tasteless lamps, a lamp so stupefyingly tasteless it makes nonsense of the tasteless-lamp category itself. Too horribly tasteless ever to have been photographed. Cameras break, eyeglass prescriptions are drastically rewritten, crowds of spectators run screaming out of exits they then get jammed up in. *Tasteless Lamp Quarterly* runs out of space to contain the overflow of readers' indignation. Is how tasteless it is, this lamp, known in underworld Esperanto as La Lampo Plej Malbongusto.

"Through some perverse law of secondary markets, the more vehemently denounced, the more valuable it has become. Lamp-collector mentality, a mystery as deep perhaps as apportation, which it seems is what's just happened to it."

The client, one of the more comfortably fixed residents of the upslope or Buda side of the river, some sort of Count, Hicks gathers, world-renowned for his collection of lamps ranging from Rather Offensive to Quite Tasteless Indeed, wants it back—"though to be honest, it may only have paused midway in its return to some more authentic owner, what we call an 'apporepo,' or apport of repossession—vulnerable, fair game for any hijackers who think they can make a grab for it en route. Who are sure to include associates of Bruno Airmont, in whom I am told you have some interest."

Requiring another get-together with Praediger, who happens to be in Budapest consulting with a flying squad out of Unit IV downtown who work nothing but apport fraud. Turns out that in response to the local ass/app situation, a trade has sprung up in *counterfeit apports*, passing for merchandise just in from the other side of whatever this is that's going on. Returns. Fake returns.

"Important therefore that you become acquainted with La Lampo Plej Malbongusto, for even the most hopelessly ill-imagined lamp deserves to belong somewhere, to have *been awaited*, to enact some return, to stand watch on some table, in some corner, as a place-keeper, a marker, a promise of redemption."

"Sure Egon, but this lamp—it could be a fake?"

"Childish, mean-spirited, exactly up Bruno's alley . . . An astounding percent of asported merchandise turns out to be lamps at least as tasteless as this one. We send our operatives out through the shopping districts, we gather data on every tasteless lamp currently for sale, we follow the weekly announcements in the trade papers . . ."

"What about lamps that aren't tasteless?"

"No such thing. Most lamps are inherently in bad taste because the design constraints are so few—when all you need is a socket, a cord, a switch, and some way of carrying off the heat of the bulb, the field is left wide-open to any ungifted amateur who wants to try his hand and get away with something on the cheap."

"This one Bruno is after—"

"Don't expect him to show up in person. He'll likely delegate one of his deputies like Ace Lomax. So keep your eyes open and do give Dr. von Kiss our best."

Suddenly La Lampo Plej Malbongusto is the topic of the moment . . . the Zoltán von Kiss shop reporting suspect faces on streetcars, in cafés, phone threats in the middle of the night—

"There is interest in La Lampo from powerful elements for whom you can never amount to more than a bothersome detail. For your personal safety, please, have nothing more to do with it," and so forth, eventually a postal delivery with an additional apportation stamp, depicting the Holy Right Hand of St. Stephen, hacked off at the wrist, dripping blood, flying through the air across Hungary holding a sealed envelope. Below stand a country woman carrying a sheaf of wheat, a soldier in full Hussar uniform, and a factory worker holding a monkey wrench, all gazing skyward in open-mouthed wonder at the flying Hand, beneath the radiant slogan sürgős, urgent, filling the sky behind it.

ZvK reads the note enclosed, nods. "All right, that's us. Let's get moving."

Rainy city pavement, fog, everything in a low-intensity blur. Hicks has no idea of where they may be headed.

First ZvK stops off at a church for a quick novena to St. Anthony of Padua, patron saint of the lost and found. "Can't hurt, kind of preventive maintenance. Lost people, lost hope, by extension patron saint of apportists."

Shaking his head briefly as if something unpleasant just alighted there, "Me, I feel like the village matchmaker. This isn't the usual collector's mania. It's desire." Explaining that his client the Count belongs to a secret community of lampadophiles, or persons sexually attracted to lamps. "You may not have run across it that much in the States."

"Spend enough time around emergency rooms, you're apt to see anything. Light sockets, vacuum cleaners, that general diameter, the minute it gets invented, some genius finds a way to put their johnson into it."

They arrive at a neighborhood of warehouses, corner taverns, cafés and hashish bars, metallic shadows, sounds of mostly invisible train traffic, train smoke in the air, uneven cobblestone pavement which demands close attention when running from or after anybody, where according to Zoltán apport-asport activities may be carried on in safety, cop-free.

A back alleyway, itself a honkytonk district in miniature, entrances and exits both alleyside and out onto the grand boulevard adjoining. The day begins at sundown, and everybody seems to be working at least one extra hustle on the side.

Csopi, who looks after the door, lounging like a shop salesman on the lookout for walk-in business, tips ZvK a friendly nod.

"*Saluto*," ZvK getting into a complicated handshake, "*agrabla revidi vin!*"

The room is turbulent with kleptos conferring in Esperanto, featuring a lot of words ending in *u* ("Volitive mood," comments Zoltán, "used for yearnings, regrets, if-onlys . . ."), hurried exchanges of goods for cash, contraband of all kinds just in from across various borders, loupes flourished like daggers, with a lot of peering up and down through eyeglasses, an unslackening interplay of hands from time-battered to just-manicured, among pockets, sleeves, lapels—traffic, scaled to the human palm and the briefness of time allotted, in antique watches, knickknacks, earrings, finger rings, cigar clippers, lenses, knives, and banknotes of several nations for making change.

ZvK smoothly adjusting a fedora of a pale off-mango shade, an Abdulla in a cigarette holder between his teeth at a jaunty angle, tossing semi-salutes left and right, now and then a gloved kiss, "Yes yes, charmed, I'm sure . . ." making his way to a table in back where three cigars seem to've been left unlit, unclipped, just sitting. Hicks goes to pick one up and *zzt*, like that they all vanish, leaving a fading iridescent halo inches above the tabletop and at Hicks's fingertips a sensation of cold, reappearing one by one across the room, clipped, lit, and smoldering in the kissers of three genial types lined up in a row, who now lift the hijacked smokes the way somebody you've bought a drink for might lift a glass, then proceed to puff on and blow smoke rings together *in rhythm* as they now approach.

"Pals of yours."

"Call themselves Drei im Weggla, which in Nuremberg is a local snack, three bratwursts on a roll. We've done some business. Here, meet the boys. Schuncki, Dieter, Heinz."

"We all used to be part of the same act," explains Schnucki. "Until it became evident that Zoltán really was apporting objects in and out. Which was getting in the way of everybody's timing—"

"Ruining the gags," recalls Dieter.

"Plus Zoli couldn't stay on the beat or in tune," adds Heinz.

"So everybody agreed that Zoli should go on with a solo career and we'd stay together as a trio."

"And less obviously as a freelance bodyguard unit."

"Because," Dieter a little reluctant, "there were also some Russians, who still keep showing up now and then . . ."

"Russians," Hicks nodding, "I guess you forgot to mention them, huh, Zoli."

"His natural modesty," Dieter explains, "though the Soviets are unlikely to admit it, they've taken a deep interest in the paranormal, especially its potential role in modern warfare. There's a narkomat set up specifically, including a secret lab run by Stalin's chief cryptography genius, Gleb Bokii—"

"Narkomat," Hicks puzzling, "that's . . . a place you go drop in a few coins, open a little door, there's a reefer, maybe a line of coke . . ."

"No. No, actually it's the Russian abbreviation for NARodnyi KOMissariAT, people's ministry. The recent climate of apportation in Budapest has drawn their attention, and someone has determined that among the resulting influx of con artists and self-deluded, our own Zoltán von Kiss may be one of very few who's the genuine article."

"And so to discourage any attempts to bring him east," Schnucki concludes, "me and the boys here have been keeping an eye out."

"So you're not really—"

"Well . . . depending what you mean by 'really' . . ."

Into the follow spot now steps a juvenile host in a lounge suit of some pale aqua shade, necktie with a good deal of burgundy and yellow splashed around in a nonlinear way, "And now! once again, as wurst comes to wurst comes to wurst, it's time to please welcome back the Teutonic! Neutronic! Drei! Im! Weggla!"

Fanfare, wild applause, and here they come, the band bouncing into brass-heavy march time as one by one the trio step up to introduce themselves—

>I'm Schnucki!
>>I'm Dieter!
>>>I'm Heinz!
>So glad you could be here, to-night—
>Still up-to-those-old monk-ey-shines,
>Always good for a laugh, and, a light . . .
>[Schnucki] Now if you smell something funny, and—
>[Dieter] It isn't the smokes—
>[Heinz] It's probably us with—
>[All together] Some more crazy jokes!
>>>>Folks,
>just hope we remem-ber, our lines,
>*Ja*, I'm Schnucki!
>>I'm Dieter!
>>>I'm Heinz!
>No, wait, I'm Heinz, and, and you're—

They fall to bickering, with the band oompahing along, about who's which, bravos and squeals from the room, which adores them, as the sleekly combed trio, knees turned inward, demurely pretend to cower behind their hats.

The act, Zoltán explains, depends on the abrupt changes of temperature which accompany any apport event. Without many pauses between, the comical threesome brew coffee, cook strings of sausages, light cigarettes, and hotfoot the shoes of those they feel are not paying close enough attention, breaking now and then into song and dance, along with quick changes of costume. The finale features a Baked Alaska over which they have first poured brandy, then, nudging and giggling, faking amazement, watched it asport away, waving it bon voyage and waiting breathlessly for it to burst into flames, ignited by the heat of passion, onto the dessert plate of some randomly selected audience member.

"Another first-rate performance, gentlemen," Zoli lifting his hat respectfully. "How long are you boys in town for this time?"

"That'll depend on your latest visitor," Schnucki losing some of his playful expression.

"*Az Isten faszára*—who is it now?"

"None of the GPU regulars," Dieter reports, "This one's clearly high-level. Said to be running a narkomat of his own."

"Keep on like this, Zoli," Heinz waving a finger, "somebody's going to start taking you seriously."

"I hope you boys can behave yourselves."

"Hasn't been easy," Dieter with a playful grin, "since we were issued the new Schmeissers," anybody's guess how much of this is being spoken in fun. As ZvK will reveal to Hicks later, one of many rumors about Drei im Weggla is that they're secretly an *anti-Soviet assassination squad*, whom Stalin and the GPU have been after for a year, but owing to a deep inventory of extrasensory skills, able to pursue unharmed a notorious career of retro-White mischief.

Suddenly Csopi has showed up at ZvK's elbow, looking uneasy, muttering in Esperanto, with a lot of that wishful *u* sound in it.

"The Lamp," ZvK up on his feet, "he says it's out in back, and we'd better grab it while it's still there."

"Right on your tail, Zoli."

They arrive about the same time as a roar and throb Hicks hasn't heard since Milwaukee, from some hotshot on a Harley-Davidson Flathead that Hicks, PI reflexes kicking in, guesses to be Bruno Airmont's deputy Ace Lomax. La Lampo Plej Malbongusto, not, as far as Hicks can tell, all *that* tasteless in appearance, trembles in the grasp of a nervous mug in a low-priced suit, who's more than happy to hand it over and disappear before

Hicks can ask for any backup in dealing with Ace, now off his bike and advancing in a way you could say bodes ill.

"I'll go get the car," ZvK whispers. "Back soon."

"That'd be helpful."

"Mind the Lamp. If it should decide to apport on out of here again, don't become alarmed."

"Ain't what I'm worryin about right now."

Hicks has been keeping Praediger's PPK heater parked in an inside pocket, undetermined tenths of a second away from being out and aimed before Ace will possibly have dropped him. However, Ace apparently is encountering some delay in disengaging from his own drapes whatever he has brought along in the way of persuasion, giving Hicks an impossible fragment of time to calculate which will cost him more, an unscheduled victim on his conscience or yet another homicidal personality out somewhere still at large and more motivated than ever to do him in. What a choice.

"You might want to think this one over," the PPK aimed and steady, "unless your week's been pretty slow."

"Go ahead, then, Alphonse or is it Gaston, you need help finding the trigger?"

Hicks motioning with his head. "You mind?"

Ace shrugs and hands over a full-length broomhandle Mauser, which he might not've been planning to actually use.

"And how do you unload this piece of artillery here?"

"Bottom of the magazine just pops off."

"Thanks." Hicks opens the magazine, dumps out a handful of rounds, pulls back the bolt to eject the last one, gives Ace back the gun.

"That's ten rounds you owe me."

"Call it a nickel apiece, we can start a tab if you want." Hicks lighting a local gasper, handing it to Ace, and lighting up one for himself. "See if I've got this straight, here we're about to start shooting over some lamp nobody's seen for more than a minute or two, some funny business too deep and far away to make much sense of, and I just happen to step into your line of fire—"

"Or me into yours. That's it, pretty much it, nothing to get nervous about."

"Big relief, thanks." What has in fact been gathering around Hicks, not fully noticed by Ace, is a peculiar nimbus, likely due to Oriental Attitude, where it's all the same whether he will now blast Ace into eternity or let him go on with a life in which, from what Hicks can see, there isn't that much to object to. Another colleague in the same racket, just happens to be working for a different outfit. Of which there are already on this ticket more than enough to keep track of.

"You're the gangster from Chicago."

"On the schnozzola, pal, bad as they come, worth an El Producto at least, remind me sometime I owe you one of them."

"How's 'ose Cubs doing since they traded Hack Wilson?"

"Startin off the season pretty good, lost a couple to Cincinnati, Brooklyn."

"Hornsby still playing second?"

"Nah, it's this kid Billy Herman. First time at bat he swings, slams it into the plate, it bounces back up, hits him in the head, knocks him cold. Meantime the Rajah ain't playin much, they've got him in as manager, the Commissioner's after him, front office ain't happy, everybody figures his days are numbered."

"Know the feeling."

"That bad?"

"Looks like I'm going back empty-handed tonight, and it ain't as if I don't have enough trouble already."

"Your boss really wants this lamp, huh."

"Not that much, the lamp is just an excuse to see me off the roster. Which with his outfit, when you're dropped, you're dropped."

"Wish I could help."

"Not unless—"

"What."

"Somebody said you know Al Capone."

"Couple years back maybe, a little business now and then with pals of his, last I knew some of them could even be still alive, but since he went in the pen I'm not sure how much of an introduction I could guarantee you."

"And . . . if I just skipped, tried to, I don't know, seek asylum someplace . . ."

"Cops in Vienna tell me they're after your boss, but any deal you make with them . . ."

Shaking his head slowly, "Not about to happen."

A deep rumbling felt more than heard passes through the invisible world and around the edges of this one. From beyond any zone of civic safety something has begun to pulsate, soul-strumming and growing louder, finishing with a great thump reaching citywide. Just like that, no more Tasteless Lamp, only the familiar empty volume of post-asport cold.

"Well what in the heck," Ace after heart rates return to normal.

"Zoli said this might happen."

"Did he have anything to do with it?"

"No idea. Think they'll buy the story back at your shop?"

"Sure hope so. What are we supposed to do now?"

"Guess I could be lookin the other way while you make your escape . . ."

"Soon as you put away that weapon, bid me godspeed."

"Till you find more ammo, reload, and start shooting at me."

"Last thing on my mind." Ace already up on the kick-start pedal. "Next time, amigo."

"Lookin forward." But the roar of the bike is all anybody hears.

23

Meantime, Pips Quarrender has materialized in Budapest, gone platinum, a finger-wave, a smart little nearly ultraviolet cocktail hat with a veil, earlobes dazzling, as if beginning to pick up from somewhere a grasp of what goes with what in the doll-up department.

"Well." Hicks taking her hand, giving her a twirl.

"I am, from head to foot, as Marlene might say. And does, actually."

"This might take some getting used to."

"All part of the craft, give whoever's watching something blonde and shiny to fix their attention, then should one need to disappear, simply get rid of it and fade into the mobility. Whoosh, and away goes this," flipping a curl, "and it's back to the old cottage loaf again . . ."

"Had you figured somehow for prim, once."

"You didn't know what you were missing."

"Nothing new. Don't see that Alf around."

"No one ever does till it's too late," Pip with a toss of her bob and a brief side shift of the eyeballs flipping open a cigarette case with a guilloche design in silver and violet enamel, full of swanky Egyptian smokes, black with gold crests, sliding one between her lips. Hicks without asking reaches himself one just as she snaps the case shut again.

"Ouch."

"Oops, didn't draw blood there or anything, did I. These happen to be Ankhesenamuns, never that easy to come by and perhaps not quite up your street in any case."

A smoke is a smoke, but, "Hep to that," handing it back, "wouldn't want to . . ."

"Oh, keep it."

"You're sure."

"After your hands, previous whereabouts unknown, have been all over it . . ."

"You're a sport." They light up. As if there might be something weird and Oriental in the smoke, Hicks politely makes a point of holding it a while before exhaling through his nose.

"Delightful, aren't they."

Could use some menthol in fact, though Hicks only beams and nods.

"Getting along all right with Egon Praediger these days, seeing things eye-to-eye, one trusts?"

"More like nose to nose, he keeps saying it's all about Bruno Airmont, but I can't shake this feeling he's up to something else."

"You've twigged by now he isn't really a policeman."

"That would explain a lot, but maybe you shouldn't be tellin me—"

"He's one of us."

"Good luck with that, whatever that 'us' is."

"The Directorate in Vienna is a convenient cover for him, besides their helpfully vast collection of dossiers. His chief remit has to do with Croatia, which ever since being absorbed into the Yugoslavian state has been trying to become independent again, by way of a goon squad known as the Ustashe. They regard Yugoslavia as nothing but a new version of Serbia, which Austria still hates as bitterly as before the War and so have been pursuing a hands-off policy toward Ustashe mischief, including a good deal of train bombing and sabotage and that sort of thing."

"So when you two handed me over to Praediger—"

"He'd been in Belgrade," Alf manifesting out of nowhere, "helping to further one more deep Ustashe design against the Yugo entity, no doubt. Hullo, McTaggart, you again, listening to Mata Hari here telling tales out of school, though you mustn't believe a word."

Alf has arrived in a jaunty turnout including a trilby hat which draws looks of disgust from Pips. "Thought we'd seen the last of that thing."

"That was the Herbert Johnson. This is the Mühlbacher."

"Every spy in town wears one," Pips explains, the town at the moment being Vienna, where the Quarrenders are currently based.

If you happen to be a spy, one big selling point about Vienna is there are no laws against spying, as long as the spying isn't on Austria. "Spies all tell you they want to live in Vienna—culture, sophistication, friendly police, legal immunity. And once Vienna really was that cozy, nothing happening, one never had to venture out of town, everyone knew each other, same round of cafés, agents of various nations, if that's your preference, once fairly sluggish going for anyone trying to scratch a living wage from International Intrigue, till of course the Nazis changed all that. Now it's as dangerous as anyplace in Europe. Right, left, ultra and infra, everyone armed and out in the street and the police worse than useless."

Alf has begun to locate at this stage in his career a "sensitive" side, a development Pip admits to being less than enchanted with. "Oh, dear, no. No, best of luck with that, some quivering retro-adolescent hoovering up everyone's precious time, that would just stuff the haggis, wouldn't it!"

"Pip Emma, my peach, you always did read me like a bus advert."

"Not attentively enough, it seems, who'd believe that I once took you for a jolly lad only looking for a bit of fun—certainly not the *tiresome complexo* one observes before one at the moment."

"Always marry a loquacious woman, McTaggart, less work for one's own lungs, more room for smoking. In fact I have here two brilliant Havanas, if you'd like to step round the corner."

Given the British appetite for alternate meanings, the Secret Service has long angled among the sizable pool of cryptic crossword solvers looking for potential code-buster talent, which is what Alf is taking a break from at the moment.

"Need to clear my head, been all morning at the Crossword Suicide Café."

"The . . . um . . ."

One night a few years ago, Alf explains, around midnight, an unemployed waiter named Antal Gyula steps in to what was then known as the Emke Café, just down the block, tried to make a couple of phone calls, no luck, disappeared into the toilet, next thing anybody knows, ka-pow, the Budapest Suicide Bug has bitten again. In Antal's pocket they find a farewell note in the form of a crossword puzzle he designed himself, whose solution will reveal the reasons he did the deed, along with the names of other people involved.

"It's been some time now, and nobody's solved it yet. A crypto bonanza potentially and yet just as easily somebody's idea of a practical joke." The longer it goes unsolved, the more confusion and dismay. Devout cruciverbalists from foreign countries have learned Hungarian, sometimes to a quite advanced and literary level, even quit their jobs, just to come to Budapest to work on the notorious Mystery Crossword, "and sooner or later they all show up at the toilet of the fatal café."

"Wait—there are Hungarian crossword puzzles? Written in Hungarian and everything?"

"The alphabet's a bit more complex, fourteen vowels, for one thing, double and triple consonants. One imagines old Dilly Knox would be the bloke to see about that, if one were interested—but hello, what's this then, someone busy pawing my wife, come along, McTaggart, I may need you to 'put the arm on' someone."

"Pipka!"

"Vassily!"

One of those left-right-left Russian kisses, repeated indefinitely, intended, as near as Hicks can tell, less for Pip than for the irascible husband approaching.

"Yes, well, cue the balalaikas, Charing Cross Station clock around here isn't it."

Known to Alf and Pip by his British code name Vassily Midoff since shortly after the War, when he was running around London go-betweening, shifting cash, pawnable jewelry, microfilm, wire traffic, one alias in fact among so many that by now he's begun to forget some of the earlier ones.

Impressions of what he looks like also vary widely. Not that he's invisible, exactly, people see him all the time, but they *don't remember* that they saw him. They'd better not. He has too much invested, he's given up literally years of intra-Party maneuvering to slip away to workshops in the Far East, where the training among clandestine orders of brothers and sisters is relentlessly devoted to the arts of passing through the world without leaving a trace.

They find an inconspicuous café, Vassily sitting with the best view of possible street approaches.

"We haven't seen you in Vienna lately. Hate to think you've been avoiding us."

"He was there," Pip suggests, "we just didn't see him."

"You do seem nervous, Vassily, more than usual."

"You know what it is. Don't pretend you don't know. Everybody knows what it is."

"If it's anything we've done or neglected to—"

But Vassily's attention now is elsewhere. He is staring into the street, as if trying to see around the corner, where a slow clattering engine sound, advancing out of the inaudible, is now nearly upon them. "Pizdets," with a rising inflection that will after another breath become a scream of terror. "It's them!"

Who turn out to be nightclub apport trio Schnucki, Dieter, and Heinz, seated one behind another on a Böhmerland Long Touring motorcycle, ten and a half foot wheelbase, red and yellow paint job, riding patrol, keeping an eye out for Russians who may be in town plotting to put the snatch on Zoltán von Kiss. Just doing what they're hired for, though try to tell that to Vassily Midoff.

"Tourists out for a spin, Vassily, what's making you so jumpy?"

"Can't you see? riding back on the extra seat? The invisible rider!"

"There's no one," Pip carefully. "The seat's empty."

"Steady, old radish," advises Alf. But Vassily is up and off hysterical down the street. There does exist an experimental military version of the long Czechoslovakian bike, with a second gearbox in back, to be operated by any rearmost or fourth passenger. In this case, invisible. As Vassily Midoff, were he not at the moment running for his life, would no doubt have pointed out, for a trinity to be effective, and not just a set which happens to contain three members, there must be a fourth element, silent, withheld. A fourth rider, say, working a phantom gearbox . . .

"We won't see him again," Pip dismal. "Something has spooked him back into invisibility."

Alf indignant, "Wasn't—"

"Ssh. Not us." Patting him on the hand, "His extra rider."

24

Reporting in to an all-purpose governmental office converted from a Royal Gendarmerie station where Praediger conducts ICPC business when in Budapest, Hicks finds Praediger obsessively brooding about his latest failure to entrap and arrest Bruno Airmont, not only flying into rages but introducing barrel rolls and Immelmanns as well. Today he has also hauled an oversized *soup spoon* out of someplace and begun energetically to shovel cocaine into both nostrils at once.

"And yet each trap I set for him, some he could not even have been aware of, he has always, through some perverse turn of fortune, managed to evade. I can't show my face around the Directorate without some idiot sniggering about Criminal Genius, as if Airmont is another Dr. Mabuse or Fu Manchu... Can you *appreciate*, how *infuriating*?" a tendency to scream through his nose, "how *insulting to me personally*, to, to be mentioned in the same breath with this feeble impersonation of a crime boss? To waste my talent not on an evil genius but on an evil moron, dangerous not for his intellect, what there may be of it, but for the power that his ill-deserved wealth allows him to exert, which his admirers pretend is will, though it never amounts to more than the stubbornness of a child..."

"Could be worse," Hicks tries to murmur sympathetically, just managing to avoid adding, "like if it turns out he's just smarter than you." How far is he expected to go along with Praediger's obsessions, how copasetic is he supposed to be with any of this? Who'll be the next well-wisher to pull him aside and warn him, "This ain't your beef, this leaper here is heading for trouble you don't want to be in, better get clear of him while you can."

Steps do need to be taken, sooner rather than later, before everybody's dodging airborne furniture or reaching for their roscoe. The Gumshoe's Manual here is not as helpful as it could be. Hicks has even written them letters about it, never answered, sometimes even sent back unopened, despite such real and widespread concern in the business, you see it every day—"What if I get teamed up, unwillingly, with somebody who's off their rocker? What's the best action to take? Prompt reply appreciated."

"Not meaning to add to your troubles, but I had a visit from Ace Lomax the other night, detained him at gunpoint, expecting you to show up any minute, next thing I know he and that lamp both give me the slip."

"*Ach*, der Lomax, *kleine Kartoffel*, meantime I seem to have run out of investigative supplies . . ."

HICKS, HEADED FOR the street at last, grabs the paternoster down to the lobby, where he runs into Terike just emerging from her latest run-in with the authorities over her motorcycle, a 500 cc Guzzi Sport 15. "It's a racing bike, which doesn't keep them from hauling me in and demanding registration documents, which there were never really any of to begin with. Plus some work of my own on the bore and stroke so she'll do better than 100 miles an hour, which they're calling illegal unless I pay a fee, along with the usual threats of inspection I have to come up with excuses for avoiding."

They arrive at a revolving door to the street. Terike motions him on ahead. "Hungarian tradition, the man always goes first, in case of trouble." Hicks steps in first, Terike behind him, and somehow by the time they get outside she's ahead of him and halfway down the block. "Huh?"

Sometimes in Hungary, and this is sworn to by any number of tourists and travelers, you can step into a revolving door in front of a native Hungarian, who will nevertheless then step out into the street ahead of you, as if you somehow have *percolated through* each other, actually occupying the same space, no memory, no expectation, simply the coercive sweep of the moving door drawing you along, molecules for an instant all intermingling, simmering together like, like *soup* . . . and how intimate is that?

Word of this gets around and pretty soon among cognizant tourist traffic there's a noticeable increase of those who *want to have this happen to them*, it's a craze, another must-do for the sophisticated globe-trotter, like crossing the Equator or kissing the Blarney Stone.

Out in Vörösmarty tér, Terike once clear of entanglement, *having remembered how*, it seems, to reassemble into the same solid Hungarian person again, takes a glance back, like a dame will sometimes to see whether anybody's conducting a posterior survey.

"Mind if I ask—"

"Ask Zoltán. He thinks it's apports . . . you understand how apports could come into it."

"Sure. Well, no—you mean the Hungarian person, which is you, somehow . . . apports herself a quarter-turn ahead—"

". . . of the non-Hungarian, which in this same example could be you."

"You can say is. Is is good."

"On the other hand, maybe you just fell asleep for a moment, and I was in a hurry, so . . ." with a quick hip gesture.

"Can we try it again, just to—"

"No."

Before he ever actually met any Hungarian women, Hicks typically imagined them as, well, kind of . . . Mexican. Latin spitfire kind of dame. "Because of the paprika, maybe . . . hot peppers, hot women, so forth?"

"Whereas American men, you in particular, seem the kind of *kemény gyerek* I was brought up to stay well away from."

"It could be worse. I could be paying you to be nice to me."

"Here she is." The Guzzi. The original bright red factory paint job by now faded to a road- and weather-beaten field magenta.

"New sidecar, just about to take it for a test spin, works better with an 80-, 90-kilo carcass in it, anybody interested?" The sidecar has a sleek teardrop shape, the kind of teardrop that only gets shed on purpose, to further some undisclosed scheme, a glamorous teardrop you might say, as if drafted in one single, emotion-free gesture of the pen.

"Unapologetically Guzzista . . . I love this bike, intense relationship, she's seen me out of more trouble than I'll ever talk about, 'cause it'd only sound like more tall tales from the wild highways. The bike, let's face it, is a metaphysical critter. We know, the way you'd say a cowboy knows, that there's a fierce living soul here that we have to deal with."

Hicks in the sidecar, off they go, the rig speeding over cobbles and under arches, flying, it seems, above broken road surfaces and up impossible grades, through gateways, down indoor-outdoor corridors that seem too narrow for a bike let alone a combination.

You want a gearbox disassembled and repaired while on the move, time and a half if you're doing over 100 miles per hour, she's your gal. She can get anything that'll fit in a sidecar across the worst terrain you can think of, war-damaged cities a specialty, master of urban obstacle-running, she can go straight up the sides of walls, *pass through* walls, ride upside down on the overheads, cross moving water, jump ditches, barricades, urban chasms one rooftop to the next, office-building corridors to native-quarter alleyways quicker than a wink.

Into a tunnel—colder all of a sudden, blasted at by their own echoing, down into a city beneath the city, grown over the years according to the demands of history, gunpowder logistics, mineral springs everywhere, saline, radioactive, violently boiling, laminar as sleep, bringing in coachloads of well-off Europeans rolling on a yearly cycle spa to spa along routes as closely mapped and annotated as pilgrimages.

Terike's first time beneath the city as a dispatch biker, though she tried not to admit it to herself, was one of those unreal entrances that actors recall making now and then. "It looked like just another tunnel" has been a comic tagline down here for years. She didn't join so much as blend, unaware at the time of any formalities, into the motor-dispatch community with its traditions of best practice, honor, coolness under fire, a mission to connect anywhere in space-time, any set of points, anything they had to do, obstacles no obstacle, ignoring cozy indoor axes, Biedermeyer xyz plus time dutifully ticking away over in some corner, zooming around through the tunnels under Budapest. Crossing back and forth under the river, keeping to their own dedicated routes, including a long-term easement through Budafok, twenty-five miles of wine cellar tunneled through limestone, requiring special exhaust work to cause as little noise as possible so the vintages might lie undisturbed . . . a silent patch in the undercity clamoring with youthfulness, as messengers in dusters, helmets, and goggles pull out of the traffic to gather briefly for quick tunnelside smoke breaks and, finding themselves enticed by surfaces whose acoustics promise to be kind to those who can't sing but must anyway, gathering for eight or sixteen bars or so, echoing up branch tunnels, exit ramps, up to the street, which now seems like daytime to a resident of the night.

They head north along the river. "Where we going?"

"Újpest. Pickup and delivery. Only be a couple of minutes."

They arrive at a factory gate at quitting time. "What's this?"

"Tungsram. We're going around back." Hundreds of women, on foot and bicycles. "Some girl-heavy workforce here."

"Assembling radio valves is delicate work. Needs a light touch. Breakage rate's too high, sorry boys, young ladies only. I hope you're not as clumsy as you look. Here we are."

They pull up by a loading dock where she's handed a wooden crate, weighing hardly anything at all.

"Try not to break anything."

"What's in here, light bulbs?"

"Vacuum tubes. Experimental, specially designed for the theremin."

"The . . ."

"It's a musical instrument."

Dimly, "Electrical gizmo, comes on the radio now and then. Mostly when there's something weird happening."

"As you're about to see."

Day shifts expire into the evening, city mobility all crossing paths, heading into town for a good time, hauling back out to homes in the outer districts, making the last pickups and deliveries of the day.

Club Hypotenuse is cheerfully neon-lit, so far having kept a dignified distance from the slobbering embrace of urban redevelopment, which has already destroyed Tabán, formerly a Serbian neighborhood on the Buda side, once known as the Montmartre of Budapest.

Around back, screeching into the tradespeople's porte cochere, on into a dedicated elevator, which takes them zooming up to a rooftop terrace, a slowly rotating dance floor, an orchestra with not just one soloist on theremin but a half dozen, each expensively gowned tomato with more or less identical platinum bobs, waving their hands at these units and pulling music out of some deep invisibility, swooping one note to the next, hitting each one with pitch as perfect, Terike assures him, as the instrument's reigning queen, Clara Rockmore. The joint effect of these six virtuoso cuties all going at once in close harmony is strangely symphonic.

"You're just in time," Terike's friend Zsófi greets them, "we're running through these tubes like nose tissues at a Garbo movie."

"Sealex machines at Tungsram aren't quite up to speed yet, they're cranking these out as fast as they can by hand."

They find a table in a corner. "Here," taking the cigarette that was in her mouth and putting it into Hicks's.

"What's this, it ain't tobacco."

"Known here as fű. Where'd you say you were from again?"

"We have this in Milwaukee, don't smell exactly the same, is all."

TERIKE GREW UP in a bourgeois zone if not often enchanted at least comfortable, no idea of what it was costing to maintain till it all came to pieces at the onset of the Béla Kun government, which in less than five months caused incalculable damage in Hungary, families driven into ruin when not stood against walls and shot, wars on two or three fronts with armies of brand-new nations stooging for the Entente that created them, not to mention Miklos Horthy down in Szeged with his own government of bloodthirsty vigilantes, eagerly on the lookout for the vacuum that would suck him into power . . .

Still a girl in those days, easily frightened, not yet political, watching her family slide closer to the social abyss as the days passed . . . till Horthy came marching into town, churches celebrating Te Deum masses, much loose talk of "deliverance" . . . soon enough understanding that this self-styled "Regency" was only to be the next form of terror, White Terror replacing Red, out to settle its own scores.

For years she thought she'd been named after the Empress Maria Theresa. When she was fifteen, not the best time to be finding out, her mother admitted that it was really after Ste. Thérèse de Lisieux, known as "the Little Flower."

"You wanted me to be a good girl."

"And it's what you've grown up to be."

"Mama, we both know better, all the candles you must've lit, see if somebody won't give you a refund."

Now here comes this oversize American gangster . . . Is there time to steer around and keep going? Should she stop and take a look?

"I can corrupt you, you know."

"Where I come from, that's where corruption got invented, so you might want to save yourself the trouble."

"Oh. Well, maybe you could corrupt me, then."

"Sure. Might have to clear it first with the Home Office back in Chicago. Meantime here's 'Embraceable You,' if you're interested."

She borrows a pair of shoes from Zsófi and off they go. The rhythm situation in here is more up-to-date than expected, owing to the bass contratheremin that's keeping the beat. After a few more numbers Terike's off in the ladies' lounge and Hicks has almost drifted into one of those hoofer trances when a voice from somewhere, likely the bar, pipes up in English—

"Hi, I'm Judge Crater, any phone calls for me?"

Hicks has a doubtful squint at this energetic arrival, "Slide" Gearheart, freelance foreign correspondent, loud, hat slightly off-angle, old enough to know better but still playing eager juvenile and wised-up newshound. "Evenin', kiddies, who's got the smokes?" Chiseling cigarettes two at a time ("OPs, my favorite brand"), one to hang off his lip, another to stash behind his ear. "I try never to kid a kidder," he addresses Hicks, "so here it is, straight up—" with a jay facial expression it's taken him years to perfect.

"Uh, huh, Slide, I'm just about scrapin through on per diem down in the coffee-and bracket, which ain't even always waiting for me at the pay window, OK, so if any of this is gonna cost me money—"

"Know the story, got some expenses myself, couple of bad habits, tell you what, meet me here," handing over a small business card, "tomorrow, if you can use any of it, pay me what it's worth to you, we can work out an installment schedule." Hicks glances at the address and when he looks back up Slide isn't there, which from experience with quick-fade artists leads Hicks to believe maybe he should follow this up after all.

Terike returns, back in motorcycle boots, and that seems to be about it for the evening.

SLIDE IS OFTEN heard whistling "The Best Things in Life Are Free." "Which," he likes to remind people, "means the *next* to best things in life are cheap," usually when introducing a sales pitch of some kind.

"The way I hear it is, is you're looking for a certain cheez heiress, who is informally attached to a certain swing band, correct?"

"That's what the ticket says, but I keep hitting detour signs."

"Hate to be the one you heard this from first, but . . ." Seems at some point the Klezmopolitans have broken up. Daphne and Hop's whereabouts are suddenly unknown, changing the ticket from a common or everyday skip to a skip into the current disarray of Central Europe, a terrain nearly 100 percent unreadable. "Swell dame and all, but if you find her don't mention me, she considers me for some reason gutter press at its worst." Slide catches this sort of thing daily, another bum's rush and so what, "My job, after all, and more educational than it looks," shaking a new set of wrinkles out of his suit, ambling off down corridor or alleyway, bleakly chuckling. "Hey, it's Hungary, insult is poetry here, where else would they tell you to go climb onto Death's penis?"

"Whoo. Really?"

"Try it sometime out in the street, *Menj a halál faszára.*"

"Yeah but . . . wait, now, you're saying Death has a, a penis?"

"Who knew, huh? Don't worry, it's only for minor annoyances, on the full spectrum of Hungarian insult it's just an everyday howdy-do."

"Not an easy language to get a handle on."

"Listen to me, this population, nobody from anywhere else is ever going to fade into it, the best we can hope for is maybe they'll think we're German. Hundreds of dialects out here, if you even look like you speak any of them somebody will figure you for a spy and take steps, so best stick to English and there's a chance they'll take you for an idiot and leave you alone. It might help if you could also pretend now and then to hear voices they don't. Idiots get respect out here, they're believed to be in touch with invisible forces."

To be honest Hicks would much rather be back on a westbound liner, steaming express, back to league bowling nights, Friday fish fries, cheering on those Badgers again . . .

"Don't get ahead of yourself, Slugger, this is just the first stage, you're not even homesick yet."

"OK, maybe this ticket is takin longer than it should, but that don't mean—"

"Yeah? How about forever? That doesn't strike you as a possibility?"

"You mean forever like 'always'?"

"Well, till you screw up, anyway, and somebody decides to bump you off."

If Hicks is looking for sympathy better he should seek it elsewhere. "This ear is not for bending, only for getting thrown out on."

Meantime Slide keeps up on all the latest inside dope, from trivial to world-historic. After years spent around copydesks and journalist hangouts, he's learned to tell when something's being kept back so readers don't get too nervous. "The smart money is on war, sometime in the next ten years."

"Thanks for the tip, where can I put down a bet?"

"No place that won't be wiped out in the first day of fighting."

25

Things pick up a day or two later when Slide reports that Daphne has been sighted at the Tropikus nightclub, in Nagymező utca, the Broadway of Budapest.

Night business here is going full tilt, sedans, roadsters, and motorcycles prowling the overlit bustle, pedestrians dodging in and out of the traffic, maybe no Dearborn and Randolph but bright enough.

Tropikus, an all-night dance-cabaret on a nautical theme in the metropolis of a landlocked artifact of Trianon, whatever it might answer to emotionally, must've looked to owners Imi and Jóska like a surefire ticket, especially with commercial real estate so cheap at the moment. Looking down the street and seeing how well the Arizona and the Moulin Rouge were doing, it seemed reasonable to ask, Why shouldn't there be room for one more joint to catch the overflow?

Waitresses in abbreviated sailor-girl getups back and forth with Unicum boilermakers and fruit-heavy house specials in coconut and conch shells, ceramic mermaids with purple Cellophane drinking straws emerging from the tops of their heads, smoke hanging like tropical weather. As Imi works the tables, making with the repartee, Jóska attends to the cash drawers, the liquor supply, the security, the girls.

The band, camouflaged in the scenery here, itching to go Latin all evening, impatient little raps and flourishes among the percussion and brass, apparently misplaced beats in the waltzes and foxtrots till at last helplessly collapsing into a Latin American fanfare, conga drums suddenly apporting in hot from the tropics along with claves, güiros, timbales, and cowbells, and sure enough here's Daphne Airmont, same lengthy red flow of hair Hicks remembers, backless evening dress, arm-length gloves, long strides, apparently solo tonight, straight to the bandstand where she's ushered to a microphone, takes off one glove, scratches the mike with a fingernail, puts the glove back on, and with a practiced swing-vocalist bounce right in on the beat—

    Yes . . . here . . . comes . . .
                             that . . .

Strange-ly trop-i-cal rhyth-m!
Yes! Strangely, hauntingly so—no
Mat-ter how, gring-go, you
Might-think-you are, some-
-thin lights up 'n' goes "Bing-go!"
and you're suddenly far . . . far
                       away, at some
un-expec-ted fi-esta, just as
syn-copated-as sin—one
Min-ute you're Ang-glo, next
Min-ute-you're not,
The stars seem to hang low,
The or-chestra's hot—
Tell ya what—
               take

[bridge]

a-break from Prohi-
-bi-tion, wave
hasta la vista to the Feds—
one li'l te-
-qui-la inter-
-mis-sion,
Pretty soon you're Lupe Velez! like
the fella sez, it's a pleas-
                      -ure steppin

Right, a-long, with-that rhyth-m—that
Pan-Ame-ri-can jive, dive-
-in into the deep end, lettin 'em
know, you're, alive . . .
down where fate is philanthropical . . .
mis-apprehensions mic-ro, scop-ical . . .
not-to mention all that tropical,
strange-ly trop-i-cal, rhyth-m!

The room by now lit up in some unearthly color process, timed in a faraway film lab so as to present an outward and visible sign of some strange underacknowledged link between Hungary and tropical Brazil, energetic dancers in vivid flashes of parrot colors and fanciful hats gliding elaborately by, camera angles growing dutched and dizzy, as it all goes sweeping down a long depth of focus away toward, and perhaps at last funneling into, an elaborate ladies' lounge or toilet, and who knows what further vistas of streamlined modernity . . .

Slide was tipped off to Daphne's whereabouts by Pancho Caramba, one of the percussionists, a bandmate of Hop Wingdale's from the old Klezmopolitans. Hicks has to make his way through a crowd of smitten debutantes just to pass him a quick word of thanks, Pancho apparently enjoying some success not only with his extravagant solos but also working the ladies' man angle in between. "Ironically it was never me but Pancho Caramba's many fans who brought him into being, Casanova with a drum kit, all-round swoon material. 'Course it helps to be crazy. I go into this kind of trance, when it's over they all come rushing up to tell me all about it. But very little of it's on purpose, 'cause in public basically I'm shy."

"Except when he cuts loose on the cymbals," Daphne materializing from someplace, "then it's 'bashful.' Saludos, Pancho, thanks for not stepping on my number."

"Ever tried that I'd be counting my toes. You two already met, I think."

"Been carrying around this daydream about it happening again sometime," Daphne trying not to sound like she's complaining, "you know the one."

Hicks can guess. "Basic rule of the business ain't it, Miss Airmont, one person's big romance is another's time and a half for overtime."

"You can say Daphne, that worked OK before." Not one of these after-dark sophisticates partial to cigarette holders, she counts on lipstick alone to keep the gasper attached to her lower lip, whether dancing, chatting, sipping cocktails, even eating sometimes. Admirers grow fascinated as to when and where butt and ashes, often still glowing, will drop.

"Yes," one eye in a squint for the smoke, "stylish as hell, and you'd better know I also chew gum. Something you'll have to deal with if this bittersweet reprise is going anyplace."

"This what? Miss Airmont, Daphne, come on, it must be years by now, one high-speed boat ride, once, that's the complete rap sheet."

"Certainly one way to look at it."

"Since then, only been following your career from a distance, Chicago papers, gossip mags, and so forth—"

"Another way to look at it, Snooks," along with an emphatic flare of cigarette smoke out her nose, "you breezed in at just the right moment and kept me away from that North Shore Zombie Two-Step, otherwise I'd still be inside and lost. You are a key factor in my history, like it or not."

"Boating conditions," he protests, "at the time, see, I was only thinking about making it back in again without runnin out of gas."

"While what I was thinking was, was if they *had* pulled me back into Winnetka Shores it would've been the last time, that's how desperate it was for me. So . . ."

"Daphne, if you're gonna start in again with that Chippewa hoodoo . . ."

By which point they're dancing, having glided into it from some everyday moment, like reaching across him for a cigarette . . . after no more than four bars of which he can feel her begin to relax, and unless Hicks wants to start deliberately stepping on her feet or tripping over his own, he's stuck once again with being Oversize Fred Astaire here.

By the time the band takes a break she has a peculiar look in her eye. Speculative.

"What?"

"You're not what you seem."

"Maybe it's you makin me look good."

"Ever dance professionally?"

"Back in Chicago, ballroom act, didn't work out."

"Personal issues, artistic differences?"

"Gang war."

"That thing where it looked like you were walking forward but you're really sort of gliding backwards?"

"Yeah, Cab Calloway showed me the basics one night at a joint up on Walnut Street. Calls it The Buzz."

After thinking a while, "See," she lets him know, "there's the other fella."

"Hop Wingdale."

"The only one for me, case you're wondering."

"Hmm, and would that ol' Hop happen to be around tonight, it'd sure be nice to meet him sometime—"

"Hoping for a twofer, were you. Sorry, flatfoot, I don't know where he is, and frankly it's beginning to worry me."

A familiar mental prowl car now begins to drive back and forth across Hicks's brain, gonging high-low-high-low, signaling trouble for somebody, which Hicks would prefer to be anybody but him.

"Don't know what they told you about me and Hop except these days it's not running off with, but more like running after. Since the morning I woke up to find the Klezmopolitans dissolved into solo acts and once again life's vaudeville hook emerging from the wings and latching around Hop's neck, and off he goes staggering to boos and whistles, wondering what he did wrong this time . . ."

No, not exactly the way it happened. Or not without what she should have recognized as the tip-off one early evening at the Hotel Grand Pignouf in Paris, where all up and down the corridors transoms are open, a dozen invisible plumes from illicit cigarettes, out-of-town cooking, perfume being overapplied as if in romantic spasms, each a different nasal melodrama.

The Klezmopolitans, reformatted by electric xylorimba virtuoso Curly Capstock from his original Back Alley Rhythm Cats into a progressive swing band, continually bringing in chords glamorized with up-to-date accidentals, lines with chromatic licks, Latin percussion, a less inhibited or as some might put it screamingly insane brass section where the Harmon mute despite being the hep dance-band introduction of the moment goes generally underemployed, an openness to non-Western scales especially in the solos of reedmen, each as crazy as any trumpet player in the band, since Curly only hires crazy to begin with . . .

"They want *freilach*, that's what we give 'em. They want hot Latin rumbas, that's what they'll get. The customers can have whatever they want. Any comments?"

"Do we have to smile, like in the movies?"

"Depends. Sometimes you'll want to go more for that earnest hardworking style, which you'll have to tell me what it looks like, I don't see much of it around here."

The last thing resembling a pep talk till the dismal day Curly announces, "Could still be some loose change to be made here and there, though we'd be running it close. If we liquidate now, money's there in the bank in Zurich, but don't wait too long, 'cause it won't be there forever and neither will you."

Meanwhile as the prospects for anything like reliable work go fading, "I've been trying to keep my nerve," Daphne admits, "but it's too dangerous over here anymore, I know that going back to the U.S.A. will only be buying time, that sooner or later no place will be safe. We need to relocate before it's all Storm Trooper chorales and three-note harmony. You're thinking about it, so am I. When can we leave?"

"Of course there's still work," Hop a little grumpy, "house orchestras at some of the hotels, bands pretending to be Lud Gluskin on tour, but if you want, sure we can make our way to Zurich, cash in my shares if they're still there . . ."

"Cheap talk, Hop, and it won't fix anything about you and me—you'd rather keep playing till the sun comes up, alone with your clarinet, unless it's some little Swing Fräulein, which I could understand, maybe even pick up a few fashion tips in the course of, but not this, this is a magic act, you're disappearing from me, into all the trick lighting, and the big band glare and shine. 'One of these days' might've already come and gone, for all I know, you might be gone anyway."

"Nothing you can't get used to, is it."

"Ah, there it is once again, like a monster in the Tunnel of Love—Bruno, evil Bruno, family crimes, bad blood, never good enough for the biblical prophet here."

"Who can assure you that the ways of God are not for us to even puzzle over. Bruno in your life is a mixed blessing which is only likely to get more so."

"You keep saying. But then remember, he isn't in my life, hasn't been for a good while."

"Sit back and let me bring you the evening news. Awkwardly enough, it turns out more of your life than you think is being run on the Q.T. by none other. Look at the things that don't keep happening—Bruno doesn't make any surprise visits, doesn't die or go bankrupt, you watch the market reports for signs of cheese being hoarded, sold off, yes, and not only the Board of Trade and other cheese trading floors but also grazing conditions in pasturelands so far away the cows go oom for all we know, the movements of refrigerated trains and fleets, dairy operations local to nationwide, herd dynamics, any quivering li'l deviation from normal that could turn out to be Bruno's invisible hand . . ."

And so they have hurtled on into that warm patch somewhere between heartburn and mittelschmerz at the immensity of everything they don't want to happen to them, together or separate. She wants to dissolve into some "Oh, please, Hop . . ." but instead out comes, "I could always get it changed into small bills and rent an airplane and just fly around pretending I'm the weather, dumping it on people, till I get my net worth down to a number you're comfortable with, how'd that be?"

"Gosh, honey, you'd really do that? For me?"

"No."

A patch of silence, short and also long enough.

"There's a train for Le Havre I can be on before you get back from work." She almost said "before you get home."

No more than a dotted whole rest this time.

"Well, Daphne. See you around the circuit."

"You bet, Hop." Yes, it's the Norma Shearer turn she's always being accused of, "Oh how I'll miss you," plus "Whew, out the door at last!" Everybody's got her number, all right, and so what?

26

For a while Daphne, flown into a dither, was chasing all over the map, trying to be there waiting wherever the puck might be on its way to but not always guessing right, along with wires going astray, trains running late, street-fighting and barricades to detour around and so forth, sleeping and eating when she can, usually within earshot of railway stations, steered along by tattered notices stuck onto public surfaces, helpful Swing Kids, Eukodal addicts with their own notions about the sequence and speed of passing events, Daphne continuing to run a train and a half, a day or a night or a street address behind, till eventually the charm wore off and she wound down to this pause in Budapest, where she figures to take a rest and wait to see if the band or any of its unknown fragments might find their way to her.

". . . but perhaps I'm telling you more than I should . . ."

"I'm interested, really."

Hicks could point out that keeping still and listening to a story isn't always the same thing as falling for it, but sees no reason to start an argument, being no stranger to the time-honored routine men have had to sit through since the world has been the world, listening to desirable women banging on about their love-life history in hopes however remote of some payoff in the cheerfully jangling currency of present-tense whoopee.

Talk about meeting cute. You'd think she'd have known better by then. It was in Chicago a few years back, still deep in her teen playgirl phase, Hop remembers some block-long Chicago speak while Daphne remembers someplace more intimate . . . getting set to move along, when shots ring out. A cocktail she has been looking forward to making the acquaintance of goes flying one direction, and the person bringing it another, ending up under the nearest table.

Hop touching his hat brim, "That may've been meant for me, Miss, awful sorry."

"Well, you should be. You owe me a double Aviation . . . and for drycleaning this dress," realizing, in one of those thunderclaps that can roll in sometimes and last for more than the average length of a jukebox number, that this is the goods, the one she's been looking for forever.

What am I thinking? she then proceeds to spend a good deal of time asking herself. Forever? Who am I kidding? Long before taking her first gowned step into the Grand Ballroom at the Pfister Hotel, she's been aware of men hanging around who thought of themselves as prime domestic material, showing up with diamond charm bracelets, wristwatches, cigarette cases, often overpriced, always annoying. None until Hop had ever considered a serenade.

Daphne could just sit and listen to Hop on that licorice stick all day and night, especially classical stuff like the solo from Rachmaninoff's Symphony No. 2, swinging it with a respectful jazz-band approach. Gets her every time. "I mean he's not that bad on 'Embraceable You,' and 'Siboney' can always get my ticker to doing the rumba, but when he starts in on that Rachmaninoff, a girl's no longer legally responsible."

"For . . . ?"

"Anything."

After listening politely to this sort of thing for as long as he figures he has to, "Truth is," Hicks confesses, "as I move into mid-career and begin to specialize, I've been trying not to work any more of these romantic scenarios than I have to."

"Maybe you just don't like women much. Afraid of us or something."

"Who isn't? Even women are afraid of women. Scientific fact, so I hear."

"Nothing to get defensive about, is it." Along with a look implying "You big gorilla."

"You'll want to keep watching my left, sometimes I let it drop."

Taking a long backbeat, "You don't think much of us."

"Which 'us' would that be again?"

"Whoever sent you over here after me."

"All being handled out of a law office up on North Wabash—your mother who misses you, family, relatives, all chipping in on the fee and let's not forget that Rodney, your, which he keeps reminding everybody about, fiancé?"

At the mention of whom she maybe doesn't wince but does blink expressively once or twice. "Well. It's not like *he's* hopping the next liner over here, is it. No, instead Li'l Million-and-a-Half hires a goon to come and do it for him. Can't trust men? Jury's still out, a girl lives in hope—but damn sure there's not one woman I'd ever trust for as long as it takes to blink a set of fake eyelashes, and especially not Mrs. Vivacia Airmont, my own mother." A pause, as if for thought. "Of course she's been busy with pals at the State Department, making a nuisance of herself, desperate to have me back, maternal as it gets, gosh yes, can't wait, deported back to the mother country, how humiliating is that?"

"About as much as being played for a sucker once again, after all these promises of advance money and per diem hard to pass up, now it's lookin like the only way I'll ever see a payday out of this ticket is if I can get you back Stateside."

"How inconvenient for you, to come all this way for so much less than nothing, and in the middle of a world Depression too," shaking her head slowly. "You seriously believed everything they told you? For a beat-up old-timer you're pretty naive."

"And you're way more fly than the junior party regular the papers still like to write you up as, too young to know any better, uh huh, instead here's Greta Garbo, all gussied up and out on the prowl and looking for trouble."

"And thinking to herself, Oh jumping catfish, once isn't enough, here comes another rescue job, big sentimental sap, lumbering on in, all reflexes, never asking if anybody even wants to be rescued."

"Except for right now, o' course."

"Oh, you've got a nerve."

"Fact it looks like I come rollin into town just in time, ain't it."

"And me wondering when some hired bloodhound will show up, never dreaming it'd be you— Ahh! how down in the world I've sunk—this is all

I'm worth anymore, look what they're sending over here to *put the snatch* on me, shanghai me back in a drugged stupor—"

"Don't know that I'd put it that way," Hicks trying to keep hold of his amiability, "for one thing, no snatch job was ever mentioned in the ticket, maybe something about tactfully passing along an offer to reconcile with folks who care enough about you to be paying Unamalgamated's 'Top Insider' rate to see you back with them safe and sound, what's wrong with that?"

"All just one more pickup and delivery for you, isn't it, well, go on ahead, tough guy, what're you waiting for? Slap on those cuffs and bring me on back to the U.S.A."

"OK, maybe not 'bring,' bring is how *they* put it, what they thought they were hiring me for. Which always turns out to be a mug who won't mind getting beat up."

"Maybe you're one of those Krafft-Ebing cases who enjoys it."

"Just another kind of hard labor's all, part of the paycheck, still better than diggin ditches. Where it gets real uncomfortable is the time you lose when somethin gets fractured. Putting in for the insurance. Cheapskate adjusters always trying to blame it on you. 'What were you doing in that neighborhood, that time of night?' all that malarkey."

"Tough guy. Cement block all the way through. And still can't keep yourself away from any woman even looks like she's in trouble."

"What other kind of dame is there?"

"Hope you're listening, here, Repossess Man, 'cause nothing's going to change. I won't go back to the States without Hop."

"Whereabouts," Hicks giving her his quit-fooling squint, "unknown right now. Swell. Does this— I hope this doesn't mean you want to hire me, locate him for you, nothing like 'at 'cause see, that'd have to be written up as a whole new ticket? New case number, forms to fill out?"

As the Gumshoe's Manual advises, always be watching for the next ticket to be sprung on you with no advance word, no front money, plus that all but certain promise of uncompensated overtime. Someday you may be lucky enough to avoid it, but for now get used to making out the forms in your head anyway.

"Hadn't occurred to me till you brought it up, but it's beginning to sound like an idea. Maybe you're brighter than you look."

"And all I'll have to do, let's see, is track down Hop for you, and you'll pack right on up and head for home?"

"The minute I see his smiling face."

How many times has he sworn the same New Year's resolution, nights posted outside somebody else's love nest, shivering in freezing rain or Lake-effect snowfall, chances for personal whoopee remote at best—No More Matrimonials! Ever!

"I need a ticket OK'd by the Home Office, if I step into this without one it'll have to be for free and out of my own pocket, which maybe I already mentioned is empty. Not to mention overtime, carfare, travel and entertainment, extra ammo, each with its own set of forms to be filled out sooner or later, at length and often in triplicate."

"Suppose I pick up the tab and we do it all in cash?"

"Wouldn't happen to have a typewriter around?"

"I used to always bring one along in a hatbox, I think this time I left it back in M'waukee, but don't worry, just a detail. Does this mean that you *might* help me find Hop and get him out of any trouble he may've gotten himself into? Oh, how can I ever . . ."

Prolonged exhalation. "Let's go over the rates. Just for the heck of it, understand."

"Meantime," after a while, riveting him with one of those sudden gazes broads like to throw around, "fair warning—I might still have to run away from you anyway, maybe even go after Hop on my own. And would you be put to some trouble then, shamus, to get me back, 'cause nowadays I'm a wised-up ol' fugitive, see, who knows how to get invisible in a hurry." Twirling elegantly nail-bitten fingers, "Like Champagne bubbles into the night. As the hepcats say, gone. The Absentee Hall of Fame? Midtown Manhattan someplace? Well, last year they gave me the Judge Crater Award. They call it the Joey? Little pedestal with nothing on it?"

"OK, but what if after what's sure to be a lot of work I find ol' Hop is just out doing the horizontal Peabody all this time with somebody cute and don't want to be interrupted?"

"My, you're sure dwelling down there in the mudflats these days ain't you, Sport."

"Must be why the pay's so good."

"It had better be, because now there's also Hop you need to worry about. Plus he might also leap to conclusions, and then you'd be up a creek or two."

"Wait, let me write some of this down."

"You don't approve, I can tell."

"I think it's the kind of stuff that killed vaudeville, but I'm a professional hey, people care about who they care about, if they didn't I'd have to be lookin for another line of work."

"Hmm. Tell me what you think," turning into a sudden three-quarter profile. "People say I look like Norma Shearer."

"Well maybe in the society pages, right after you've kissed off one more of them career lounge lizards, you get almost that same look on your face— ain't it grand the sacrifice I'm making, and at the same time, whoo, what a relief."

"You've been . . . keeping a scrapbook or something, how charming. That's really how I come across?"

"Heck, Toots, I don't even know *if* you do."

"Talk about suave. How's that one work back in Wauwatosa?"

"Have I been mashing on you? No wonder I'm such a hit with the dames, out there pitching woo, half the time I don't even know it. "

"I wouldn't exactly call it that, but . . ." shifting her gaze downward for a beat and a half, then back to his face again.

"Occupational handicap, ignore it."

"Planning to, thanks."

"I mean if you want suave, I can be plenty suave, if I have to."

"Of course with me you don't have to."

"Daphne, no offense, but now and then you strike me as . . . a little insecure despite in real life being blessed in all directions as few of your type of dame ever are? Is?"

"Why, how sweet. A girl could get confused."

"About what?"

"Your intentions." They both know that runaway fiancées and their duty-bound pursuers are expected to fall in love—stage, screen, and radio are full of it. Hicks angles his head, hoping his eyeballs are lubricated enough to flash highlights of warning, in case she plans on rolling any further up that particular stretch of scenic highway, offers her a smoke from his last pack of duty-free Spuds from the *Stupendica*, which she tucks into a crease of her gown and switches for one of her own Melachrino cork tips, bending in toward him carefully, an intimate of flame at many levels from candles to arc lamps . . . knowing how different sorts of briquet light will work with a given makeup job, how long to remain lit up before ignition and withdrawal, how deep to inhale, so forth. Flashing him another look, and this time, what a look. Remarking in a reasonable tone, "Whoever's alley this may or may not be up, don't be expecting any easy spares."

"Come on," taking her by a hand not holding a cigarette, which is parked instead on her lower lip. A murmur to the bandleader, "You gents know 'Cigana de Catumbi'?"

"Gotcha," with one of those complicit grins.

Ordinarily it's not a good idea to dance the Maxixe with somebody till you really know them well—not that the steps are that tricky, but since you do have to look good, it helps to feel as sincere as you want it to look, keeping always pressed close, with a lot of swaying, till it becomes hard, so to speak, to pretend your intentions are that nonsexual for very long, as it were.

"You must, you know." Daphne lamplit in one of the two or three possible varieties of surefire fatal . . . the line of her neck . . . the corners of her eyes . . . "You must get clear of this. It isn't for you."

She's been watching him with that how-much-can-I-trust-this-one look he knows all too well. ". . . once, in one of these mental fix-it shops I kept getting sent to, up on the office wall was a motto of Carl Jung—*Vocatus atque non vocatus deus aderit*. I said what's this my Latin's a little rusty, he sez that's called or not called, the god will come."

"And . . . back then when you were out in the woods—how'd that work, you called, you didn't call—what happened?"

"Once, twice, something showed up, don't know about any god, but," shrug, breaking off eye contact. "Something."

"Your old pals from the rez think it's spoze to be a critter."

Takes a deep pull at the Egyptian gasper and thinks about that. "When you first saw me did you ever wonder—is she really crazy after all, maybe they actually have every right to keep her inside their laughing academy?"

"You were on the run, that was enough."

"One more North Shore subdeb who needed to be rescued from something, you figured."

"I did?"

"What I do know," alluringly shrugs the Cheez Princess, "is you've let yourself in for plenty. When the Ojibwe tell you somebody's on your duty list forever—"

"A-a-ack! Reminding you again, Tootsie Roll, how this ain't my ticket, no matter how many of these Chippewa curveballs you keep throwin me."

"And of course everybody in M'waukee knew all about the speedboat."

"Not from me."

"No," Daphne nodding, "from me actually, and so what."

"So I had to put up with Ole Evinrude remarks, job offers from undercover G-men for midnight hooch runs and booby-hatch crash-outs. Had me starting to feel like Fairbanks Junior or something—you discombobulated my workday as much as I did yours, but am I insisting on some contract clause? Heck no, never asked for no fugitive heiress ticket, not my specialty and did I also mention— where you going?"

"If I wanted a fifteen-minute sob story, I'd have the radio on, wouldn't I."

HICKS MAY HAVE strolled by Daphne's hotel once or twice but hasn't till now set foot inside, being reminded of places he tends to get thrown out of or at best told to move along from. Tonight however, seems Daphne has been busy sweet-talking the management. "What a pleasure to meet you at last, Mr. McTaggart. Madame expects you, please follow me." Delivered with a face just managing to avoid the well-known bellboy smirk.

The second he clears the doorsill, before the door has even latched behind him, Hicks understands that Daphne has timed this whole routine so it'll look like he's catching her by surprise. "Oh—I must be early, hey."

"Didn't want you to miss the aldehyde fractions." She's sporting one of these black yet see-through negligee getups, while with some *powered atomizer*, valves and gauges all over it, she now triggers into the room an enormous cloud of scent, slips off the fancy kimono and steps, pale as a crescent moon, this freckle-dusted beauty, into the patch of fragrance that hangs in the air, strangely coherent, like it's waiting there for her. "Brand-new, House of Tuvaché, Jungle Gardenia. Come on in, it isn't riot gas."

"Try to tend to business smelling like this all through next week? thanks, Toots, I don't need the attention. Jungle what?"

"Too late, you're in trouble now, way past the five-second limit in fact, nothing can resist it, not even the shine on that cheap suit—"

"Off the rack, maybe," Hicks protests, nevertheless toppling on in, "but it probably cost— hey, careful with that, what do you think you're doing—"

"You know what I'm doing."

"Yeah, but do I know what I'm doing."

For a second he thinks he can see past the nightclub eyes, the scarlet lipstick, back to the nervous kid climbing off that rumrunner's special like an explorer facing into who knew how much unmapped land, Nicolet or one of them, stepping ashore once upon a time thinking it's only a short day-sail from Green Bay to China, its deep splendor, its mystery . . .

And then back comes the postdated debutante on the run, to reclaim this present hour of shenanigans, hammering away in clouds of jungle perfume and cigarette smoke . . .

"Forget what they sent you for . . . be the lost and found just for me . . ."

Which you'd think would be an improvement on all the "You big ape" types of remark he's gotten used to, not that sometimes it isn't agreeable to be taken for a big ape, especially one with what's known as a One-Track Mind, many's the dame who enjoys that and why shouldn't she?

Later, no closer to being back out of unfamiliar territory, sentimentally swaying to music on the Victrola. "Swell that we finally got around to this."

"That night on the speedboat? you know you could've made me do anything."

"And it ain't till now that I find out, swell, here just let me flag down a—oh . . . oh, Time Machine? uh huh? over here?"

A number of pauses to flip the record over, or sometimes forget to.

"Yes and while we're on the subject, you're sure, Daphne, now, about your—about, um, that Hop Wingdale? who could come strolling in here any minute—you're sure he don't mind that we . . ."

"Not that it's any of your business, but we have a free and forgiving arrangement, yes many's the time I've come upon him in the sweaty clutches of some Swing Girl barely into her teens, Louise Brooks hairdo, nighttime makeup in the daylight hours and all, ah but then why *brewed*, as Schlitz said to Pabst, as long as Hop and I each do get to have our own adventures you see. Are you waiting for details? I hope not."

"Had my mouth open again, didn't I."

"Hop is dear to me," she advises, "beyond anything a kicked-around peeper such as yourself may be able to grasp, and frankly I don't mind admitting as an off-and-on praying person that I'm praying for his safety right now. Which is already more than you need to know."

"Fair enough except for maybe one or two details, like, oh would he be packing a heater of any kind, and how ready would he be to, you know . . ."

"This isn't Chicago."

Pretending to look the place over, "By golly you're right, it isn't, but—"

"Though now that I recall . . . of course, you haven't really seen him with the steam coming out his ears, yes, Hop can become quite excitable indeed, most ammo is like birdshot to him, bounces right off. Anyone wants to keep us apart, short of fifty-caliber, forget it."

"Faithful?"

"Maybe not 'unto death,' as Herbert Gustave Schmalz might put it, but at least unto a high level of inconvenience for somebody. Just so you know—if it will get Hop back to me safe and sound, OK? there's no depths I wouldn't go to, even degrading myself rolling around with a lowlife such as you."

"Could've just said you love the guy, I would've bought that."

"But this way you also got to have your ashes hauled."

"Now that you bring it up—"

"Looks like I have, but no."

"Aw?"

"Because unless I lost count that would make it twice, Cupcake. Very different from once, or did they forget to teach you that back at hard-boiled dick academy?"

"Ah . . . Just some one-nighter in a motorboat, yep it figures, why don't I ever tumble sooner."

Hicks isn't about to admit it, but the thought crosses his mind—stops halfway, looks back over its shoulder and winks actually—wouldn't it be a nice turnaround to bring some couple back together again, put the matrimony back in "matrimonial" for a change, instead of divorce lawyers into speedsters and limousines.

27

After a string of peculiar one-night engagements, girl vocal trios with megaphones, French horns in the brass section, white tenors putting on jive hepcat voices, reedmen who move their instruments around in the air all together, a bandleader with an electric violin whose bow he uses for a baton and whose long power cord he keeps tripping over, adding a thrill element of self-electrocution, Hop Wingdale gets as far as Geneva, where his booking agent is doing business out of a low-rent office in brisk walking or when necessary running distance of the train station, under the name of Nigel Trevelyan and behind a facial expression, carefully worked on for years, as dodgy as his name. "Half my client list, over here it's standard practice. Jewish musicians prefer these English handles for some reason."

"Well, you sure outdid yourself this time," Hop collapsing onto a beat-up divan. "Must be a Depression on or something. Dismal, desperate . . . Toilets I don't mind, Nigel. Just don't ever book me into any of these Nazi joints popping up all over, them I won't work in."

"What, you're Jewish or something?" A phrase going around lately. "Hop, wake up for a minute, how do you know you haven't been taking Nazi money all along?"

"Because Nigel Trevelyan, my agent and incorruptible standard of truth, keeps reassuring me it's all kosher."

"Here's something at least pareve, next week through the end of the summer, motorcycle gig, the Trans-Trianon 2000 Tour of Hungary Unredeemed, dance band including vocalist, transportation by luxury road-Pullman, excellent bar on board, one fashionable wayside lounge after another, it sez here, all through Lower Austria, Slovakia, Carpathians, Transylvania, Slovenian Alps, Adriatic coast, Fiume . . . Motorcycle riders plus their friends and admirers. According to this, 'Each night will be like the czardas in reverse, peppy and crazy to begin with, yet soon relaxing to almost a soothing and stately lullaby, as one by one, motor-vagabond audiences go toppling drugged into night's oblivion.' Any flicker of interest here, Hop?"

"Long as nobody minds if I stay awake."

"Bringing us to the clarinet. Lately, to a certain type ear, clarinet playing of any kind screams Jewish, anything else you could double on, how about trumpet?"

"Anything in A-flat, sure."

"So each number you play, to what could turn out to be a houseful of violent Jew-haters, gambling on their collective tin ear, you'll need to calibrate how klezmeratic, not to mention how Negro, you can afford to present yourself as. Anybody begins to suspect that the bright thread swooping out of your instrument might somehow be Jewish saliva, well . . ."

"Gotcha, Nigel."

"We'll call this a definite maybe. Now," hitting switch buttons, disconnecting jacks and plugs, drawing the window blinds, and checking the lock on the office door, "moving to the real business at hand."

Hop's "booking agent" turns out to be a bureaucrat working at Continental scale, field supervisor for an agency seldom specified as to nationality and, like many offices in Geneva, exempt from a broad range of governmental controls. Hop gazes, fascinated as Nigel proceeds through a smooth frame-by-frame personal transition, gaining a couple inches in height, mustache narrowing to little more than a lip gesture, discreetly tinted indoor specs.

"You may have noticed the antisemitism situation has picked up some steam since the last time you were over here. As the momentum builds, it's increasingly likely that Jews, maybe even in unprecedented numbers, will soon be needing to change their address, and quickly, and now'd be the time to start making arrangements—exit routes, dummy post office boxes like those already in Lisbon and Shanghai, fuel dumps, secure places to sleep . . .

"Not that there's a hell of a lot of money available for this, nobody in London, Washington, anyplace helpful is willing to step an inch out of line. We're in for some dark ages, kid. Dim at least. This could turn out to be thousands, maybe tens of thousands of lives, and we'll have to be the ones with better logistics, infrastructures of resistance and escape in place and at hand . . . we'll have to become supply officers, postal clerks, expediters, switchmen, every day, fact-compliant, inescapably committed to the given world . . ."

"And this motorcycle tour . . ."

"Will give you a chance to look at possible escape routes from Central Europe should a sudden exodus become necessary. Keeping you outside the borders of Hungary, where since the mad bomber Matuska, Jews are drawing more than the usual unwelcome attention. The key connection will be to Fiume, also known as Rijeka, partitioned, variously occupied, paperwork, bribery, and larceny everywhere, nobody's first choice right now for a port of embarkation, but in the near future, along the edge of which we're all blindly groping our way, it worked once and please God might again."

Hop finds the road-Pullman all lit up, size of a railway sleeping car, futuristic as something just rolled off the cover of *Amazing Stories*, reflected in wet pavement, three decks high, intake manifold outlined in purple neon, giant stabilizing fin on the tail end, brightly lit control cabin and crew's quarters up on top, where personnel can be seen bustling about. He walks all around the vehicle, squinting doubtfully. Too high and narrow to take any kind of curve at any speed and stay upright, in fact breathe too hard and this rig could tip over right here standing still, is the impression it gives. How's a weary music maker supposed to get any sleep speeding around dangerous curves in the middle of the night on board a buggy like this?

As it turns out nobody will be sleeping that much.

28

Sometimes all Hicks wants is to be back in Milwaukee, restored to normal life, to a country not yet gone Fascist, a place of clarity and safety, still snoozy and safe, brat smoke from a lunch wagon grill, some kid practicing accordion through an open window, first snow coming into town off the prairie, barrooms where the smell of beer is generations deep, women in round little hats. Penny scales, newsstands run by war veterans named Sarge, everyday street doors that lead to nothing deeper than friendly speakeasies, El Productos in glass tubes, fried perch and coleslaw on Friday nights. Buttermilk crullers, goes without saying. A fantasy of old-time Milwaukee, dairy-colored surfaces through the leisurely days imperceptibly continuing to darken behind a bituminous haze safe to breathe, never as bad as Chicago . . . Back when you spent more time on the interurban than in a car, work just unexciting enough to keep a gumshoe happy, matrimonials with little to worry about except now and then some dainty pearl-handled Housewife's Special in a kitchen cabinet someplace . . .

"Well-known condition," nods Slide, "you might call it post-American, some choose it deliberately, some not, but whatever it is you're headed for it, and on the express track too, allow me to point out."

"Maybe someday I'll get tired enough of all this to just turn around and go back to M'waukee. No reason not to, is there?"

"None at all. Ticket offices'll be open bright and early tomorrow morning, anybody's free to walk in—first, however, allow me to point out, seems to be, why look, it's another Central European night to be got through, in the course of which anything might happen, even giving you a reason *not* to turn around but to continue ahead, the way you've been going, into winds of the sort that tend to pick up east of midnight."

It doesn't improve the situation to learn that Terike will soon be off on a 2,000-kilometer scramble, maybe farther, in mostly, call it 90 percent, male company. Hicks isn't sure how comfortable he feels about that. Allowing for rare examples of fidelity to absent wives or girlfriends, time taken up by field repairs and improvised parts redesign, men with little to no interest in women, that still leaves a hell of a lot of bikers at loose ends for Hicks to worry about, though Terike doesn't seem to, especially.

"You and Daphne won't mind."

"Terike—"

"Excuse me, are you confusing this with an emotional exit? Do you see anybody storming out of here? What do you know about it anyway? This is the Trans-Trianon, *Haver*, not some local hill climb."

"Leaving me to deal with the bughouse cheez heiress, plus a skip ticket I never asked for . . ."

"Cheer up, it'll give you two a chance to recover that long-ago speed-boat magic."

"Yeah, a-and what about you and that Ace Lomax? Maybe I should install a lens in my belly button, so I can see where I'm going with my head up my ass."

"Don't take it personally," she recommends. "I'm not what Ace is looking for."

"Thought you two go way back."

"That's just it. I know him better than he thinks anybody can, and that's the last thing he wants."

"To the world," as Ace likes to put it, "I'm the notorious V-twin Valentino, bike-happy cuties topplin over like bowling pins, too many to know what to do with. But in sad truth the real-life Ace Lomax you see just goes grimly rolling on, older every day, out on constant patrol searching for that one-in-a-million road mate of his dreams."

"You really think that sounds romantic, Ace? It doesn't, it's pure resentment's what it is, you're just a big soup kettle bubbling over with sex prejudice."

"C'mon, no—me? I'm a li'l more sociable than that, ain't I?"

"Don't see too many ladies looking to ride pillion."

"I need the space. Oil if you want to know. This machine is known far and wide for losing oil in its sleep."

Then there's Praediger, in whom Hicks has begun to feel a certain wavering of trust.

"Only a cordial suggestion," the inspectorly smile making up in curvature what it lacks in sincerity, "if you should happen to run across our dear friend and conditions allow, why, perhaps, in some way to be determined—"

"Here it comes, it took you long enough. Would I mind putting the bump on Bruno for you. Your tough luck, Egon, I've been off the torpedo crew for a while now."

"Most of you'd be flattered."

"Not that kind of publicity, sorry, no, draws too much kiddie outlaw attention, and the history to follow don't ever turn out too happy."

"Yet I notice you're still alive."

"Sure but have I earned it? There's enough of us hard cases who'll kill for pay, dangerous-looking but inside quivering like a plate of Jell-O in a dining car from too much thinking, too many thoughts running wild, prices that are never right, deals that fall apart . . . somebody in your shop must keep a list of bad actors who'll work cheaper, why bring me into it?"

"Have you ever really looked at your employment history? One high-risk orangutan job after another, always in the service of someone else's greed or fear?"

Imagining that Slide Gearheart might at least be halfway willing to incline an ear to the subject, "Slide, is it really that bad? I thought I was past all that. Will they always be throwing that once-a-torpedo routine at me?"

"You think you've found redemption via Cheez Princess? That anybody owes you forgiveness, that you won't surrender to the old torpedical impulses the minute somebody makes it worth your while? I've seen it happen, sure, that and stranger than that, once or twice out in the long and slowly deepening twilight of our nation's history, but if you're looking for guarantees, them I don't do, find a used car dealer or something."

What was Hicks expecting? "It's all OK, Slide, no more of that riding to the rescue for me, rather be out all night in the M'waukee weather, watching nothing happen behind some bedroom window. No more runaway rich dame tickets for li'l old H. McT., thanks, this one so help me'll be my last."

"Ah yes," Slide out the side of his mouth, "and how familiar the refrain."

"You say somethin?"

"When—that's not if, but when—you sign on to your *next* Dame in Distress ticket, and you suddenly realize, here it is all over again, try not to spare a thought for the old embittered newshound who predicted it, in as much detail as you could stand for."

"I keep thinking Praediger might be some help at least."

"Are you kidding? All he's after is a coke dealer who won't charge him a month's wages for what'll turn out to be half a pound of Alka-Seltzer. Don't expect a philosophical cop. Drug habits are no guarantee of advanced thought, some of the least educational people around here are devotees of the nasal bobsled run. Don't imagine that when the moment comes Praediger will choose anything but peace and quiet, whatever he has to go along with to get it . . ."

"Except for goin screaming bughouse whenever the topic of Bruno Airmont comes up, o'course."

"Well, Bruno . . . you ever meet Bruno in person?"

"Not yet."

"Take it from a longtime veteran of copydesks throughout the land," advises Slide, "seen so many tough customers I could write you a bird book identifying all the different types, ain't often comes along as deep of a desperado as Bruno Airmont. Maybe your grandma told you there's some good in everybody? Well, Bruno in the neighborhood'll even send Granny reachin for the squirrel rifle . . ."

And why should Hicks be all that surprised, recalling how often a stray tip or even bum steer has converged to the same list of bad actors, however feeble the memory or elaborate the lie, Bruno keeps showing up, the same low point everything nearby seems fated to go draining into, as if there's some powerful whirlpool of modern crime invisibly at work that gumshoes have been known to go mystical about, sloping off into long speakeasy monologues, fate versus free will and so forth, sometimes getting so cranked up on the subject that they forget to buy the round when it's their turn, and nobody takes the trouble to remind them.

AMONG MANY PRIVATE matters Daphne hasn't mentioned to Hicks is a recurring dream about Bruno, on some faraway island, stepping outdoors every day at noon to shoot the sun with a ship's sextant, just to make sure the island isn't somehow, day to day, *changing position* in the sea, off on a voyage by itself to an enchanted landfall . . . Of course it's an island, complete with hula-hula girls, a sleeping volcano, a leaf-thatched saloon that's become a local favorite for dodging into each midday as the clouds rise over the vast ocean, backlit some till-now-unimagined shade of red, rushing in at express speed, the skies letting loose . . . which is usually about when she wakes up.

Till one night with sleep out of the question, in a turbulence and drift of multiple unlikelihoods, she and Bruno meet up.

At Night of the World, inspired by the multi-floor cabarets of Berlin, what circles of depravity may be found do not rise from street level but instead go corkscrewing down beneath it, ten floors down it's said, ten known of and more rumored, down through boiling mineral springs, toward ancient depths few have been willing to dare, each with its own bar and dance band and clientele.

Running on what's left of her old international playgirl reflexes, which she still thinks of as nerve, Daphne has a look inside. Each table here has a small circular cathode-ray tube or television screen set flush in the tabletop, throbbing more than flickering with shaggy images of about 100 lines' resolution. Viewers sometimes do not agree on the nature of the image. Pareidolia is common. You look down into it, like a crystal gazer, and faces loom unbidden. Numbered push-button switches allow you to connect to any other table in the place and watch each other as you chat.

"The future of flirtation . . . here they call it Gesichtsröhre, or 'Face-Tube.'" He doesn't look insane, but as Daphne has long come to understand, you never know. He does keep on referring to a hydropathic which could easily be of the mental sort, "except for the nights." Shivers dramatically. "The fountains all night, same frequency range as human speech, soon enough you begin to hear the spoken words, which can drive you quickly as insane as any of the inmates, a yardful of head cases who scream all night in different languages and by the approach of dawn have become invisible. Miles outside of town in any case. Securely locked at nightfall. Better to stay here where the light is more forgiving, and pretend that outside this establishment waits only a long patch of darkness we must somehow make it through."

"Someplace," she lectures him, firm but friendly, "you must've picked up the notion that ladies of my vintage are automatic pushovers for tragic older types. Do everybody a favor, old-timer, let it drop. Nobody's gazing into your eyes, if we're watching anything it's your feet and whatever it is those there are in, which in this case ain't exactly John Lobbs."

"Damned if you don't remind me of a daughter I used to have, talked just like that."

"Heard that one too, easy to whistle, no more'n half an octave range."

"And yet, can't get her off my mind. Last I heard she was in some trouble and didn't know it."

"This'd be years ago, natch."

"Some of us are still brooding about it."

"Because you could have done something once to fix it, but you did nothing and now it's too late."

But for the moment a simple brush-off would somehow cost her more than she's brought with her in her evening bag. Curiously, this conversation seems to be following a different storyline than the usual Old Goat Looking to Get Laid. Some payoff beyond that, some wild hope . . . as slowly, untrembling as stage light brought up by a skilled hand at the rheostat, she recognizes that of course it's been Bruno all along, as meantime he, maestro of timing, reverting to a Wisconsin dialect from years back, thoughtfully taking her hand . . .

"Of course," some Viennese know-it-all who happens to be eavesdropping (did anybody ask?) will be sure to comment, "each knows perfectly well who the other is."

In fact it seems the right moment for them to have a look eye-to-eye, dizzy and deep, except wouldn't you know it, just about now a Russ Columbo–style crooner steps into the follow spot, starting off slow and expressive, with a zither backup—

> Drinkin my way up, th' Dan-ube,
> missin that pep, in my shoe . . .
> Can't really blame me much, can you, b-
> but then, what else,
> was I s'posed, to do?
>   without you . . .

[speeding into jump tempo, rest of the band joining in]

> Back here in Boo, hoo, hooo-dapest!
>   Yes!
> Ever-since our love done, flew, th' nest . . .
> I've been out on the town,
> wouldn't say I was down, oh,
> maybe-a touch of moo-di-ness . . .
>
> Eatin' so much past-er-y, mm!
> Can't even find the space to re-
> -volve around on mah stool,
> just a face-stuffin fool, the rule is
> don't-get, too-depressed—

[bridge]

> Back on the Oktogon there,
> the music playing so soft,
> for the end of, me and you . . .
> (Truckin' off to Tim-buk-tu!)
> what a chill in the air,
> when we finally kissed it off—
> Down, by, that, Dan, ube, so, blue!
>   No-way to
> mis-con-strue th' rest,

though who'd-a guessed we'd
con-clude th' mess, in
Bu—da-pest?
But if that's how it goes, well
lemme just blow my nose, 'n' close
by wish-ing, you-the-best—
outa here, gotta fly,
No more tear in my eye,
Bye-bye, to Boo, hoo,
hoo-dapest!

Enough of a toe-tapper that Daphne doesn't mind being hauled up for a brief spin around the crowded dance floor.

"You don't look too different."

"You do. I wouldn't have known you."

These days the Central European backwoods, Bruno explains, are full of "scientists," elsewhere known as witch doctors, working miracle effects in chemical defiance of time—swift, smooth enough yet often purchased with long months of transfusions, injections, cell salts, and proprietary hormones at finely calculated phases of the moon. "Anyplace east of Karlovy Vary seems like once a week there's another damn new gland clinic opening for business." Ancient plutocrats who should be wrinkled and skeletal by now instead go bouncing around among us with a spring in their step and that same old itch in their BVDs, ill-behaved even in bright daylight as teenagers out after curfew. "I was lucky to keep even this much maturity in my face. Had to shell out extra in fact."

"Yeah, you could pass for somebody's junior sidekick now."

"Started off with just a simple Steinach, everybody was getting them, though I don't suppose you—"

"Semi-vasectomy where they tie off one testicle so it starts producing male hormones instead of sperm cells. Hardly a night goes by I'm not hearing the details, thanks."

"Pretty soon I was feeling twelve, thirteen again."

"Up to you of course, many of us would rather not go through that a second time."

As if Bruno can't figure out how exactly to bring it up. "I keep waiting for the question."

"Which one, there's dozens."

"Why did I skip out on you and your mother like that."

"You mean without telling anybody. Just from a quick look through the paperwork you left behind, didn't seem like you had much choice."

"How much did you see? Who else saw it?"

"Nobody, I burned it. Lit a couple cigarettes. Toasted some marshmallows. Took the federals a while to show up anyway."

"You saved me. How do I ever thank you?"

"Just another housekeeping chore, don't mention it."

"Have you been to the movies lately? We used to do that a lot. How about a date?"

"Sure, April 23rd, 1928, that good?"

"I mean it, today is Thanksgiving for me, and you're the most precious pumpkin in the world."

"Nemnemnem!" a bouncer in a hussar outfit goes muttering by, "it's like eating your way through Gerbeaud's around here, would you two mind going easy with the sentiment till I'm out of range, thanks, knew you'd understand."

THE MOVIE HOUSE is in an underlit neighborhood of dilapidated saloons and bathhouses, solitary men with appetites open to question hugging what scraps of urban shadow they can find . . . a neon marquee in the fog, radiant tubing hung in midair reading MOZIK. Inside they find a cozy hideaway below street level and the picture just about to start. Streetcars roll overhead, after a while blending unnoticed with the soundtrack.

"Enjoying that popcorn, there," Daphne observes, "and the lights aren't hardly down yet."

"Mighty unusual taste, besides the paprika, I mean, it's not butter exactly—"

"It's goose fat. Normally it'd be restaurant lard, but now and then, special movies call for special recipes."

"Aahm-hmng!" through a mouthful of giant exploded kernels fiery with erős paprika, drenched in goose grease, vanishing by the fistful till soon, shamelessly, Bruno has started grabbing at Daphne's popcorn as well.

"Here now, none of that—" batting his hand away.

The feature they're here tonight to see is *Bigger Than Yer Stummick* (1931), the latest hit starring child sensation Squeezita Thickly, which is about, well, eating, actually. Back in the States, every showing of this movie, no matter where, has collapsed well before the second reel into civic disorder—screens across the nation presently inscribed with knife scars, fork tracks, spoon indentations as audiences, many of whom haven't seen a square meal since the start of the Depression, sent into collective chuck horrors by giant images of turkeys, roasts, tenderloin steaks and birthday cakes, pots of soup big enough to swim in, go running up to physically assault the screen hoping in some magical way to forcibly enter the paradise of eats being so meanly denied them, only reluctantly pausing when Squeezita, adorable as always, comes marching into the shot with a determined twinkle in her eye, brandishing a sidearm, and swinging dimpled li'l fists back and forth, and singing in 3/4,

>   Ooohh,
>   Eat-ing, eat-ing!
>   My, what a thing, to do!
>   When it's pea-nut but-ter and
>   jel-ly time?
>   Right, down-in-to-yer
>   Bel-ly time!
>   Who'd ev-ver wanna stop, eea-ting?
>   Pass that ba-na-na cream pi-i-ie—
>
>   Ooh my!
>
>   You don't want conversation? well
>   nei(heehee)ther do I, when we're
>   Ee-ea-ting!

A pot of soup, approached from overhead, now smoothly lap-dissolving into a giant swimming pool full of bathing beauties, bordered by palm trees and food pitches, offering an array of snacks from roast turkey drumsticks to deluxe hot dogs smothered in sport peppers and dripping green-blue pickle relish strangely aglow, even though the movie's supposed to be in black-and-white, and gigantic Italian sandwiches quite a few feet long, and glutton-size ice-cream extravaganzas and oh well that sort of menu . . .

Soon enough, however, the music has shifted grimly minor, as overhead now looms a *giant soup ladle*, about to dip down and scoop up one or more of the aqua-lovelies, as if, in the *distant world* from which the ladle has descended, they are considered edible delicacies. The girls cast theatrical glances skyward, scream, squeal, submerge in the soup trying to escape, yet smiling all through the shot, having just the greatest fun, while pretending to croon, in tight inside-the-octave harmony.

> Sir-loin steaks-from-the bar-
> -be-cue—
> Hot fudge sundaes 'n' lob-sters too, It's my
> own business what I've been
> Ee-at-ing,
> Never mind how much I ate—
> Long as you keep yer lunch-hooks a-
> -way from my plate, when we're
> Eea-ea-ting!

The setting is someplace vaguely outer European, not Russia exactly, everybody talking with a different foreign accent, and even more peculiar, for a Squeezita Thickly movie, now and then also *shooting at each other*, both semi- and fully-automatically, not always in play, plus setting off spherical anarchist-style bombs which appear to wreck one expensive set after another, causing Bruno, each time one of them goes off, to shiver agreeably, which Daphne can't help noticing.

"Little blast-happy, Pumpkin," he explains. "Something the mental docs call Ekrexophilia."

"New one on me, thought I'd heard 'em all."

"Shh!"

"Vanilla 'or' chocolate, Yer Excellency? 'Or'? Really? I could always just gobble 'em *both* up, couldn't I, one right after the other, 'n' see how ya like *that*."

"Oh but I say—"

"Who's gonna stop me? You?"

"Well, upon my word."

"Do you mind? I'm in a hurry and I'm hungry."

Turned out in stylish little Soviet-inspired uniforms, Squeezita it seems has recently been appointed Food Commissar of a recently installed People's Republic, where she lives with her Daddy (Wallace Beery), a chef with a big soup-soaked mustache and top-heavy chef's toque who keeps drifting out of the frame on secret missions for the new regime, while everyone continues to regard him only as the everyday amiable lout Wallace Beery often gets to play—a perfect cover story, at least until Squeezita, whose respect for her parent lately has begun to slacken, finds out by accident about this other secretly heroic identity.

"Aww, Sweetie, and here all this time I thought you hated me."

"Ooh, Daddy, it's only because I mistook you for one more spineless drudge . . ."

"Well, that'll learn ya, kid . . . lemme just tell you how it was in the old days . . ." Born in fact into a minor branch of the former ruling dynasty, roaming the prerevolutionary halls of stately homes and summer palaces he found himself pausing in various kitchens whose helpful personnel before long were showing him how to bake pies, cakes, and pastry, smoothly drifting into an alternate identity, the soon widely discussed "Chef Raoul," pâtissier to the elite of three continents, rumored to be a jewel thief on the side, a casino gambler, a breaker of aristocratic and too often innocent hearts.

After the movie, in an adjoining subterranean café, streetcars still rumbling overhead, "So what'd you think of the picture?"

"Didn't care much for that firefight at the end. The rifle grenades and so forth."

"Did seem to go on a little too long."

"Well . . . not long enough, actually."

"Don't you think Wallace Beery deserved some comeuppance, working for both sides like that?"

"If that's what it was, only it looked to me like somebody was setting him up. Unless I missed something when I stepped out for seconds on popcorn, mine having somehow mysteriously disappeared."

"That funny Italian guy who kept hollering at everybody—you think that was supposed to be Mussolini?"

"Everybody's afraid of the Duce, even in Hollywood they might not want to offend him."

If Daphne has been hoping for something incestuous yet romantic, she's once again reminded how very little anybody can put past Bruno. They are somehow soon deep in financial discussion.

"Apparently your Gramps left you some herds."

"How many cows would that be about, do you figure?"

"Ten thousand head at least, up to a hundred thousand, maybe."

"Kind of a spread there."

"Helps sometimes to think in orders of magnitude, Pumpkin. They're all over the state. Some of them your Grampa owned directly, plus all the other herds he had controlling interest in. Someplace somebody's been keeping complete records, I'm sure." Scribbling on his napkin, "Even with prices brought down to where they are, that's still a hell of a lot of milk—if those goldurn Bolshevik collectives would let us sell it, of course. Right now they'd rather block all the shipments and dump them trackside. Even back when prices were normal your Gramps's bookkeeping was impossible to follow, and given current conditions you might not want the trouble it's likely to cost you for the eentsy li'l percentage you'd end up with."

Time for another of those profound gazes, except that Daphne's right now is looking more like a squint of suspicion. "Let me guess. You can put me in touch with somebody who'll be willing to take all the bothersome details of herd ownership off my hands, right? Plus the bookkeeping. Realizing maybe a fraction of pre-1929 value, of course. All I'd have to do'd be sign that impressive-looking piece of paper you've been fidgeting with there."

"Oh. This. Just a standard release form. We can fill in some figures later."

"Uh, huh. Surely, Pops, now you're not trying to euchre me, your own daughter here, out of money that's rightfully mine, nothing like that?"

A broad sort of "Who, me?" shrug, a comical face he thinks is endearing. "Well yes I suppose I am, in a way. It's time you grew up, and sometimes it's a father's job to speed things along. Just 'cause I call you Pumpkin doesn't mean I want my li'l Cinderella turning into one."

"Um, Pop, I don't think it's actually Cinderella who turns into a—"

"Whatever, maybe I wasn't paying that close attention, mostly remember reading it all snuggled together when you were little . . ."

Probably not the best time to do a double take, and she tries not to, but . . . Creepy? Maybe a little.

"I need the money, Daph, I'm on the lam. Some very bad people are after your old Pop, itchin to take down the Al Capone of Cheese. Forces I once had no idea even existed."

"Who's chasing you, Pop, and why?"

"Somebody wants to run the Cheese Outfit, and frankly if they want it they can have it, fine with me, though it'll take more to keep the sawed-off shotguns away. When did I ever ask to be the Al Capone of Cheese?"

"May or June of 1930—you forgot already?"

"Just never say I didn't warn you. Here, here's a 'Kleenex,' wipe your nose and try not to fall apart into too many pieces." Reaching for a Unicum bottle that happens to be nearby, meantime wondering, What's wrong with the kid? she used to have some sense once, there was even a time he'd expected to bring her into the Cheese racket someday, teach her everything he knows about the different cultures and processing, how to read the markets, buy and sell, options and futures . . .

Heck with it. Fatherly pipe-dreaming. By now she's stepped out into a life of her own. Bruno may understand that this is something he needs to come to terms with. Then again, maybe not.

OF COURSE IF anybody has the inside dope it's Slide Gearheart. "One way to look at it," Slide busily pretending to redefine his hat brim, "except maybe she's known everything about it all along. Word around is she's been working her own counter-scheme, luring Bruno deeper into a sordid and forbidden sex affair while hired photo crews secretly record every last shameful detail—"

"Wait, wait. Daphne? A-and Bruno? come on, her own father, that's illegal, ain't it?"

"Not too much of that going on in Milwaukee, I bet. Here, catch up on the news of the world," tossing over a back issue of *Lowlife Gazette*, in which Hicks finds snapshots of Daphne, early adolescence, posing ambiguously on Bruno's lap, each with the same self-pleased expression on their kisser. Easy to mistake for the imperfectly contained smirking of a girl and a secret lover.

So of course next time he and Daphne cross paths, Hicks figures he ought to bring it up.

"And . . . what's it to you again? One evening recently, you and I did some kidding around, with a lovely time appearing to've been had by all, but I'm not sure how much of the story of my life that entitles you to."

Next thing he knows Daphne has gone AWOL. Looking for Hop, according to Slide's sources, which include Heino Zäpfchen, a much sought-after Judenjäger, or Jew-tracker, familiar with ranges and habits, and secret migration patterns . . . In for 10 percent. The rest goes to the client, all on spec," Slide explains, "he sends them over, gets as much as he can, if they're not for one customer they'll be for another."

"And when he brings in somebody who turns out to be not Jewish—"

"Never happens. Heino gets to make the final call. If he says they're a Jew, whatever they were when he made the collar, by the time he brings them in, they're a Jew. Leading to a lot of complaining because Jews don't proselytize, plus it's not uncommon for Heino to turn around and convey to safety a Jew he's already shopped and collected bounty payment on—pursuit and rescue, playing both sides of the racket."

"And we're paying him . . ."

"All on contingency. Fact, I have him nearly convinced he should be paying us."

Heino's list of useful leads happens to include Nigel Trevelyan, and so a rough idea of Hop Wingdale's whereabouts is not long in arriving.

"He's booked onto a motorcycle circuit of some kind, which would be a breeze ordinarily, except that it's heading him straight into Vladboys territory."

Of the many paramilitary gangs that have been proliferating ever since the departure of Béla Kun's Lenin Boys and the arrival of the White Terror with its open season on Jews, the Vladboys have come to be considered among the worst. Their hatred of Jews is pure, free of remorse, they aren't in it for the ideology, they just want to damage as many Jews as they can, taking as their inspiration Béla Kun's triggerman Tibor Szamuely, who cruised the Hungarian Soviet aboard his personal death train with a platoon of Lenin-fiúk, and wherever it stopped people were hanged.

"They're merciless, this bunch, unbribable because nothing the law-abiding world knows how to offer them has ever been enough . . . We've got to go search and rescue," Slide figures. "If the Vladboys get hold of Hop, they're so desperate for Nazi approval that they'll do some creative damage before handing over what's left of him. And now he's about to play a Vladboys rally. Wishing him a hatful of luck, I'm sure." Slide up on his feet and down the street. "See if I can't promote us some transportation, back in a flash."

Which is more like a day and a half later, when Slide shows up out of nowhere, which turns out to've been Bratislava, in an Alfa Romeo 8C Touring Spider, accompanied by Zdeněk, who claims to be an authentic Czechoslovakian golem, in a Bugatti Type 50 sedan, his face not easily read, something like a bowler on a bowling trophy just at that split second before the ball's about to leave his hand, a face prepared to react as needed to whatever gutter balls, strikes, difficult-to-impossible splits may lie seconds away down the alley in an untranspired future.

"Nice buggies, boys, where'd you pick 'em up?"

Happened to run into a Concorso d'Eleganza translocated from somewhere, Lagondas and Delahayes and Hispano-Suizas, a parade of snazzy coachwork and chrome, drivers worried more about receiving so much as a scratch than getting hijacked, which being unthinkable was what Slide and Zdeněk went ahead and did, and next thing anybody knew there they were, tooling on down the highway each in his own elegant ride.

For centuries, Zdeněk explains, ever since Judah Loew was Rabbi of Prague, a body of powerful golem lore has been passed down, rabbi to rabbi. At present, owing to a secret rider to the Treaty of Saint-Germain, written in invisible ink, no one in the newly patched-together Czecho-Slovak entity has been allowed to build any golem above a certain size. If a customer should, however, find they needed a smaller, single-purpose unit, making up in pugnacity for what it lacks in dimension, a sort of snub-nose golem, there does happen to be a clandestine works near Pardubice, of which Zdeněk is a Versailles-compliant alumnus, up to modern spec.

"And how many of you are there?"

Not as many as there should be, thanks to BAGEL, the Bureau Administering Golems Employed Locally, whose agents are always snooping around, hoping to interrupt funny business in progress, working in cahoots with various late-capitalist entities to whom a golem is only a primitive form of cheap robot. Lately Zdeněk has been coming in for unwelcome attention, and Slide obligingly was giving him a lift out of town.

"Only checking in with the shomrim, more Jewish tough guys in Bratislava than anyplace east of the Purple Gang."

Bratislava, once Pozsony, before that Pressburg, kept trying to be a free city, but each time the Czechoslovak Legion came in, started killing people, threw their weight around enough to slap on the kibosh. The wind unrelenting all year long is believed by some to be the vestige of this free city that never came to be, as the breath of ghosts may sometimes be felt in haunted locations—a great history-wide sigh of unrequited political desire.

"And shomrim, that's, um . . ."

A self-defense group, meaning "watchers" in Hebrew, formed a couple of years back, when Nazi students in Prague began staging anti-Jewish riots, which soon spread to Bratislava, where currently the shomrim are busy inventing a close-quarters form of combat soon to be known as Krav Maga.

"We've been keeping an eye on the Hercules Gymnasium . . . there's this Lichtenfeld kid, already a champion wrestler, takes a particular interest in street fighting. Understands that there are no rule books, this isn't sport, it's Nazis who are out to kill us, and the less well-mannered we can be about it, the more effective. Nazis prefer an intellectual cosmopolitan Jew who lives mostly inside his head, a Luftmensch, easy to push around, little or no means to defend himself. Surprise! In Bratislava they're developing a more dangerous model. Idea is to always keep moving, keep hitting, never have both hands doing the same thing at the same time."

"Sounds kind of Japanese."

"You could think of it as Jew-jitsu," sez Zdeněk, who's actually just as happy to be away from Bratislava for a while, an uneasy triangle having developed featuring himself and a glamorous, indeed sultry, *robotka* or female robot named Dushka, who has a crush on him, and the local rabbi nominally in charge of golem affairs, who despite being unsure if Dushka is human or mechanical, wouldn't mind dating her himself . . .

"Ahhhgghh!" Slide rolling his eyes upward, side to side, around and around. "Do we have time for this? Wasn't there some business in Transylvania we needed to take care of?"

Later, breezing down the highway, "Appreciate the company, Slide, seein this ain't exactly your type of ticket."

"You kidding, it's the scoop of the century," replies Slide, "cheap at half the price and thanks for asking."

"Cheez Heiress on the Run? thought that'd all be yesterday's news."

"This is bigger."

"And," Hicks nodding more in encouragement than understanding, "the headline will read . . ."

"We will know it when we see it, as the hat-check girl said to the private eye."

29

By terms of the Treaty of Trianon, concluded in 1920 at Versailles, the former Kingdom of Hungary got dissected by the Entente into pieces to be handed out to the newly reformulated nations of Romania, Czecho-Slovakia and the Kingdom of Serbs, Croats, and Slovenes, soon to be known as Yugoslavia, which also got the old kingdom's access to the sea, the port of Fiume, nowadays known by its Croatian name Rijeka. Leaving a broken ring of unredeemed territory around the fragment still known as "Hungary," a halo, as some would have it—battered, insulted, compromised.

The route of the Trans-Trianon 2000 runs inside this shadow zone between the concentric Hungaries old and new—in some places dating back to the legions of Roman Dacia, all conditions of roadbed from hoofbeaten to fresh-poured, ranging from marshy flats up into the Carpathians, Velebit, Karawanken, anywhere a motorcycle can roll, climb, or jump, headlong down high-percentage grades, airborne over gulches, across rivers by raft or ferry, through great forests which, though not endless, for some riders might as well be.

Sometime in the period 1920–25 the first tentative motorcyclists set out on low-horsepower machinery, army dispatch bikes, city-street models. While the '20s roared in Chicago and American expats whooped it up in Paree, while Dziga Vertov and Boris Kaufman went gliding through the city traffic of Petersburg filming a newly tsarless and not yet Stalinized people, while Berlin still offered unparalleled freedom and refuge to heretics and asylum seekers of all persuasions, this is what was going on in the strange ring of historical debris that had once belonged to the Kingdom of Hungary—bikers in motion, some riding clockwise, some counter-, not a rally, not a race, not a pilgrimage, no timekeepers, no grand prizes, no order of finish, no finish line for that matter, though some, speaking metaphysically, say if there were one it'd be at Fiume. Rijeka, whichever.

Riders can join in at any point along the route. There are no restrictions as to sex, nationality, or engine displacement or how much of the 2,000-kilometer circuit anyone is obliged to ride, since as quickly becomes clear, it's not for everybody, though it continues year-round—riders get iced or snowed in, flooded out, caught in lightning storms that come out of nowhere, "Is what it is, takes as long as it takes," as you hear often out on the route.

Some riders are here on intelligence-gathering operations, reconnaissance, mapping, some are zealots who regard the XT2K as outward and visible expression of some geophysical redemption to come, while others, looking back, are chroniclers of unfinished business, tellers of and believers in geopolitical ghost stories. There's always more than terrain to get through, or old tribal boundaries to get across—some duty taken on as if under a flag of truce, in the dark, silently.

Out on open stretches of road with her Guzzi up to speed, Terike feels it now and then, some inward ignition, a willingness to risk more, for all she knows everything, drawn mysteriously by something beyond her own perimeter . . . Run-ins are frequent, with armed and jittery young men in uniforms newly designed or assembled from pieces of earlier ones, appearing at ridgelines and river crossings, out to intercept anything they can, being extra-attentive to motorcycle traffic, the most common excuse being tobacco smuggling, regarded as a capital sin out here, where everybody smokes all the time. Brought for a moment out of the snooze of routine, they'll often just let Terike go rolling on through. But not always. One nightfall some semi-uniformed mountain patrol start throwing their weight around. Nobody can find the right papers, safeties on sidearms are being nervously toggled off and on again, pretty soon there's a queue of machinery backed up out into the twilight, riders now and then allowing their engines to rip into silences felt to've gone on too long. At some unexpected point in the middle of which, into the overspills of light electric and acetylene comes rolling Ace Lomax, all throb and opacity, aboard his Harley-Davidson Flathead, waving genially, poised to launch his widely recognized insane laugh. A stirring in the small unit, nothing observed actually changing hands because everybody out here has picked up a repertoire of drops and passes and other low-visibility transfer skills. Business soon taken care of, the patrol smile and salute, jaunty as operetta tenors.

"Nice runnin into you, Terike, guess you're clear to roll."

"Anything else you noticed out there that you might want to tell me about? Oh and did I forget to say thanks?"

"Don't imagine you'd be interested in riding point for a little."

Her gaze narrows.

"Who's after you now, Ace?"

Ace realizes he probably could have hesitated longer before coming out with, "You mean besides Bruno."

"You're supposed to be working for Bruno. Did I miss something, hear something wrong?"

"Dunno, but sure is looking like I must've."

In this backcountry saturated with suspicion, where strange bikers are less than welcome, drawing an evil eye from the locals into whose midst they go speeding so carelessly, women on motorcycles are apt to be located safely beneath disbelief, composite critters like sphinxes or mermaids, sightings reported, few confirmed.

"What's with these people, they act like they've never seen a motorcycle before."

"Some have never seen anything with wheels on it."

Ace by now is drifting into middle age. Beginning to find himself approached by practiced fingers reaching from the other world, to bring him away, one stitch at a time, into a crazy quilt he might never know more of than a few of the patches adjoining, crazy and lost as himself. The appeal of pure adventure may have begun to fade for him as early as 1919—decisions once automatic, based on maintaining a blind forward momentum, have more and more come to include how much discomfort is likely to result.

After the War he found he couldn't return to the U.S., something there had gone screwy, it was badlands now, to be avoided. "But . . . there's no money over here, all the money's back in the States, how can you afford to even put 'gas' in that rig?"

"Turns out it's oil I'm spending more on, but there's money here all right, if you look long and close enough." Some old and well protected, some newly created. It was only a matter of time before Ace, inconspicuous citizen of the pavement, creeping about smelling of Motalko exhaust, found himself drifting into the motorcycle adventurer racket, taking on jobs as they came along, at first carrying confidential messages, presently small cargoes of undefined legality . . . trading up from an Army FUS dispatch bike to higher displacements, up to the Flathead he's currently on. Stretches of the deep highway opening up to him, geography once only a set of names becoming real, flowing from either side into view, rushing by, next thing anybody knows he's interurban, moving in unexpected circles, finding early celebrity, after a while international. How much of a surprise could it really have been that one day he would drift into range of Bruno Airmont, and presently find himself, hat in clenched fist, joining the long, unchronicled queue of hired stooges making their way up the back stairway to the boss's office door?

THROWN TOGETHER IN the Trans-Trianon 2000 ride an assortment of exiles and misfits, some disappointed in romance who hopped on their bikes and joined the tour thinking it'd be like the French Foreign Legion, a lonely pilgrimage where they could brood their way out of the blues, even manage to avoid women for a while, and bonne chance with that, fellas. They are of course mobbed out on the road by village girls, farm and city girls, female bikers, to be found these days in numbers greater than expected, even grown women, locked into the same everyday routines, when suddenly here comes trouble, fly-boy goggles, resolute jawlines, a way of bending the light. Christian and virtuous is fine as far as it goes, but narrow and sleepless are the beds of those whose lives shining apparitions like these have gone throbbing in and out of, young men too often regrettably unaware that local girls belong to families apt to own firearms ranging from single-shot to full automatic, resulting sooner or later in one more sad tale of romantic misjudgment.

For some, magical events are reported. Creditors are outrun, bets pay off at long odds, death, injury, and wreckage from terrain or weather built into the deep structure of this route in some way nobody wants to go into detail about are narrowly avoided. For the most part, an unexceptional mud-spattered mobility, obstacles looming at every curve not always easy to read as to size or placement especially at sundown, cargo spaces stuffed with hooch, drugs, ammo, all manner of taxable goods, especially tobacco. "Not exactly a vegetable truck, but as you find out sooner or later, small loads can often fetch high prices."

30

The Vienna branch of MI3b, daytime, a modest-size office decorated with a movie poster of Lilian Harvey waltzing with Willy Fritsch in *Der Kongreß tanzt* and an ancient map of the Hapsburg Dual Monarchy, bentwood office furniture in the local Workshop style. From a distant open window can be heard an unremitting suite of Wagnerian works transcribed for zither. A green and magenta carpet of eye-catching design no one wants to be called up onto, which is where Alf and Pip find themselves at the moment.

Station chief Arvo Thorp sits in front of an ashtray overflowing with Woodbine butts, frowning at a document still smelling of duplicator-machine fluid. "It's your Bolshie lot," he growls, "this Vassily Midoff again."

In the daylit office space, a patch of bitter weather impossible to explain away as harmless now appears, spreads, begins to thicken. The Quarrenders risk a quick moment of eye contact, but the certainty of some crisis long deferred and at last arrived at is too intense. Thorp, as usual, has just gone blithering ahead. "Since you last saw old Vassily in Budapest, we gather he's been on the run. No concern of ours either way, but upper levels have apparently found it troublesome. Their best guess is that he might sooner or later be seeking to join a motorcycle rally in progress at the moment, Soviet elements of which have lately set up shop in Transylvania. No idea what he's thinking, some idea of mobile asylum possibly. We're keeping a close eye, but you appreciate that someone must be sent round, and soon."

Alf on his feet, beginning to pace back and forth as far as dimensions here allow. "Certainly can't envy the poor miserable sod who'll have to— oh here now, Thorp, what's this look?"

"Ehrm, 'Best of luck,' I imagine, take note of the Fateful Initial in green ink, this is direct from F. himself, and if you and the missus wouldn't mind both signing off... here, and here... Official Secrets releases... civil-action waivers, usual bumf, insurance, so forth..."

"But he was ours, Thorp." Pip's voice drained of civility. "Our bloke."

"Someone else's by now. Not pining away, I hope."

"Meaning only," Alf reasonably, "why not deploy some new faces instead, that he wouldn't recognize as easily."

"Housekeeping clause," Thorp shrugs. "Your lad, your inconvenience, you go see to the tidying up."

Pip's eyes fidget longingly toward her purse, where the Webley lies waiting to be brought out. Alf, pretending concern, taking her gently by the elbow, both getting to their feet and off the carpet, "Thanks for locating him, Thorp old turnip, you and your lot."

"Ever so grateful," mutters Pip.

"We'll see you have carte blanche down at the motor pool. Least we can do," Thorp benevolently spreading his palms. "Off you go, children, and do try not to slam the—"

Slam.

"—door on your way out, cheers."

"WELL," ONCE THEY'RE someplace unlikely to be monitored, "so much for expecting this to be done with by now. Thorp brilliant as ever."

"Makes no sense. What do you suppose it could be? One more vendetta no one bothered to tell us about? Has someone found him at last simply too inconvenient, too much effort to keep all his allegiances straight?"

"Less paperwork," Pip making no effort to keep the contempt out of her voice, "in exchange for a human life. Cold-blooded reptiles, this lot."

"Puts us in something of a pickle, luv. Can't expect to be given an easy way out. At least it'll be my turn this time," if Alf remembers correctly.

Philippa sits gazing into a Keepall Bandoulière with built-in compartments for short- and long-range weapons and ammo plus fashionable getups for a range of occasions indoors and out. She's learned to inhabit this stylish bag, it's become a portable flat for her no matter where in the world she and Alf get sent off to.

"Oh, they're assuming it'll be me again. You aren't remorseless enough. Might be you that finally nags me into it, but it'll be my finger on the trigger, as usual."

Limited clarification arrives presently in an intercepted message from one I. P. Khvostov at the GPU to his opposite number in British Intelligence, who awkwardly it seems has just been sent into unwilling retirement while the enigmatic block of text goes on wandering the mazes of Secret Intelligence till eventually finding its way to MI3b and the already overloaded desk of Alf Quarrender.

The news, encoded a bit more elaborately than expected, is that Vassily Midoff, far from being the scattered moral casualty he seems, has apparently been promoted to deputy operations officer of an unacknowledged narkomat, a Blavatskian brotherhood of psychical masters and adepts located someplace out in the wild Far East. Stalin, it's assumed, hedging his bets. A rumor that his chief crypto genius Gleb Bokii is also running a secret lab specializing in the paranormal . . . Beyond this, the plaintext rapidly proves elusive. An encryption that somehow cannot, *must not*, be broken, allowing Alf only glimpses behind a cloak of dark intention at something on a scale far beyond trivialities of known politics or history, which one fears if ever correctly deciphered will yield a secret so grave, so countersacramental, that more than one government will go to any lengths to obtain and with luck to suppress it. Which will no doubt also mean a death sentence for any poor blighter unlucky enough to have broken it.

Better, obviously, to leave it alone. But he can't quite, can he, not Alf— as if something, some invisible power, is counting on his curiosity, his obsession . . . Luckily only occasional fragments are making it through. "Russia remains the world's largest untapped reservoir of pre-Christian faith . . . magical and shamanic arts . . . Dialectical materialism will never succeed with a people who regard the material sphere as essentially spiritual . . . Objects with souls . . . Bolshevism only a passing phase . . . ephemeral cannot begin to describe . . . As long as Gleb Bokii is safe, the narkomat is safe. But if we ever get to the point where Stalin believes himself actually threatened by supernatural forces . . ." An indecipherable patch, perhaps a string of possible scenarios. "Even then he'd probably go after Jews first."

"No idea," Alf clutching a cold cigar tightly between his teeth, "what to make of this confounded Blavatskian narkomat of his. He may have gone mad, he may in fact have crossed a line forbidden or invisible to the likes of us, thrown by some occult switchwork over onto an alternate branch line of history, where Stalin and his crew are no longer possibilities . . ."

By which point Pip has reached out her Webley, ascertained that there are indeed rounds in all chambers, and calmly aimed it in Alf's direction.

"Oh well if you're going to be that way about it . . ."

ALF AND PIP arrive at the Russian Trans-Trianon caravan to find the expected ideas of merriment, Russian bikers up at all hours—drunken uproar punctuated by the not always playful discharge of firearms. Any of these motor pilgrims could be GPU, posing as pit mechanics or cameramen or even star act Yuri and Yelena, riding IZh-1's, appearing in the international illustrated press posed side by side, semipro enough to wonder how much longer they're meant to get through on youthful glamour. Yuri, now in what he thinks of as government work, sports a prison tattoo of Marx, Engels, and Lenin across his chest, needled in years ago in the semireligious belief that no Soviet firing squad would ever damage imagery this sacred.

"*Udachi*. Of course all it takes is one renegade willing to spare your holy trinity and just go for a head shot."

Yelena meantime back on low-traffic byroads and dead-ends, seldom passing up a chance to entertain pit crews, bikers, and propaganda units of other nations, everybody but Yuri, her supposed partner in motorcycling romance and adventure, one day happens to be in the middle of a rendezvous with Vassily Midoff, in whose air of hysterical desperation she has found a strange appeal, when their stolen moment is interrupted by a small crowd of local folks running around excitedly gesturing at the sky hollering, "*Lubeniță zburător! Lubeniță zburător!*"

"What's this?" Vassily with a wild and jittery upward gaze.

"Means 'Flying watermelon! Flying watermelon!' Looks more like a zeppelin, doesn't it?"

Sure enough. Seems that for a couple of years now, deep in the growing season, a passenger zeppelin has been detouring briefly from its route between Friedrichshafen and Rio de Janeiro to touch down at a Transylvanian watermelon field only a short ride from here, bestowing on the crop a brief benediction not altogether free of political motives, then flying off again. Today it has also occurred to somebody to paint the ship with light and dark streaks of green, so it will look something like a watermelon in flight.

An early autumn day in Transylvania, giant pear-shaped haystacks in the fields, heat of passion and so forth, but Vassily is shivering nonetheless. Likely something to do, Yelena guesses, with the pair of British visitors—Alf and Pip in fact—who arrived yesterday in a not inconspicuous Austro-Daimler 635 and have since been observed lurking around the Russian encampment. "Asking after someone who could easily be you, claiming you're all long-time comrades. But after a while one picks up a sixth sense for this kind of thing, and these two sad to say scream nothing but Capitalist Assassin."

"No four-seat Czech motorcycle, or."

"No. Something like what's headed the way right now," head-gesturing back down the road, where a roadster of somewhat swank design has just appeared.

"Pizdets. These two. They've sold me out, I knew it."

"Ever flown in a zep before?"

"I have a choice?"

"We might make it in time. Hop on."

On the road, before they can get up to speed, here come a number of rifle shots close enough that Yelena at first mistakes them for high-speed bumblebees. "Your old comrades. You could've said something. I sure know how to pick 'em."

A temporary landing site has been set up with a local concert band and a chorus of presentable young women singing "Székely Himnusz," the Transylvanian regional anthem.

By the time Yelena can get close enough, the Blessing of the Watermelons has concluded, and volunteer zeppelin ground crew have begun to release mooring lines, except for a stray length of cable dangling from the gondola. Better odds than Vassily is used to, grabbing hold of the line just as the immense dirigible, as if taken by some reverse gravity, goes plummeting into the sky.

"*Paka paka,*" she calls. "*Prashai.* Forgive me."

A desperate few minutes' struggle, swaying over an abyss deepening by the second, hand over hand up to the gondola. A hatch slightly ajar, which seems too far away to reach, given the fatigue he's begun to feel in his arms, but at the last moment, he's hauled up and in. Passengers in the lounge are too busy swilling down Caipirinhas, listening to Carmen Miranda's hit record "Ta-hi" on the Victrola, and exchanging merrily evasive quips, not about sex or alcohol so much as the millions of cubic feet of hydrogen gas just above their heads, to pay much attention.

A brass-buttoned purser in a dark suit approaches. "*Es war knapp,*" one of the few useful German phrases Vassily has picked up over the years, attempting a three-stage Russian-style kiss, from which the purser takes a professional step back.

"That'll be $450 U.S. to Pernambuco, $475 to Rio."

Far below, dwindling, through the slanted windows of the promenade, Vassily thinks he can just make out the foiled assassins, arrived too late and reluctant to risk any more gunplay. Instead of jumping up and down and shaking their fists at the ascending zep, however, Alf and Pip have become noticeably more relaxed.

"Thank heaven," Pip gazing aloft, "out of our jurisdiction at last."

"Knowing that idiot F., now he'll send us to Brazil in pursuit."

"I suppose I shall need a new turnout, one of those elaborate hats, at least . . ."

31

Beneath an archway with a neon sign, ÁTFOGÓ ALKATRÉSZEK, visible for miles as an electric blue nimbus above the treetops, Hicks, Slide, and Zdeněk come rolling into a parts depot deep in the Transylvanian forest, around which in recent years has gathered a collection of roadside taverns, overnight flophouses, fuel stations, eateries, repair shops plus an inventory including local workarounds of every part of every model and make of bike on every road, priced attractively, asking for as little paperwork as possible and sometimes none, coffee always just brewed, pill-vending machines from which various miracles of modern German chemistry drop twinkling, a laundry, radio sets that folks come in from the evening countryside to listen to, a terrace to go out and get romantic on, sometimes even when the weather isn't exactly right, indoor palm trees, a small dance orchestra who come around on weekends, easy credit, a bar where riders can drop off mail or pick it up from an array of carpentered pigeonholes, bartenders with pockets full of folded messages, gal-mechanic cuties in Paris-original crêpe de chine boiler suits strolling around, as if looking for something to do. A Transylvanian oasis, glowing like a holiday tree ornament, among wind-driven waves of forest. According to those who've never visited here and can somehow not find out how to, all a mirage resulting from route-side folklore and hopeful yarn-spinning.

Well so this is it, it now occurs to Hicks, actual Transylvania, the vampire motherland itself, not in movie black-and-white but autumn colors and countryside aromas, forests filled with shadow, early previews of the winter ahead. It rains and blows, and wolves come out and address the night, chamois pose up on ridgelines, farmers' daughters who have let go of much of the cheerfulness of months earlier settle in again to ride out this particular pivot into darkness, as mountainsides in the distance go whitening each day, throwing strange, almost theatrical back and fill lighting to alter faces grown familiar over the summer.

Stretches there's little choice but to drive through, hairpin turns frequented by vengeful spirits, passages cursed by some local shaman, marsh life you wouldn't want swarming around you after dark, "And the bats of course," adds the golem, who for some reason is informed on the topic, "bats lurching all over the scenery, some carnivorous, not the shy twilit blurs we're used to, no—these can come any time of day at all . . ."

"Wait, now you're talking about—vampires?"

"Unavoidably. Common as beetles out here, but these days, to be honest, they're mostly for distraction, allowing other forces to pursue deeper schemes . . . If they were ever known to breathe, we would call it conspiracy, but these are the Unbreathing, who go about their business in a silence not even broken by pulsebeats."

To cover the supernatural angle, Slide has brought along a little 35 mm Leica, but for all his cranking, aiming, and snapping, each time the photos are developed, once again it's the same sorrowful story told so often out here, one blank frame after another, a vampire's allergy to silver, an ambivalence as to light itself . . .

What seems to've begun happening out here on the route with some regularity is that impulses disallowed in normal society are surfacing unexpectedly and being acted upon. Some more benevolent than others, spontaneous pig rescue, for example.

Unaccustomed bustle one day in the repair shop, where the ill-tempered Sándor Zsupka, across whose path few who have ever ventured care to do so again, currently on the run from a number of felony charges, including actual bodily harm, is putting together a pig-customized helmet and goggles combination revealing along with his criminal activities a gift for millinery.

"This is your . . ."

"Spirit guide, and even a spirit guide can do with some extra windproofing now and then. Further questions?"

"Never seen a pig quite like this..."

She's a Mangalica, a popular breed in Hungary at the moment, curly-coated as a sheep, black upper half, blonde lower. And that face! One of the more lovable pig faces, surrounded by ringlets and curls. Squeezita Thickly should only look half this adorable.

No more than idly cruising the countryside, Sándor happened to get off on one of those fateful back roads, and there in a steep farmyard were a family and their livestock, a cute meet, you'd say, though not half as cute as the pig herself. "Oh and this is Erzsébet, we're eating her for Christmas."

Hell they are. Sándor and some barroom accomplices perform a snatch-and-grab in the middle of the night, the pig pretending to be asleep, as she is picked up, installed in the sidecar of Sándor's rig, and spirited away, just like that. Next thing anybody knows she's riding in the sidecar, done up in helmet and goggles, beaming, posing like a princess in a limousine. Anybody feels like commenting, they don't.

HICKS WANDERING THE COMPOUND one day hears a piano in the distance, recognizes the tune as "Star of the County Down," a longtime favorite of Irish drinkers he's known. He follows the thread of melody to a temporary dance pavilion and finds seated at the instrument, a tear track not entirely free of mascara slowly making its way down one cheek, who but Pips Quarrender, singing, in better tune than the piano, all but subvocally, "As it fell out upon one day..." Till now he thought he had the details of silent approach down pretty well, but not with Old Pips here.

"Gordon Bennett, you again."

"Nice tune there, Pip."

"Dives and Lazarus. Old story from the Gospel of Luke, rich bloke throwing a party, down-and-out leper starving outside on the pavement, technically it's a Christmas carol, though uncomfortable for the average churchgoer given its rather keen element of class hostility, not always first choice when the youngsters go round caroling..."

"Congregational Methodist, myself," as it dawns on Hicks, breaking like the day, that Pip must once have been an actual English kid who celebrated Christmas with her family, and probably sang this once or twice when she was coming up.

Reminding him it does happen in fact to be almost Christmas season. Snuck up on him as usual.

Busy now with her compact mirror, "Shall I hide this eyebrow, do you think? Or this one?" More though far from final touches. "Right. Wicked enough for the Ku'damm."

TAKING A SHORTCUT through a parts department swarming with clerks and customers, Hicks notices a young woman in road gear, unlikely to be who he thinks it is, illuminated beneath a rainswept skylight.

"Pretty gummed up, float needle is nearly shot, you might want to just replace the whole unit, Guzzi will be switching to Dellorto Rex for this new model year but we still have some Amals in stock so we could give you a discount on a replacement . . ."

A gust of rain and shaken-off tree debris goes racketing across the roof.

"Nice one to be in out of," Hicks remarks.

She looks up from the catalogue page, leaving her finger where it was. And what do you know, it really is Terike, with a carburetor situation. Rainlight wavering across her face. Happy to see Hicks? He wouldn't bet the rent.

Despite frequent warnings in the Gumshoe's Manual not to consider hairdos as more than secondary factors, let alone deal-clinchers, Hicks now finds himself unprofessionally gazing . . .

"Your hair's longer."

"It needs a shampoo." Her stylish aviator helmet having not altogether kept the wind from getting in and leaving behind deposits of farm dirt and atomized road oil.

"Happy to give you a hand with that."

Which gets him a look. "Come to think of it, what are you doing here anyway? Have you been following me?"

"That would explain it all right, but—"

"Not that it's any of your business, yes, Ace has been on the run, what from he's not telling me, he never tells me anything, but he still needs looking after, if not by me then by who, I'd like to know. Anytime you want to chip in and help, feel free."

AFTER SOME MYSTERIOUS shortwave conversation with Heino Zäpfchen, Zdeněk the golem has located Hop Wingdale en route to a Croatian guerrilla training camp near the Hungarian border. "Think I'll go down there and see what's what. Might get lucky. You better stick around, wait'll you hear from me, don't want to be too conspicuous. Fact, much as I like the two-tone paint job on the Bugatti here, maybe it needs to blend in more with the landscape."

32

As the road-Pullman plows its way through the night, moving deeper into Vladboys terrain, underlit landscape furling silently aside, the band find themselves growing less enthusiastic about the Trans-Trianon 2000 Tour of Hungary Unredeemed. Loose cocaine isn't always practical on these beat-up roadbeds that send happy dust flying all over the coach interior, in which you can't depend moment to moment on where your nose is going to be in relation to line or spoonful, exactly, so to maintain a chirpy outlook everybody prefers a veterinary-size pill combining cocaine and morphine, known as a speedball.

"What's with that sign out the window, FAL A HALÁL? Hungarians at Christmastime?"

"Means 'Wall of Death.'"

"We're supposed to be playing a gig at one of them?"

"Good ol' Nigel, done it again."

They pull in by a towering wooden cylinder set in a clearing, filled with the snarling of low-displacement bike engines, light of beacon intensity thrown skyward, Motalko exhaust and smoke from bike engines and spectator tobacco rising slowly up the bright column into outer darkness.

The management here want music not only for drinking and dancing but also to accompany Wall of Death activities, not that ascents, descents, and time on the Wall between aren't dramatic enough already. Sheet music copied from Erno Rapée's *Motion Picture Moods* is available.

Ace Lomax, taking a break from the Harley-Davidson he rode in on, has been working aboard a local brand of bike about the size and horsepower of an Indian Scout, zooming up, down, and around, collecting tips paper and metallic in a number of different currencies as he goes circling around the top.

"And welcome to amateur night! Your turn, hotshot."

"Me?" Ace a little embarrassed, "Can't carry a tune in a bucket."

"Take a look at this crowd. Nobody'll notice."

"Anybody here know 'O.K. Corral'?"

"Didn't Smith Ballew cover that?"

"Whistle us a couple bars."

[clip-clop cowboy rhythm]

> Down by the O-K, Corral,
> That's where we usually met,
> our little corner of Tombstone,
> Where folks seldom get . . .
> Just passin' the day,
> Me and my fiancée,
> when sud-denly ev'ry bless-
> -ed fire-arm in town
> Starts blastin' a-way!

[the drummer goes temporarily crazy]

[bridge]

> "It's your family!" I cried,
> As she smiled and replied,
> "Better both keep our heads down,
> 'n' go along for the ride"—
>
> Now the gunsmoke's all gone,
> Looks like she's moseyin on,
> When I ask about next week,
> All I get's just a yawn . . .
> Talk about the miles, of chaparral
> between a trail hand and his gal!

Things were so jake, at the O.K. Corral—
Till those Earps and Clantons came along—
Good luck to you, my femme fatale,
Yep and to that old O.K. Cor-ral . . .

Later in the evening, about to get back out in the wind, Ace goes over to wave so long to the band, spots Hop, and does a double take. "Well, 'at's 'at there Hop Wingdale, ain't it."

"Last time I checked. You're . . ."

"Ace Lomax. Recognize you from your mug shot, nice to see you're still vertical."

"Was I not supposed to be?"

"In fact Bruno Airmont offered me the job of seeing to it you wouldn't be, but I said no thanks and now I'm on the run and it's Bruno and them that's after me. Not sure you're the reason why exactly."

Could also have dated back to once when, having put the arm on someone for a trifling sum grown overdue, Ace approached the boss with a gentle reminder.

Usual practice around here being to stiff his smaller creditors, Bruno got slightly annoyed. "I sent it to your last known address by trusted messenger, in a deluxe paper bag embossed with my personal monogram, you mean it didn't get there? Well, land sakes."

"No harm done, just look in your petty cash drawer—smaller bills if you wouldn't mind."

"Or we could do it another way, which is, you see Gunther there?" an office fixture maybe two meters high, with a background in bill collection. "You leave right now and we won't have to ask him to help you find the way out."

"Um. Well then if that's all, guess I'll just . . ." heading for the door.

"Or there might be one thing," in a tone of voice that goes along with thumbing off a safety.

"Sure. OK if I turn around?"

"Say we upped the ante and there was more cash in front . . ."

"You want to give somebody the bump."

"Nobody you know personally, nobody special, you must have done it plenty during the War—"

"I was a dispatch rider, needed both hands just for getting point Ack to point Beer."

"Oh? What's with the face? knew you were such a virgin I'd've shifted into Sunday whites and classed up my language."

"Just a two-bit grifter here, Bruno, trying to stay even with the upkeep on my bike. Don't sound like anything much in my line."

"Give you a day to think about it."

Ace, with no idea how unusually generous this is of Bruno, spends his day of grace decoking his exhaust, looking for parts at the junkyard, avoiding people he owes money to. Next day, "Well. Here's the mug shot, I can suggest times and places but it'll be up to you really."

"Why me, you've got plenty of talent around here to choose from."

"Turns out the lucky stiff-to-be is Jewish."

"And I'm not. So what?"

"You're the top performer at HIJAC right now." This being one of Bruno's many sidelines, Homeland Integrity through Jewish Asset Conversion, where Ace has been specializing lately as a sort of strong-arm repossess man cashing in on selected Jewish citizens who've decided to flee their countries in a hurry, leaving behind enough property to be worth the effort of stealing it.

"Which makes me what, prime Jew-killer material? Are we working for Hitler now?"

"You might want to mind your mouth, grease monkey, who I do business with is none of yours, is it."

"Nope, no more than who your daughter keeps company with, Boss," Ace having learned how not to look away from eye contact at moments like these. Daphne's story has been an open secret around the shop for a while. Which isn't helping Bruno much with his composure.

"I don't have time for this. You want to keep going with it I'll ask Gunther to drop around later," meantime pretending to get busy with some pieces of paper.

When Ace gets to the stairway he decides for some reason not to take the steps but slide down the banister instead. It is a long enough swoop, the breeze blowing in between his ears and clearing out any number of cobwebs, that by the time he hits the street it's pretty clear where things go from here. By nightfall he's in Bratislava and slipping unnoticed in among a convoy of Trans-Trianon machinery in the 750-cc-and-above range. Nobody is speaking English and they all seem to be heading roughly south and west, which is fine with Ace.

Meanwhile, as if Jewish clarinet players aren't bad enough, Bruno, to whom it has more than once occurred that Ace himself also might be smitten with Daphne, ends up shifting Ace over into a higher category of risk. Ace is now, as they used to say in the business, a marked man. "Wall of Death work is a sort of working vacation," as he describes it to Hop Wingdale. "Living on tips these days, just dropped by to pick up a few pengoes. The Harley is expensive, but those lightweight li'l rigs just make me nervous."

"Somebody said it's safe long as you keep moving fast enough, something about centrifugal force."

"Ridin the Wall of Death, ridin the Trans-Trianon, same only different. Problem down here at ground level is goin too fast, somebody hits the throttle, gets slung away on a tangent, ending up who knows where. Maybe forever. 'Course then again, ridin in circles all day, a man's brain does start to spin."

"So that cheese kingpin is after us both," sez Hop. "Sorry you got dragged in."

"Me too. You packing any heat?"

"Little Frommer STÖP, I keep it in with my clarinet." Ace's eyebrows go up a little. "It comes in handy now and then. Not everybody over here is a jazz lover."

Ace climbs aboard his Flathead. "Don't think it could have anythin to do with that, uhm, that Daphne Airmont, do you?"

Uh-oh. Hop has no idea what Bruno knows, how much he may have told Ace, how interested Ace might really be in Daphne, round and round yet again. "Crosses my mind now and then. Why Bruno should want either of us out of the picture that much."

Here is one of those openings for the kind of discussion two men with an interest in the same woman might get into, when both understand that she plays in a league more advanced than any either has ever heard of . . . Except for the lingering few percentage points of a chance here that Ace might still be working for Bruno.

But Ace by now has kick-started his machine, flipped a salute, and, calling back "Don't tell anybody you saw me," is rolling off and away.

TERIKE HEARS THE NEWS from a bartender with a shortwave set in the back room. "Radioed them at Cluj, they said he'd be checking in, but nothing's been heard since."

Her face, her cryptic road-adventuress face, begins to drift into disarray, though nobody would notice who hasn't been gazing at it as earnestly as Hicks. Her mouth going askew, eyes unable to look anywhere, forehead losing its smooth serenity.

The wind outside has grown louder, reached a high, disconsolate edge likely to last through the night, a wind not even eccentric or daredevil bikers tonight are eager to get out in. Everybody assumes that Ace has been in some kind of a crash. In the mountains, climbing through rain just at the edge of turning to snow, night coming earlier, Ace forgetting as usual to check the carbide in the headlamp, the light flickering, failing, dwindling to darkness and the metallic smell. Even with a reliable working headlamp, he's always had this habit, or maybe practice, of riding faster at night than he should, of not staying safely inside the space lighted ahead of him. Like many Harley Flathead riders of the period, Ace has disconnected the new front-brake cable and grip arrangement, looking to avoid any more braking skids than what he's going to get into anyway—possibly some annoyance, bordering on resentment, at the whole idea of braking itself, of any limits or interruptions to motion forward.

Hicks figures he's somehow beaming telepathic messages of caring and support directly into Terike's brain, puzzled that she doesn't at least gaze back, slowly understanding that she wants not to be looked at at all. Fine with Hicks, who couldn't have watched this collapse for much longer anyway.

Which as it turns out he doesn't get to. One day it's the carburetor. Then for a few bothersome days, a countershaft bearing situation. Next time he goes looking for her she's all set to leave.

"His trouble might not've been mechanical, dispatch riders usually know better. Your chain acts funny, you're always ready to break, press, rivet. Your tire goes flat, you stuff it with grass and ride on. Ace can be careless but he's not stupid. This could be anything, even some run-in with locals known to get unfriendly. I have to go see. Try to understand—if it was me, wouldn't you?"

"Sure. How about Ace, would he?" regretting it the minute it came blurting out.

"And that really is stupid, Hicks."

Maybe, but he won't let it go. "What if all it is is that he's met—"

"Suppose he has and what's it to you? He always knew how to ditch me, so natural that it took me a while to catch on that I was going to be alone again, so simple, no goodbye note, just some empty oil cans and cigarette butts lying around, and then one day there he'd be again, all right? Listen, if you're going to get all *investigative* about this, swell, it'll be up to you, but meantime if you don't mind there's a couple thousand bugs should have been in my teeth by now."

Turns out that in some walled-in maze of a mountain town Ace has missed a turn or taken the wrong half of a fork and ends up running on fumes, miles out of his way just about the time the wolves come out. Wolves and as it happens Vladboys, who also run this terrain in packs. Aware of the danger, Ace has gone blasting on in anyway, thinking he had an edge, but these riders are not touring. They're hunting. Small, nimble, predatory, full of pep—dirt scramblers, hill climbers, creek crossers. Ace's weight and displacement work against him, he's been listening for a throb as deep as his own, anything higher-pitched or faster will take him a tenth of a second too long to sort out, and that's their edge. It proves decisive. The snow comes down more heavily, deleting other options. Ace finds himself in the hands of the Vladboys.

33

A Hungaro-Croatian terrorist training camp, located right on the borderline, not, like the notorious Jankapuszta, aimed at Yugoslavia in particular so much as flexibly all-purpose Fascist, quivering in readiness to be deployed anywhere . . . specializing in lightning putsches local and continent-wide, chaste as any of nature's killer species, briefly innocent as Fascism in its "springtime of beauty," as the old anthem goes, before it descended into paperwork and brutality . . .

Fascist adventurers have journeyed here from all over, Austrians sporting blue cornflowers and black grouse feathers, secret police, anti-Red goon squads, revolutionary cells, convicts escaped from internal exile and not sure where they are right now or what language they're supposed to be speaking, colonial stooges in civvies in from as far afield as Indo-China and South America, irredentist aristos from the old Hungarian kingdom adrift in nostalgia, Polish freelancers working on spec for all of the above.

At the gate, sentries welcome the bus with the standard Ustaša exchange, *"Za dom!"* right hand striking chest over the heart, to which the bus driver replies, *"Spremni!"*

Like "Heil Hitler," somebody, probably the bass player, who knows everything, explains, only different.

"History rolls on," Storm Leader Dubendorff, apparently in charge of the entertainment around here, greets the band, "toward our Fascist future, immense and stately, we here being only the squalls and tornadoes breaking out at her edges," cranking aside a drapery of some kind to reveal through multipaned floor-to-ceiling windows a vast stretch of the puszta, a sweeping view of tank-friendly countryside aswarm with vehicles the colors of local earth and dust, thundering and hurtling, squads scrambling around shooting at dummy tanks or machine-gun nests, practice detonations at all hours out in the brush.

"In this current exercise we are pretending to invade Fiume, which any number of potential clients want back, requiring only a simple pincer movement—in from the Adriatic, down out of the Velebit, all over in a day or two. *Anasa supo.*"

TONIGHT VLADBOYS HAVE gathered from all over, to dance to the beat of this tiny orchestra making with swingtime straight from the night cities of capitalist decadence, in this ruined limestone amphitheater, once dedicated to bloodletting presented as amusement, back when the Fifth Macedonian Legion were busy here invading and occupying. Nazi bikers creep around furtively chiseling cigarettes from anybody they can as long as it's not the official Storm Trooper brands they're only permitted to smoke.

"A Gay Evening with Vlad Țepeș," including "Vlad's Vegetarian Chef."

"*Et voilà*—just out of the oven, Your Excellency, dig in!"

"Turnip loaf again, remind me to have the chef impaled."

"What, again?"

"It's simple—ease up on the vegetables, I do less impaling—pari passu, fair play, am I being so unreasonable?"

"Vlad at the Office."

"Criminal code? Nemnemnem, too elaborate, first-degree this, second-degree that, too much paperwork . . . instead how about one penalty for everything—simple impalement! Murder, queue-jumping, double-dealing and false shuffles, easy to remember, no case law to look up, no judges to bribe, no lawyers' fees—in fact, no lawyers! Find a stick, sharpen it, *zzt*! done in a flash, another of those reductions in government spending for which I have become famous. But do they ever call me Vlad the Spending Reducer?

Not likely! Since I took power, the threat of Turkish invasion has fallen to zero—do they call me Vlad the Invasion Preventer? No . . .

"But! *Run one stake* through one small-time chiseler . . ."

KEEPING PACE WITH the lunar cycle, tensions within the Vladboys have been building up, sending them out after prey each time in a more dangerous state of arousal. Trivial disputes are apt at any moment to erupt into violence. Local women go more and more in fear of their safety, cover their hair, stay in groups. The weirdly erotic charge accumulates, until *vrrrooom!* here's the Vladboys out on another massive prowl, unmuted machinery slowly thundering through devout villages where nothing mechanical is allowed—filling up the lanes and alleyways, while shut behind doors suddenly unreliable, guarding doorframes no mezuzah can protect, Jews wait, anxiety growing meantime among the Vladboys as the population of Jews available for persecution seems to be getting smaller lately, and any phantom, any report of a sighting in low light, any unexplained density passing among the streets and alleyways after nightfall that can be shot at, is apt to qualify as a "Jew." Ace is an understandably welcome catch, with the Flathead an unexpected bonus, which the boys keep insisting is a Jewish motorcycle.

"Weiss Manfréd makes one," Ace tries to point out, "but the displacement's under 100 cc's. This engine is much bigger, 750 or so."

"Harley. David . . . Son, this is son of David, no?"

"Two guys from Milwaukee, I don't think they're Jewish."

"American, same thing."

Meantime when nerves are on edge and everyone is in easy reach of a weapon, never get into an argument over cards.

Somewhere close by, an ordinarily friendly cruce game has unexpectedly flared into violence when a visiting Fascist, maybe only unfamiliar with the ornately detailed Hungarian deck, fails to follow suit. Demands that his hand be examined, considered impolite but not illegal, don't help much. Voices are raised, then fists, then hands as firearms are produced and aimed.

Within minutes of the first shot, gunfire has become general. "We'll be back. Csongor, keep a careful eye on the Jew."

"I'd rather come along with the rest of you."

"No telling how this will develop. Better to have somebody in reserve."

Csongor is a sort common in these parts, an apprentice vampire doomed never to develop past journeyman, despite which everybody's afraid of him because they think he's mad, as in mad dog, a glitter in his eyes telegraphing trouble long before he's inside *Za dom!* radius, by which point it's too late . . .

Punctuating the rifle and machine-gun fire, hand grenades and tank and anti-tank guns can now occasionally be heard. Because in situations like this it soon becomes advisable to get flat and under cover and wait there for longer than you think you might need to, Ace and Csongor presently find themselves sheltering under a good-size Czechoslovakian army truck, a Tatra six-wheeler. "Don't suppose you know what's become of my Mauser," Ace in a friendly enough way. "Unless you people think that's Jewish too, like my bike."

"We meant no disrespect. We only assumed—"

"Yeah, nothing personal, forget it. You boys sure get cranked up over anything Jewish, don'tcha."

In the bursts of light from explosions and military traffic on the move, Csongor finds himself gazing at a tattoo on Ace's arm of a mad-eyed zombie on a BMW bike as seen from a few degrees below flat-on, an angle providing a good stretch of apocalyptic sky to frame him against. "*Die Todten reiten schnell*," the Vladboy reads from the Gothic lettering there. "Something about the dead ride fast."

Ace shrugs. "Some old poetry." The tattoo artist in Berlin, years ago, threw it in for free.

Csongor can't let it go. "And do they? the dead. Ride fast?"

Ace is smiling, though not sociably. "I never spent much time in math classes, too busy learning how to hot-wire cars, but from what I recall you're never allowed to divide anything by zero. Over there, among the dead, time has no meaning anymore, so to get distance per hour you'd have to divide by zero, which even if it was legal would still give you infinite speed. OK so far?"

"Is this what they call Jewish physics?"

"No idea. But I already may've begun to cross over to the next world, not dead yet but pretty damaged. Maybe worse than some little troop of amateurs know how to do."

"Tough Jew."

"If you like. But now stand by, you're about to see the genuine article, heading our way."

It's the pocket-size golem Zdeněk, his elegant touring car fueled up and raring to go, its original finish now camouflaged in brushland shades as if he's expecting to be in trouble sometime soon. With him is Hop Wingdale.

"Saw you go under the truck, thought you might need a ride out of here."

Zdeněk's left arm turns out to be a modified ZB-26 Czech light machine gun, with the magazine built into his shoulder. "This is one of many earthly variants of Azrael, the Angel of Death," he informs Csongor, "a Jew less forgiving than some you may have hoped to come across, who has been keeping a busy schedule and is still a little backlogged, though be patient, shmuck, you're at the top of the list, it'll be your turn before you know it."

"Best be on your way," Ace suggests, "while you've got him in a good mood. Nice chatting with you, Csongor, hope you won't get into too much trouble."

"This isn't over," replies the Vladboy peevishly.

"It never began. Stay safe, pal."

Zdeněk hits the gas.

"Thanks for the lift," Ace mutters from the tonneau. "You might have bumped the punk off and saved everybody a lot of trouble."

"UTOPIAN caveat in effect, I'm afraid," explains the golem.

"Which would be . . ."

"Wired into every current-model golem—Unless The Opportunity Presents Itself, Attack Nobody. You want to keep your head down, or are you having too much fun up here in the wind?"

"We'll need to get to my bike," sez Ace.

"Not going to happen," sez Hop. "That Flathead has long been taken away to a fate unknown."

"Good, let them have it, it's a rolling death trap anyway. Too heavy, clutch never could handle the weight, flywheel's too small, go any faster than 50 it starts trying to shake itself apart . . ."

"Well, but aside from that—"

"Hate to interrupt but," Hop pausing as something shadowy goes whizzing by close overhead and explodes deafeningly nearby, "I think that was for us."

"I'll make a note, thanks."

With the first of the Vladboy pursuit screaming into the edge of his vision, Zdeněk, bouncing behind the wheel muttering in Czech, makes a wide U-turn, sending up a plume of dust and gravel, back onto the road headed the other way. A line of brief dirt explosions goes racing left to right just ahead of them. "Hmm. You want to hang on—" Off the road into unpaved terrain torn up with ruts from heavy machinery and littered with shell casings from the recent activity.

From behind woodlines nobody can even see, field howitzers have begun to lob shells, abrupt small craters creeping closer in a tightening ellipse. Gas rises in dense flare-struck columns.

Nothing but fence as far as the eye can see. "There was supposed to be a gate around here someplace," Zdeněk somewhere between perplexity and annoyance.

"Could use a Bangalore torpedo," Ace supposes.

"Might happen to have a pocket-size model here," Zdeněk rooting around in back and coming up with a few sticks of dynamite thoughtfully borrowed last week in Transylvania off of a freelance firefighting crew passing through en route to a Romanian oil-well fire everybody could see from fifty miles away.

"Ought to do the trick," Ace figures. "Somebody got a light?"

Obligingly Zdeněk snaps his fingers, which begin to glow red. "Here we go, everybody mind their ears now . . ."

34

Not that Daphne would admit to being lost, although it hasn't taken her long to regret this impulsive attempt to find Hop. She has blundered out into a territory she thought she knew, which in fact the political situation has changed to something unrecognizable and poisonous. The best plan she can come up with is to retrace the old Klezmopolitan routes she remembers. Wear solid hiking shoes and watch her step.

Hamburg, once the Swing Kid metropolis, is especially depressing for Daphne to visit. Dockyard neighborhoods solidly Social Democratic and Communist are suddenly all infested with brownshirts, singing Nazi lyrics to the tune of "The Internationale," *"Auf Hit . . . lerleute, schließt, die Reih-en"* and so forth, known as the "Hitlernazionale." Local citizens try to drown this out by singing the original anthem, which might be charming enough for a travelogue, amusing even, except for the physical violence it always degenerates into. Negroes have vanished from the Reeperbahn jazz bars, leaving unlighted windows and Rooms to Let signs all through St. Pauli. Blues licks have largely given way to major triads.

Now and then she thinks she sees familiar faces, Swing Kids aged into the hopeless awareness that what may have been possible for them once is no longer so. Girls who used to dance their braids all loose before the end of the first set are now en route to children, church, and kitchen. No greetings of "Swing Heil!" anymore, not even in a whisper. No more gathering up closer to the bandstand to listen, humming harmony, sometimes to just hold each other and what they called "sway" in time to the music.

Daphne understands that she has already seen the last days of Klezmania, traveling parties of Swing Kids and Red Front fans, Jewish and otherwise, fraternizing shamelessly, who knows what expectations tumbling through their minds. The sort of thing Jew-haters don't like to see but cops do, because it means overtime. To call yourself a Swing Kid was to count on a fight every time you went out to hear music, or dance, or even just hang around, running on little more than beer and their own adrenaline, while the Hitlerboys would be cranked up to unnatural levels of speed and force by the latest pills intended for Army use, some still under research at IG Farben. Creeping their way after the last set, dazed and apprehensive, back out into the deep hours of a future where not even furtive reprises can any longer be counted on and the streetcars home are few if running at all anymore . . .

One evening just past sundown Daphne wanders into a beer garden the Klezmopolitans once played at, formerly named the Midnight Mouse after a poem by Christian Morgenstern, now converted to a Sturmlokal, Der Schlagstock, with SA, since it's legal to wear the uniform again, all over the place, amateur Nazi choir music, not so much sung as shouted in unison, tables crowded with boys in identical shirts and haircuts . . .

About the time her foot touches the doorsill, Daphne, who must have slid somehow into a nostalgic daze, is reminded it's back to the present tense.

"Looking for me, Schätzchen?"

"Long way from Friedrichstraße tonight."

She tries to turn and step back out but her way is blocked by Hitler-happy adolescents, faces already familiar by way of the newsreels, imagining themselves predators but when observed more closely, fated after all to suffer, to be brought down as prey, even at the hands of those they thought were brothers in a struggle for which they themselves were always too fragile.

Congratulations, Cheez Princess, she snarls to herself, you're about to become fondue.

Providentially, overhead, approaching out of the dusk, comes a god-awful racket.

"*Ach nein!*"

Alarmed gazes skyward. "This one again!"

"Take cover!"

Catching the last of the departing sunlight, a white apparition comes sailing ominously in.

Shouting down through a megaphone, "Need a ride, sister, I'll be right with you." Since she began flying the autogyro, something in Glow Tripforth del Vasto has begun to stir, something deep and each time less disposed to forgive. Across her face now and then there will drift, only for a second but ominous while it lasts, some sign of a counter-angelic presence that lives to do harm, till all goes flickering back to normal, likely nothing more than one of those twitches in the everyday weave and reweave, you'd like to think, and yet . . . There are times when enough, frankly, is enough. Some annoyances do really have to be seen to. In the interlude of waiting for the rotor to get back up to speed in a loud rising scream, as Sturm kiddies mill about, cringing, taking snapshots, raising steins in salute, Daphne runs and climbs into the mother-in-law seat in front of Glow, hollering, "Noisy rig, ain't it?" except nobody hears her over the racket, bedazzled by the twilight flickering between the vanes as they slowly begin to roll, to pick up speed. She falls into a light trance, next thing they're headed down the road at about the local speed limit for farm wagons, and up into the sky they're taken. Or what, with a gyro, passes for sky. Because down this low, as Daphne is soon to learn, the ground also figures as part of the flight . . . not really transcending the earth, not soaring into some higher element, but following perfectly the nap of the terrain, every hollow and haystack, every turn of creek, tobogganing hill, and lover's leap . . .

"Thanks for the lift."

"Halo's in the shop or I'd blink it at you."

"I want to believe they're only being obnoxious but I think it's worse than that."

"It's worse." Glow and her skycraft have tangled more than once with Hitlerist gunboys in biplanes and sport zeps, and it hasn't ended well for any of the lads. "Flight these days isn't as much fun as it was once upon a time. Borders less easy to cross, sharpshooters, ack-ack fire, airborne pursuit and interception."

At first, too busy to feel anxiety, each time she stalled or lost the engine Glow undramatically settled in a long and serene lapse to earth as the rotor vanes slowly, deeply folded her to a safe landing, till one morning, as she flew along a ridgeline in the Pyrenees, there came to her unbidden the certainty that she would never crash in this thing, along with its corollary vision of the future of autogyroing—a flood of no-talent stumblebums barging into skies already crowded enough, fools smiled on by the gods of flight, guaranteed happy landings every time, parachuting down on those pale vanes graceful as wings . . .

"Gyros are forgiving ships, 90 percent foolproof—and there's the danger. The idiot appeal. Man in Indiana taught his dog how to fly one, now the dog flies him everywhere, a sky chauffeur, wears this li'l sort of outfit, hat, goggles, and so forth . . . Fools will flock to this machine, attracted by the simplicity of operation. Romance on the cheap. Too many will do things wrong and have accidents far enough short of tragic to give the rest of us a bad name, with insurance companies and loan officers suddenly all over the place.

"But look, right down there's a tavern, it's cocktail hour, and the least you can do is buy me a drink." Gliding to earth with the accustomed racket which brings half the customers outside to have a look.

Glow's been a longtime regular here. "Place back then was no bigger'n a hiker's hut, and Miklos here was running his own distillery down in that patch of woods."

"Back when you were using your own wings, the way the people tell it," Miklos bringing glasses and bottles. "We never quite got used to you being mixed up with that Spanish guy."

"Aha," Daphne lifting her glass, "I knew it, romance in the air."

"I was still only a subdeb, too busy breezin' through the season, disrupting lives, and thinking I was so seductive. Then one night in Berlin, at the Femina-Palast, I think, though Porfi recalls it otherwise, I was approached by this slick-haired tango juvenile in an all-black turnout, you could say unpromising relationship material, you know the sort, no point risking even a distant nod unless a gal's confident enough she can handle herself through any escapade, which in those days I thought I was. My error and oh sister was it." Suddenly up close came this thin mustache, high collar, an elegant briquet snapped open, suavely extended, a sleek art deco–shaped flame . . . How can a girl resist, she wondered, just audibly enough, and didn't, finding herself dancing some Gardel and Le Pera number with the as it turned out notorious Porfirio del Vasto, doing business at the time under a different name that no longer comes to mind.

"Gracious," Daphne pretending to fan herself, "how soon is the movie coming out?"

"My undoing," Glow with a comparably sincere sigh. "The gyro, that damn loud billowing thing, is what did the trick, more than Porfirio himself, even when I could hear him over the noise, murmuring, 'I couldn't let one go for any less than such and such,' and 'I'd consider monthly installments, if we can agree on the interest,' which I'm hearing as playfully coded romantic declarations . . .

"Smooth? George Raft could've taken lessons. Shows you how desperate for attention a girl can get."

"Couldn't've been that bad, could it?"

"There were moments. Our honeymoon in Mallorca . . . really something, would you like to hear the details? They're sure engraved in my memory, I can tell you."

"OK with me if you care to skip it."

"I'll take that as please do go on, oh very well, if you insist . . ."

DAPHNE FINDS HERSELF next day almost relieved to be clamorously back in the air, moving at pretty much the altitude and speed of lucid dreaming, slipping along the terrain so unexpectedly close below, fields of cloud stretching away like prairie, then all at once a hell of a lot of trees. Glow's laughter streaming across the altitudes like a white silk aviator's scarf.

A cloud comes out of nowhere to enfold them. Glow cuts the engine and they volplane through. In the relative quiet, they can hear bells of livestock from somewhere below, conversation among invisible steeplejacks whom they seem to be hurtling through this zero visibility within feet of, apt at any moment to hit a hillside, self-impale on a treetop—

Then abruptly out again into blessed sun glare, sky blue, Glow starts up the engine again . . . the racket resumes.

Late in the day as factory shifts are ending, commercial windows catching the last fume-broken rays of the sun suggestive as fortune-telling card layouts no one here quite looks upward to read. Another sizable country town, once believed safe, independent, overrun by the War and broken, left to a diminished history in its seldom traveled corner of the old empire. "Quite a few of them out here, take your pick."

Evening falls, the gyro goes sailing into and through a Searchlight District where public lamps of varying colors and intensities abound, thickets of electric arc beams crossing from every roof, prismatic, cylindrical, masses of shadow, flanges and vanes of light.

Daphne and Glow have found one of the few cafés to remain open after dark. The garish sky above like an anxiously held breath.

"For the moment it's enough work just trying to stay away from Porfirio, meaning away from Spain. He has this notion that Spain is my destiny."

"Meaning that he is?"

"I'm not so sure. I keep running into these psychical types, readers into the future, all telling me I'm on the way to . . . some kind of anarchist sainthood. Spain supposedly being known for its anarchists the way other countries are for their wine, their cooking, or the quality of whoopee within their borders. There's also the church, the military, the old dictator Primo de Rivera, his son who's putting together his own phalanx of Fascists. Hatred between the Right and the Left gets worse every day, Asturias is ready to explode. Soon as I can get hold of a tommy gun I'm just going out before breakfast and start shooting Fascists."

"Not very saintlike."

"Gets worse. I'm nearsighted too. Maybe you think these are pilot goggles—nope, they're glasses, and even with them on, I'm a terrible shot. I can just imagine myself trying to get cute in Spain, 'But *compañera*, no, you must not use this weapon, you are a danger to us all, to yourself.'"

Daphne is giving her a look saying, yes, but at the same time it's not too late, you can still peel off from this sainthood trajectory you think you're on, get back down here with the rest of us, remember what we have to wrestle with every day, before you just go blasting away into some vertical beyond. At least take a vacation from El Smootho. But is not about to start handing out free advice to any gun-happy autogyro pilot.

"Whatever it is that's just about to happen, once it's over we'll say, oh well, it's history, should have seen it coming, and right now it's all I can do to get on with my life. I don't care to know more than I need to about the mysteries of time," snorting briefly, lopsidedly smiling. "You're expecting spiritual wisdom from little G. T. del V.? you'll be waiting a long time, sucker."

BELOW THEM a cheerful march tune can be heard—mandolins, a concertina, a sort of amiable jangle to it all, a moving collective on their way to Fiume, young fighting-age men and women carrying banners with the old D'Annunzian slogan *"Me ne frego,"* another nostalgic descent on what used to be Hungary's exit to the sea, rolling down into town together, down out of the Karst, to waterfront cafés, window boxes spilling over in scarlet turbulence. In the distance, out past the breakwater, evening pleasure steamers in the Quarnero bound to and from different islands.

"I can drop you here in Fiume," Glow offers, "you may have some business here."

"Glow. You've heard something."

"Fish-market intelligence. Something to do with motorcycle traffic."

Her heart jumps but she pretends to gaze at the Adriatic, "Can't help noticing that good-size stretch of water there. On the off chance I'm fed up at last with the fool's errand you found me mixed up in, this might also be a good place to kiss it off and catch a liner the hell on out of."

"Come, come, no way for a cheez princess to talk, keep that chin up, lady."

"Sure, so somebody can take another swing at it."

35

Once a major port of embarkation for the New World, bright and bustling, Fiume now is a tattered ghost city with a sordid history of secret treaties and sellouts, edging its way through what the Fascist Italian regime calls Year Ten, continuing to collapse in on itself, unlikely to be redeemed, barricaded and wire-fenced, corroded, sentry-boxed, moonlit some nights brighter than what flickering neon remains . . .

Some blame Fascist Italy, which absorbed it. Others point out that any attempt to go up against the liberal bourgeois order is destined to fail. Rollicking youth grow old, the middle-class condition goes on forever. So forth.

One day of rain and fog, secondhand light here in the streets and piazzas reflecting off the wet pavement, a day meant for slow silver emulsions and long exposures and few chances for color, Daphne hears a woman somewhere invisible singing "Daleko m'ê moj Split," an operetta tune from a few years back, grabs an umbrella, walks out the door, down an alleyway, then another, trying to find the source. The sky brightening a little, then dark again with more rain.

Adrijana, who works at the cigarette factory, is off shift today and just about to put in earrings representing a black Moor's head in a fancy white turban, which Daphne has been noticing on ears elsewhere around town.

"What wonderful earrings."

"There's something like it in Venice, but you'll find the Morčić only in Fiume. Our little Moor, our protector, our good luck."

They locate a café with a piano in back, Adrijana teaches Daphne the song. "They'll excuse your accent, but miss a double-dot on the beat and they'll never let you forget it."

A COUPLE NIGHTS LATER, after hours, they show up at a sympathetic room in a roadhouse on the Yugoslavian side of the line, where neighborhood musicians like to get together, tonight a C-melody sax, banjo-uke, trombone, piano, an underlying beat from snare brushes and woodblock. Daphne understanding before she's eight bars in, not without goose bumps, that this is likely not the last time she'll be singing it in public . . . a warm peach-colored spot picking up sun streaks in her hair she's forgotten were there, a smile at the band for going easy with practical jokes such as unannounced key changes . . . and after the vocal, an instrumental break, joined out of somewhere by a clarinet, all too immediately recognizable as who else but Hop Wingdale, klezmerizing all over the place, salaciously wiggling his licorice stick in her direction, understanding with some seldom used fraction of his brain, about the same time she tumbles, that like it or not here they are again.

"Caught me right in the middle, couldn't believe it was you, had to stop and go back to the tonic and wait."

"I noticed."

"Liked your number."

"Still needs some work, but thanks."

"Hope you weren't thinking I ran out on you, or—"

"Did cross my mind."

"Daphne, I would never have—"

"Sh-sh. Yes, of course, I've been out there looking for you ever since."

"Thought by now you would've just gone back to the States."

"I would never have done that. Not without you." Eyes gazing nowhere for the effective beat and a half, and when she does look back into his, even a stumblebum like Hop understands the emotional disarray this has already begun to collapse into.

He reaches for a highball glass, where he's been keeping a couple of reeds soaking in slivovitz, drinks what's there, pours in more.

"U-uhck! That's disgusting!"

"Dunno, gives it a sound somehow."

A BUSY ECHOING interior comfortably dim with all-night cigarette and kitchen smoke, young runners who never fall asleep in and out bringing seafood fresh from the Adriatic, a continuous wind outside, down from the high limestone, a theremin of uneasiness, sliding around a narrow band of notes, in which it's said you may come to hear repeated melodies, themes and variations, which is when you know you're going bughouse, with only a very short period of grace to try and escape before it no longer matters.

"What'd I do now?"

"How about what you were doing then." Daphne lights up and sits there deadpan and puffing.

Hop goes through it again and of course it keeps coming out even less convincing, as it has each time around.

"So . . . all this time you were pretending to be a klezmer clarinetist, romantically involved with an heiress to an American cheese fortune, meantime gathering intelligence on the sly, sending faithful summaries, about what and back to whom, exactly, not for the likes of me to imagine."

"Not exactly the way I'd've put it. But—"

"But we both know the headline, Empty-Headed Good-Time Girl Finds Love at Last, meantime falling for one of the sorriest routines in the history of male deceit, congratulations, lady-killer, what it must've cost you—my yes, the stamina, the patience. All those tea leaf readers and penny scales were right all along. Cheeziness is my destiny. Should have stuck with Rodney, least there'd've been some class in my life."

"Wait, second thoughts about—"

"You bet. Especially since he went literary."

Having reluctantly given up on scheming after Daphne's fortune, G. Rodney Flaunch has recently published *How to Lose a Million and a Half and Bounce Back Smiling,* already named a Book of the Month and picking up a devout group of followers growing larger every day, including indicted embezzlers, retired moonshiners, and perpetual litigants, with plans for a further series of *How to Lose* books plus a Dale Carnegie–style lecture-seminar to go along with each. "I can get you signed copies, if you like."

"You have every right to feel this bitter—"

"Just your sensitive, caring side coming out, don't let it bother you, it won't last long."

"Someday this will all ease up. Someday, some heat wave of danger and crisis safely behind us, released into the first autumn breezes of rational adult behavior, I'll be tracking some long-held secret bank account, you'll be shopping for a hat to celebrate the new fashion season. We'll cross paths in the bar of some grand hotel . . ."

"Traveling sales-rep talk, yes spare us both, Hop, or whatever you're calling yourself these days. Don't even bother to come looking, you won't find me that useful anymore."

"Useful. I want useful, I go to a hardware store . . ."

But she's already out the door.

HICKS RUNS INTO Daphne down at the harbor, busy wrapping up some arrangement with Drago Pebkać, skipper of a little coaster making break-bulk runs to Split, Dubrovnik, Corfu, and points beyond.

Focusing in on his right earlobe, "We're both wearing the same earring, that Morčić."

"Wouldn't cast off a line without it."

"Never thought I'd need that kind of luck, but— Eek! why Hicks, you did make me jump."

"Only havin a look, no need to act furtive or nothin, jake with me if you're hightailin it, Daphne, long as you don't mind signing a release, keep 'em all happy back in Milwaukee."

Drago casting a look of speedy appraisal, "Special rate for two, if—"

"Not me," sez Hicks.

"Not him," confirms Daphne.

"Buy you a quick cup of Joe, you got time."

They find a café. "That boat trip isn't for me, as if you didn't guess. Me, I'm taking the next liner back, you'll be happy to hear."

"Must be Bruno then. Don't tell me nothin more, I'm still technically workin for Praediger, who thinks I'm helping him haul Bruno in."

"You won't say anything, will you?"

Shrug. "Not my ticket, even if somebody tells me what in heck's going on, which ain't about to happen. And with Praediger I can't get a word in edgewise anyway."

"What did you think would happen?"

"No idea. Besides which, the gumshoe's code, no daydreaming on the job, so forth."

"He's in real danger, seriously on the lam this time. I can't not help him, Hicks."

"Gotcha." They observe each other carefully in the precarious sunlight. "Well, Daphne, now, there might be one thing—"

"Ha! The speedboat! I knew the moment would come! Look at him, he can't stand it anymore, can't keep away from those *motorboat memories*, yes, damned if he isn't turning to Jell-O right here before my eyes!"

"Well only a small favor, but if you're gonna be that way . . ."

"No. What I really mean is thanks forever for saving me way back when from the kindly attentions of the Winnetka bughouse, and consider yourself released. It was an impulsive act of rescue and thus may not incur recompense, let alone lifelong obligation, U.S. versus somebody, federal case, I looked it up once."

"You're lettin me off that Chippewa hook? About time."

"There was also something about—"

"Oh. Well, in case I don't get back to the States as soon as you do? if you wouldn't mind getting a message to somebody?"

"The girl you left behind you."

"More like grown woman, married, family to raise, unknown numbers of gun-totin Calabresi in the picture, but if it was being brought to her personally, see, by the actual daughter of the Al Capone of Cheese in Exile . . ."

"My pleasure, I'm sure, and that object you keep carrying around all the time there? I hope you're paid up on your fire insurance."

What one of them should have been saying was "We're in the last minutes of a break that will seem so wonderful and peaceable and carefree. If anybody's around to remember. Still trying to keep on with it before it gets too dark. Until finally we turn to look back the way we came, and there's that last light bulb, once so bright, now feebly flickering, about to burn out, and it's well past time to be saying, Florsheims, let's ambulate.

"Stay, or go. Two fates beginning to diverge—back to the U.S., marry, raise a family, assemble a life you can persuade yourself is free from fear, as meanwhile, over here, the other outcome continues to unfold, to roll in dark as the end of time. Those you could have saved, could've shifted at least somehow onto a safer stretch of track, are one by one robbed, beaten, killed, seized and taken away into the nameless, the unrecoverable.

"Until one night, too late, you wake into an understanding of what you should have been doing with your life all along."

Something like that. If anybody was still there to hear it. Which there isn't.

36

Bruno had been hearing about Fiume since it was still an independent state under D'Annunzio. What brought him there in person was a scouting assignment on behalf of the InChSyn, which by then had grown more global and sinister in scope, avoiding central headquarters, instead choosing a more distributed model, free-zone hopping, setting up shop in short-lived entities emerging from the World War and the Russian Revolution, preferring mixed populations, disputed territories, histories of plebiscites and provisional government, currencies printed on inexpensive stock in fugitive inks.

Fiume, despite a rumor Woodrow Wilson was once considering it as a site for the League of Nations HQ, turned out to be one such focus of impermanence. Bruno himself by then, keeping on the hop, expecting the door to be kicked in any minute, avoiding paperwork, file cabinets, anything too heavy to pick up and vamoose with, took little more than a look and was instantly charmed, acquiring a villa just across the border from the new Yugoslavian entity, in fact having no agreed-upon location unless "Currently in Dispute" is your idea of a postal address, at times partly situated in Serbo-Croat-Slovene territory, and part in Fascist Italy . . . from which if necessary a cheeze magnate on the move could easily step from country to country as long as he's willing to put up with sentries, delays, routines of the borderline that require constant attention to grease and gratuities.

For Daphne the villa is a place she would gladly have come "home" to, even to live in. Her prayers for Bruno having once almost included the hope that he grow into somebody who'd understand and deserve someplace very like this, however much South Sea cooch-dancing tabloid scenarios might turn out to be more up his alley.

The villa dates from just after the War, when d'Annunzio's republic was young and Fiume had a reputation as a party town, fun-seekers converging from all over, whoopee of many persuasions, wide-open to nudists, vegetarians, coke snorters, tricksters, pirates and runners of contraband, orgy-goers, fighters of after-dark hand-grenade duels, astounders of the bourgeoisie . . . Bridges, archways, views of the gulf and the islands, floor plan like a native quarter, with a lengthy history of re-surveys and legal shouting matches in various international courtrooms. Easy for visitors to get lost climbing up and down among levels, running mazes vertical and horizontal, navigating an indoor geography they fail to learn much about before it's time to move on. Nobody knows how many rooms there are, scale enough for suites and wings, alliances and betrayals, storms of armed emotion sweeping through the house unannounced.

At night the lights of the villa shine far out over the sea, all night long, behind each window, someone is always awake late and up to something— night owls, freeloaders, accidental walk-ins, practitioners of esoteric arts, fearers of the dark, compulsive socializers, secret police, jewel thieves, firefly girls, drug dealers, cigarette-factory workers, tobacco smugglers, a dependable number each evening lately of Trans-Trianon bikers, though it hasn't taken local authorities long to outlaw group motor sorties after dark. Not that anybody complies or that there are enough personnel on hand to do anything about it.

One afternoon out on the Korzo, Hicks runs into Terike, who's in town looking to head off Ace "before he gets into something he can't handle," is how she puts it.

"Riding point again."

"Not exactly. There's more to this."

"Always is, and someday if anybody's still alive you'll tell me all about it. Meantime, if I knew you were this cold I'd've asked you to keep a bottle of beer for me close to your heart."

Seems Ace has blown into Fiume aboard a 976 cc Royal Enfield plus sidecar, forced after a good deal of sentimental bikerly brooding to admit that this current ride is no substitute for his old Harley Flathead, which, though less of a coherent machine than a history of maintenance melodramas each waiting its turn to be enacted, he now misses heartbroken as a cowboy in a song, convinced by now that it is Bruno Airmont who's responsible for its loss, seeing how it was Bruno who chased them into Vladboys territory to begin with, and thus obvious to anybody that Bruno must also bear the cost of its replacement, estimated at 200 quid, which Ace will accept in dollars, dinars, Reichsmarks, or if necessary—such is the state he's worked himself up into—blood. "Actually I can do without the blood, too much cleanup, just the sucker's head would be enough."

"We don't do heads ordinarily, but there are people we could put you in touch with. Do you speak Albanian?"

"Then again maybe I'd settle for his last known address, how'd that be?"

Accordingly, one otherwise tranquil evening, down out of the hailstorms and lightning of the Karst, surrounded by a blinding halo of disgruntlement, Ace arrives at Bruno's villa with no clear plan in mind.

In one of several loosely defined Grand Salons, the nightly spirited uproar has continued to pick up speed. As if somebody has found the ignition key to a time machine, the secret equations of social turbulence are once again in effect as in the days of D'Annunzio. People are keeping company here who, if history had a shred of decency, would never be allowed within miles of each other. Rogue nuns in civilian gear are two-stepping with bomb-rolling Marxist guerrillas. Fascist daredevil aviators are playing poker with Yangtze Patrol veterans who believe all that airplanes are good for is to be shot down. Wagnerian sopranos are learning the hillbilly guitar chords to "Wabash Cannonball." Pirates are getting soused with peddlers of marine insurance. And Porfirio del Vasto, having tracked Glow here in her autogyro after she dropped off Daphne, loitering wistfully, looking for some excuse to get into a duel with somebody, though lately nothing's been going right. Torrential rainfalls at dawn that the gunpowder always manages to get left out in, blanks swapped for live ammo. Last-minute apologies, sometimes accompanied by cash. "It's like the material world telling me this is the wrong path to take . . ." He sells his perfectly matched Wogdon dueling pistols to an indecently eager collector in Chipping Sodbury, Gloucestershire, briefly considers switching to sabers, which may account for why he's been in and out of Hungary lately. Taking saber lessons. He's gotten pretty good on the backs of horses accustomed to this sort of thing, carried at a gallop down rows of champagne bottles and whacking the tops off.

At the moment Porfirio is deep in earnest dialogue with former Berlin chorus girl Lady Forsythia Bladesmith, who's trying to remember if they've met.

"Buenos Aires, perhaps, around the time of the coup? Teatro Colón, performance of *Tosca*, Apollo Granforte sang Scarpia. You were busy down in the stalls among the marriage brokers, though pursuing business less respectable—"

Through some deep unacknowledged Freudian means, Porfirio's old jewel thief reflexes crank up again, but just as he's reaching, zap! they asport away, diamonds of just under two carats each plus palladium findings, vanishing off of her earlobes clean as a whistle. Feeling the sudden release, she gives Porfirio a long, funny look.

"Not me." Hands spread in puzzled innocence.

"Mind turning out your pockets?"

"*Cómo no*," revealing a silver and enamel case full of stolen smokes, a flash roll diverse as the League of Nations, a fob shaped like an Alp holding a couple of keys for car, house, autogyro. "This has happened to you before, *¿verdad?*"

"Never perhaps with so light a touch, or without some kind of romantic business to divert my attention. One reason I prefer a screw-back style, they take so long to undo before anyone can slide them off. Necklaces are what you people tend to go for, the clasps are far easier. All common knowledge among your sort, I expect."

"Allow me to point out that I'm only a used-autogyro salesman."

"Of course, and who's been using you? And—aaggh!" at which point her earlobes are suddenly milligrams heavier again as the missing earrings apport back into place, and across the room there's Zoltán von Kiss winking and beaming, lifting another glass of Pommery from a passing tray and angling it amiably their way.

Ace Lomax wanders by, spots Hicks and Zoltán von Kiss. "Sorry about those Cubs, four straight in the Series like that, damn."

"Murderers' Row," Hicks shrugs, "what did anybody expect?"

"And Babe Ruth calling that shot, huh?"

"Never heard the details."

"Top of the fifth, count is 0 and 2, after each strike the Babe steps out, points toward center field—next pitch looks like it'll be strike three, instead wham, he sends it out to deep center, past the flagpole into the stands exactly where he was pointing at."

Zoltán is intrigued. "Such precision is common in baseball?" with a mischievous look Hicks recognizes.

"Not very."

"Then . . ."

"Don't say it," sez Hicks, "it's 'em apports again, what else, it's how Zoli explains everything, ain't it."

"That lamp back in Budapest," Ace recalls, "that same mental whammy, you're saying that's how Babe Ruth—"

"Puts a homer where he says he will," Hicks nodding. "We know all it is is a perfect eye, perfect timing. But—"

"Some might call that supernatural," observes Zoltán.

"Especially Chicago fans," Hicks adds. "What're you doin down this neck of the woods anyway, Zoli, you're supposed to be in Budapest."

"Business, I'll be gone again before you know it, like Petőfi in the fog. Our mutual pal Praediger has a screaming obsession with the mysterious disappearance off the dock in Hamburg—Praediger says a hundred kilos, possibly more—of raw Peruvian coca paste en route to the lab, allegedly intercepted by a gang of apportists based in Budapest with whom I have always done respectable business, transferred to a submarine, at present here in Fiume, to be delivered to points beyond, one of whose crew members is not unknown to you, a Mr. Keegan . . ."

"Stuffy. Him and that sub, they're here in town? He said they might be."

"I'm only the go-between here, as usual. Mr. Keegan seems anxious to confer with you."

"This sub—you've seen it?"

"Maybe. It was at night, they told me that's what it was. If it apported in, it was on a scale bigger than I've ever been comfortable working at . . . in any case I'm told not everybody gets to see it."

"I went through the same routine back in M'waukee."

Sudden screaming, followed by a tremendous crash full of jingling crystal drops and brasswork, as three partygoers sitting up in a chandelier too flimsily anchored in the ceiling to hold them for long land without injury on a conveniently located overstuffed sofa, one of whom seems to be Egon Praediger, nose merrily aglow, presently able to scramble away on hands and knees, giggling. Bruno gazes after him. "Well. So-fa, so good . . ."

"Congratulations," Hicks with a touch to his hat brim, "there goes the collar of his career, he's been after you forever."

One of the deeper lessons of grand opera for the working gumshoe that Boynt forgot to pass on to Hicks is that even the most villainous of bassbaritones may turn out to be a nervous soul trembling with anxiety for the high notes just a few bars ahead. "Time to be making tracks then, ain't it," is how Bruno puts it.

"You'd really be better off in the Gray House," ZvK assures him. "Trust me, I can read the future. Compared to what's waiting for you out there on the run, the Josefstadt lockup is a suite at the Ritz."

"My combination's just outside," Ace offers. "Case somebody needs a ride in a hurry."

"You?" Bruno fooling with his hair like Hitler in the newsreels, "a free ride from you? Sure, straight into the clutches of that Austrian flatfoot you've no doubt been stooging for."

"Aw, lookit, his feelings are hurt 'cause I skipped? You had me on your target list, Bruno, what was I supposed to do?"

"Maybe all that time I was trying to educate you on the sly, even about to name you as the official Deputy Al Capone of Cheese—you're telling me you never saw it happen back in the War? C.O. gets put out of commission, wise old-timer of a sergeant steps up, brings the outfit through?"

"And me thinking I was always just cannon fodder. You coming or not?"

Takes them a while to find their way out among early departures from the all-night jollification, the reluctant, the fugitive and piratical and later, emerging somehow untouched into the yet unbroken day, bickering in whispers, looking around for their shoes, even a few drowsy advertisements for love at first sight.

"You might want to keep an eye peeled," advises Bruno, "for anybody looks like Praediger's posse of Inter-police down from Vienna. Any of them we can shake, so much the better."

At the parking lot finally, "Here's the bike, climb on in the sidecar, we'll be on our way."

"What happened to the Harley-Davidson?"

"Thanks for asking. I was about to bring that up. You OK in there? Good. Hang on."

Local coppers out in the street are no happier than they ever are around here with motorcycles after dark, but as if Bruno is broadcasting do-not-disturb signals or something, the route to the elegant Hotel Bonavia remains strangely clear all the way.

"Now as to the matter of who'll be springing for this combination here. How exactly I came by it need not detain us, but at some point I do recall passing along your name and address, and they said they'd send you an invoice. Should run you in the neighborhood of a grand, U.S."

"Me? Somebody took your word that I'd—and, and then they just let you—ride off?"

"Your name must still work magic."

"My daughter says you have an honest face."

"Sure, that must be it. Thank her when you see her."

"She might be here at the moment, if you—"

"What's this, Boss? Branching out into the lonely hearts racket, now?"

"Why not, you'd make a handsome couple and the job offer stands. Head of Operations, Adjutant Kingpin, call it what you like."

"How about 'a dark delayed and a smacker short'? Sorry, Bruno. I'll stick with freewheeling solo for a while."

Offers of steady work keep rolling in. At a shipfitters' bar in Kraljevica, Ace runs into Hop Wingdale again. "That was a tight spot you got us out of, back up the road there."

"Not me, it was really that Czechoslovakian robot should get all the credit."

"We could use you both at our shop. Sort of underground work. Escorting Jews to safety, one at a time or in truckloads, become a sought-after specialist in a fast-growing field, bright earning possibilities—"

"Earn Unlimited 'Gelt' in Jew Rescue, sounds like the back pages of *Popular Mechanics*. You know what I used to do when I was working for Bruno, right?"

"Antisemitic grand larceny, so what? even better. Gives you a chance to reform."

"Let me think about it." He's still thinking. Meantime a spot of aggravation with his triple tree rake angle is demanding some attention.

37

Abandoned after the War, the old Whitehead factory, where the torpedo as we have come to know it was invented, has fallen into ruin, occupied these days by unhoused squatters and motorcyclists passing through. Few care to stay much longer than overnight, because it's said to be haunted by the ghosts of submarines long dismantled which feel compelled to return to their birthplace. More objects-with-souls gobbledeygook, Hicks figures. Hopefully.

The map Stuffy drew for Hicks seems clear enough. The beer joint is easy to walk up to and into but no guarantees about getting back out. Hicks has a look around. Enough light to see by, despite a blur of smoke out of which anything can come hurtling unannounced, a couple of industrious barmaids whose smiles are not unconnected with having just come on shift, circulating among assorted submarine sailors, if that's what they are, on liberty, plus a few homegrown tomatoes rolling in and out.

"Nice joint, Stuffy. Been in worse."

"What'd I tell you? Come on, like you to meet the Skipper."

Ernst Hauffnitz is set up at a corner table behind a smoldering pipeful of some Latakia blend and a half-liter beer mug. Hicks isn't sure what kind of story the sub skipper's had from Stuffy, but apparently the cheez heiress ticket comes into it by way of Bruno Airmont.

"Who is about to be taken, as we speak, off on an undersea voyage of uncertain extent. We and our client apologize for any inconvenience this may be causing you."

"This client wouldn't happen to be a Viennese copper named Praediger—"

"Ach, der Praediger." A chuckle plus two or three puffs of pipe smoke. "Ustashe operative, cocaine enthusiast . . ."

"That's the kiddie."

"It doesn't matter. The vessel is invisible to him, as it is to the Vienna Police Directorate, none of whom have been exactly alone in their plodding pursuit of Mr. Airmont—there's been quite a long list, headed by the International Cheese Syndicate, who happen to be the ones breathing down our necks at the moment." It isn't only the hefty amount of Syndicate money that Bruno has embezzled, but also everything he knows about the inner workings of the InChSyn. "The secret overlords of Cheese are understandably anxious for that to remain in confidence, even—in fact—at the cost of Mr. Airmont's life. Working ourselves generally more in the search and rescue line, our objective is to see that Mr. Airmont is safely relocated where he can neither commit nor incur further harm. You might consider us an encapsulated volume of pre-Fascist space-time, forever on the move, a patch of Fiume as it once was, immune to time, surviving all these years in the deep refuge of the sea . . ."

Doubts began for the Skipper early in the War, when Max Valentiner torpedoed and sank SS *Persia* in the Mediterranean, killing 343 civilians in direct violation of Chancellery orders to spare passengers and rescue survivors. "I remembered Max from U-boat school in Kiel. Before the War he had become famous for saving lives. A hero, many times decorated. But command of one's own U-boat can do strange things to a man."

"Yet you managed to avoid that."

"Spent my time in the Mediterranean Theater bottled up in the Adriatic behind the Otranto Barrage, playing cat and mouse with British destroyers and drifters, no casualty count that I know of, idiot's luck no doubt . . . Some of us, if consciences had toenails, would be hanging on by just that margin. Yet conscience must find ways to go on operating inside history."

In the late summer of 1921, U-13 was ordered to proceed to its birthplace, the Óbuda shipyard in Budapest, to be broken up pursuant to Article

122 of the Trianon dictate. About a day out from port the Skipper had one of those moments. The K.u.K. Kriegsmarine had ceased to exist in 1918. Orders from some bureaucratic successor made no sense at all. The Skipper tied up at a disused quay near Csepel, left a skeleton crew, and sent everybody else over on liberty and went on a meditative bender himself in Budapest, his thoughts far from festive. The city had a long history of suicide, attracting pilgrims from all over the world seeking a Lourdes not of hope but of despair, assuming that suicide in Budapest, like love in Paris or greed in New York, would be somehow more authentic.

One night on the Chain Bridge, gazing down at the river, in an alcoholic trance, he was approached by a small delegation of his crew members, out looking for him, as it happened. "Evening, Skipper, hope we're not interrupting anything."

"Trouble with the boat?"

"The boat's fine. But we've been wondering, some of us, why you're not bringing her into the yard."

"Why I'm disobeying orders."

"Something like that."

"I admit my command had more to do with running enemy blockades than disrupting their shipping, but I still developed a strange rapport with the boat, you could almost call it a sort of psychical connectedness . . ."

Not exactly muttering but producing the subvocal impression that the old man had gone off his rocker at last or, as some would put it, again.

". . . so you can appreciate that to hand over the U-13 to the ship-breakers makes no more sense than it would to commit suicide myself—wait, what'd I just say . . ."

Indeed. As he would later come to explain it, that moment was the beginning of his new career of nonbelligerence, though other forces were already at work, running, you could say, deeper—fear of and desire for oceanic depths despite the U-13 having been originally designed for shallower missions, for actually creeping about on *retractable wheels* over harbor floors at modest depths, still there will come over him an urge more ancient than anything he knows of to go deeper, to descend, rivets creaking, into depths legendary as those of the Valdivia Expedition of 1898–99, which brought up into the daylight a pitch-black critter known as the Vampire Squid, by whose name, these days, the U-13 has since come to be known.

"WHAT WE EXPECTED," Bruno handing Daphne an account number at a bank in Geneva, "it's here. I was going to leave you this at the last minute and now's about as last minute as it's going to get, so here you go, my li'l midnight pumpkin, all for you."

"Don't want your money, never did."

"Better than money."

"No such thing."

"It's information. Enough on the secret history of the InChSyn, and the full membership, anonymous and otherwise, to send the whole business up in one giant fondoozical cataclysm."

"And whatever's left gets grabbed up by pikers and riffraff—Kraft, Unilever, the Cheese Exchange in Sheboygan, oh, Pop, no, how can I—"

"All safe and sound in a vault under a remote Swiss mountain range just waiting for you. You'll know when, if, and how to use it. Everything the Al Capone of Cheez was Al Capone of is now in your hands, you're the Alcaponissima."

"Di Formaggio, thanks, Pop. The boat's all set to go, Drago says he does this all the time, a look-alike in a beat-up old jalopy with 8 cylinders under the hood will lead them miles out of the way and then go invisible, meantime you're off with Drago's crew doing a little harmless night fishing. Skipped before anybody knows it."

"Where'd I ever get the idea you were just some kind of innocent bystander."

"Gossip columnists will say anything. Better you find out now than when it's too late."

"Oh, Daphne—"

"Don't know why I said that. Forget it. It's not too late, Pop, never will be, not for us."

Quick look at a Rolex Oyster Perpetual he does not seem to recognize, as if thanks to the psychical ambience he's been in all evening it has just apported onto his wrist, "Could be if we don't hurry."

CLOSE TO DAWN, a pale foreglow revealing clouds sweeping over and down from the Karst, Drago Pebkać, at the wheel of his little coaster, having threaded his way innocently among a number of islands, out in the open Adriatic at last, is presented with an unexpected dilemma—is the dark shape now looming ahead a solid real-world vessel, or some fragment of nightmare reluctant to withdraw into the early light?

"Not a mirage," his Moor's-head earring in a whisper only he can hear. "Solid steel and on a collision course."

Drago stops the engine and heaves to. A hatch in the U-boat's conning tower opens, and Ernst Hauffnitz, in an old-time Austro-Hungarian captain's uniform, brass buttons, visor cap with gold braid and so forth, comes out with a megaphone. "You have an American passenger aboard."

"Looks like that won't be for much longer."

"Where were you taking him?"

"Hadn't decided. Dubrovnik?"

The Skipper hauls out his pipe and lights up as Bruno emerges on deck in a state of agitation. "I thought we had a deal."

"A young woman handed me an envelope full of banknotes. I took you aboard. In your country that may pass for a sacred covenant. Out here . . ." A shrug.

"How much more will it cost you to let me off in Dubrovnik?"

"Take it up with this gentleman and his U-boat. I have no inclination this morning to be torpedoed."

Captain Hauffnitz puffs away, mischievously beaming. "Dubrovnik's loss. Come along, Mr. Airmont, and welcome aboard."

The hatch is secured behind them and the metallic command to dive is heard on the loudspeakers. Bruno is escorted to a snug though not uncomfortable cabin and handed a cigar compliments of the U-13. He lights up, sits awhile smoking and stupefied. Goes over to a porthole and observes a tuna looking back in at him showing every sign of wanting to communicate. Is this the brig I'm in, he wonders. No, submarines don't have brigs, they *are* brigs. The tuna winks its visible eye and swims off. Bruno turns abruptly. Lounging in the doorway is somebody he thinks he ought to recognize.

"Howdy, Bruno."

"Who are you?"

"Christopher Keegan, but everybody calls me Stuffy."

"Whose bright idea was this? It's that goddamned Praediger, isn't it?"

"Somebody else, some cheese syndicate. A while ago they say you skipped with a good-size piece of their cash, and they still want it back."

"I've spent some of it."

"No regrets, I guess."

"Why? What else do you do with money? Eat it, smoke it? Take it out on a date?"

"They're OK with whatever percentage is left. But they intend to be less than courteous if they ever get hold of you."

"And how much are you delivering me for?"

"We're not working for them."

"Who?"

Shrug. "See, there's a difference between the Al Capone of Cheese and the AC of C in Exile. One sooner or later gets the paving-material overcoat. The other goes where he'll do no harm. Our racket happens to be exile."

"You're telling me there are death squads going around with a list of targets while friendly submarines meantime are also cruising around benevolently picking them up before any harm can be done. This is crazy."

"Latest from Stateside," handing over a copy of the *Chicago Tribune*, delivered out of the darkness by transoceanic radio facsimile. Seems revolution has broken out in the U.S., beginning in Wisconsin as a strike over the price per hundredweight that dairy farmers were demanding for milk, spreading across the region and soon the nation. Milk shipments hijacked and dumped at trackside, trees felled across roadways and set aflame to stop motor delivery, all-night sentinels, crossroads pickets, roundups, ambushes, bayonet charges, gunfire, casualties military and civilian.

"They're out to destroy Cheese," is Bruno's immediate assumption. "To destroy everything I'm Al Capone of." Nobody wants to hear about it. The real Al Capone can't help, he's in the pen now and the Outfit has other problems on its mind. The Red Hour has struck at last. Bankers, capitalists, clubfellows, Fascists locally and abroad ignore Bruno's pleas, offer no aid or comfort, fail to return ship-to-shore phone calls, often too busy thrashing desperately themselves against the relentless vortex of a sinking world order, others relying on their faith in the realities of blood and soil, which never go away, to save them.

"I knew it. The minute that damned Bolshevik Roosevelt got into office—"

"Only for a minute and a half. There was a coup. Gang of millionaires including a couple of Roosevelt's own Brain Trusters, like that Hugh Johnson. General MacArthur is in command now."

"The one who broke up the Bonus Army."

"Says he understands the insurrectionary mind."

"Old Milwaukee family. I think Doug went to West Division High around the time I was in Chicago Latin."

"Might be a useful contact for you back there."

"We never met, we didn't move in the same circles."

38

Meantime on the Korzo who should show up one morning at Caffè Impresa but Dippy Chazz Foditto, wearing a Borsalino, a bespoke Neapolitan suit, and Lenthéric Men's After Shave Lotion, waving around an unlit full-length Toscano. Being deported, in style it seems, back to his ancestral Sicily, in fact on the way down there right now after a quick detour through Naples to see about another suit fitting with Bebè himself, "That's Gennaro Rubinacci to you."

Chazz has become something of an international adventurer, having at the moment just signed on to a scheme hatched and run by U.S. ruling-class elements who are betting that the island of Sicily will be a strategic factor in the next war, and that therefore a local anti-Fascist guerrilla force, trained, armed, and ready to roll, might someday prove helpful.

"They hate Mussolini, who's been trying to bring the island under Fascist control—sorry, Duce, no sale—which has not been lost on my principals."

"Which is who again?" Hicks inquires.

"Rich white guys I used to see all the time in that chop house next door to the Union League that Jake Guzik worked out of, Saint something . . . It was ol' Greasy Thumb who introduced us, in fact. The deal is I do them this one li'l international intrigue job, and they drop everything they got against me which if you add up the beefs just since I saw you last is already plenty. Plus now I'm on a federal swindle sheet with a nice-size wagonload to spend."

"Better watch it, Dipster, this could put you only about a sawbuck short of respectable."

"Stepped right into it, can't remember how long ago anymore, and now I'm stuck. There's no catch and release with these trawlers, they eat what they pull in. They call it duty to my country but it's really penance for my sins including all that double-dating you and me did back in the olden days, remember, hey, that Lois and her crazy friend," kissing his fingertips, "couple a tomatizz, huh? strictly San Marzano." By now they have strolled as far as the *ribarnica*, or fish market, where they are gazed back at by the bright though regrettably dead eyes of a full assortment of recent dwellers in the Adriatic.

"Your lucky day, Dips, if we ever double-dated I don't recall none of that and seein I'm the only witness you get a full pardon, OK? I'm not giving you the jitters, here am I?"

"Me? Cool like the *giadrul*. How about you?"

"Keep lookin like you're just about to say somethin, then you change the subject."

"There might be one small news item, somebody should of passed it on to you, but if I do it then you'll blame me, so maybe I better not."

"M'waukee, everything there's all right?" Along the payline of Hicks's uneasiness, reel by reel, full-color fruit images have begun to click into place.

Dippy C. shrugs, Hicks shrugs him right back. "I'm supposed to guess?"

"Everybody else would've by now."

"C'mon, Chazz, for a pal?"

"That's right, muscle it outa me, hired torpedoes, it's all y'z ever know how to do, ain't it. Swell," less a snort than an articulate release of Toscano smoke. "You asked for it," reaching under the cracked ice for a gold-headed sea bream and speaking into it like a microphone, talk about a fish in the face, "Bulletin just being handed to me, dateline Kenosha, hot off the society page, is that sometime later this summer local songstress April Randazzo and 'Ndrangheta kingpin Don Peppino Infernacci are expecting a blessed event, and we don't mean no audience with the Pope, all right?" After watching Hicks just sit there idiotized awhile, DC, nervously, "Your thoughts on this, Mr. McTaggart, if any."

Hicks lights up a local Croatian cigarette, inhales and exhales a couple times. "Sure snaps a silencer onto the conversation, don't it."

"Didn't expect you'd be so calm about it—me, hey, I'd be eaten alive by jealousy."

"Thanks, Chazz, I knew you'd understand."

"Yeah, I'd be on the next liner back to the U.S.A., stow away if I had to, so what if it's that whole outfit down there in Li'l Cosenza, even if you could beat the morning line on that, both o' yiz somehow making it out of Wisconsin alive, on the run forever . . . Even with no baby in the picture—"

"All right, all right. See if I've got this straight now . . ."

"Kidding aside, it's no place you want to go tap-dancin into, even by accident, I can name you a dozen reckless youths who have met with grievous fates for so much as even once maybe twitching an eyeball at some *goomara* of Don Peppino's as she went gliding by."

"Gotcha. Reading my mind, Chazzy, and excuse me for wondering, but what's it to you?"

"Just want to be sure you're not mistaking this for the usual evening at the opera, some elderly basso trying to keep the leash on a soprano that's in the mood to get out and scramble, see, instead of which you got April here, married to and pregnant by the exact type who normally she'd've only been out kidding around with . . ."

"Tryin to tell me—"

"Got enough to worry about already without some comedian from her past shows up with romance on the brain . . ."

"Me?"

"You, and you're only the *picciotu*, don't expect much sympathy, old flames are a dime a dozen, West Madison of the labor market of love, sad, desperate, and cheap."

"I'm supposed to just—"

"Wake-up time fa yiz, Hicksie, time to be up off of the linoleum and don't look too forlorn, you're out of a bad situation, nobody's here to endanger a hair on your head, speakin of which yours could use some attention," producing a pocket comb and advancing on Hicks.

"Don't," dodging away, "much go for folks bein all in my hair's the thing, Dippy C., 'f that's OK."

Comb disappearing, empty hands spread in innocence, "Take the tip, is all, it's over for you in M'waukee, Hicks, Chicago too, not many old pals you can count on anymore. Not even ol' Lino the Dump Truck, gone too respectable these days to be seen with mugs like you, sorry to say. Believe me, I'm an expert, what's happened is, is you've been deported, same as me."

"What now, this is somebody's sending *me* to Sicily?"

"You should be so lucky. Just better not count on gettin back to the States anytime soon. Best thing for you'd be change your name and get into some other racket, like international intrigue."

"Sounds like government work, anything like what you're doin, fat chance."

"Long as you don't start believin none of the propaganda they all keep throwin at you, remember to trust your own judgment," picking up a concertina, ". . . and like the great Luigi Pirandello always reminds us, ooh—"

> "Co . . . sì è,
> *(Se vi pare)*,"
> Yes and so it is, if
> That's-how, it-looks, to you . . .
> no use say-ing,
> "Whoa, oops, I'm sor-ray,"
> Just 'cause you don't see
> What all them others do . . .
> With the sky full
> Of storms and thunder,
> Thinkin they're under
> Some heaven of blue,
> Ehi, don't worry!
> mah ol' *goombah-ray, co-wo-wo-*
> *-sì è . . . se, vi, pa-re . . .*

SOMETIME IN THE dawn hours of the first day of a post-American life, passing from a brief moment of hopefulness into the outer fringes of whatever it is that's coming, Hicks has been dreaming he's someplace back on the prairie, in an old lopsided telephone booth warped by the wind, snowed and hailed on, run into by cars and farm wagons, assaulted by hungry drifters looking for all those nickels in the box.

Onto which he drops in another, dials a number without thinking much about it till later, when he remembers it's a TRIangle exchange number in Chicago, same as Al Capone's mother has. After a few rings, "Who's this, and it better be good."

"It's Hicks, who's this?"

"Hicks, what the hell."

"Ma?"

"Last time I checked. How about you?"

"Where are you?"

"Better not say much. They listen in."

"Who?"

"The ones I work for."

"Same ones?"

"Yep."

"Ma, can't you see what they are?"

"It's not for everybody, Sunshine."

"But if you decided to quit—"

"Keep meaning to look into that."

"You always said it was wrong."

"Maybe I didn't know what I was talking about. Maybe it's too late. Just mind what you see and hear in the sky. Ain't likely to be wild geese on the wing. If you're lucky you'll have some shelter ready to jump into, someplace you can believe for a while will be safer. Please stay safe, my Carload o' Kisses."

"Your what?"

"I used to call you that when you were little and we kissed a lot. Carload of Kisses."

"Don't remember."

"I do."

"Long time ago," trying to find it, maybe with just a glimpse of something blowing away into the night, something it's already too late to chase in this windbeaten emptiness taking possession of his heart . . .

39

Somewhere out beyond the western edge of the Old World is said to stand a wonder of our time, a statue hundreds of meters high, of a masked woman draped in military gear less ceremonial than suited to action in the field. Nothing else around for uncounted miles of ocean, only the lofty figure, wind, weather, ocean. Her facial expression, hair and brow at their forbidding height undefined, an openwork visor of some darkly corroded metal protecting, some say hiding, her identity, though now and then aircraft at this altitude have reported glimpses of something like a face behind the mask, more specific and somehow more familiar than faces commonly found on public statuary, keeping a direct gaze at the viewer, as if she's just about to speak. Like somebody we knew once a long time ago.

The U-13, surfaced, passes slowly, everybody out on deck for a look. She can be seen for miles till night unmeasurably vast falls around her.

"Statue of Liberty," guesses Bruno.

"Nope," Stuffy replies, "and we ain't Gallagher and Shean either. There is no Statue of Liberty, Bruno, no such thing, not where you're going."

"You said you're taking me back to the States."

"We are, and then again we're not."

"Meaning what?"

"It's the U.S. but not exactly the one you left. There's exile and there's exile."

All night long, between watches, sleepless, not always sure what they're dreaming and what they've drifted out of dreaming back into however briefly . . . faces turning from time to time to gaze back down their wake, turning together and drifting upward as if for signs of intention from above, if not quite yet in terror or wonder, at least put on notice—their sight lines briefly converging at the same place in the sky where clouds invisible till dawn are towering toward an altitude still to be reached, a shape as yet untaken, unimagined.

Whatever counter-domain of exile this is they have wandered into, they will be headed not back into any sunrise but west, toward a frontier as yet only suspected, as the days sweep over them—

As Hicks begins to understand he's not going back to the States right away, that what he thought mattered to him is now foreclosed and he's stuck over here maybe forever, he has a moment of panic. "What'm I spoze to do, I can't even speak the language."

Terike zooms right in. "Time you started learning, isn't it. Here, a tomato. Say '*paradicsom*.'"

"Which one, you or it?"

"Too difficult, let's try '*csókolj meg*.' Means 'kiss me.' Go ahead, try it."

"*Csókolj meg*."

"Oh all right, if you insist." She kisses him. "Hmm, could use some work, let's hear it again."

"Wait, stick around, like to take a quick snort here—what is this now, ain't Shalimar, ain't Jungle Gardenia—"

"It's called Mitsouko. You like it?"

"Can't be sure till I know where you put it exactly, if you can just hold still a second—"

"*Mi a kibaszott*," not entirely to herself, "what am I getting into now?"

Hicksie, it's me—

This is what you call a "quick out and back in"? Hope you found that "big-time" payoff you were hoping for.

On the hop myself lately, somebody must be hiring extra truant officers, every time you turn around there's another one. Paddy wagons, dogcatcher nets, arrest warrants, the works. Not so many places to hide as there were, not even safe under our old Viaduct anymore.

Riding the Beerline around town, thinking one of these days I should just stay on and keep going, all the way out west. You remember Zinnia, she gave me that glow-in-the-dark watch? I've been teaching her how to get on and off slow freights, she has a natural gift for it, and it looks like things are getting serious. She keeps throwing hints we should team up and go cross-country. There's supposed to be plenty of work out on the Coast, paying better than this burg. I can't be boosting cartons of Luckies all my life, and Zin, no big surprise, she wants to get into pictures. They're always looking for "us Ruby Keeler types," she says. How would I know. Too much else going on in movie theaters to be looking at the screen.

I wish you could meet her, wish you were around even just to talk to about this, everybody else's got their own problems. Not complaining, but could really use some advice, even yours.

People up on Walnut Street send their regards. Otto and Hildegard say fish fry ain't the same without you. Hoagie Hivnak turns out to be a regular Joe for an old guy, tries to pass me a free cone sometimes if nobody's looking.

You said I should stay in touch with the U-Ops office. Honestly I tried to but soon as Mr. Crosstown saw it was me, he made a face and reached for the phone and not needing any more gangbusters in my life just then, it was on with the breeze machine and I haven't been back since.

Luckily Lew Basnight saw what was going on and says he'll lend me and Zin the fare out to California. "God help you, kid," he keeps muttering at me, "like a dope habit. You think you're having fun, you're really miserable but can't let it go. Meantime somebody just started shooting at you." So on— forks in the road, close shaves, mistakes he wished he didn't make, another one of those pep talks you guys are so good at. "You and every would-be private eye west of the Rockies drawn into that old L.A. vacuum cleaner, little offices opening up all over town, everybody hungry, still mostly divorce cases so far. Eternal youth, big Hollywood playpen, whatsoever—but someday they'll lose that innocence. They'll find out."

"Maybe they'll keep finding new ways to be innocent."

Which got me a funny look. "Better if somebody tells you now—innocent and not guilty ain't always the same."

No idea what that means, but I have a feeling I'm about to get it. Time to put them street kiddie days behind me, not so little and speedy no more, if life was a ballpark you'd say maybe time to move from shortstop out to where I can range around, keeping long ones from going into the stands. While I can still hit.

Your first question will be, have I shot anybody yet. Don't argue, I know how you think by now. Sure would like to get into details on that, but like you always tell me, put anything in writing and it's only buying trouble down the line.

Really wanted to say about Stuffy Keegan—I know what happened to him and so do you, we both saw the same thing under the ice but who'll ever believe us? Just to keep everything professional I went out and tried to track down everybody I remember Stuffy doing business with, which was plenty, talk about legwork, kept ringing up No Sales, and after enough of it, seemed like that U-boat was the best bet after all.

Don't know how late you've been staying up, but if you can get next to a shortwave set nobody minds being on all night, keep it warm, tuned and biased, sometimes if you're lucky you can pick up by skywave some news about the U-13, maybe a direct broadcast from the boat itself. Frequencies keep changing, but it'll be somewhere inside the 3- to 30-megacycle band. Sometimes there'll be a voice I'm pretty sure is Stuffy in person. You'd have to listen and see what you think.

Meantime there's the Santa Fe Chief whistling all aboard, so I'll stop here and pick it up again when Zin and me get to California. Hope you'll come out sometime and see us. Right now, we've got a couple of sunsets to chase.

Best pals always,
Skeet

Thomas Pynchon is the author of *V.*, *The Crying of Lot 49*, *Gravity's Rainbow*, *Slow Learner* (a collection of short stories), *Vineland*, *Mason & Dixon*, *Against the Day*, *Inherent Vice* and *Bleeding Edge*. He received the National Book Award for *Gravity's Rainbow* in 1974.